PLATO'S DREAM:
Crisis of the Employment Singularity

Topher Cliver

Published by Georgia Business Internet Solutions, Inc.

This is a work of fiction. Names, Characters, places and incidents either are the product of the author's imagination or are used fictitiously. Any resemblance to actual persons, living or dead, events, or locales is entirely coincidental.

ISBN-13: 978-0-9970870-2-4

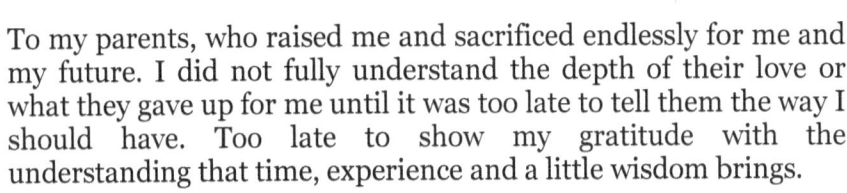

To my parents, who raised me and sacrificed endlessly for me and my future. I did not fully understand the depth of their love or what they gave up for me until it was too late to tell them the way I should have. Too late to show my gratitude with the understanding that time, experience and a little wisdom brings.

To them I dedicate this book.

"Imagine that the keeper of a huge, strong beast notices what makes it angry, what it desires, how it has to be approached and handled, the circumstances and the conditions under which it becomes particularly fierce or calm, what provokes its typical cries, and what tones of voice make it gentle or wild. Once he's spent enough time in the creature's company to acquire all this information, he calls it knowledge, forms it into a systematic branch of expertise, and starts to teach it, despite total ignorance, in fact, about which of the creature's attitudes and desires is commendable or deplorable, good or bad, moral or immoral. His usage of all these terms simply conforms to the great beast's attitudes, and he describes things as good or bad according to its likes and dislikes, and can't justify his usage of the terms any further, but describes as right and good the things which are merely indispensable, since he hasn't realised and can't explain to anyone else how vast a gulf there is between necessity and goodness."

— Plato

Chapter 1

Meeting Matthew Ligarck as a boy

"There is truth in wine and children"
— Plato

    We like to classify things neatly into categories based on an ideal we have conjured up of what that thing is. We do this with decades by remembering elements of them and defining the whole decade by these stark images surrounded by fuzzy memories. We tend to forget that the first part of the seventies was more like the last part of the 60's, which we fondly think of as the decade of protests, hippies, and Vietnam. We lop off the first part of the 60's also where things looked a lot like the end of the 50's. The seventies most people tend to think of started around the time Nixon resigned at the end of 1974 and that is roughly where we are at.

    Philip Kingsley was a brilliant but naive boy all of six years old with black, side-parted hair. He wore baby blue and white checkerboard slacks with a matching jacket covering a white ringer t-shirt tucked in above a thick white belt and was sitting on the floor out of site. He was playing with five or six different Matchbox cars behind the sofa on the hardwood in a room that looked like more of an exhibit of a living room than an actual living room.

The sofa, and cushioned high back chairs were white and formed a three-sided rectangle on a huge Persian rug in the middle of the room. The cars lay scattered between the rug, which extended beyond the back of the sofa for a short way, and the grandfather clock which sat against the wall on the hardwood floor. The edge of the rug offered a bump the perfect size to facilitate car crashes from both cars propelled forward and cars carefully guided by the godlike hand of the giant who owned and cared for them.

A blond haired blue eyed boy wearing green slacks and a gray long sleeve turtleneck appeared out of nowhere looming over the boy playing cars. He had his hands on his hips and judgmental expression on his face.

The blond haired boy said, "They won't let you play with toys at boarding school." His hair was on the edge of what was considered short for the times for something that wasn't a buzz cut like the sons of many veterans were forced to get. It was in a no man's land. It was long by the standards of most decades but was somewhat conservative for these times. Like all styles of this era, it looked like the barber had been tripping on acid and sculpted the hair by cutting a random pattern, hacking off anything that stuck out too far. There was a sense of fear that this boy instilled and a sense that he was an authority figure even though only a six-year-old boy with a white belt and matching shoes.

The black haired boy had stopped playing and just held the red, 1967 GTO in his hand as he replied with total innocence, "What's boarding school and what's your name?"

The blond haired boy said, "I am Matthew and boarding school is where you are going in a few weeks. I know because I'm going too. I know all about it and they don't let you have toys or candy or TV."

The black haired boy said, "My name is Philip. No TV? That's not true, my Mom and Dad told me I would have my own TV in my room this year."

Matthew laughed and said, "They are shipping you away and they lied to you. You are going to have to sleep on the floor. My brothers go to that school and I am going too. We can get you a bed, but you have to do everything I say."

Philip, looking terrified could only shake his head in agreement as his lip started to quiver ever so slightly.

Matthew sensing victory said, "Ok, I will be in a lot of trouble if anyone finds out I told you so you have to swear not to tell anyone."

2

Philip straightened up and said, "I swear I won't tell."

Matthew looking skeptical said in an accusing tone, "Swear to God, cross your heart, hope to die, stick a needle in your eye?"

Philip, "Yes."

Matthew, "Say it!"

Philip said, "Swear to God, cross my heart, hope to die, stick a needle in my eye."

Matthew said, "So if you tell you will have a needle right in your eyeball so you better not."

Philip said, "I won't I promise. I want a bed, will you get me one?"

The boys sat through another boring dinner overdressed and forced to eat horrible adult food and listen to the adult conversation all while not being allowed to utter a sound. Matthew Ligarck left with his parents after dinner and Philip did not see him again until he arrived at boarding school several weeks later. Philip did not confront his parents about the TV or about school as that simply was not done. Philip Kingsley's parents were of the mind that children were like the family silverware, to be brought out and displayed when company was here but then taken away by the servants to be cleaned and then to be cared for and polished once they left. Philip's parents were simply not a part of his day to day life in a meaningful way which would make leaving for boarding school easier for him than for others

Philip's day to day oversight was seen to by Ms. Abby, one of the Kingsley House staff. It was not like the movies where there were very specific roles like maids and butlers. There was simply tasks to be performed and three ladies who worked rotating shifts to take care of them. While this was true for most things, each lady did gravitate toward what they were best at. Ms. Abby specialized as the primary caregiver for Philip, but all three ladies had more influence on his day to day life than either of his parents. The Kingsley estate was huge, perhaps a hundred years earlier it would have required a large staff, but the staff of 3 was large for the times. There was also a groundskeeper who was the husband of one of the three house staff. The Staff lived out back in what was essentially a small detached three bedroom, two story house.

Ms. Abby had a son named Frederick who was a year younger than Philip and his constant companion. They were each others best and only friend as this was before the time of play dates. In this neighborhood, a child did not simply get on their bike and

3

ride down a cul de sac to meet his friends so it is not like they had an option. That was ok though because they were very compatible and enjoyed each other's company. Frederick, or Freddy as he was called at the time, was the beneficiary of second-hand tutoring. A series of teachers came and taught Philip all manner of things from French to ballroom dancing to astronomy, all year round from the time he could walk. Whatever tutor was there, Freddy was almost always off to the side with a book waiting for Philip Kingsley to be finished so they could play. Freddy was the beneficiary of quite an education, soaking up almost as much on the sidelines as Philip Kingsley did front and center, in various fields of learning.

Philip's parents may have rented people to take care of their son, but they did not skimp on his education. There were more books at his disposal than most small towns had in their libraries. While Philip loved to read, Freddy was a voracious reader, a hobby that filled his time while he was waiting for one thing or another. Neither boy watched TV. Freddy, because they couldn't afford one and Philip, because his parents would not have one. The boys, when not reading themselves, would sometimes read to each other. Often they discussed the concepts they read and would have fascinating discussions that would have made many a college professor well up with tears to witness actual passion in defense of ideas. They also both possessed a lack of insecurity such that they both had the ability to graciously concede a point when a better argument or theory was presented. They fought to change each other's mind. When one or the other had a winning argument, the other would not only embrace the winning idea but would radiate a sense of admiration and appreciation to the other boy for having set them straight with the greater and purer truth.

They carried on like this every day until Philip left for boarding school only to be interrupted by the trips that Philip actually got to go on, which were few. Philip's parents were liberal in a fashionable sense but were always elitists at heart and if they were to ever realize how much time their son spent with Freddy would be appalled by it. While some of the disgust would be at the thought of their son spending his days with a Negro, the more revolting thought would be that their son spent his days with, and around, poor people. Once Philip left for school, Freddy was all alone and if an avid reader before, became consumed by reading until his companion would return home during holidays, breaks and then summers. Freddy walked two miles to and from his school bus stop and attended a school consisting of almost all white

4

children. His classmates were not rich enough to go to private school as many of the kids in this part of town did. They were not nearly as smart as the black child whose presence reminded them that this was, in fact, a public school. Freddy learned after a few beatings to bite his tongue and to save his lively debates for Philip.

Matthew Ligarck, even at age 6 knew how to use knowledge as a weapon and used his slightly greater knowledge of what was coming to torture Philip. That was Matthew. He manipulated Philip in such a way that he didn't know he was being maneuvered. It could be argued that Matthew was doing him a service because while he had his fun with Philip he never really caused harm and he protected him from those that would indeed cause harm. Matthews's older brothers provided him the same "service" although sometimes their torture was genuine. While the occasional public humiliation infuriated Matthew, it served to both make him look tough as he endured it as well as making him actually tough for having endured it. No peer would dare lay a hand on him for fear of retribution from one of his crazy brothers who, unlike Matthew, were all jocks.

Throughout the years, Matthew continued to torture Philip much the same way until the incident in the 6th grade. Matthew's brother Tommy was two years older and by far the most sadistic of the brothers. He was usually kept in check by their two older brothers, but they both had their own high school lives to tend too while Tommy was at the pinnacle of the elementary side of the school. He was feared by his classmates and brought terror to those younger than himself. This large and strong bully was particularly angry at Matthew for who knows what as Matthew could have the effect of bringing out a particular rage that only he had the ability to conjure.

The school yard was very crowded at recess as all the grades went at the same time and there were areas around buildings that were hidden from the direct view of the teachers on recess duty. Matthew found himself in such a place and Tommy circled him with a look of fury on his face. Tommy had blond hair too as all the Ligarcks did and he wore it in an unkempt mop. He was physically mature for eighth grade and was muscular already at that age. Matthew, who was tall for his age but only worked out the muscle between his ears and so was lanky, stood with a look of pure insolence tempered with hatred. One thing about Matthew is he would not back down, ever.

5

Normally how this would play out is that Tommy would do something like frog Matthew, who would drop in pain, but would not submit and instead would endure the pain. The way he did this earned the admiration of his classmates and their pity for having to live with such an animal. Frogging, of course, is when you extend the middle knuckle outward when making a fist so that the force of the punch is concentrated at that one point which digs into the flesh. When it hits square on, it often would leave a nasty bruise and always brought intense pain. When Matthew was a jerk, people cut him some slack for this reason. You see, Matthew too was a feared bully, but he beat people up with his words.

That day, Matthew would have very little to say. Tommy was determined that this would be the day that he would once and for all break that smug little bastard of a brother. He would make him pay for correcting him in front of Amy Henthorn and embarrassing him or at least that was the reason he would let people think. That day was different because while Tommy always inflicted pain he also always left humiliation out of it. Tommy circled Matthew, who stood in the grassy mini lot that sat hidden from the teachers view by the two small one-story buildings that were built after the main five-story brick building that housed the classrooms. The two smaller buildings were far enough apart that the space between them was not secluded but close enough to create cover so that certain parts of the courtyard between them were hidden from view. These places were well known to the kids and Tommy, like a general picking his ground, had skillfully positioned Matthew there to spring his trap.

A Small group of kids gathered around and as the event went on that number would grow as did the intensity. Matthew was by no means loved and many kids were excited to see him get his comeuppance. Today though Tommy seethed as he circled Matthew.

He looked at Matthew and said through clenched teeth, "On your knees and you kiss the bottom of my shoe."

Matthew just stood there in his schoolboy uniform with an expression that looked almost British in its combination of resolve, defiance, and superiority. What you could not easily notice behind that blue blazer with the school crest or the gray shorts and socks was that Matthew was shaking in his black laced up shoes. He knew Tommy all too well and he had never seen him this angry. He was not sure what was going to happen next, but he knew it was not going to go well for him no matter what he did. Tommy kept circling

6

him slowly like a shark measuring its prey. He would periodically repeat a variation of the command to kiss or lick his shoe or foot and to get on the ground or his knees or all fours to do it.

Most schoolyard fights are noisy as the spectators heckle or jeer or make some kind of noise. This scene was eerily silent so when Tommy uttered his demand it came out of his mouth like a suppressed yell that lingered in the air and filled it with suppressed rage and malice. You see Tommy was the least bright of the Ligarck boys and while also the strongest and meanest of all of them, accounting for age, he was also less athletically gifted than Matthew. That was saying something as Matthew had no athletic ability but unlike Tommy he didn't try to be an athlete. Today's rage was not about athletics, it was about intelligence. Their Father had told him he was a disappointment after seeing his average grades, which he had actually worked hard to get, and told him over the phone he should try and be more like Matthew. Tommy only knew one way to expunge the demons in his head and this was it.

Matthew knew that even if he humiliated himself in front of all these kids, which in his mind was not an option, he would still take a beating once on the ground. The problem was Tommy was not yelling and he wasn't enjoying the torment and this was something new and it was scary. Tommy did not have the talent to catch, throw or hit balls and he had no speed or grace. He did have ungodly strengths such that if he pushed your head down into the dirt your head would feel like it was being crushed in a vice. If repressive dictators held a draft to select the top talent in the torture league, Tommy for sure would be a number one draft pick.

Tommy got closer and closer to Matthew's face and what no one there but Tommy knew was that it was sheer willpower that kept him from unleashing hell on Matthew. As scared as Matthew was, Tommy was every bit as scared for him because there was a fury unfelt before by him fighting to get out. Feelings of inferiority exasperated by parental disappointment and brotherly jealousy from a middle child that had none of the gifts cherished by a gifted family. Tommy, trembling, grabbed the back of Matthew's neck and dropped him almost immediately to his knees as he didn't have anything close to the strength to resist this force despite his best efforts.

There with Matthew helpless on all fours, Tommy swung his leg back in the beginning move of a kick that would surely maim or kill Matthew such was the wind up when all of a sudden it happened. Philip had been missing from the scene. He had been on the other side of the playground and came over late to the drama unfolding here. He did not know Tommy nearly as well as Matthew, but he did see enough to realize Tommy was in a bad frame of mind and that something bad was about to happen. Everyone's attention was focused on Tommy's foot being drawn as far back in a kick wind up as it could physically go. Then seemingly out of nowhere, through the air Philip came flying, feet first, like one of the two by fours you hear about being hurled at high velocity by a tornado that then goes through cinder block walls. Philip's feet hit Tommy just above the side of the kneecap of the planted foot that was not only in a twisted and stressed angle but was supporting all of Tommy's weight. The impact and stresses of all these forces were more than bone could handle and Tommy's leg broke in that instant.

The near silence that had prevailed in the battle zone was instantly snapped as Tommy screamed in a long, extremely loud wail that brought teachers from every direction. Kids dispersed and an entire crowd melted away to avoid being involved in the sure to follow investigation and inquisition. But they watched from the corners of their eyes to see Tommy on the ground writhing in agony. Philip sat on the ground with knees bent slightly upward and arms extending behind him like ropes extending from a tent to the stakes in the ground. Philip was stunned and in a state of shock as he just sat there looking at Tommy with an expression of horror at what he had just done to him.

Matthew, as was his nature, immediately soaked up the situation and the consequences and immediately went into action. He stood up and started waving his arms as if to get the attention of the oncoming teachers. As he did this he said to Philip in a voice only loud enough to be audible to him, "Philip, get out of here. Go blend into the crowd while there is still time."

Philip, of course, did nothing but sit on his backside until it did become too late. Matthew took charge of the scene as soon as the teachers arrived he acted hysterical asking for them to help his brother and to get a doctor. He ranted apologetically taking the blame for the incident saying, "We were just goofing around, why did this have to happen? It's these shoes that made him slip and break his leg, we should be able to wear tennis shoes! Why did this happen we were just horsing around and bam his leg snaps." Matthew went on like this acting distraught and repeating the elements of the story which came off as believable and served the important purpose of establishing the story in such a way that everyone around could hear.

Most of the former crowd was back and there were many new arrivals. Once it looked like it was no longer going to be a crime scene, thanks to Matthews quick thinking, people filtered back over to watch the show. The members of the crowd when interviewed stuck to the snippets that Matthew had droned into them like a raving pneumatic tool. "They were just horsing around and his leg broke." or "The older boy's shoes slipped and he hurt his leg." Philip was sure to confess to the whole crime.

Matthew had foreseen that too and at the scene with plenty of teachers there made a point to call out Philip saying, "I can't believe you just missed the whole thing. How could you be right there and not see a thing? Why were your eyes closed?" He threw enough questions with feigned outrage, interspersed with the other story elements, that when a teacher finally took him aside to calm him down, that teacher had heard this misinformation a dozen times, whether they were aware consciously or not. In any case, it worked because they never called Philip in to talk to him so the opportunity to confess came and went as he waited to be interviewed over the course of the days that followed.

That day fundamentally changed the actors and the relationships to each other. There was no retribution from Tommy. He wore a cast for two months and the need to save face was long gone by the time it came off. Tommy later discovered wrestling and channeled his aggression into that sport. Matthew had his demon removed and was free to become more confident and much more arrogant than he was before. Philip got past the guilt over time and although he would not admit it even to himself, standing up to Tommy and risking the beating of a lifetime was brave and gave Philip an additional level of confidence.

The biggest change was to Philip and Matthew's relationship. Like it or not, they were friends from this point on. That didn't mean they were any more likely to agree on anything as they still seldom did. In fact, to the outside observer nothing appeared to change as they still continually verbally sparred and made fun of each other. But something fundamental changed and they had bonded in a way that is not easy to see as it was a psychic bond that was formed. Matthew replaced the brother he was genetically saddled with for the brother he chose and from that day forward they would be so. Tommy would, later in college after a night of heavy drinking, smash his Porsche into the small compact

9

car of a nurse returning home from a long shift at the ER. He ended both their lives and left three children without their mother.

Topher Cliver

Chapter 2

High School

"Be slow to fall into friendship; but when thou art in, continue firm and constant."
-Plato

The early eighties were marked by one of the worst economic downturns since the great depression. Kids graduating college were looking at a job market filled with blue-collar layoffs that were the result of the normal economic cycle fluctuations but something deeper, somehow different. The IBM PC was introduced marking a turning point in the computer industry as it became a standard and was "cloned" en masse. There were PCs before this, but this became a tipping point and computers have been an integral piece of our lives ever since.

This downturn was about productivity. Business inefficient and the computer had the ability to allow one worker to produce the work product of several workers using analog alternatives. A spreadsheet was more efficient than a row of people punching calculator keys or writing down numbers to sum. Typing was not as highly prized skill when any schlub could key in words, fix them until in the form desired and hit print. Computers are really good at keeping track of stuff as well from warehouse inventory to hours worked to workers needed.

Not to be overlooked in this transformative time was a mass increase in women entering the workforce in numbers unseen in memory. There had always been women in the workforce but, for the most part, they had been stuck in specific roles such as secretary, nurse, and school teacher. Now they were breaking through these barriers and working jobs that had traditionally been held almost exclusively by men. This gender democratization, as well as the technologizing of business, would continue onward from here, but both gained momentum during this downturn

The view from the higher perches of society, as always, was different. The Kingsley and Ligarck families would not simply endure the recession as working class people hoped to do, they instead hoped to, no, expected to, profit from this opportunity. In turmoil, there was always an opportunity for profit and while the Kingsley's did well, the Ligarcks did exceptionally well as the family business became focused on mergers and acquisitions. They bought inefficient behemoth companies organized around the old model of strong organized labor and high-skilled workers doing jobs that required specialized training and experience. Like many of the companies the Ligarck's acquired, the system was being torn apart and each constituent part was being reordered, reorganized and remade from the ground up. On the other side, business became stronger but at the cost of the workers, as a part of the equation, becoming weaker.

Philip was home for the summer before his junior year in high school. Philip was tall and lean with a boyish look in a man-sized frame. The ritual had been that the beginning of the summers found Philip at his most conservative and most elitist. Meanwhile, Frederick, as he had come to demand people call him, was his most left wing and most anarchist. None of these terms being meant as an absolute describing either boy, but rather as a far point on a spectrum. Each was further toward the absolute relative to their normal distance from it at other points in the year. It was as if each was gathering research for the debate that began each summer and it was always an exciting time filled with intense discussions that would often go into late hours of the night.

Philip had arrived home in the morning. The groundskeeper, who was also the driver, carried his bags upstairs and put his stuff away as he had a formal lunch with his mother, as was the tradition when arrived home from school. Sometimes the special meal with Mother would be afternoon tea or if later, then a special dessert together after a family dinner. Victoria Elizabeth

Kingsley was a proud and lovely lady dressed very formally and conducted herself when greeting Philip as if greeting him as a guest in the receiving line to a formal ball. They sat at the large table across from each other near the middle of the long rectangle that it was.

"Do tell me how you are getting on at school Philip?" his mother said.

Philip said, "Things are going great. I have decided to run for class president next year,"

Mrs. Kingsley said, "You will need to discuss that with your father dear. Have you met any nice girls this year?

Philip said, "You do know it's an all-boys school, don't you?"

Mrs. Kingsley said, "Don't be ridiculous Philip. I'm quite sure you have had several social events which would have afforded you the opportunity to make the acquaintance of some proper young ladies."

Philip said, "We had a few dances and mixers with our sister school. I met plenty of girls, but none of them really caught my eye."

Mrs. Kingsley said, "Oh dear, for heaven sake please do tell me you like girls Philip."

Philip said, "Of course Mother, I just felt like I was on a job interview with these girls. I really didn't get to meet that many as we only had so many opportunities and the ones I did meet were mostly obtuse snobs."

Mrs. Kingsley said, "Be distrustful Dear of any young lady who does not treat it as a job interview as that is essentially what it is. Who you are does matter and you should be inquiring about her and her family as well. Just because a young lady attends a nice school does not mean she is suitable for you."

Philip said, "I did meet one girl I especially liked."

Mrs. Kingsley said, "Do tell."

Philip said, "She is tall and elegant. She came once a week to visit her father who washes dishes in our cafeteria."

Mrs. Kingsley said, "Stop it this instance Philip. Why do you torture me so?"

Philip thought to himself that he could ask the same question but kept it to himself. They continued on catching up like two regular people would who run into each other at the grocery store, hitting the highlights and superficial details. Once lunch was over, they parted ways and Philip made his way to see Frederick. He knocked on the door to Ms. Abby's apartment out back and gave her a big hug when she answered the door. She squealed with delight at seeing him and gave him a big kiss on his cheek.

She said, "Philip you handsome devil you must have grown a foot since Christmas. You are nothing but skin and bones I swear if you don't start eating I'm going to take the bus up to that school and start cooking all your meals right there in your room."

Frederick hurried down the hall and then suddenly stopped and jerked himself right as if he caught himself drifting off to sleep in a chair. He then walked calmly the rest of the way to the front room where Ms. Abby had now pulled in Philip, continuing to shower him with hugs and affection.

Frederick said, "Mom stop it already you're embarrassing him."

Philip said, "Oh this is the best part of coming home. You didn't really think I came by to see you, did you?"

Frederick said, "Mom, really."

Ms. Abby said, "Oh you can be embarrassed all you want when one of my boys comes home to see me there it going to be some hugging. You made this old lady happy, now you too can go off and talk about girls or whatever teenage boys talk about."

Philip grabbed Ms. Abby and gave her one more huge kiss on your cheek and headed toward the door and said, "Come on let's go out to the gazebo."

The boys ran down the exterior stairs that led up the apartment and headed out across the property.

Philip said, "Damn Freddy, sorry Frederick, when did you get glasses?"

Frederick replied, "About two months ago. I'm still getting used to them.

Philip said, "Going for the full on nerd look eh?"

Frederick replied, "Shut up you bastard. Have you been made someone's wife up at Boys Town yet?"

Philip sat staring out across the pond next to the gazebo and after a moment of silence said, "It's amazing how different everyone and everything is and yet it all seems the same."

Frederick said, "That's quite a paradox. You should write that down, you are probably the first to notice that."

Philip smiled and said, "You can laugh, but things like that become clichés for a reason. These are universals that you can intellectualize all you want but like a rite of passage they must be experienced firsthand. Freddy, we have to get out in the world and

16

make a difference and not just read and think and talk about it. Not to seem too immodest, I am upper percentile smart and on my best days you are twice as smart as me. We can do great things in this world."

Frederick punched Philip in the arm and said, "Good Lord, so I have three months to pound that pretentious aristocratic bullshit out of you. I guess I have my work cut out for me."

They noticed the rotund groundskeeper, Mr. Charles, walking out toward the gazebo. Once he got within about ten feet, he said, "Mr. Philip, your father wants to see you right away in his study."

Throughout his life, Philip had been summoned to his father's study which, in essence, was his work office in the home. The term home office was just taking off and that would be too gauche a term for the Kingsleys. It never failed to bring a sense of dread like being called to the principal's office or seeing flashing lights in the rearview mirror.

Philip's father was tall and thin with a frame that was sturdy and yet not worn or strengthened by a day of hard labor in his lifetime. He always wore a suit with a vest and gold pocket watch that his father had given him. His face was chiseled from granite and in it was etched a permanently serious look with lips slightly downturned at the edges and bushy brow that was just slightly furrowed. His ears were large but not ridiculous and his face long but not oddly so. He wore rounded wire rim glasses that made him look professorial and he had stern eyes behind them. Strangely Philip could not remember ever seeing him laugh, or smile for that matter, and the family photos seem to support that maybe he just never did.

Barton P Kingsley IV was born about two years before Philip. Mrs. Kingsley had given birth to his new brother Philip just two weeks earlier when the nanny got distracted by a vase broken by the innocent toddler. Barton Kingsley IV staggered, as those new to walking do, down the hall and to the stairs where he fell with momentum forward down the stairs to his death. The dark cloud of that event hungover Philip's early childhood and his father lost more than the heir to his name, he lost the heir to his throne. Some people have talented siblings they have to grow up in the shadow of but they, at least in those instances, are up against real people earning real accolades. Philip grew up in the shadow of an idea of a

17

human being and all that the dreams of his father would have him aspire to.

Philip's mother smothered him for much of his early childhood as she had the maternal love stored up for two sons and only one to express it on. He was not allowed upstairs until he was six. Usually what BK said went in the Kingsley household and an impractical rule such as this would usually never fly but Barton supported it and it was law. Barton for all his flaws was a good husband and he tried to be a good father and sometimes succeeded. Philip's parents loomed large in his life like all powerful gods until he came of school age and then they became the relatives he stayed with on the holidays and took vacations with.

Barton Kingsley III was an extremely well-educated and well-read man but one who held very few original thoughts. Philip's father resented him when he had different, or worse yet, original ideas that varied from his own. This resentment grew as he, at least on a subconscious level, realized that Philip was more intellectually gifted than he ever was. One would get the impression that if Barton Kingsley III were born into a more humble setting he would have achieved, through hard work, a middle managerial position and a gold watch after an uneventful and long career. Several million dollars and social connections tend to change outcomes.

Barton Kingsley III finally straightened out his papers and stacked them in a pile which he neatly put to the side of his desk. He did this in a manner that suggested that that's not only where he was going to put them, but that indeed was where these papers go, where they belong. He looked at Philip for the first time since he entered the room and said, "Philip, it is time we prepared your CV for Green."

Philip thought, "Gee I'm fine Dad, I had a good trip home and I missed you too."

But he said, "Father, I've given this a lot of thought and I think I will get a more rounded education at Harvard, not to mention the greater number of potential connections I can make there."

Although you would think this impossible, Barton Kingsley scowled a little more than usual and said, "Don't be ridiculous. Harvard is for the men people like us hire to run the day to day operations of our businesses or to defend us from lawsuits."

"But Father both President Adams" attended as well as both President Roosevelt's, not to mention JFK."

Barton Kingsley replied, "Surely I will not mention him and you are proving my point. These men ran the day to day operations of the country for the real men of power who attended exclusive colleges like Green."

"Father, I want to be in a leadership position and maybe, if things go right, join that list of Presidents who attended Harvard."

Barton Kingsley thumped his fist down on the desk. Not hard enough to imply potential violence or be intimidating at all but just hard enough to emphasize his point. He said, "No son of mine is going to be a politician being led around on a leash begging for scraps from the tables of the men who really run things and make decisions. If you want to make decisions, then that is what you should aspire to and that is what Green will prepare you for. Matthew has applied to attend I hear."

Philip's voice quivered just a bit as he said, "Why do I care where Matthew goes? Why do you care?"

Barton Kingsley calmly replied, "Matthew's father was bragging at the club several weeks back on how Matthew had found out from one of your classmates that a merger was going to take place and the Ligarck's netted over $10 million." That was far from the most clever or most profitable story he has told. Matthew has not only paid for his education he has apparently actually learned something. How much has your GPA and accolades earned? Men who want awards and titles and who seek office are vain and naive as they think these things matter. While it may be significant to some floozy waitress or actress, the men of power are unknown to the public and happy it is that way. You have a lot to learn Philip and you will learn it at Green. That is the end of this conversation."

Barton Kingsley calmly picked up a new stack of papers and began separating them into piles directly in front of him. Philip seethed but bit his lip, turned and left the room. He knew he handled that argument all wrong he should have brought up some of the business leaders Harvard had produced, but the problem was his Father was right. He could name politicians, Supreme Court justices, and Nobel laureates all day long but no names that his father would respect. He decided to live to fight again some other day.

Topher Cliver

Chapter 3

Spring Break

"Strong minds discuss ideas, average minds discuss events, weak minds discuss people."
-Plato

In the spring of Philip's senior year of high school and Frederick's junior year, they took a road trip to Fort Lauderdale Florida, the spot to be if you were young and carefree. They could have flown but decided to make it a road trip adventure. Philip had convinced his father to let him borrow his Aston Martin Lagonda, which offered the ideal balance of luxury and power without drawing attention. They had a state of the art radar detector, a box of cassettes, including a stack of mixtapes for the ride, some maps and Philip Kingsley's platinum card for everything else.

The first hour or so of the drive was filled with catching up as they really hadn't had time to talk since Philip was home at Christmas.

Fred said, "Ok I've been waiting to tell you this, I got my SAT scores back."

Philip said, "And?"

Fred said, "I nailed it, man, I nailed it, I got a 1,520!"

"Holy shit Fred that's totally radical! The highest I got between two tests was 1,410. That is so awesome." Philip said.

Fred said, "This puts us one step closer to being at Harvard together. I'm feeling good about a free ride now as long as I don't blow my grades over the next year."

Philip suddenly looked like a sail that lost its wind as he said, "Fred about Harvard."

Fred interjected. "Tell me you didn't back down. There is no better place to study law."

Philip said, "Look, I compromised, I'll go to Harvard law once I complete my undergrad at Green. We can get a place together your senior year there. This just sets us back a few years."

Fred said, "I can't believe you man where's your spine?"

Philip said, "I'm not like you Fred, I can't live by ultimatums of principle, I find compromises that allow all to come out better."

Fred said, "That's bullshit man you just didn't have the guts to stand up to your father, that's all."

Philip said, "Look I know you had this idea of us dominating Harvard together but my father was not going to let that happen. He was not going to accept me going anywhere other than Green and he certainly wasn't going to let me go to Harvard. I have gotten him to concede Harvard Law. He's giving me a chunk of my trust fund once I start Green with a generous yearly stipend and the remainder once I graduate."

Fred said, "So it's about the money."

Philip said, "Don't be naive Fred, of course, the money is a big part and it's not like I'm compromising a good education or good connections at Green. I could spend my youth fighting my father but what would that get me. If he wins, I still go to Green and if I win, I'm cut off and without the means to jumpstart events or help those I want to help."

Fred said, "Jumpstart what, watch out for that idiot!"

The car swerved onto the bumpy shoulder narrowly missing a sedan that breached their lane."

Fred continued, "What events and help who?"

Philip said, "Jumpstart my career and help you and your...our Mom."

Fred said, "What do you mean, help me? I don't need your help and I didn't ask for your help. And what do you mean, help Mom? Help her do what?"

Philip said, "Calm down for god sake. I'm not going to force anything on you, but I would like to be in a position to help even if you refuse it. As for our Mom, you know her arthritis is getting worse and I can't imagine she has much saved up after supporting your needy ass. She raised me. She saved me and I'm going to make sure she is taken care of as soon as I get the first chunk of money. She needs her own place near her son and she will not have to work if she doesn't want to."

Fred turned in his seat looking at the road as he mulled this over. It angered him that someone else would be the hero for his Mom. Philip certainly had the right as she did so much for him but also he knew it would be 5 more years before he even got out of school let alone had a job. He knew he would have to let this go and letting it go would be the thing he could do for his Mom.

After a mile or two of silence Fred said, "What do you think is going to happen when half the Third world declares bankruptcy because they can't repay their debt?"

Philip said, "That won't happen, they will just restructure their debt again to get them through this recession and to a place where they can pay again. No one wins if they go belly up."

Fred said. "It is economic enslavement getting these countries heavily indebted and then controlling them like puppets because of what they owe."

Philip replied, "No one made them accept the loans and if they used the money as intended there should have been a return sufficient to pay it back."

Fred said, "When you are desperate you take what you can get and you can't afford to be choosy. They were hustled by con men in nice suits working a sanctioned con game all through the 70's."

Philip said, "They became desperate in the first place not because they lack money but because they couldn't manage their resources or their economies. They would be in the same trouble if that money were a grant instead of a loan only a grant would have let them ask for more money to waste. As far as the organizations who loaned the money wanting a say in how it is used, that's a good thing. Obviously the countries have a hard time making the proper decisions to begin with and are motivated by things other than getting a return on investment where that is the main motivation of the investors."

Fred said, "And you act as though that's a good thing."

Philip said, "It is not the ideal thing, but it is better than the same decision making that got them into the mess to begin with. Their problems aren't a lack of money, most of these countries have

23

some sort of resources, it the fact that they are always at war with someone or themselves and the main reason is corruption. You stop the war and set up a legal infrastructure strong enough to eliminate corruption and these countries will prosper in a generation or two. Japan and Germany did it after World War 2."

Fred shook his head in amazement and said, "So you have boiled down the problems of the third world to stopping war and corruption and with that they will blossom into first world countries."

Philip interjected, "Now I never said that last part so let's stick to what I did say."

Fred smiled and continued his impassioned rant, "You're of course right, you gave me enough to work with already. I mean let's look at a couple of other things you didn't say. What about disease, lack of sustainable food crops, potable water, or how about a lack of infrastructure to distribute all the fixes to all these problems. There aren't many Rome's in the third world for all the roads to lead too. In Fact, there aren't many roads. What about a lack of education and training not to mention the technologies they should be training for. How about the lack of an educated class as most of the intelligentsia of these countries go abroad to study and then stay there instead of bringing those skill back to their countries. What about diverse ethnic and religious groups forced together artificially as a legacy of imperialistic colonization that drew arbitrary lines on a map that these modern countries are now stuck with?"

Philip jumped in with, "Ok let me respond to a couple of these things before you go too far down the road here both literally and figuratively. What I identified are the two things you need to solve before you can even begin to address these myriad other problems. They are of course paramount, but you can't start equipping a guy to farm his land when he is going to be carried away and drafted to fight in a civil war in a couple weeks. You can't hire contractors to build roads when all the money going into the project ends up in the pockets of corrupt government officials and their crony contractor friends. While colonialism was tragic for those colonized, most every country in the world has its stories of being conquered. Most every line on every map was arbitrarily drawn to benefit some small group of benefactors or conquerors and not the greater number of people who actually live there. As far as diverse peoples being forced to live together, they need to figure it out like the rest of the world and come out of it a better and more enlightened people."

Fred drew back with a look of astonishment and said, "Please tell me you don't include the United States in that group of countries as better and more enlightened."

Philip said, "Of course I do."

Fred smirked and he began, "That is a typical privileged white man's view of the world to think this country is somehow morally superior to poorer peoples in other places around the world. We have all the exact same fundamental underlying problems we have been talking about right here in this country. They manifest themselves differently because of a list of reasons, but the most important is the level of economic development. You are looking at the problems from the perspective that they are the actual problems and not the symptoms and of dollar signs to fix these symptoms while the disease ravages the host."

Philip looked thoughtfully at Frederick and replied, "Ok convince me. What is the inability to feed your own country a symptom of, and how do we have that problem here?"

Fred looked at Philip in disbelief as he said, "Yes, it is a symptom and I don't even have to look for a moralistically equivalent symptom here in the US. We have millions of people right here going hungry right now, many of them children, even though we have the means to feed every single person in the US generously several times over. We have food, roads, trucks and even a certain amount of political will to fix the problem and still people go hungry. We are rated as having very little corruption compared to the rest of the world

This is not a problem of resources, it is a product of the flaws in humanity. It is greed that directs food overseas for profits. This underlying human problem manifests itself as greed in government by way of the administrations of both parties directing resources the government has accumulated in taxes. They then distribute them in such a way as to help groups and people other than those who are hungry. Furthermore, most of those distribution decisions create economic opportunities and gains for people aligned with the people making the distribution decisions. Therefore, plain and simple, it is greed."

Philip responded,"If I were to concede right now, you have said the problem is greed and that greed is manifesting itself as corruption. That was one of my original points that corruption is one of the first things we must eliminate.

But if that is the problem I must ask what about welfare, food stamps, and unemployment? Those are all government resources that people in government decided to make available to the people who you say are going hungry here. Why can't they use these resources to get the food and then the jobs to eliminate the problem? Help is fine but at some point people have to be accountable for themselves, they have to pull themselves up by their bootstraps and move past needing the help."

Fred replied, "This is the same thing we were talking about before and the same mentality. You don't even realize that there are some third world countries right here inside the US. They have much better infrastructure and resources than the third world countries outside these borders, but they share many of the same underlying problems. You throw loans at Africa and welfare at the poor. As the ancient proverb goes, give a man a fish and he eats for a day, teach a man to fish and he eats for a lifetime.

So you give these people a fish, what do they do tomorrow? The third world country still has no means to fix the problems they have and a huge loan debt to service as well. The poor person in America, when given the proverbial fish, has only the ability to get a minimum wage job. That job will not even earn them enough to live on, offers very little hope of career advancement, and virtually no hope of training.

Before you come back with some anecdotal story of the single mom with two kids, who flipped burgers all day. You know the one who then went to night school until she got a better job as the manager and then, with more night school, a district manager of the fast food chain. I concede there are stories like that, but she had to have help and she had to be exceptional. Help is not enough. You cannot hold a group accountable to do that which the most exceptional of that group does. It is not fair and not reasonable. If you reset the bar to the level of the highest achievers, you don't raise the group, you make the highest achievers look average and the rest of the people look lazy. You wouldn't do that to kids in school. You wouldn't fire everyone at a workplace who didn't perform to the level of the highest performer, you would have a couple employees and a huge list of unfilled positions. Yet, that is what we do to our poor people here and abroad.

To fix the problem, you must address solutions to the average person afflicted and their situation. There will still be people on one side of the average who are lazy and people on the other side who are still exceptional. The difference is the average people should have the means and opportunity to advance ahead. The exceptional people should have the opportunity to be exceptional and not at the expense of ever seeing their kids. They should be able to aspire beyond managing grease houses and to use their abilities to benefit society as a whole."

Philip smiled and said, "Fred, are you writing?"

Frederick looked at him bewildered and said, "A little but mostly focusing on school, why?"

Philip now also looking bewildered replied, "Because people have to hear what you are saying. You just opened my mind more than any high school class ever did. You are brilliant and people need to hear this. I'm not BSing you. I generally don't lose debates, even when I'm wrong and you have made me want to stop debating you and start listening. Do you know how rare that is?"

Frederick looking embarrassed said, "Stop that shit, Philip. You need to be a politician with that nice complimentary redirection. I can spout this stuff all day and it means nothing because I have no power. It's when people like you start saying it that it matters. I could write a book that a million poor people read and that would boost my ego and my back account. Only if I convince the right rich man with the power, then these words can change the lives of all those poor people."

Philip, propping his knee beneath the steering wheel used both hands to open the soda Frederick had grabbed him from the cooler some time back and took a long guzzle that ended with an obnoxious belch.

While Frederick chuckled, Philip said, "Ok so let's look at a middle ground here. I don't know how to fix greed but what about corruption? I was talking about good old fashion bribery. Your argument would seem to be that it exists here and yet I rarely ever hear of government officials taking money in exchange for a favor and when I do, it is because they were arrested for it. I certainly don't see people working payoffs into their business plans as a cost of doing business as they do in some parts of the world so where is this corruption here?"

Frederick replied, "Corruption in more developed countries is more subtle. We have set up a system that is dependent on politicians to raise money if, for no other reason, to let the electorate know they exist. Then hopefully beyond that, if there is money, time, or interest left, they can let people know where they stand on the issues. This is a perfect microcosm of corruption throughout the world. The politicians need money so the logical place to acquire it is from the people who have money. The people with the money expect a return on investment for that money which will likely come from the use or misuse of government services and or powers. To realign these services or powers, they must be taken from somewhere. The most logical place is the poor. They are generally a large receiver of services while at the same time unable to contribute to the political process financially and do not participate as actively in the process by way of votes.

The group I have not mentioned in this equations is the middle class. Politics is a show put on for the middle class. Politicians take money from the rich to convince the middle class to vote for them and then take resources from the poor to compensate the rich. The middle class get as little government services as the politicians can give them and not lose votes but just enough to keep them from complaining. This system is all controlled by messaging, manipulation and manufactured narrative to keep people doing what the system wants them to do.

Corruption exists throughout society, though. How many jobs in this country are controlled by connection rather than abilities? Sure people have to have certain skill sets to qualify for a job but beyond that it is connections that matter. This is this great mythology about the jobs wanted ads but really the only jobs that make the classified section of the newspaper are the ones that people with connections would never want. The good jobs are never advertised. Sure people get a good education at Harvard, but I could have gotten that at my public library. We go to Elite schools because of the connections we are making and those are what will define our careers rather than if we get an A or a C in calculus. That is why your father insists you go to Green.

These corruptors are subtle in the west and yet extremely powerful and all consuming. These corruptors define the rules of our society. Take these basic perversions and magnify their power in society and we end up with the cesspools of 3rd world corruption. In politics, the dictators have no middle-class voters to have to earn votes from and no need to ask the rich for money. They simply do as they will and take what they want and as long as they are generous enough with the military and police then their success is guaranteed. It is this very stranglehold that often causes the other major issue which is war. War can be used to justify whatever actions the a dictator wants. The need to remove a dictator can be used by good men to also justify horrible things and in so doing make them as horrible as those they would replace.

Philip, one day you will be an integral part of a group that holds power and you may, indeed, be the head of that group. At least I hope it will be you and not someone like Matt. Don't get me wrong, I have nothing against Matt and, in fact, I have a tremendous amount of respect for him but he is the enemy. He knows all that I have said to be true. He will use all his connections, wealth, power and intellectual gifts to make sure that he and members of his club remain where they are and things remain as they are. That makes him the enemy. But you Philip, are the hope. You can change the world."

Philip belched again loudly and kept it going for a count of five and then laughed as Frederick too smiled and laughed a bit. "You had me up until the last part where you made Matt into Lex Luthor and me Superman. Look, I don't disagree with you but how would someone overturn what has been thousands of years in the making?"

Frederick grew intense again and said, "Look to your history Philip. Opportunities for change happen all the time and it is just a matter of who's in power and what is the nature of the change that matters. The Revolution, the Civil War, any number of recessions, the great depression, World War II, the Cold War, and any events that have the potential to alter the status quo in terms of the distribution of wealth and power. What is important is to be in power when these opportunities arise."

Philip, replied, "I'm a little surprised that you left out the civil rights movement and the Vietnam War."

Frederick smiled and said, "Don't you see, those are just things to keep the people distracted. They are bread and circuses. Ending Jim Crow didn't change who was powerful in this country or hinder their ability to exploit the system to make money. Vietnam was that and a money maker through defense contracts. It's only when the elite has a legitimate fear that the power structure could change is there an opportunity for change. The Civil war was sold as about humanitarian issues but it was economics and who held the power. Nazism and Communism were threats to that power structure. There will surely be more threats and some day one of those threats will strike and change things in ways we can only guess."

Philip pulled into a gas station and the two got out and did all the things you do at a rest stop after driving 3 straight hours on a long road trip. After they got back in the car and were down the road a bit, Philip looked at Frederick with a strained expression. It was like he just couldn't let this go and said, "Ok so if we were in power and the opportunity presented itself, how would we fix it?"

Frederick finished chewing his candy bar and said, "For corruption you would have to rebrand it, as the marketing people like to say, and tie it to something sacred. Then make its violation a betrayal of the sacred and the community and worthy of a very serious and very public punishment. Campaign finance...well I guess you get a public outcry but good luck with that. The people who want to keep the status quo would just start waving the flag and the constitution and yell free speech until enough of the country blocks it from going anywhere."

Philip was more pensive and more serious than earlier in the conversation. He said, "That would be a challenge but if there were a greater crisis that could be sold it could be done but to change the nature of hiring and firing seems an even bigger challenge."

Frederick replied, "It would take a monumental crisis to facilitate change. The current system of job allocation is horribly inefficient and wastes a tremendous amount of untapped resources. The right crisis could prompt change. Maybe something worse than stagflation? People without jobs have nothing to lose and nothing better to do than move history."

That spring break would be the last time Philip and Frederick would spend a significant amount of time together for many years. They both had fond memories of the drunken debauchery that followed, but the debates are what they missed most and having someone they could be intellectually honest with.

Chapter 4

Meet Penne in college

"Love is a serious mental disease."
- Plato

It was early fall and the summer heat had just recently departed and now the sun was dialed back and a cool breeze trotted out from the shadows where it had been hibernating. The Campus of Green University was alive with Coeds in sweaters of every type exploding with patterns and colors as this was the golden age of the sweater. Yes, there was the occasional sweatshirt or hacky sack playing preppie going with the layered polo look instead, but, for the most part, sweaters were everywhere.

Philip Kingsley and Matthew Ligarck each had a little clique of orbiting freshman acquired from the rooms surrounding their respective dorm rooms. Philip and Matthew had purposely decided to go their separate ways in college despite both attending the same school. Green University had been the place for the intellectually elite sons and daughters of the financial nobility for generations. They had no big sports program and were not part of the Ivy League. Established by a generation of Robber Barons in 1883 in the Green Mountains of Vermont away from the hustle and bustle of modern life. It was purposely secluded so one could immerse oneself into the classics and engage their fellow students in debate and speculation. The motto: "Thought is Power" was displayed in Greek rather than Latin, as vulgar Latin was for the masses and formal Latin was for engineers and those who oversaw the masses. Greek was reserved for the educated and refined. There was a whole mentality in this that if you wanted to find a man to run a successful empire you looked for an Ivy Leaguer. But if you wanted an empire built, you found a man from Green.

The school was filled with the brightest children of the richest families in the nation, which means that they have also attended the best school with the best teachers and had the most knowledgeable tutors. Green was ridiculously expensive and, as a rule, did not broadly offer financial aid but did give full scholarships to the equivalent of 5% of the freshman class each year. These scholarship students could go the full four years for free if they could survive to the end, but they were otherwise on the same playing field as the rest of the students there. Most anyone with the tuition check for the full four years up front, a letter of recommendation from an alumnus along with certain minimal academic scores was let in. In some years, the freshman class was quite large, up to a 1,000 students. Green worked such that the bottom 50% the first year and 20% each succeeding year would be sent packing, often to the Ivy League. A freshman class of 1,000 would be a graduating class of 320. By gentleman's agreement, there was no manipulation or influencing a student to better grades and if the son of the richest man in the world doesn't make the cut, then that is it. Harvard or Yale will surely be destined to receive a large endowment for accepting that transfer.

Philip Kingsley and ML were part of such a class and it could have exceeded 1000 except for the rule capping the number there because the campus could not support a larger class. The freshman had to double up in the dorms and the living was tight. It was a dormitory, but that is not to say it didn't have the amenities that these children of the elite expected and demanded. They did not go there to spend time washing clothes or making beds, they were there to develop their minds so that they may use them to reshape the world. The rooms were broken into sets of four that shared a common area where they could relax as well as a separate and silent study area available anytime. Freshman were known as Knights, Sophomores Lords and Ladies, Juniors Kings and Queens and Seniors were Aristocrats.

One day in the first week or so of that freshman year Philip entered the St. George Pub, the only place on campus open to all. Significant to its patrons, it also served alcohol to anyone of legal age, which was 18 at the time. He nearly collided with one of the workers, obviously late, running to clock in. He looked to her to apologize just as she turned to him to do the same and their eyes locked for a moment that transcended time. It was as if Cupid's dart stuck him and injected him with that toxic poison love, for his heart raced like it seldom had, pumping infected blood throughout his body. The light of this goddess's visage was burned into his brain.

She was 5"7" with olive skin and dark, black, long, wavy hair that flowed like a silken waterfall. It was long and teased and puffed into a sexy tussle that was stylish at the time. Even though she was in a uniform of a long sleeve white dress shirt, black slacks, and black tennis shoes, her shapely proportions could not be concealed. Her piercing green eyes mesmerized Philip through her oversized brown glasses. Everything about her outfit was made to detract or at least conceal her beauty, but Philip saw through all of that and is his mind's eye saw her in a flowing gown. He later realized how strange this was that he didn't visualize her naked or at least in her underwear.

Philip sat at a table with some of the boys from around his dorm and collected himself. His mouth was dry and heart finally slowing down but he felt tired suddenly or perhaps drained is more accurate. He had never felt like that and was caught up in trying to snap out of his trance, but it was difficult. It was as if he washed up on the shore and was trying to piece together what had happened out at sea but was still in a fog. Then he saw her come out of the kitchen of the pub/restaurant and stand at the counter where she took food orders. Her hair was up now in a bun and she looked less disheveled and Philip was smitten.

She worked there three days a week and Philip always ate there those days. She was part of the 5% on a full scholarship and worked at the pub as a way to make some spending cash over and above the generous per diem build into the scholarship. Philip asked her out while she was away from work and she turned him down explaining her studies came first and she would date after college. He asked her out while she was at work with the same result. He asked her in the morning, in the evening, in her dorm and in class, all with the same result. After three months of this he had worn her down and she agreed to have coffee with him. It was history from there as she could not help but succumb to his charms and they were together from that moment on. She made him work for every milestone as he had to prove worthy of her love and he always did.

She was a hard worker who had a chip on her shoulder and was always trying to prove that she deserved to be there. She was brilliant and could debate with the best of them but would always fold before winning an argument. She would get nervous and lose confidence and not go for the jugular when her opponent was weak. This was true until one day when a smug boy with an average mind infuriated her insinuating that she should go home and have babies. She eviscerated him and re-discovered that anger gave her courage. Philip was more important than ever as he became her safe place where she could leave anger behind. That was essential because she took it to class and to work and that is what got her through the first year and what propelled her to the surviving upper 50% of the class.

After that grueling year, Philip wanted her to come to his house and meet his parents. She talked him out of it as she was terrified of this. She was terrified that she would be judged and found to be inadequate as she was the lowly daughter of a single mother and a departed deadbeat father. She grew up in a working-class neighborhood and went to private schools her whole life and she was always the poorest kid at every school. Poverty like everything else is relative. She lived in the greatest nation in the world and had a mother and large extended family who loved her and provided her with everything she needed and every opportunity they could. That was nice but didn't pay for the designer clothes and fancy accessories her classmates wore. Every day at each private school she went to she was surrounded by reminders of how relatively poor her family was. She knew the type of family the parents of a boy like Philip Kingsley wanted him to marry into and hers was not that type. She deftly postponed this inevitability as long as she could.

She enticed Philip instead to go away with her on a summer adventure. He brought her to the beach house of some friends of the family. They arrived in a huge private beach house which they had all to themselves. They were there hardly an hour when they found themselves entwined in a passionate embrace. Neither were virgins, but they had not slept with each other yet. Young bodies burned with desire and they ended up in the bedroom. They kissed deeply and tenderly slowly moving to the bed and shedding clothes. They

36

made love gingerly joining their bodies in a rhythmic dance of two souls in love. This love which radiated from their eyes as they stared deeply into each other's is what saved them from this sweet and romantic disaster. They climaxed and laid awkwardly wrapped in each other's arms in silence. Something was missing.

Fortunately, the awkwardness stayed in the bedroom and they reconnected outside it. They went for a swim and when they came back, Penne stumbled across a full bar. They were 19 and at the beach so of course they proceeded to get plastered. That night while drunk and kissing Philip picked Penne up as she wrapped her legs around him. He carried her to the bedroom and threw her down on the bed and a sparkle entered her eyes. She slipped her hands between the buttons of his shirt and while scratching her nails across his midsection tore open his shirt. No love was made that night but incredible mind blowing sex was had instead. They moved like dance partners feeding off of each other's intensity and passion. They pushed each other to the next extreme and experienced pleasures they had never known before this night. They would never make love again after this night, but they explored the extremes of sexual pleasure together while leaving romantic intimacy to other areas of their relationship.

Some couples are bonded emotionally or share interests or a sense of humor and they have good sex that occasionally borders on great sex but inevitably devolves into boring sex. Other couples have great exciting sex but are a bad fit outside the bedroom. This is typically the good girl with the bad boy stereotype or the crazy girlfriend scenario. Penne and Philip were the best part of the two relationship types. This was good and bad. When it was good, it was great. When it was bad, it was because each knew they would probably never find another person who they could connect with on a personal level. Almost certainly it would not easily find someone of the same sexual predilections they shared. The latter is always the tough one because while most everyone has certain turn ons that can seem unusual to those who don't share them, it's hard to find compatibility too far off the main path.

That leaves two choices, one could own the desire and look for a community of like-minded individuals whether that be through clubs, classifieds, or a look or a style that advertises it. Or, one could look for people they envision may behave that way in bed while not really knowing until they have sex. The latter choice is the one most people make because to advertise their predilection categorizes them and has consequences in every other area of their life. People want their partners to just do what they fantasize them doing without having to explain it or give instructions. What they don't want is someone who isn't into it and is doing it or enduring it because their partner asked them to as any of these scenarios detracts from or out and out kills the fantasy. These same people can't very well have a conversation on the first date about these preferences. Depending on what they are, this may be a conversation that is never had because of the embarrassment or fear of judgment.

The enjoyments Philip Kingsley and Penne shared were not of the sort people of their destined place and stature would advertise. They would certainly make for a very awkward talk several dates into a relationship, or worse yet, a risky leap of faith in the bedroom with the hope of not freaking out their partner. No, they were very lucky to have found each other and also in a way, trapped. They both knew that despite what may happen, they could find another compatible companion if they were willing to settle. The problem was that they would likely not find another person in their circles who would instinctively take them to the heights of desire and pleasure such that they did for each other. The bonds they occasionally shared in the bedroom extended metaphorically beyond the bedroom and each knew it.

Penne's family history was not unlike one typical of a Green University student, up to a point. Theodoros Plutous had taken the family business to undreamed of heights and even during the depression found ways to expand their shipping business when everything else was failing. Theodoros married his childhood sweetheart Laskarina. Together they had seven children, the youngest named Nikolaos. The Plutous family of Corinth had risen to be one of the wealthiest in all of Greece.

On October 28, 1940, the Italian army invaded Greece but was repelled forcing the German army to divert crucial assets away from the invasion of Russia to finish the job their allies bungled. During this second invasion, Theodoros Plutous put his family, except for his wife who stayed to fight, on a ship with a good part of the women, children and old people of their village. There were 142 of them in all. The ship came to America with a considerable sum of money to ensure that the group would be allowed in and that they could be settled. They ended up in Boston and assimilated into the local Greek community that had sprung up in the decades prior.

Theodoros Plutous had trusted his youngest children as well as his fortune to his Uncle Kostas, who was 69 when they made the trip to America. Kostas found an apartment building that met their needs and purchased it. It fit all the members of their group and had some extra apartments which were rented out for profit. The bottom floor of the apartment was meant as shared space and was underutilized. Kostas paid to transform it into a restaurant. It not only brought in money and gave many of the people who lived in the apartments work but made sure everyone had good food to eat and served as a gathering place for events and celebrations. It was also a place where they could mourn as word came of deaths back home, fallen heroes of the struggle against oppression.

While the patriarch of the Plutous family fought the Nazi's in Greece with his wife and two eldest sons, the other five children lived in adjoining apartments. Three of the children lived with their Aunt, who was an old maid and had always been around to help raise them. The eldest daughter, Maria aged 19, lived with the youngest son Nikolaos who was just five. She raised him as if her own and they lived in that apartment for years as the group survived the many hardships of the times. At the end of 1941, America too was at war with the Nazi's and the Plutous family did all it could to support the war effort.

Nikolaos was nearly ten when the war ended and by then only a handful of the family he barely remembered had survived back in Greece. His mother and one of his older brothers had lost their life as well as several uncles and many cousins. His father and brother were fighting communists now and both eventually lost their life to that struggle. Kostas had died just before the war's end and with him the drive to collect everyone and return home as a group. While some residents of the apartment building went home, most stayed and they came to love America. Kostas had set up trust funds for all the residents of the group with generous amounts set aside for each villager to get on with their life. Of course, the remainder of the fortune put in trust for the Plutous aires.

Nick had moved out of the apartment once he received his first sum of money from the trust at age 20. He had blown through it in less than a year and was back in the apartment building by the time he was 21. The next sum came at age 25 and was substantially larger. He lived the life of a playboy, without a job or income and partying until all hours of the morning. Within a few years, his money started to run out again and he panicked as the next sum required him to be over 30, married and with at least one child.

Nearly broke again, he married a blond party girl but they failed to have a baby. She had not told him about the back-alley abortion that left her sterile. They divorced a year later and Nick, penniless, divorced and humiliated, once again moved back to the family apartments.

Nick, a broken man, was put whole once again by a neighborhood girl named Popi, who was widowed, without children at age 25, and was on her way to becoming an old maid. They found strength in each other and got married. A year later, when Nick was 33 they had a little girl that they named Pennelope. Nick and his new family received his final inheritance which dwarfed the first two. What had already been a large sum of money in the trust grew substantially larger as the country prospered and investments flourished. The next generation would receive their inheritance when they turned 18 and that would be the end of the trust Kostas had so wisely established.

Nick and Popi bought a large house, much larger than what Popi wanted and much smaller than what Nick wanted. Penne received all the toys she wanted, the best education, and her daddy even got her that pony that every little girl was supposed to want. Nick and Popi fought, always over money. Even though Nick spent a lot and did not work, Popi did temper his spending and made some wise decisions that helped preserve the fortune that, if used wisely, should have lasted 6 lifetimes. One day, a foreclosure notice was tacked to the house they had owned free and clear. Nick had taken out a mortgage without Popi knowing. Nick had spent a lot of money without Popi knowing as he chased harebrained get richer quicker schemes and gambled until he owed bookies all over town.

Nick loved his wife and daughter and spent a good deal of money spoiling them both. While well intentioned, he was weak and indolent. One day he left and just never came back. Penne was just 13 and would only receive the occasional postcard as the only means of contact with her father for the rest of her life. Popi was left penniless and saddled with debt. She was forced to sell off everything and would have been homeless had not the family welcomed her with open arms. They moved back into the old apartment building and Popi worked in the restaurant. Penne was at a vulnerable age and imagined that her mother drove her father away and that he would return one day and take her away back to the privileged lifestyle she had known. She tried to run off across town to see her old friends, but these were disasters for her as they made fun of her clothes and that her family was humiliated. The thought of trucks pouring into the neighborhood to claim the cars and furniture days before the house was auctioned off still burned. Penne was a sad little girl.

Popi was a great mother and weathered this storm of resentment from her daughter. She got Penne to focus this anger on showing the world what she could be. Nick was very intelligent which made his story even more tragic as he had money and brains and managed to squander both. He did at least pass on his intelligence to his daughter and combined with the untrained and unappreciated intelligence of her mother, it destined her to always be one of the smartest kids in the room. Popi helped her focus that anger and intelligence into a competitive fire that had her seeking to be the best in her high school and she was.

She scored very highly on the SAT and was offered scholarships and grants to several college and universities. She became intrigued by an offer for a full ride, guaranteed stipend, and a job at Green University in Vermont. She had never heard of it but was fascinated by the prestige of the remote and obscure university that had apparently been educating the power elite of this country for generations. Penne took that competitive fire, incredible IQ and tremendous chip she kept on her shoulder and moved to Vermont to prove she belonged with the smartest and bluest of the blue bloods. She would redeem her family's noble stature. She would make her father proud...wherever he was.

Chapter 5

Communism Socialism Capitalism

"It is our duty to select the best and most dependable theory that human intelligence can supply, and use it as a raft to ride the seas of life."
— Plato

Philip, Penne and Matthew had survived the first year's grueling cut and made it to their sophomore year while half their classmates did not. Meanwhile, Frederick had received a full scholarship at Harvard which in a time of great recession and federal cuts to financial aid for higher education, was an accomplishment. Philip, Matthew, and Frederick met up on a skiing trip at a cabin Matthew's parents owned on Red Mountain in Crested Butte Colorado, in mid-December during winter break. They had skied all day and were relaxing in the central great room of the cabin. It was huge, more like a lodge than a cabin and Philip's mom and dad had hired some local help to staff the cabin while the group was there.

Penne was in total awe but did everything she could to hide it. Until a few months ago, the odds had been highly stacked that she would have been the help as opposed to one of the guests. Philip knew she came from a modest background and was working her way through school while taking on debt at the same time to supplement her scholarship. She was smart and ambitious and Philip was already starting to develop deeper feelings for her. This was her first long time exposure to Matthew and the first meeting of Fred.

Fred and Matthew had both brought companions as well for this fun couple's getaway. Fred had brought Teresita, who he had been dating for four months. It had ended shortly after this trip, but they were pretty serious up to this point. Matthew had brought a bimbo named Julie. Well more precisely she was from a well-off family and had scored well enough to get her into Green, but they were manufactured. Her resume was massaged and manipulated to get her in. From there she became one of the girls seeking a specialized degree, the MRS degree. These girls had a short shelf life at Green as the best they could do is make it to the end of their freshman year and guys like Matthew were the perfect mark. Guys like Matthew, of course, knew all that and used it to their advantage. As long as he kept his condoms hidden and puncture free and didn't otherwise lose his mind, he could have all the fun he wanted. He knew a fresh batch would arrive next year willing to do everything to please him as long as there was a hint at the possibility of marriage somewhere down the road.

Each evening, after a day of skiing and fun, the couples would meet back at the cabin to enjoy drinks by the fire. Of course, they were college students and it was never as sophisticated as all that. The first night they gathered around the big oval wooden table and played quarters. The object of this game was of course for everyone to get drunk, but specifically for your opponents to get drunker than you. To play, each person took a turn as the shooter whereby they attempted to bounce a quarter off a hard surface into a shot glass or cup. When they made a shot, they could select someone at the table to drink a cupful of beer. The volume of which was agreed upon by the players prior to the start. In a mixed group such as this, was a relatively small amount, like one-eighth or one-quarter of a plastic cup.

This universally loved college drinking game had regional rules and variations. For instance, the no pointing with a finger rule, no saying any variation of the word drink (drinking, drank, drunk, etc.) and various other things they couldn't say or do. Most, but not all versions of the game allowed players the ability to simply pass

44

their turn. This would be penalty free upon missing their first attempt however they could take a chance with a follow-up shot and risk having to "consume" the cup themselves if they missed that one.

Philip was the best shooter of the group, which, of course, meant no one would be foolish enough to send too many drinks his way as he could crush that person in return. Matthew was a decent shooter as was Fred. Teresita was a horrible player and a depressing drunk until she got horny and then came Fred's reward for suffering through the depressing part of the evening. Julie was an ace but was interested in getting drunk herself as much as making anyone else drunk so she could then molest a drunken Matthew and hope to have his pedigree seed take hold in her womb. Penne was a rookie at the game and had she not been under the protective cover of Philip's streak shooting she may have been the first of the group to commit a party foul.

It was Philip's turn and he repeated the sound of a quarter ricocheting off the table and clinking into the cup 14 straight times before finally missing two in a row and drinking himself. He punished Matthew and Fred a little more severely than the ladies. Penne followed him and had, under Philip's tutelage, gone from horrible to progressively better. Something must have clicked because she rattled off 6 hits herself which she distributed among the ladies.

Julie jokingly said, "God, you two are like the Evil Empire of quarters over there."

Teresita quickly corrected her, "If this were the Soviet Union we would share the drinks and not be told to drink when the bourgeoisie desired."

Julie angled her elbow at Teresita and said "Consume! You said the "d" word."

Penne jumped in and said, "First, I think she was joking and not making a political statement. Second, a handful of people telling everyone else what to do is a perfect metaphor for communism."

Teresita retorted, "The Soviet Union is no more truly Communist that the US is a true Democracy or purely capitalist, which is the real evil in the world."

Julie said incredulously, "How can you sit here in this country, in this cabin and call capitalism evil? GO U-S-A!"

The men were conspicuously quiet. They seemed to sense that this was the type of discussion that could disrupt a fun night of drinking followed, hopefully, with drunken sex."

45

Teresita glared at Julie and said, "I can't believe this is a big joke to you. There are people right now risking their lives to defend one or the other set of principles."

Philip sensed the change of attitude in the room and also that Penne was about to blast her. He slightly squeezed Penne's hand and said, "Ok our game of quarters is fizzing out and since you insist on talking politics let's make a game of it. Grab four pieces of paper. You have to write down a pro or con of either capitalism or communism depending on what you roll with the dice. 1 is a pro for capitalism, 2 is a pro for communism, 3 is a con of capitalism, 4 is a con of communism and of course 5 you just drink. Yes, I said it, drink drink drink!"

Philip stopped for a moment to chug a cup of beer while Matthew and Frederick chanted "Here's to Brother Philip who gets fucked up tonight, drink motherfucker, drink motherfucker drink!"

With that final word Philip slammed down the empty cup on the table.

He continued, "Where was I? Oh yea, and if you roll a six you can make someone drink. If you can't come up with the pro or con for your roll, then you must drink. If you say something already on that list, then you must chug a cup. If someone challenges an answer, there will be a round of debate followed by secret balloting. The loser of the vote chugs and if a tie, both the person who said the answer and the person who challenged must chug."

Julie was obviously excited by this redirection of the mood back to drinking and added, "How about if you say someone's name you must also drink?"

Matthew, getting into the spirit of things said, "And you have to drink if you say, bear, eagle, red, white, blue, pink or any patriotic or nationalistic derivation thereof."

Fred then said, "If anyone names a capitalist or communist country or the past or present leader of either a capitalist country or communist country the group must toast them. Same with anyone famous or held as an important figure on either side, like a Trotsky or Adam Smith."

Julie gave a quasi-cheer of "Wooo" and said, "We need a name for this game."

Penne responded with, "How about Cold Beer War?"

The group looked around at each other and no one had anything better so they all agreed, Cold Beer War it was. Julie volunteered to start things off and rolled the dice and got a one. This was a pro for capitalism. Julie grabbed the appropriate sheet of paper and wrote her answer which she then said out loud, "Freedom."

Teresita immediately said, "I challenge that. The Nazi's were essentially capitalist and I would not call them free."

Julie glared at Teresita and you could feel the laser beams shooting from her eyes cutting her in half.

Philip jumped in and said, "I guess we need more than just an economic system and if these are going to essentially be stand-ins for the US and USSR. How about we further define them as Democratic capitalism and totalitarian communism. Julie, given that, do you want to rephrase your answer?"

Julie, while still staring at Teresita said, "Freedom."

Teresita again said, "I challenge that. That is a broad term and I could argue that we are not free in the US and also that there is freedom in the Soviet Union."

Matthew raised his cup and said "a toast to the US," whereby they all took a drink. He followed that immediately with, "A toast to the Soviet Union" and they all drank again.

Julie replied, "You are such a little wannabe commie."

Fred interrupted, "Drink."

Julie took a sip and continued, "...how can you say democratic capitalist societies are not free?"

Teresita said, "How can you say they are?"

Penne said, "In fairness, you didn't say there was some freedom or they enjoy a high degree of freedom, you stated it as a one word absolute."

Matthew said, "So are you saying there is no country in the world that enjoys freedom because it is not absolute? So is no country large, or rich, or just or anything?"

Fred chimed in with, "Well if the answer is vague then it is open to lots of interpretation. Can we say Nazi Germany enjoyed freedom because the people were free to hum polka tunes while doing the dishes?"

After a moment of silence, Philip jumped in and said, "If no one else has anything, let's vote." He proceeded to hand out slips of paper and a combination of pens and pencils gathered from around the cabin. Everyone wrote out their vote, folded the paper and tossed them into the bowl, devoid of its plastic fruit, which became their makeshift hat.

Philip tallied the votes and Julie lost, four to two. The room was silent for a moment in wait for a response and when Julie poured a beer into a cup and proceeded to chug it while the room sat in awe. She slammed down the cup and proceeded to let loose a reverberating belch that seemed to last 30 seconds. The room broke out into applause and cheers.

Next up was Matthew, who rolled a four and answered "A con of communism is that it provides little choice in the marketplace."

Teresita rolled a one and said, "A pro of capitalism is that it" pausing slightly, "sometimes, leads to higher degrees of creativity and innovation."

Fred rolled a five and drank.

Philip rolled a two and said "a pro of communism is that there is no unemployment."

Penne rolled a six and made Philip drink.

Julie rolled a four and said, "A con of communism is that workers are not provided incentives to work harder or produce more."

Some people at the table noticed that Julie was smarter than she let on. Some smart girls act dumb if they want to trap rich guys.

Matthew rolled a six and made Philip drink

Teresita rolled a three and said, "a Con of capitalism is taxation, used a tool of policy and oppression."

Fred rolled a two and said "A pro of communism is there is an abolition of classes." He then rose up his glass and said "A toast to Comrade Trotsky" and the group drank and Julie let loose a "Woooo."

Philip rolled a three and said, "A con of capitalism is that speculation leads to bubbles."

Next up was Penne, who rolled a one and said, "A pro of capitalism is that free markets allow capital fluidity."

Julie rolled a two and said, "Comrade Marx always used to say a pro of communism is that there is an equal distribution of wealth. Raise your glass to comrade Marx." They all raised their glasses and drank.

Matthew was next up. He rolled a five and chugged a cup of beer, cringing as he finished.

Teresita rolled a six and gave it to Julie, who poured a cup and drank it enthusiastically again burping loudly when done.

Fred rolled a five and chugged himself slamming the cup down and twisting his face as he fought to keep the ice cold beer down.

Philip rolled a one and said, "A pro of capitalism is that prices are optimized automatically by markets."

Penne rolled a six and made Matthew chug a beer. He did so followed by a resounding belch that just slightly topped Julie's. Julie offered up her hand saying, "high five" and Matthew slapped it.

Julie then rolled a 3 and said, "Crap, we haven't been filling out the sheets."

They spent the next few minutes filling in the sheets as a few people took advantage of the stoppage of play for a bathroom break. Once she had the list in front of her, she said, "Con of capitalism is that the general outlook is short term as in the next election or board meeting."

Matthew rolled a six and sent it Penne's way saying "Payback is a bitch" Penne smiled, poured a cup and chugged it down in an instant then said, "And so am I."

The people at the table all looked impressed including Philip. Julie offered her a high five and said "Totally righteous."

Teresita rolled a two and said "A pro of communism is that there is equality amongst the sexes and races."

Matthew pointed to a cup just on the other side of Teresita and asked "Teresita, can you pass me that black cup next to you there?"

She looked to where he was pointing and said with a corrective tone "Do you mean the blue cup?"

Matthew responded with "No I mean the drink a cup, you said the "b" word."

Teresita glared at Matthew as he poured a beer into her cup. She drank a gulp and stopped.

Julie said, "The idea is to chug it, not sip it like a glass of chardonnay."

Teresita took another gulp which left two-thirds of the beer remaining and in a pained voice said "give me a second, I'll get it. Go on and play."

Matthew said, "Nope, we'll wait for you to chug the rest of that cup. Only half to go."

Teresita took another gulp and was down to a third and was hurting. Fred declared "Pinch hit" and grabbed the cup and finished it for her. Teresita gave him a look of gratitude like he had saved her from drowning.

Fred was next up and rolled a 4. He said, "A con of communism is that there is slower development generally because of less incentive to innovate and group decisions which take longer."

This went on like this as the group was getting pretty drunk and Julie rolled a six. She gave it to Teresita who was starting to look a little wasted. Julie smelled blood in the water and between her turn and Teresita's just start spouting out names that initiated more toasts. Next she tricked Teresita into saying white and made her drink again and it was all over. Teresita stumbled to the kitchen threw up in the sink. Penne and Fred went to comfort her as Julie and Matthew slid out and into the bedroom.

Penne took her back to take a shower as she could not stand and had thrown up over a good part of herself. Fred and Philip Kingsley sat on the couch for what seemed an eternity in the huge open room that literally had a bearskin rug and drank a beer, realizing Matthew was having wild sex just yards away.

Philip said, "I guess it could have been worse, she could have thrown up on you."

They chuckled for a moment and then a sliver of silence before Fred said, "It's not all bad I mean this exercise proves that. There is plenty of injustice in the world, but even the worst political systems have aspects that work."

Philip responded, "True enough. Every system has its flaws as well as their strengths. It would be nice if we could create a hybrid and pluck the best things from all the various political systems that have been tried. What would be a just system? What is justice for that matter?"

Fred smiled as he loved this sort of big thinking. He said, "Justice? That's easy. It is an outcome that is fair and distributed amongst the participants in proportion to what they deserve."

Philip asked, "Who decides what is fair and what is deserved?"

Just then Matthew came out, grabbed a beer and cracked it open. He said, "Those who have the power make the rules, those in power determine its application."

Philip said, "So Justice is what the strong determines it to be?"

Fred said, "You can't call that justice, that is simply what happens in the real world and that does not make it just. An essential element is fairness and that is what is often missing when the strong determine justice."

Matt said, "Well you can talk all day inside your ivory tower about justice as an ideal but what good does that do you if it is never applied in reality?"

Fred said, "Because it is not just the ideal, it's the definition, the baseline for success. You know when you see injustice only when you know what justice is and compare it to what is actually happening."

Matt replied, "That's the problem with you bleeding heart liberals, you want to pluck an ideal from its glass case and apply it to this world where it doesn't exist naturally and doesn't belong. There are no absolutes, everything is relative. It's like you have been raised in a room in front of a TV and you have blinders on your eyes so all you ever saw was the TV. Then one day you come out of the room and see the real word but all you can do is relate it to what you saw on TV. You must come to realize that the coyote can't defy gravity or death and the Roadrunner wins after the first scene of the first episode."

Fred replied, "I will concede that absolutes are rarely seen in reality, but they give us the target to aim for. The archer may never hit a bullseye but he can get close to it and he can only do that if he sees a target to aim at."

Philip said, "It is essential to know what you are shooting for but if all the shots miss their mark, then the conversation must at some point focus on the targets they are actually hitting."

Fred said, "Back to the political system. So what features do you sew together in this political Frankenstein?"

Philip had perked up because he too loved discussions like this and said, "Well I think we would want the freedoms of a democratic society and the competition of a market economy. I think you start with that and build from there."

Fred drank his beer with a thoughtful look on his face and said, "Ok, two problems we should address are unemployment and wage inequality as in the teacher vs. the ball player."

Philip replied, "Ok so the communists just have everyone work for the state, unemployment solved. Why don't we just hire all the unemployed to work for the government ala FDR's Civil Works Administration?"

Matthew said, "The problems with that are many. First your Neo-CWA is nothing but a huge tax suck. You are taking the most unemployable people, the ones that no business wants, and giving them work doing what no business can find profit in doing? You sensitive liberals don't want to say this, but this is the sick and the

51

dying of the herd. If this were a million years ago, these would be some of the humans that would be identified by the predators and picked off making the human herd stronger overall and preventing them from successfully passing on their genes. Today these people are not blocked from passing their inferior genes but instead are supported with housing and food so they have more time and opportunity to procreate."

Philip replied, "Ok Mr. Social Darwinist, assuming we are not going to literally throw these people to the wolves how do we make them productive?"

Fred said, "We educate them and train them to do the jobs that are in demand."

Matt replied, "Ok so you tell the kid who takes out $20k in student loans that now that he has a job, he not only has to repay the loan but he has to pay more in taxes to give someone else a free education?"

Fred said, "Should he feel better about paying more in taxes to build a bigger prison?"

Matt replied, "Should, is a loaded word as it brings is to questions of morality as opposed to practicality."

Philip Kingsley said, "Insurance companies spread risk by having a large number of people so when that predictable number get sick and rack up bill there are a lot more who are healthy and don't have claims digging into the premiums they have paid. The problem with our system is that business gets to pick all the "healthy" workers and leaves the "sick" ones for the government to take care of."

Fred said, "Communism would have them all employed by the state which then has the benefit of having all of them to then absorb the costs of those who are less employable. There are no need for taxes then and the state can use the profit from one to pay the costs of the other."

Matt sat with a bag of barbecue potato chips and said, "No taxes, that's hilarious. More like 100% taxes and you can see in an open society such as ours how easy it is to get your money back once you give it to the government. There is no "profit" from workers to offset the other costs because communism strips their incentives and motivation to be more productive and create profit."

Philip said, "Ok so what if to maintain the motivation and incentive to maximize production you take the things driving that in capitalism and combine that with the full employment of communism. What if you added competition to communism? What if you eliminated the business cost of labor and let them form and compete with free labor and reward success with financial bonuses."

Fred said, "Success could then be more broadly defined to fit the needs of society and balance those with the wants that currently drive profits. You set it up so that soda companies are incented not only to make a popular drink but a healthier one too."

Matthew said, "And who determines what is incented?"

Teresita had been put to bed and now from their bedroom Penne called out, "Philip can you come help me for a minute?"

As Philip walked away, Matthew looked at Fred and said in a low tone, "You know he's not coming back, right?"

Fred smiled and said, "Yeah, I know."

Matthew then went to his room for round two and left Fred to himself.

Chapter 6

Law School

"Employ your time in improving yourself by other men's writings, so that you shall gain easily what others have labored hard for."
-Plato

Philip Kingsley, Matt, and Penne had graduated Green and were off to get graduate degrees at prestigious schools as most Green Grads did. Matt was off to the London School of Business to add some worldliness to his already savvy character. Philip had planned to go to Harvard law but was convinced to hold off on that by Penne. She wanted to move to Berkeley so she could get her Masters in History focusing on late modern Europe. Philip Kingsley rolled with this detour from his life plan and picked up an MA in Classical Studies. Berkeley is where Philip really fell in love with Penne and almost asked her to marry him there but feared it would be a distraction and waited. Penne was smart and determined and independent. Philip admired her as much as loved her, but she could not understand the former although she cherished the later.

The two years on the west coast brought them closer together and the change in pace and in attitude was refreshing.

Philip also got a glimpse of the budding technological revolution from ground zero and this had a profound influence on the rest of his life. Two years later they were back on the east coast in Boston, or more specifically Cambridge, so Philip could finally go to Law School at Harvard. Frederick had started the previous year and it turned out he was the one who ended up one year ahead of the other. Penne looked for a job but primarily wrote and did so prolifically.

Philip rented a house that belonged to the family of a connection he made at Green. The boy Philip knew had just finished law school the year before so it worked out nicely. The next three years were some of the most enjoyable of the trio's lives. Philip convinced Frederick to move in with Penne and himself as the house was huge and easily accommodated them. Philip and Frederick loved law school and they loved arguing about everything until all hours of the morning. Penne enjoyed writing as much as they enjoyed arguing and in between scribbles on the legal pad she had with her at all times, she was occasionally drawn into their debates. She would put up feign resistance, but she loved to argue as well and could have made a formidable attorney.

Philip had grown to be 6"3" tall and had dark black hair and a natural, slightly dark complexion. He was thin but with a well-defined musculature like you would see on a well-rounded athlete but more so like a decathlete than a linebacker. He had rugged good looks and you could tell that he had been handsome his whole life as he didn't seem to even notice when women swooned over him as if it were just part of every man's life. He radiated confidence without a trace of conceit or vanity. He tended to look into women's eyes just a little longer than most men in what may have been on the verge of creepy if he were ugly but because he was far from it came off as a subliminal invitation to dive naked into those blue eyes and let their inhibitions behind. This had a strong effect and was just one component of his charisma and charm and, of course, would help him along in a political career

Men saw him quite differently. He was supremely confident and yet did not come across a confrontational or competitive. Competitiveness inherently contains the possibility that the other guy may be better than you and Philip had more of the air of a graceful winner who easily crushed you at everything. Philip was seldom the first to speak and he wasn't the loudest but when he did speak men listened. He was a natural leader and had the power to subordinate powerful men to his will. He could do this without

56

having to first defeat them in a battle of mind, spirit or body to earn this right although he could have and that is the notion most men took away. Men usually only challenge those they think, rightfully or wrongfully, that they have a chance of beating and men never felt that that was a possibility around Philip.

Frederick was 5"9 and just chubby enough to make him a little awkward. He wore black frame glasses that were like slightly oversized wayfarers. He wore a modest hi-top fade and dressed in an intentionally non-threatening fashion although he probably could not pull off threatening if he tried. He had a reserved confidence and seemed to nearly always have the look of a man who respectfully disagrees with you about something or maybe it was everything. He was incredibly smart and very well read which would have taken him far but throw in the work ethic of a Calvinist and he was more like an unstoppable intellectual force.

Penne had blossomed and become a striking beauty with long black wavy hair that glistened as it moved and brought out her green eyes that were mesmerizing when you stared into them. Her beauty was apparent but did not jump out and club you over the head but instead slowly poured into a room as she entered until the room subtly and almost unintentionally filled with it. Beauty occurred in Penne's life much the same way as she was a late bloomer acquiring the personality of a nerdy, skinny bookworm with acne before later blossoming into the olive skinned goddess she became.

Her breasts were not huge but erupted perfectly formed from her chest like two navel oranges. Her teeth were perfect at first glance but upon looking for a moment more you noticed that wasn't true. They were almost all straight, but some were slightly crooked like she didn't wear her retainer as often as she was supposed to. She was always that awkward, ungainly girl just below the surface but had already filled a person with awe before that realization if they were one of the very few allowed to get to that point. For those who could snap out of the trance-like aura, she induced and actually had a meaningful conversation with her they were usually blown away a second time by her insightful intellect that she kept tucked away like a concealed high caliber handgun and used like a marksman when the topic worthy.

Philip and Frederick piled into the house through the side door after coming back from the library lugging backpacks stuffed with books. They were a little sweaty from the bike ride even though it was just above 60 degrees outside. The house was taller than it was wide, being three stories high. They entered through the kitchen and found Penne sitting in the front room in a chair staring out of one of the several windows into space as her legal pad sat idle in her lap. Penne wore sweat pants and sweatshirt and snapped around as if being shaken out of a trance.

"Deep in thought?" Philip asked as he walked over and pecked a hello kiss on her cheek.

"Yeah I've been kind of stuck and I can't seem to write my way out of it," She said.

Philip said, "Can I help."

She said, "Yes talk to me about anything but writing. Did you two get all your homework done?"

Philip said, "Well technically that is discussing writing as I finished my paper but I also got a good deal of reading done."

Frederick said, "Same here, but I have a ton more reading to do. For now though I need to give my eyes a break. I remember when I actually used to read for enjoyment."

Penne said, "So you never read up on the finer points of patent law in your spare time for fun before now?"

Frederick said, "And still not now. The patent system is important, but it's dull from a legal perspective."

Penne said, "But I thought that's what you wanted to specialize in?"

Frederick replied, "Intellectual property, not physical property. I want to argue the ownership of ideas, not stuff. Stuff is boring."

Philip said, "The whole system is rigged anyway. You have to be a huge corporation to be able to afford to defend a patent even after the jumping through all the hoops to get one in the first place. We should give patents away freely and pay for the resources needed for individuals to file for patents and to defend them. My gut tells me the indirect return on investment in tax dollars would be break even at worst and much more likely return many times the cost. Patents lead to businesses and jobs and expand the overall economy. Hell, we could even slap a meager small percentage tax on sales for the life of the patent which would go away when it becomes public domain."

Penne said, "Didn't I read that we already produce more patents than any other country?"

Frederick said, "That is very true, but 75% of them are awarded to corporations."

Penne said, "What's wrong with that?"

Frederick replied, "There's nothing wrong with corporations filing for patents. It is so disproportionate because corporations not only have the upfront money and resources to invest in the R&D and patent application process but they have the resource to defend them and then also bring them to market. Individual inventors have to invest their personal capital or do fundraising and then they also have to be good salespeople. It takes a separate skill set to sell or license the product or be entrepreneurs and start up their own companies to make and sell the products. There is a vast harvest of ideas that rot in the silos."

Penne said, "But what about all those commercials I see for companies that help inventors bring their ideas to market? Isn't that the answer?"

Frederick said, "Unfortunately these companies are almost all scams of one degree or another who exploit the very problem we are talking about and make money by catering to the dreams of these inventors and giving them false hopes in exchange for a large sum of money. If these things were legit, they would work on a contingency basis and do the work in exchange for a percentage of ownership, but they don't.

You see when a corporation invents, it is to solve a specific problem that they have identified as being profitable to solve and within their wheelhouse of knowledge and resources to solve. When an individual invents, the business aspects are a huge added expense. They have two options. One is that they can either throw in all the added costs for the infrastructure of building a company around the idea. The other is that they must employ a marketing and sales effort to find and convince an existing company with the means to use the idea, to pay for it. They must convince the company that there is money to made in doing so and that they should pay the inventor to do it. This actually happens, but only for the savvy minority who have knowledge of the system and the resources needed to work within it."

Philip said, "This one of those situations where a problem in the marketplace has not been solved within the framework of the market. To make this work you need government to step in with the goal of them interfering as little as possible and still getting the job done. Maybe a tax credit for investing in a new invention or make the filing process for individuals free. This is doable."

Frederick said, "I like where you're going, but I see some problems. A tax credit would put money out in the water like chum

59

for the sharks already there. Making the process free for individuals sounds good but I would want to think through the unintended consequences of that. Maybe corporations have their employees file while at the same time signing lifetime licensing deals for a penny or something like that."

Philip said, "There is such an opportunity for capturing the ideas that go nowhere now. The ideal system would result in every idea getting patented quickly and ready for the marketplace to then see and use the ones with utility for a fair fee."

Penne said, "Why do a one size fits all? Just give inventors and company's options and let them choose. Maybe there is a free option that defines the licensing terms alongside the patent including a nominal percent going to the government. Then the winners can hopefully earn enough to cover the losers."

Frederick smiling hugely said, "That just might work and if that is an open licensing agreement so that anyone could use it non-exclusively as long as they pay the licensing fee then it can hit the marketplace right away. Corporations who want a traditional patent can file the current way and maybe some other options for small business and individuals with more breakthrough ideas where they would get more for keeping the rights or license exclusive."

Philip laughed and said, "You see, the three of us can fix the world."

Versions of this scene would play out as the three got along well and Frederick never mentioned what he heard in a house with walls that could only contain so much sound. Philip and Penne never gave Frederick any crap for some of the incredibly unusual women he would bring home to bed. Frederick convinced himself he did not have the time nor the desire to be distracted by a girlfriend so he didn't allow himself to have one. Meanwhile urges did need to be met and being an awkward, albeit witty, nerdy little fellow, he could not always be discriminating when looking for a good time.

These were the final relatively carefree years of anonymity. These were enjoyable years at Harvard. Frederick earned his SJD focusing on Intellectual property and technology. He went on to become a professor at a string of schools and then ended up back at Harvard. He taught himself computer programming along the way. After graduating at the top of his class, Philip had his choice of jobs and chose a prestigious firm in Atlanta Georgia. Penne kept trying to write that commercially successful book while living with Philip in Atlanta.

Chapter 7

Early Marriage-Love for the ages

"By all means marry: if you get a good wife, you'll become happy; if you get a bad one, you'll become a philosopher"
-Plato

It seemed very difficult to get Penne to move again three years later to Atlanta. Philip was offered a job at a prestigious firm that would fast track him to partner if he just lived up to his potential. She went and he felt guilty for forcing her into it. He hadn't given her an ultimatum as he said he would stay for her but really that was just the love talking. She owed it to him after the diversion to Berkeley and she had no roots and no friends in California and she no longer kept in touch with her family in Boston at all.

In Atlanta, it quickly became apparent that Philip was not going to become a partner based on long hours or number of cases. Not because he wasn't a capable lawyer, he was brilliant, but because he loomed large in life. For him to spend so much of his time on the mundane details that comprise a law case seemed wasteful and almost ridiculous. His bosses identified that in him and were all busy latching onto him before his star started rising.

He was invited to seemingly every social function that came along and met every person of any significance in Atlanta and charmed them as well. Philip owned not one but three tuxedos and Penne had a new gown almost weekly. Philip's social standing quickly exceeded his professional standing

Penne went through a bought of depression during this time and the social events were exactly what she needed as a distraction. She finished her first book before leaving Boston. It was from the heart and was about what she wanted to write about and received good reviews but no sales. For her next book, she sold out and wrote a book designed to appeal to the masses and she hated every minute of writing it. It got lousy reviews and to add salt to the wound and also didn't sell so she didn't even get paid for selling out. She realized that writing could bring happiness or at least peace, but she would not find success in terms of fame or fortune. Unfortunately for Penne, and for most people, they ignore the things that actually make them happy in favor of the things they've come to believe are supposed to make them happy. She thought you had to be happy as a result of certain accomplishments, actions or things or it didn't count. Penne would not write another novel.

Philip would become a well-liked and respected figure and Penne, by virtue of being his beautiful wife, was envied and coveted. He built a cadre of rich and powerful people that proved invaluable when after about a year in Atlanta an opportunity came his way. The City Councilman for District 6 fell ill and had to abruptly step down from office leaving his seat open for a special election. A couple of the senior partners of his firm urged him to run as it was only a part time job would bring connections and publicity to the firm and certainly wouldn't hurt Philip's career. After discussing it with Penne he decided to run and with the help, and money, of his important connections, easily won the job.

Later in life, Philip's memories would often drift back to this period of time when he was running for office for the first time. It was during this time that he asked Penne to marry him. He had wanted to ask her in a memorable way and struggled with something that was a grand gesture, would be something Penne would appreciate and would show his love for her. She had lost her way in life and was at times depressed so Philip settled on a traditional setup at a swank restaurant which also allowed him to abort the plan if something wasn't just right. Philip set up a fancy dinner that was supposed to be with a very rich new supporter who had to cancel at the last minute but insisted they stay and enjoy the evening.

Penne said, "Philip, can you come help me with this zipper?" loud enough for him to hear a couple rooms over but not so loud as to be shouting.

Philip said, "Sure. Did you pack the overnight bag like I asked? I'm not saying it's going to happen but from our research, we found he loves to show off his Casino in Mississippi and if that happens we will want to stay the night."

"I certainly hope he is bringing his checkbook if we are going to have to endure a Mississippi casino and the toothless hillbillies playing penny slots."

"Be nice, those are hardworking folks and I was hoping a little later to play some Penne slots myself."

"Behave yourself, Councilman. What time will the car be arriving?"

"We still have another 15 minutes. Got something in mind?"

"Philip, you naughty boy. Maybe later if you minimize the torture of this dinner."

The car came 15 minutes later just as Philip had said. Philip was wearing a dark custom-fitted Italian suit on the conservative end of the spectrum. Penne looked stunning in a conservative, full length, Prussian blue, one-shouldered gown. She wore her luxuriant black silky hair up and around her neck hung a single strand of pearls. Philip walked into the room to see the finished masterpiece and stopped in his tracks when he saw her.

"You take my breath away you are so beautiful and elegant. I am the luckiest man in the world. Our chariot awaits if you are ready."

"Can you grab my bag for me, Baby?"

That was a good sign as she only called Philip Kingsley baby when she was in a happy place.

"Got it," He said as he walked over and grabbed her hand and gently pulled her closer to him as he leaned in to kiss her, staring into her tranquil green eyes as he did.

They hopped into their Town Car and arrived at the restaurant in a night, not unlike other similar nights they had experienced since Philip Kingsley started making connections. They were seated and after just a few minutes the Maître d came over letting Philip Kingsley know he had an important phone call.

When Philip Kingsley came back to the table, he said to Penne, "I have excellent news of sorts. At least for us. Their son was arrested for some minor thing, but they want us to continue on with the evening compliments of them."

They had some drinks and ate their food enjoying what Penne did not know was a contrived and meticulously planned out romantic evening. As they completed their entrees, Philip found himself nervous. He stood up to excused himself and went to the restroom to regain his composure. As he returned to the table, he walked up to Penne and took her hand in his and stared into her eyes. She smiled and then felt the awkwardness of the moment as Philip neither said anything nor sat down. Her eyes nonchalantly and unconsciously darted around the room to size up the scene that Philip may be creating.

That's when he dropped to one knee and said, "My life has been great. I have no complaints, nor should I. Yet with no one there to share the best life has to offer and no one there to help or be helped by when troubles appear as they do, life is empty. It felt empty until that day I first saw you at Green University and have felt full ever since. I don't want to ever go back to the time when I don't have you to share the stories of our day, our thoughts, our hopes and dreams with each other. I never want to be without you ever again."

Penne choked back tears of joy as Philip spoke these words. The activity of the restaurant stopped for this moment in time and all attention was directed to their table. Philip was not speaking exceptionally loudly however it was somehow apparent to all there that something was happening. The people at all the surrounding tables stopped what they were doing and watched this scene unfold, mesmerized as it played out. Philip slipped his hand into his pocket and pulled out a ring with a large stone in a tasteful setting and held it with his right hand as he held Penne's hand in his left.

Philip Kingsley continued, "...Penne Plutous, will you honor me with your hand in marriage?"

The restaurant had not only stopped but now held its collective breath as the look on Penne's face went initially from embarrassment to shock. It then went to holding back tears of joy and finally, with elation, exploded with the yes she had wanted to blurt out the second Philip Kingsley started his proposal.

"Yes, yes I will marry you, Philip Kingsley!"

Philip slipped the ring onto her finger and kissed her as the restaurant exploded into applause. Even cynical older couples were touched by this scene of true young love and added a spark of romance to all who witnessed it. The waiter and a team of busboys appeared on cue with a bottle of champagne an ice bucket and glasses. Philip Kingsley turned to the waiter quietly told him he would like to order champagne for the room.

They received congratulations and thanks for the next few moments, but suddenly they had to get out of there and so Philip took care of the bill they headed back out to the car. They embraced in the back seat and Penne held her hand out in front of her and stared at the new ring that adorned her hand with a huge grin on her face.

She said, "Pennelope Kingsley. Penne Kingsley. Mr. and Mrs. Kingsley. Yes Mrs. Kingsley, right away Mrs. Kingsley."

Even the most exotic and unpredictable of women acts as a cliché at times.

Suddenly it occurred to her that they were not headed home.

She asked, "Philip, where are we going?"

Philip said, "To Paris!"

"Philip, don't toy with me are you serious? What about my passport and luggage."

Philip leaned in, gently and slowly kissed her and then said, "It has all been taken care of, just relax and enjoy."

They went to a small airport just south of the city where they boarded a medium sized private jet loaned to Philip by Matthew Ligarck as an engagement gift. They got on board and settled in with another bottle of champagne that was waiting for them in a bucket of ice in the cabin next to a bowl of strawberries. They enjoyed a few glasses and fed each other strawberries as the plane took off.

Philip took Penne's hand as the flight attendant closed the door leading toward the front of the plane. He leaned down and kissed her gently at first and then more vigorously as Penne became more aggressive in her kiss back. She bit his lip in the process and he momentarily pulled back with surprise. She looked up at him with a look that was one part innocence and one part the cat who ate the canary and one part devilish grin. He grabbed her and picked her up out of the chair and carried her back to the bedroom.

They did not make love or stare tenderly into each other's eyes and no harp music played and no unicorns trotted out of rainbowed landscape. That was not how they were. They shared their intimate lovey dovey moments, but they were not in the bedroom. There they had sex and it was great, mind-blowingly great sex in the clouds. Penne was a great artist and her canvas was a bed. Actually she was a performance artist and Philip was her co-performer and biggest fan. They never spoke of their sex outside of the bedroom and never held back anything inside it. They were wild and free and brought each other to unparalleled heights of ecstasy. Nothing was off limits and everything was explored. That night they joined the mile high club several times and several ways and Philip would find himself remembering this night often.

In fact, Philip would fantasize about any one of several specific nights and sometimes days spent in pleasures of the flesh. Philip would never tell anyone that he thought about Penne this way because men just didn't fantasize about their wives and especially sexual fantasies, but Philip did. Another woman would likely be a boring disappointment and Penne had always surprised him and fulfilled him. There was no inhibition, no embarrassment, and no regrets. He was obviously in love with her, but he was also obsessed with her.

They enjoyed their honeymoon and were the talk of the Atlanta social set. Philip finished out the councilmen's term and in that short time made many connections in the Mayor's office and continued to expand his social circle and influence. He had made several connections in the DA's office including the Atlanta District Attorney himself and after his term as councilman ended decided to take up an offer to join the DA's office in the prosecution unit. He, of course, skipped over some of the dues-paying steps which won him no friends but who needs low-level friends when you have high-level connections. Philip loved the opportunity to work in the courtroom and was exceptional. He fast-tracked to Senior ADA and made a name for himself throughout the area with his high conviction rate and telegenic presence which the press gobbled up.

While the DA's stroke caught everyone off guard, it was not really a surprise as the man had been DA for over 20 years and lived on steak, cigars, and scotch. Davis Johnston was made the interim DA pending the special election he was almost certain to win. No one saw Philip Kingsley coming and just as his candidacy against Davis was a surprise his hugely successful campaign and victory were even more surprising. The wild card in the whole campaign turned out to be Penne. She was superb in the role of candidate's wife. She was charming and whatever else she needed to be to get the support and money out of whoever was in the room at the moment. She studied the field and knew all the players better than anyone on Philip Kingsley's staff and made sure he knew the right buttons to push from moment to moment.

Three years later when Philip ran for Lt. Governor, they almost pulled it off again. While they wrapped up all the key support in Atlanta, Philip was practically unknown to the rest of the state and lost a close race. Philip needed a change and stepped down as DA to run and so was technically unemployed after losing the election. They took a break after that and saw the world a bit before coming home to decide on next steps.

Just about that time Matt came into town and invited them out to dinner. Matt had jumped into the business world out of school and exercised his considerable talents. He could recognize the potential of a company underperforming because of mismanagement or because they were upstarts. He could also see the potential of upper management types and where their abilities could best be utilized. This latter skill was what brought him to Atlanta as it was no coincidence that he arrived just as Philip was looking the next adventure in his life.

Philip and Penne arrived in the limo Matt had sent for them and were escorted to the private room that had been reserved for this dinner. Matthew Oliver Ligarck was sitting with a lovely woman who was pointing to some papers and glanced up at Philip and Penne as the door to the room opened and then looked to Matthew as if looking for direction. Matthew nodded and mumbled something to her as she quickly gathered the papers and departed the room nodding hello to Philip Kingsley and Penne as she left.

Matthew was five feet ten inches or so and his strikingly blond hair of his youth had become sandy with age. He was not fat but not skinny either and perhaps better described as soft. He lacked musculature and was round in the places where more athletic men were defined or angular. His looks were average at best, but everything else about his appearance was top shelf, from the shoes and clothes to the manicured hands and meticulously combed hair that made you just want to stab both hands into it and muss it up. His blue eyes were piercing and with his blond hair and arrogant attitude gave him a bit of a Gestapo vibe. Of course, the idea of Matthew Oliver Ligarck feeling superior to any subset of humanity was ridiculous as he felt vastly superior to all other humans without prejudice.

Matthew rose out of his seat, spreading his arms in a welcoming pose as he smiled broadly. He said, "Come and sit. Penne, you look simply ravishing. College sweethearts surviving out into the world. You give the rest of us hope."

While saying this, he kissed Penne on the cheek and embraced Philip. "Philip, you look great too. Still working out I see."

Philip looking a bit off balance looked quizzically at Matthew and said, "Just who the hell are you? I was supposed to meet Matthew Ligarck here this evening and instead have been greeted by a personable, friendly, socially adept, charming man who I have never met in my life.

Matthew replied, "Come now Philip, I've added some European refinement to my American cynicism. You don't mind if I show it off a bit do you? In all honesty, it's a little hard to turn it off."

Penne, in all seriousness, said, "Please do turn it off Matthew, I rather always enjoyed the pompous, arrogant prick we came to know."

Philip glared harshly at Penne and then apologetically to Matthew, "Penne was never one to speak her mind."

Cutting him off Matt replied, "Yeah right, don't be ridiculous Philip and don't be embarrassed by the truth. Penne thank you for cutting through the bullshit. You're right, I have my guard up because I wasn't sure how this reunion would go.

Penne, I owe you several apologies. I was always an ass to you because well, I thought maybe you were a gold digger and I didn't think you were good enough for Philip. I'm happy to have been proven wrong on both counts."

Penne smiled just a bit and said, "Ah there's a glimmer of the jackass but now tempered by the diplomat. I'm not buying it, but I'll play."

Philip jumped in and asked what he had been doing and the conversation took off. Various courses were served slowly over several hours as the exquisite wine flowed as did the conversation. They caught each other up on the details of their experiences since college. Each knew the other had followed the other's career and had prepped for this meeting, but they shared the funny anecdotes of what was not publically known. This went on for hours and dinner came and went as did dessert and more wine.

Penne had played along but by this point she had enough and asked what Philip was thinking, "Matt, thanks for dinner but what is it you want? Why are we here?"

Matt laughed and said, "I did not think you would endure this long and I was really just seeing how long I could go before you'd call me out. Fair enough, we've had enough chit chat and reminiscing for one night."

Matt's face, now more hardened, looked Philip in the eyes and said, "Philip, what the fuck was that election fiasco? I don't even know where to start. First, why would you not go ahead and go for Governor? To lose to that bum is embarrassing enough but for Lieutenant Governor no less. Now you have to go back and win just to prove you can. For Christ's sake, I understand you won't come to someone like me for advice for fear of feeling beholden. Really though, if you are going to be serious about this then you need a serious team and one playing at the level of the ultimate goal and not just DA or Lt Governor. The mistakes you make today will hurt you in your presidential bid when it comes. Where is your long term thinking? Ahhh Philip, you are so much better than this JV bullshit."

Philip Kingsley looked at Penne and then back to Matt, "If I didn't know any better I'd think the two of you were conspiring against me but I think maybe it's just the truth aligning itself. You are right it was a blunder. I dipped a toe in the pool on a whim. I thought maybe I wanted to be a lawyer for a moment, but this time off has given me time to reflect and I do want the White House."

Penne nearly spit her wine out as she said, "You want what? Where did this come from?"

Philip feeling the wine said, "I was going to talk to you and this timing forced my hand. I want to lead and there is no better place to lead from."

Penne said, "You lead with power if you want to change the world you should be doing what this nimrod is doing. I have gone along with this political career as I thought it was about connections, but now I'm not so sure this is what I signed up for."

Philip said,"Matt my apologies, I don't mean to air our laundry here."

Turning to face Penne he said, "Look it was and that is why I lost. I thought I could go that route, but that is not who I was born to be. That is not who I am. All I ask is let me give it a shot. If you give me your full support in this, if I fall short of the goal I will throw all my energy into becoming the richest most powerful man on the planet."

Penne sat in thought for a moment and then said, "One run. I don't want to be married to the perennial losing candidate who then tries to sell books before his fifteen minutes of fame expires or accepts a position beneath him as a gesture from some politician who beat him. One run with no mudslinging and an honorable exit when it's time."

Philip said, "Agreed."

Penne laughed and said, "See I can compromise. It will just delay my gratification and make it that much more enjoyable. You are too pure and too righteous to ever be President. You will not sell your soul and that is the price of admission."

Philip smiled and said, "You are probably right and the best I can probably hope for is to influence the national conversation, but that would be something. But, don't underestimate me too soon. I may just have a trick or two up my sleeve like the offer I can't refuse that Matt is about to propose."

Matt grinned, "That transparent?"

Philip grinned back and said, "Just to me."

Matt said, "Very well here are my cards. I am planting several seeds so that when the time is right I have a man in the Oval office that will take my calls. If you do what is smart, I will help you get to the starting gate with no quid pro quo. I will assess the situation when it's time for the race and I will likely not back you or more likely you will not be willing to commit to what I will demand in return for victory. I offer advice, connections and access to money. I will commit some money of my own but only if it doesn't cost me when all's said and done. Write-offs and the like. I will get you unscathed to the starting gate. That is my commitment. From you I need a commitment to get there and a clean record. Do the smart thing and you will have my support. Do something stupid that hurts the big plan and we are done. That is the offer."

Penne said, "Wait, first why am I here for this?"

Matthew said, "Because Philip would bring it to you anyway and I would rather be in the room to overcome objections."

Penne said, "Smart. Ok, let's say I buy that and most of the other crap, walk me through the scenario in which it benefits you to have Philip in the White House. You two haven't agreed on a single thing or been on the same side of an issue since I have known you and I suspect ever."

Matthew replied, "I love the way her mind works Philip, I've gone full circle from thinking you're an idiot to being extremely jealous. Penne, you are quite right. My deal is not to put you in the White House, it's to put you in the starting gate. You would be an unlikely option but an option nonetheless which is an asset. Philip, your candidacy may very well hurt the opponent of the candidate I back. You may end up being worthless to me in which case you are simply a hedging bet that didn't pay off. Those are the two most likely scenarios but as I said it gives me options, some of which may not be known until the day comes.

In any case, you get a powerful backer that brings strategy, connections and money to the table without requiring a slot on the agenda in return. You will be on your own in the end and will ultimately go down in flames, but we both get what we want and need from this."

Philip Kingsley said, "Ok, the Lt Governor move was a mistake. What would you do from here?"

Matthew said, "Well with your background, the Senate would have been a better route for you and certainly not from Georgia, but what is done is done. A governorship is a great launching pad, but the timing and state have to be right. You need to wipe away the specter of this loss so I would have you win the Georgia Governor's office for one term. That is about all you could hope to fool the conservative suburbanites and the hicks of greater Georgia out of. Then after one term we move you to a Northern more liberal state with an available and vulnerable Senate seat opening up and get you to the Senate. The next step would be to wait until the right race came along and enter it. What you do from there is on you."

Philip looked at Penne and then back to Matt and said while raising his glass, "Then I propose a toast as I have an agreement with both of you."

Chapter 8

The Bets are Placed

"He who wishes to serve his country must have not only the power to think, but the will to act"
— Plato

"Senator, Mr. Ligarck is here to see you," said the secretary as she popped her head in Senator Kingsley's door.

"Thank you, please send him in" replied the Senator.

Matt walked in with his coat slung over his arm and Senator Kingsley stood up and the two shook hands vigorously.

"How are you, Matt?"

"I'm good Phi...Senator. You ready to grab some lunch?"

Philip said, "Sure, let me grab my coat."

The two men went out together to the front of the building where a black limo pulled up. A very serious looking man in a suit got out of the passenger side and scanned the surroundings as he held the door to the back of the limo open while the two VIPs took off their coats and climbed into the forward facing seat.

Philip tossed his coat onto the rear facing seat and buckled up. He said, "So is that man new?"

Matthew sat quietly for about ten awkward seconds and then started to reply, "No Ben's been with me for about a year and a half now."

Philip had seen what Matthew was looking at asked "What is that light?"

Matthew replied, "It indicates there are no surveillance or other electronic devices so we are free to talk."

Philip smiled and said, "So I guess this is a good time to ask you what this is about. I mean I enjoy catching up, but I thought your team will have this next election wrapped up at the ball seems to be bouncing back to that side of the fence. Is this where you tell me good luck and you're cutting me off?"

Matthew, with a look of total sobriety, said, "We need you to save the republic."

Philip laughed as he heard this until he realized Matthew had maintained a straight face throughout.

Matthew said, "I am dead serious. This is one of those times like September 1929 or August 1939 or August 2001 for that matter. The coming event is not so singular as those events would be but no less transformational and pivotal to world events. We can either be in a position to take advantage of what is inevitably coming or we will be the victim of these events.

We have had think tanks wargaming this for years and there is no way at this point to avoid what is coming. The potential outcomes range from scary to disastrous so you would be shocked at the things that may be tolerated in order to preserve the American way of life."

Philip looked aghast but then recovered and responded,"So, "American way of life" sounds like code for us rich guys keeping our money and power. Things 'tolerated", I take would mean someone with radical ideas from someone such as myself as opposed to a puppet. What I can't decipher is this catastrophic event."

Matthew said, "It is not so much an event as a collection of trends that are snowballing and on a collision course. The need for human labor is decreasing while, at the same time, the energy supply is decreasing or more accurately, transforming. We are increasing our energy demand as well as demand for raw resources. Why do you think we have positioned our military assets all around the Middle Eastern oil deposits? Why do you think we are running huge deficits propping up a market with ever growing unemployment and underemployment?

The shit is about to hit the fan Philip and we need someone who can steer us away from it and pull it us to the other side where sunshine and green fields wait for us. We either evolve into a society that utilizes and benefits from the gifts that technology is about to bestow on us or we can fall apart on the doorstep of that, as a people who could not manage change and so were ruined by it. I believe you are the person who can get us through this."

Philip looked incredulously back at Matthew as he said, "I have never known you to be reactionary or to use hyperbole so this is a little much to take in. You sound like a conspiracy theorist instead of the ultra-conservative, old money plutocrat I have always known."

Matthew replied, "Then when coming from me you should receive the message with that much more urgency. I am a realist and I have seen the scenarios and they range from war to civil war to anarchy. The best outcomes only push the timetables for these events out but don't change them. We can act or we can let them eat cake while we wait for our heads to come off. What happens when 500 million Chinese, who have found manufacturing work and a rising standard of living for the past 25 years, suddenly see that disappear? What happens to world markets when prices spike for oil as we have moved past peak oil and the Saudis no longer have the ability to up the flow to keep prices stable? What happens to the world when the US economy is no longer strong enough to prop it up and collapses under the weight of it all? Chaos. That's what happens and chaos is bad for markets. I can make money on the descent, but that would be predicated on its eventual re-ascent.

The people I represent benefit from the status quo and aim to preserve it as much as possible, even if that means some things must change radically. When a dystopian police state is one of the better, likely outcomes, then the time to act is nigh."

The two sat in silence for a few moments while Ligarck left his words linger in the air and Kingsley let them sink in. Finally Philip said, "So what saves us?"

Matthew replied, "We don't know what saves us so we are searching for who saves us. Look, we don't agree on many things in the world of ideas as it exists now in this bubble of existence. But that is about to come unglued and we need someone with new ideas, who can act decisively and get people to follow them into courses of action that won't always seem logical.

I say this humbly, and God knows I am far from a humble man, but I have never been bested in debate or had less than the best idea in any room in my life except for the one you were standing in. I'm certainly not conceding every argument we ever had, but I have to concede a good deal of them and probably, if I'm honest, most, and that never happens anywhere else. I am the smartest guy in every room you are not in.

You have that going for and people like you. Something I only cared about when it was profitable and otherwise found highly overrated. Be it a gift or curse that you have. People like you and will follow you. Even if I thought it possible, I'm not looking to make you a puppet because that would imply I knew which strings to pull and I don't. We don't.

Take some time and think about it. If this is something you want, just run and you will win. We would never have to meet and you would not be taking part in anything illegal or immoral, we would just do as we do and use our money legally to exercise our freedom of speech as guaranteed by the constitution.

Philip, I am not asking you to save those I represent, I'm asking you to save the Republic. Your country needs you. Your countrymen need you."

Philip said, "Look, let's say I'm buying this, and I'm not saying that yet, what's in it for you and what do you expect back out of this?"

Matt said, "Look, business as usual means I lose my fortune and power. Looking at the extremes of each camp ends in the same result. Looking at dark horses on each side with some independence and a brain and we find some slight variation on the path but we end up in the same place. Beyond that, we enter the realm of the people who won't run and the people who can't get elected and you are a much better choice than anyone there. We have war gamed this all out and while we find a cliff and a void beyond it, with your Presidency it's not a certain drop and no darker than the abyss we get with anyone else. With all else being even, I would rather bet on someone I think gives us a chance and someone who, while they may not take my advice, I hope will always take my calls."

Philip said, "This seems like the lead up to Y2K all over again. Why do you think this is different?"

Matt said, "This is not about code this is about jobs. Look at just about every revolution and most every major riot in the history of the world and if jobs were not the main cause they were a main indirect cause. Even race riots can circle back to this when you consider that it is or was racial discrimination preventing the people rioting from getting a good job or fair wage that keeps them in poverty and prevents them from having something to lose by rioting.

This is coming too fast and going to affect too many jobs and we will hit a point where events take on a life of their own and things start to move rapidly in unpredictable directions with undesirable outcomes. I mean I could move to a safe haven and watch this from afar, but I can't outrun the markets. I couldn't stand to cash in and be a hermit sitting on a pile of gold watching the world unravel. Don't get me wrong, I'll have that waiting for me as a contingency plan. The end of days bunker I have envisioned is being built as we speak, but I hope to never see it let alone live in it.

That is where you come in. It is no accident that you are here in this position, well known, well respected and beholden to nobody and no party. The patient is sick and you are the best doctor I know. If you want it, this would be the last time we talk until it's over as I will be setting up a super PAC and we would not be allowed to coordinate.

As soon as you declare, things will start to happen and support will appear. You will have resources, but you will not have party machinery behind you. You will have to run as a populist outsider much as Perot did back in the 90's. There are many roadblocks set up to prevent an independent candidate so you will need a crack legal team on the ground and you will have to be playing three moves ahead and always with the end game in mind.

Your best bet is to drive a wedge down the middle of the two parties and steal as many from the middle as possible. That will force the fields to choose either their bases at the extremes or the middle, which you need to own. If they run to the extreme then beat them by appealing to the moderate middle and if they run to the middle then crush them by being a better person and candidate.

Although this was a contingency, I did not think it would come to this. It's you move from here Philip but the gates to Rome lay open and I offer you my gold and my legions. What shall it be Senator?"

Philip absorbed this speech and then replied, "How grim is it? What do your models show that has you scared enough to do this?"

Matt said, "Best case is a steady climb of unemployment with an increasing deficit to prop up the numbers waiting for a surge in new jobs that will never come. The worse case is a hockey

79

stick graph of the same thing. Either way we continue to use debt to prop the economy up until eventually, inevitably, interest rates rise as it gets harder to find buyers for the debt instruments and then it all starts to unravel. First stagflation will return along with a massive recession that will devolve into a depression at least as bad as the one in the 30's.

Back then the economy was not nearly as global as today. Once we go down, there will be a ripple effect and those other economies will have been hit by the same forces hitting us and driving up unemployment. That is where our economic models stop working because there is no quick turning of the ship and this will go on and on.

Finding a way back from here is pointless because the social models show even in the best case a breakdown of society. We won't have hobos on the rails we'll have a nation of hungry gun owners on social media flaming the fire and self-organizing. That will be our Arab Spring, but ours will carry with it tornados of revolution and chaos.

There is no profit in widespread chaos. There is no controlling chaos. There are no limos and fine dining in chaos. From chaos, humanity tends to revert to our baser selves and the warlords, the strong men, the petty dictators rise, manipulating anger and fear. That is not the world I want to oversee. There is no profit in chaos or what comes next. We don't fit prominently in a world of bullies and thugs."

Philip said, "You realize I can't use any of this in my campaign. The odds are heavily stacked against a third party candidate even running, let alone winning. I understand your timing now as I will have to lay the groundwork ahead of primary season which also negates any chance of catching them by surprise. I will have to run a slow and steady campaign that builds momentum like a freight train. How deep are the coffers for such a prolonged uphill battle?"

Matt said, "As deep as they need to be. I have convinced enough people of means that this is where we are heading and this is a world we must not let happen. You have free reign to do what needs to be done. At some point down the line when you are in charge, you will need us and we will have a seat at the table and we will be able to negotiate terms then. Until then we realize you may have to sicken the patient from our perspective, to save the patient. You leave your shadow support to me.

Meanwhile hire the best people money can buy and organize a strategy that takes you all the way to the finish. I would organize teams to wargame what the two parties will do so you can anticipate and beat them at their own game. Money is not, and will not be, an issue for you. Just win."

They arrived back at Philips office without having eaten. Philip exited the car with a glazed look on his face and coat in hand. He had a lot to mull over that day and every day after that.

.

Chapter 9

The Run for Office

"The heaviest penalty for declining to rule is to be ruled by someone inferior to yourself."
— Plato

Philip ran as an independent. His campaign was far enough ahead of the race that his team was able to plow through or figure out how to circumnavigate the majority of obstacles in place to prevent third party candidacies. His was a grassroots campaign in that it organized support from the ground up and was extremely savvy in utilizing all the tools available for such an effort and leveraging social media. The campaign had no big media spend and instead spent on the much lower cost and highly targeted online advertising.

While support came from the bottom up, the money was abundant from the top down. There was a significant amount of money that trickled in from the bottom that, when summed together, was a good amount. However, that alone would not allow the campaign to make winning hearts and minds the focus instead of money raising. Philip hired a team that consisted of old school campaign gurus as well as new school thinkers on the use of the internet. He hired people that had worked on the Perot campaign as well as people who had written books on successful third party bids such as those of Teddy Roosevelt, William Jennings Bryan, Robert La Follette, Millard Fillmore and even George Wallace. He wanted them to look for modern practical applications of the things they did right and to study the things they did wrong or could have done better.

Matt helped pick a team of consultants who spoke money and power. He hired strategists from within both parties and well as a team who were experts on the other third parties. The thought was that when the time was right, they could go after the other party's supporters without alienating their own supporters, who originally came from the big two parties. Philip played 10 moves ahead and was already thinking of his first hundred days in office and laying the groundwork to support that agenda and his candidacy which had not really even begun yet. He assembled experts on the different classes of American society as well as the religions and age groups to help ensure he understood the perspectives of all these groups. He had people who knew labor and people who had their finger on the pulse of the small business owner. He had over 70 consultants and experts on the payroll at any given time. This, of course, could never be done by most candidates who didn't have a large treasure chest, but even those candidates would simply have spent that money on more commercials or yard signs.

Most of these advisors would be talking to and meeting with people within the constituency they were supposed to be an expert on and met up with Philip Kingsley in person when it made sense in the travel itinerary. Others worked on a contract basis where their time was billable to the campaign. What Philip loved to do was schedule a daily call or video conference with a hodgepodge of these advisors or anyone else he thought made sense and a topic would be thrown out for brainstorming and or debate. Philip wanted each person to come at the conversation as a representative of the constituency or area of knowledge they knew about. On some calls, Philip would not say a word other than to thank everyone at the end. On other calls, he would be in the thick of the debate which often times would get heated. Philip loved the passion and anyone who didn't bring it was promptly replaced.

Another area the campaign did not skimp on was technology and especially the security of that technology, their communications, and their data. There was a whole separate bus in the caravan dedicated to tech & sec as they called it. It was adorned with antennas and satellite dishes as well as housing a whole tech support team. They made sure everyone in the entourage had a working version of what they needed when they needed it and that it was all secure and accounted for. There was physical security along as well who were like a private counterintelligence force made up of several people who had spent careers doing just that for various governments.

One of his most important advisers was Frederick. He was one of the first people he brought on board and he consulted with him on most everything. Matt, of course, was highly important as well but not as a day to day advisor but as a secret operative who brought intelligence from the front lines. Penne was incredibly influential and was in on all the strategy so could actually speak to the issues when she went out and was by no means window dressing although she could have contributed immensely as just that. She spoke well and often and brought droves of people to the campaign including a different subset of women than Philip tended to attract.

Big media, of course, ignored the candidacy as long as they could until the point where they would just look stupid if they did not acknowledge it. The internet had been successfully used by candidates up to that point to reach primarily young voters. This campaign used the technology that people used and not just technology that sounded cool to use. They went after the sites and apps and tools that people who were likely to actually vote used. They focused on arming people with easy to follow relevant memes and talking points so that support at the grassroots level could send an email or post something that would be of importance to the people they knew. They spent a fortune creating educational information in every format imaginable to help people spread the word.

Six months before either party had selected their candidate Philip had a team hard at work putting together petitions and public support for adding a third party candidate to the debates. Everything they did was based on the assumption that the things that would proceed that thing will have worked. Philip constantly preached to not look at where they were but to think in terms of where they will be as if they were already there.

The fact there would be no sitting presidential candidate eliminated what would have been a huge disadvantage. Add to that the ineffectiveness of the lame duck president and the ever lowering popularity of that administration as the economy and specifically the job situation became worse and worse. This not only moved the conversation about the election toward the very topics Philip Kingsley was focused on but also diminished the prestige the Vice President brought as he was incidentally the leading candidate for his party. Meanwhile, both major parties were at war with themselves as there were multiple camps that formed on each side in how to handle the problems America faced.

It had been a typical day and Philip was on the bus which was hauling everyone from a stump speech in a small town to another speech and photo op in another small town. Around the bus most everyone was in conversation or staring into a screen of one sort or another. Philip plopped down in the seat next to Frederick, who was just staring out the window.

Keeping his stare out the window, Frederick said, "Do you think they know what is at stake? That we are at an unprecedented point in the history of humanity?"

Philip let the question linger in the air for a moment and said, "It's not their job to know. It's our job to know. They are doing what they are supposed to be doing now and we need to make sure we do what we need to do."

Frederick said, "Why can't human beings just stop and enjoy what we have for even just a moment. If we took the energy we spend on continually advancing full throttle and instead applied it to using the technology and resources available at that moment we could fix all the injustice and inequality. So what if I didn't get a new model of phone for a decade or I have to suffer the same level of automotive advancement for a decade. Who cares? I don't come close to understanding or utilizing 10% of my gadgets before the next must-have comes out and I am forced to get the new thing because no one and nothing supports my old model? Humans have seen an entire generation come and go without a single new invention or change in day to day life. We weren't meant for this pace, we'll exhaust ourselves. If we could just be jellyfish for a moment instead of sharks."

Philip said, "We'll we are sharks though and we'll die if we stop moving. What kind of justice and equality can we provide if economies stagnate and the population grows while advances in food production stay the same? Or for that matter water purification or the use of energy and any finite resource? No, we are sharks. There is a price for that, but there is also a reason sharks have been around for half a billion years and survived numerous extinction events. Things are better now for all but a tiny percentage of people, than they were for the top 1% of people in almost any era in the past. Yes, there are costs but in the end they are worth it."

Frederick replied, "I suppose you are right. So there were more riots in China this morning and the Government forces are said to have killed a few hundred protesters. How soon before that experiment totally unravels?"

Philip said, "I'm afraid they will hit a tipping point soon and we'll see a heavy handed police state crush that country. It's like they always knew this day would come and despite all the transformation and capitalism they maintained the state infrastructure in the background waiting for this moment. I wish we could help them, but we will need to focus all our energies here to keep ourselves from unraveling. I'm also worried closer to home about Mexico disintegrating."

Frederick said, "Philip, I'll be terrified if you don't win but my God, really what are you going to do if you do win?"

Philip said, "Make no mistake, we are going to win. What I'm going to do is leverage the popular support we will have to garner in order to win and use it to do the things the smartest people I can find agree we must do."

Frederick said, "How can you be so confident. All I see are land mines and all you see is the tape for the finish line."

Philip said, "I see the land mines too, I just don't get fixated on them. I need you to keep looking for them so I don't have to fixate on them. I need to look at how I'm going to get a second term while still accomplishing what needs to be done. I need you focused on the right now so I don't have to as much."

Frederick said, "I have never known the specifics of the circumstances or the details of the path, but I have always somehow known you would be here and that you would win. I also always known that I wanted to be a part of it. Thank you for letting me be."

Philip said, "Frederick, thank you for being here and for always being a true friend. Enough of this mush. Look I have all these guys telling me how I should address race with a strategy for Hispanics and a strategy for blacks. I just feel like all of it is wrong, but I also don't feel like I have the credentials to make the argument I want to make."

Frederick said, "What is the argument?"

Philip said, "I want to address it by no longer talking about it. Most of the time when we talk about "black" issues that are really code for issues of poor people or of the inner city poor to be more specific. That is bogus though because not all "black" people live in the ghetto and not all of them are poor. The flip side is that not all poor people are black.

The very fact that we talk about black and white infuriates me. Why does this attribute matter in policy conversations other than the fact we have decided it does. I never get asked about what my plans for the red headed community or the left-handed minority so why should I have a special policy concerning those with the darkest complexion. It makes no sense that we hold on this and it creates an artificial separation between a 'them" and "us".

When I hear a white person tell a story and there is a line, something like, "and then these two black guys drove past in a car," when the fact that they had dark skin had absolutely nothing to do with the story at all, drives me crazy. If they had been very short or very tall, they likely would not have pointed that out in the retelling unless it mattered to the story, and yet, there is this ingrained mentality that people feel the need to identify it was not one of "us".

I don't think it is overt racism but just a matter of habit that goes unchallenged and leads to us thinking about differentnesses instead of similarities. If we talk about the rich, the middle class and the poor have we not talked about the African American community? If we talk about the people who live in the urban areas, the cities, and the suburbs have we not talked about the Hispanic community?

Why do I, as a rich white guy, feel reluctant to speak on these issues and why do I feel like I have to go to my black friend as a representative of the feelings and thoughts of all black men everywhere to gain permission to say any of this?"

Frederick had turned his gaze from the window to Philip toward the beginning of this rant and now a large smile erupted as he said, "Philip I could kiss you. That is what I feel must be said too. I say this as me though and not as the elected representative of all black opinion. I will be happy to stand by your side as you make the argument, but I honestly don't know where it will land you with the black or brown community. There are a lot of people with a lot of power tied to those distinctions and issues specific to those distinctions. I don't know if it will gain you more votes than it will lose you but in my opinion it is the right argument to make and the best time for the best argument is when you are on the soap box and brother.... You are on the soapbox."

Chapter 10

The First Term

"The beginning is the most important part of the work."
— Plato

Business would recover as it found ever cheaper and more efficient ways of making things and then finding more markets in the vast world at the lower selling price to sell them in. However, the workers continued to suffer and each time the economy dipped there were some who permanently lost work. While some found new work, others were adding to the largest growing segment of the modern economy, the permanently unemployed. The government fudged the numbers by no longer counting them as seeking work after they went without a job for two years, but that was just an accounting lie. Kids looking to make extra money while in school used to flip burgers but now these jobs were competitive to the point where you needed a high school diploma or better, a clean record, and good looking resume just to land those jobs.

It had slowly started decades before where the American worker suffered the advances in technology from the manufacturing robot replacing the assembly line spot welder to the spreadsheet replacing row upon row of bookkeepers tallying numbers on mechanical calculators. Actually the case could be made that this was always part of the economy, but only the most recent examples stuck in mind. Hadn't the tractor stolen work from farmhands with picks and shovels? Hadn't assembly lines destroyed the livelihoods of many a skilled artisan who had previously handcrafted items? Jobs too had gone overseas before, and the American worker evolved and developed the skills needed for the next set of jobs that came along.

Maybe it always feels different "this time" but this time it really did. Maybe the pace of change hit a tipping point where we did not have time to adjust before the next round. Expecting an office worker to learn how to use a computer is daunting but when everyone had to learn it, and when essentially it was just a new and better tool for the same job, it became viewed as doable. Those who could not adapt were the ones who were laid off as these new tools took fewer workers to produce the same or often better or more results. We had always been able to absorb those who could not adapt to the changes at hand and help them find another kind of work, even if it wasn't as good a job. We had always been able to train people so that they could rise up from the pool of the unskilled to find a job with a future. Something changed and the pool of those with dead-end jobs or worse yet, no jobs and without hope or the means to support themselves, had continued to grow.

Technology is this amazing sword that cuts through inefficiency and increases our abilities, but it is a double-edged sword. Autonomous cars had been coming for some time, but suddenly they went from novelty to being ready for prime time. Luxury cars began the trend with little bits of the technology seeping into the driving experience doing your parallel parking and sensor systems controlling the suspension and smart brakes activating faster than you could when obstacles appeared. As with most automotive technology it started at the high end and as prices dropped, filtered down to the lower priced car. It got to the point where you could not wreck a new car. You could point it toward a wall and stand on the accelerator, but you could not crash it.

While this was a wonderful technological advancement that saved lives and made driving easier and more fuel efficient, it had not been a societal game changer yet. While you could not wreck a new low-end model car, you still had to drive it. The new luxury models meanwhile slowly evolved to the point where you could turn on an autopilot, a term that became a double entendre. Of course, people started just keeping the autopilot on and like that we had driverless cars. The safety record proved that lives were saved. The elderly and young were able to be chauffeured out of the prisons of their homes. Commutes became times of productivity and cars could drive themselves to run errands like oil changes.

Businesses adjusted so that drive through windows would put the food paid for online on the seat of the car in a container that would not let it spill. Business saw an opportunity and it would not be wasted. The big change in all of this came not from our personal cars but from the trucking industry. Suddenly, in historical terms, overnight, almost four million truck drivers were no longer needed. The big rigs could drive themselves and do it cheaper, safer and without the need for sleep logs or drug tests. In the drop of a hat, those four million were unemployed with their major skill being obsolete. But it wasn't just the big rigs, the post office had autonomous delivery vehicles filling rows of mailboxes along suburban streets. Some mail still had to be delivered on foot, but millions of mailmen were suddenly a costly expense the struggling USPS could not afford.

Industry after industry after industry figured out how to utilize this technology and as salaries and benefits are an expensive component of any business it was vital to eliminate them when you could. Businesses that were slow to evolve or refused to evolve for moral reasons or were just loyal to their workers were instantly at a competitive disadvantage and suffered accordingly. Why hire some unreliable, pay demanding, liability disaster waiting to happen, packaged as a kid, to deliver pizzas when an autonomous delivery unit could keep them piping hot and adhere to strict and exact schedules and times? Sure people had to walk out of their house to get their food but they didn't have tip and you could have your food there any exact time you liked. But it wasn't just the drivers in these industries that lost their job, think about the businesses that support these drivers from truck stops to makers of over the counter pills to keep them awake. The cost of shipping dropped dramatically and sparked increases in how much and what we had delivered to us which helped some businesses. Where business and the consumer were helped, the worker and the society that had to help them were hurt.

Philip Kingsley was entering office in a tumultuous time of change and displacement and these were the very conditions that allowed a man such as him to win. Not unlike Jimmy Carter, who could only have won the presidency under the conditions present when he ran, the Kingsley presidency existed because of the alignment of circumstantial stars in the political heavens. People were doing better and worse than ever. The have and the have nots were now the well employed, underemployed, the unemployed and the hopeless. The well employed had watched first the blue collar jobs get hit and then white collar middle management jobs. Next came specific jobs that were surgically removed from the US economy and transplanted to a foreign land for a reduced cost never to return. Call centers reps were hired in India and then came bookkeepers, programmers, and every shade of technical worker in between. Jobs requiring English communication went to places like India and the Philippines while work that took nibble hands and strong backs went to China and a myriad of other countries with hungry workers.

We had finally gotten used to these realities when these next waves hit us and the rest of the world hard and we should have seen it coming. The next wave of outsourcing was different. The jobs didn't go overseas, they went to technological doppelgangers. Artificial Intelligence or AI, for many years, didn't advance like we predicted it would. It developed maybe even faster than we predicted in some ways only how it manifested itself was different than what we envisioned. There talking computers but they were not the quasi-sentient supercomputers from the movies, they were specialists all around us we didn't even consider. From search engines to automated stock trading programs and the systems that ran autonomous cars to complex automated voice mail systems it was all around us and advancing every day.

While AI was the brains of the being of the future, the body and hands were advancing all around us as well. We were expecting the robot butlers and human impersonating androids again, like in the movies. The robots and physical technologies grew not as a mighty oak but more as a billion blades of grass until one day we had a technologically sophisticated lawn. Robots cleaned floors and pools, they disarmed bombs and flew to targets they destroyed with missiles. 3D printers created anything you wanted in mere minutes and the types of materials they could use grew by the day. Companies started making industrial sized 3D printers and soon we could print just about anything of just about any size.

All these changes eliminated even more American jobs, but that was nothing like the hit the workforce in places like China and India took. We took back all those jobs we sent over there and had our smart computers and gadgets do them right here in America again. Factories in China closed down and giant container ships rusted in ports as the tchotchkes, trinkets and plastic items we wanted were printed right down the road from where they were wanted, slashing labor and shipping costs. This was the new age of manufacturing-on-demand where the item you ordered in the morning could be made in the afternoon and delivered to your front door by a delivery company's autonomous drone by dinner time. Better yet, it could be printed right in your home within minutes. Chinese workers no longer made the items that filled American shelves and that would become an issue for the new president down the line.

AI systems kept getting better and the jobs overseas were done just as well by a computer in a building right here in the good old US of A. Workers from India and all over the world were laid off by the hundreds of thousands. American jobs were not exempt as repetitive office jobs melted away, but that had been happening for ages by now. Where people felt the pain was when smart systems could project images of what was functionally the most helpful and knowledgeable salesperson of all time. A virtual salesperson who could tell a shopper the price, if their size was in stock in the back of the store and anything else they needed or wanted in an instant and they didn't have to be paid commissions or provided dental benefits. Specific jobs were removed from the realm of human work and done better, cheaper and faster by technology

The one industry that in the past had always been exempt from these work transformations was the service industry. In fact, it continued to grow in size and number of workers and the very idea of service engendered a human doing something for another human. Technology was starting to have its day here too. For instance, one entrepreneur created a hair cutting system that revolutionized that industry. It digitalized your head and hair with a 3d scan and allowed you to use a tablet to play around with styles and colors and whatever until you got the look you wanted. Next you saved it, put your head in a huge helmet-like device that gently sucked your hair in every direction outward from your head and in seconds cut each hair to the precise length necessary to achieve the style designed. Haircuts could be done for a fraction of the cost as the big storefronts with all the chairs and most importantly, all the stylists were not needed. Eventually, a competitor made a model cheap enough to own and people could cut their hair to the exact length and style once a week in about 2 minutes. This was a feat once attempted and mocked in comedy routines turned out to just be ahead of its time.

While that is only one example, it represents an impact to over 80,000 salons and over 700,000 stylists. Not all of them were replaced with technology, but probably half a million were, and they had no hope of ever getting another stylist job and most had limited skills to apply to a different career path. These were the sort of things happening across the workplace but hitting the service industry particularly hard because of recent technological breakthroughs and because they had been immune from previous waves of layoffs. Fast food companies, always looking for a competitive advantage led the way in restaurant automation and the big box stores and grocery chains brought robots out of the warehouse and had them stocking shelves.

The people who kept their jobs were taxed more to pay for the benefits of those who lost their job and societal tensions ramped up. Business saw profits increase at the same time that sales dropped. The stock market inched forward even as unemployment grew daily. Tensions grew overseas as well. Europeans protested the transformation of their welfare states as government and business couldn't afford the free perks and long vacations. Disaffected people in countries around the world were organizing. One of the great ironies of these times was that a neo-communism emerged in of all places, rural China. For the first time ever, one communist regime was threatened to be overthrown by another communist regime.

If there was good news in any industry, it was in energy. Alternative energy sources continued to get better and cheaper and looked more and more attractive as demand continued to climb and petroleum-based energy continued to rise in price. Fusion power was still this fantasy that would seem to be always 30-50 years away. Wind was great where it was practical but would probably never exceed a few percent of the total need. Solar continued its advances and solar panels spread like an algal bloom across the southern US. Where there was sun, there was a surge in solar but that was not the answer for every place and while batteries were getting better, the sun didn't shine at night.

Hydrothermal energy had always been cheap, efficient and eco-friendly but only certainly places within certain countries that were positioned to exploit it. One side effect of the oil drying up was great advances in drilling technologies in search for what remained. These techniques were allowing geothermal plants to exist in places that didn't have a natural hydrothermal infrastructure. It was way more complicated than this, but basically they dug deep wells, added water and contained the ensuing steam to create power. They were able to dig the wells deep enough and far enough away from aquifers so that they could use salt water without risking contaminating the water table. A few small plant sprung up on the west coast and moved inland.

These hydrothermal plants were a big investment, as many energy endeavors are, but there was little risk unlike there was in searching for oil. While the repayment of the initial investment takes time, it was less time than other investments such as dams. The real breakthrough came when one company used this solution to also solve a second problem, fresh water. They pumped water in pipes from the ocean down pipes into the earth that superheated it to steam that rose to power turbines and condensated into distilled water which was then pumped to buyers at a relatively cheap cost and adding fresh water to areas with little. They figured out how to purge the accumulating salt through another pipe and it too became another by-product. These plants were small, had zero emissions, were safe enough to build close to the consumers of the energy and created a scarce resource as another byproduct. There was not one answer for energy but rather many, and while one would be the best answer for one place, it would not work in another.

Philip Kingsley was the newly elected president of the country in great trouble. The economy was broken, the country was riddled with debt, the people were disillusioned and the Congress, as well as the whole political system, was corrupt. Philip was a supernova of energy and enthusiasm that radiated out from him and filled all around him. That was what got him elected. He was a bastion of hope at a time when that was what people desperately needed. While it was not a landslide, his supporters were avid and ready to act to support this messianic figure.

President Kingsley had a team that told him how it would likely go down and what causes he should make a priority and what deals and compromises he would have to make to accomplish each item. He disregarded everything they said. The centerpiece of all his attention, political capital, and momentum was a bill entitled America First. He went directly to the people and explained the problem and how he proposed to fix it. We all, of course, know the system and all its players were corrupt. We knew that for a long time that the problem was systemic, but no one ever offered us a fix.

President Kingsley went on air and announced that nothing could start getting better until this issue was fixed and he submitted the bill to the press so, as he put it, the people could see what was being done and debate it. His bill, while sweeping and revolutionary in its changes was simple in its language and relatively short. He, of course, did this on purpose because he wanted people to read it.

Among some of the revolutionary changes, it proposed was a breakdown of who or what benefited financially from each section of any given bill as determined by the OMB or Office of Management and Budget. It also created a law whereby each member of Congress was obligated to state any and all conflicts of interest with regard to any piece of legislation they voted on and were obligated to recuse themselves if the conflict was personal or financial, whether that be of personal financial gain or because of contribution to their campaign. Failure to disclose and/or recuse was made a crime. It also stated that any official of the federal government with a pay grade above GS9 or pay above that baseline for that grade would be required to sell off all investments and to buy into their choice of investments that were tied to the market as a whole (IE an Index Fund). It also required each employee above GS9 or with equivalent pay sign a non-compete type agreement so basically they couldn't go work as a lobbyist for at least a year after leaving office.

This was a bill that was both simple in its language and length yet sweeping in its vast nature. The final component of the bill was perhaps the most shocking. The corruption provisions stated that any use of publically granted power to enhance the finances of oneself, one's family, or in acting as an agent of a business or entity that did not act in the interest of those they represent, were guilty of treason which was a capital offense.

That was it. Simple and powerful. Philip Kingsley went all in on this one issue holding press conferences, town hall meetings, and speeches. He made videos with charts that broke it down and made it simple. He had people who walked around with him all day so he could tweet and upload photos and short videos of his barnstorming tour for this cause. It was like he never stopped campaigning only he went from running for president to running to get this bill passed. People saw this and were reminded of it in all the places they spent their time during the day.

Meanwhile, the Congress was receiving the full court press behind the scenes. President Kingsley was building a change coalition from the middle and ignored party lines. He made it clear he was betting all the chips on this one play and you didn't want to have voted against this if he won and he assured them he would. Most new presidents, and especially their staffs, were idealists and naive but not Philip Kingsley. He had a strategy and he had a file on each member of Congress that made J. Edgar Hoover smile from the grave and in time, worked them one by one pressing the right buttons and dangling the right carrots. He put all his political capital into this and first won over a group who would introduce and champion the bill and then a larger group who would demand a roll call vote.

He played the game in order to change the rules of the game. He was great at this and was like a charming and handsome reincarnated alphabet soup of LBJ, FDR, and JFK. He was generous in what he promised in order to make this happen and scared the hell out the people who chose to oppose him. The lobbyists ran scared and ran hard as this was nothing short of war for their very existence. President Kingsley painted this simply as you were either for or against the bill. He made it the same as you were for or against corruption and he challenged those who would vote no to explain to their constituency why they were for corruption. This put those against on the defensive and there they stayed. Philip Kingsley was a political Napoleon and this bill was his Austerlitz. They underestimated him and never saw this coming as he never even touched this topic in his presidential campaign.

President Kingsley got the votes he needed. Just barely, but he got them. The bill passed and immediately everything was made different as America First was now law. Philip Kingsley was like Jesus coming to the temple to throw out all the money changers. The FBI was suddenly parked outside of Capitol Hill keeping an eye on the lobbyists. President Kingsley had bet it all and won and the entrenched power in Washington was hit with a haymaker in the first round that they never saw coming. Now, while they were dazed he followed it up with a host of bills that under normal circumstances would never have seen the light of day but with the lobbyist running off to lick their wounds he struck.

President Kingsley was smart and left the divisive issues like gun control on the shelf. The first bills he rolled out were pork chops wrapped in bacon. The first of these was the Smart Grid bill. This was not a new idea but one that was virtually impossible given its vast scale an almost limitless amount of potential pork that Congress would have available. But in this time of growing unemployment pork spread across all the districts that was rich in jobs and was building something that would benefit everyone was just what the doctor ordered. The timing for this was perfect in that Congress needed a win at home and this would be the first test of America First and so the urge to exploit this cash cow would be suppressed. Even so, this bill meant lots of jobs and lots of money being pumped into the economy. The country needs a new electrical grid to ready it for the next phase of energy. One that, like the internet in the 90's and what it would do for content creation and distribution, would democratize and expand the possibilities of the electrical grid so that any and every idea could be tried.

This omnibus bill would cost trillions of dollars but would also be set up like a bond in that there were taxes built in so that some of the cost savings consumers would receive on their energy bill would go to taxes disguised as fees that would pay back the investment over time while still saving users money. It would allow new forms of energy creation to plug into the grid and be used alongside the coal-generated energy. It would allow individuals to sell their extra solar power on sunny days and all could be tracked with smart meters and most importantly it was purposely made upgradable so the next best thing we haven't thought of yet could plug right in. Of course importantly this was a job that required work everywhere and was spread pretty evenly across the nation so every state benefitted. Alternative energy would now have the means to spread and grow home by home.

What was missed again was that the devil was in the details. This bill provided much that was needed including jobs. One little section outlined a new concept that had nothing to do with energy but everything to do with the framework for a revolution that would transform the worker and the entire American Capitalist system. The bill created Competitive Government Agencies or CGA's. Each CGA would split the job assigned to it with another agency. They would then compete and be measured by specific goals or metrics set up at the start. The loser would be dissolved as an agency and a new competitor would be created in its place so that creative destruction and competition were infused into government.

Further lost in the details was that all workers brought on for this project would receive 8 hours of training or schooling, paid for by the employers whether they be direct government employees or subcontractors brought from private companies, for every 32 they worked. While resistance would be high when this was uncovered in the bill, the fact that it was distributed across the whole workforce so no one was disadvantaged, helped.

Furthermore, it was paid for as part of a future direct tax that in turn came out of savings and gave much-needed training and education to workers who desperately needed it. All this would also quell the opposition. Yet another benefit would be that since workers would spend twenty percent of their time training that meant that a 20% larger workforce would be needed to complete the same work. This also meant that many more unemployed people would get off of government assistance programs and instead, collect a paycheck, paying taxes and gaining the skills needed to keep them employed going forward.

While this bill consumed the rest of the productive time of his first two years as president before the midterms. It was going to happen and all the haggling was over the details and not the substance of the bill. This was an energy bill wrapped around a jobs program that also infused money into the districts of all these congresspeople up for re-election. All those who played ball on America First, regardless of party, were rewarded as they could go home and campaign as an honest politician who cleaned up Washington and one who brought home work and projects that further bettered their lives and their country. Those who fought against America First were crucified as corrupt politicians in the pocket of special interest and they were swept from office regardless of party. President Kingsley seemed above party and people were defined as for him or against him and that was how the midterms were defined and how everything changed in the two years to follow.

The midterms were a sweeping affirmation of President Kingsley, the man and his policies, not the party he belonged to. He had no more huge pieces of legislation for the rest of his term but really, what he already passed had transformed everything. He spent the rest of his term battling unemployment day by day, battle by battle. Technology sped up and people were laid off at a steadily increasing pace. President Kingsley fought for bills backing infrastructure projects like building sidewalks and homeless shelters, to service projects like tutoring or helping in schools and organizing a new victory garden movement creating local crops at the neighborhood level. These bills always used the Competitive Government Agency (CGA) model of course as well. When possible he championed bills to spread the CGA model to existing agency projects as well effectively increasing the employment rolls as he went. Despite rising numbers of layoffs and stagnant hiring in the private sector, the unemployment numbers actually went down even if just slightly and there was more importantly a sense of hope that had been lacking for so long.

Lobbyists didn't know what to do as the more money they would give to a candidate the more that candidate would have to declare. The more they had to declare, the less effective the politician was for the lobbyists and after a certain point, they would have to recuse themselves making them totally useless. They tried for a while to give money to those opposed to them to take them out of the battle, but that backfired too as suddenly everyone was against them hoping to get paid off. Special interest left Washington and instead hired Madison Avenue to go straight to the American people. The problem was that this was no longer the era where everyone sat down in the evening and watched one of three channels. Media was splintered and the younger the demographic they needed the harder it was to use a monolithic method of message delivery. Special interest certainly didn't go away or die overnight, but its influence in Washington slowly withered on the vine.

As the first term was winding down and the campaigning for re-election was in full steam, President Kingsley enjoyed soaring popularity amongst the people and tremendous support from Congress. Penne had been gone about half the term so far traveling to meet with foreign dignitaries and substituted for a good part of the dignitary role the vice president usually fills. This was, of course, fine with everyone as the Vice President was a quasi-Libertarian from Texas. He lacked a certain polish but brought in a camp of voters that Philip himself could not secure as he rounded out the ticket nicely.

This arrangement worked for Penne as she got to be treated like royalty and travel the world which was not the same as being mega rich but was an acceptable substitute since she was living as if she were. Philip didn't have to have her around as much complaining and distracting from the work so he too was fine with this. Just as they longed for each other, to the point where her absence was a distraction, she would be home again and just before her presence became unbearable, she would be gone again.

This international country hoping was actually very valuable to Philip as Penne made relationships high up in governments and with important people around the world. With their normal defenses down, she was able to gauge their thoughts and plans for dealing with the economic turmoil that was gaining strength around the globe. This energy would not be redirected domestically into the re-election effort where, while Penne secretly was fine if Philip didn't win, she had made a deal and stuck by it.

Penne was home from just such a jaunt through Central America and caught up with Philip on the campaign trail. She was excited to be with him outside of the White House, which afforded at least a chance of some private time, unlike the White House, which seemed to have no boundaries and absolutely no privacy. She couldn't remember having sex once without it being interrupted by a knock at the door. The road seemed to put up an extra barrier where that didn't seem to happen as much although it probably did.

Campaigning from Air Force One was vastly different that traveling the back roads of America on a bus. Penne caught up with the entourage just as they were leaving for California. It was past midnight and pretty much everyone, save those whose jobs prevented it, caught some sleep. Meanwhile, Penne and Philip retired to the Presidential Bedroom which was completely soundproof and Philip gave the guard permission to shoot anyone who tried to come in before the President said it was ok. They didn't even waste time converting the sofas to beds as buttons and shoes flew across the room. The world was tuned out and the room was wrecked and neither got any sleep before touching down in California.

They straightened the room up a bit and ordered some coffee and breakfast. Philip said, "So how are the nobility of the bottom of our hemisphere holding up?"

Penne said, "They are scared. They don't have the long-standing infrastructure and traditions of the Europeans and have seen turmoil in the streets. They seem to see a darker future than most. Their immediate fear is Mexico and what a wave of refugees would do to their own people. I get the feeling they would just assume shoot a Mexican "troublemaker" before letting them come in and disrupt their hold on power."

Philip said, "Who was saying this?"

Penne said, "Oh this was girl talk and I got the feeling that they had no qualms about mowing down fields of refugees in they needed to. I kept catching Sanchez's wife's friend checking me out. That saucy little vixen had naughty written in her eyes. I could have slipped into the bathroom with her and shoved her head between my legs."

Philip said, "Stop! We don't have time to go again. Oh god, I've missed you."

Chapter 11

Second Term-Education

"Prefer knowledge to wealth, for the one is transitory, the other perpetual."
-Plato

Philip had won a tight election based on convincing people his ideas for fixing the economy were right and that he needed another 4 years to see them through. He came very close to not getting that chance. Despite the efforts of the first term, the private sector was still dropping jobs at an astounding rate. The economy grew slightly as money began being pumped in from the new electrical grid project, but jobs kept disappearing.

Technologies were often the creators of new jobs but they also often left old jobs in their wake. There once were rows of desks with manual calculators in finance departments across the nation. These were replaced by a couple people with computers and spreadsheets who do all of that calculating in a few hours and still have plenty of time to do the ever more complex financial analysis. The next wave was AI systems that had the expertise of hundreds of heads of finance and CPAs and bookkeepers and tax lawyers and IP lawyers and hundreds of related professions. These AI systems were specialized to their department of focus and incorporated the laws, the tax code the external economic conditions, the competition, the details of suppliers and their competition. Jobs in finance changed from people who needed to analyze spreadsheets to people who needed to analyze complex models of hundreds of scenarios run with assumptions of different conditions and variables. Lower level spreadsheet jockeys were looking for work while companies couldn't find enough people with advanced finance degrees to replace them.

What was needed now were highly educated people who could analyze and synthesize the information the AI systems provided and act on it. People who had this ability were paid their weight in gold while the majority of people who couldn't, were replaced and without work. People who worked with systems thrived, but the many more people who were replaced by systems saw what skills they had, become obsolete. If they could pull an advanced degree from a prestigious institution out of their pocket, they would have already. Meanwhile, that accounting degree from State University didn't mean much anymore.

Automated cars didn't just appear out of nowhere. We had been hearing about them for over a decade. They crept slowly into the automotive fleet. Features such as automatic parallel parking, automatic braking when a crash was imminent and other helpful features first appeared on luxury cars. Once proven, these features trickled down the car lines. We were used to dumb cruise control, but it became smarter and was more and more like an autopilot that people could turn control over to for stints until one day the stint became the whole trip. This automation hit the trucking industry as well where millions of truck drivers drove for hours on end, popping pills to stay awake. It wasn't long until the long stretches of highway were handled by automated pilots and the city driving was left for truckers and eventually they were replaced altogether.

At one point, there were almost four million truck drivers of every sort with a little more than half driving the big rigs. When those jobs were no longer needed the jobs that replaced them were for people working in data centers tracking the fleets of automated trucks and similar jobs. These new jobs represented not only a tiny fraction of the jobs lost but also required an entirely different skill set. It wasn't just the truck drivers, it was also all the truck stop diners that suddenly had no customers and the dip in sales at the truck stop convenience stores. There was also the gains from far fewer accidents, better fuel efficiency, and trucks that could drive non-stop except to fuel up. Millions of people lost jobs and did not have the skills needed to find another as the expertise of driving was no longer needed.

Offshoring took jobs from the U.S. and technology took them away from foreign countries and brought them home although seldom to a human. Products once made in Cleveland were later offshored to China now were made by hundreds of distributed manufacturing facilities around the US. These centers made thousands of types of products utilizing industrial 3D printers to make the product close to the end user so that it never had to come across and ocean, pass through customs, sit in a warehouse or even a store. A customer could click to buy online and that order went to the closest manufacturing facility that could make that product and spit it out. Within hours or sometimes minutes, there would be a delivery company truck or drone loading packages as they literally rolled off the assembly line. Companies went from the philosophy of just in time to the philosophy of not until, as in the product was not made until the money moved from the customer's account to the seller's. Customers would have products in their hands still warm from the manufacturing process.

The tech revolution didn't make all the jobs more complex although that was the general trend. Package delivery continued to transform as a service. With more products created domestically, shipping to one's home became exponentially cheaper than from around the globe. A massive change happened in how packages were transported as well. First there were automated trucks that no longer required a driver. These vehicles were smaller and more fuel efficient without humans driving but also incorporated a fleet of varying size drones. Trucks became like aircraft carriers for squadrons of drones that, when in the area of a given delivery, could have one of the drones fly the package to the door and deliver the package. The drone rang the bell, collected the signature and picture of the recipient and was off back to the truck for its next mission landing on the roof, like a helicopter on a naval vessel. The drones came in a variety of shapes and sizes ideal for different missions. One drone, in particular, became known as the meatbot. This drone was human because sometimes that was the best tool for the job of taking a package that last 100 yards to the customer. This, however, was a job that required no driving ability and much less skill than the former delivery driver had and now paid minimum wage.

Another company started using airships that people usually just referred to as blimps, but these were so much more. These could carry tons of packages and a fleet of drones and worked like an unmanned distribution center in the sky. They didn't need to be really fast because they lofted over traffic and flew straight to an optimal delivery hub point for the fleet of drones to deploy packages in every direction around it. They were also covered with solar panels but could operate with batteries to fly on cloudy days or in the dark predawn hours to get into position for morning deliveries.

With more deliveries came more efficiency and these companies started delivering 24/7 and stole from another delivery system that was ravaged by the changes. Suddenly the amount of overseas shipping dropped by a significant amount as automated factories and 3d printing brought manufacturing home. Delivery companies bought up these unneeded shipping containers and used them as moving distribution points for their field vehicles which would rarely have to leave their routes. They would rendezvous with an automated truck carrying a shipping container filled with the latest collection of packages for that territory as well as fully charged replacement batteries for the truck and fleet of drones. The swarm from the trucks transferred packages and each was off to its next stop.

Some products skipped this step and could be made at home by 3d printers at people's houses. People printed up a new mug the way you could print a picture of a mug on a piece of paper and in only slightly more time. These 3d printers continued to increase the complexity of design they could handle and the variety of raw materials they could incorporate. Industrial 3d printers began to look like automotive assembly lines completely filled with robots and conveyor belts. Items were assembled only if they couldn't be printed at a single print station, as they were made. These printers scaled to be able to actually make items the size of cars or down to the size of a match. The housing industry was transformed as what came to be known as Lego houses made the idea of onsite construction quaint. People could design their house virtually and have the components printed in nearby factories and delivered on site in days or hours ready for assembly. Millions of construction jobs disappeared as it took only a fraction of the workforce to assemble the pieces.

Even the last bastion for the unskilled worker was not safe from this wave of automation as robots learned to flip burgers too.

A chain called RoboBurger swept the country with a combination of the cookie cutter franchise system and the automation of the cutting edge technologies being developed. These restaurants allowed a person to drive up to one of many parking spaces all equipped with a large screen that displayed the menu, as well as the current order and total. They also allowed people to order ahead online and the app would let the restaurant know the customer's precise ETA so their meal could be ready the moment they got there. There was no line behind you so there was no pressure to rush your order and you could ask questions and see a picture of the food or caloric information. Once your order was complete, you could wait a few seconds while a drone whisked out your food and you could drive off on your way or eat it in the car right there. You could also choose to dine inside and a tracked robot would meet you at the table you chose, bringing food and willing to fetch napkins or whatever you needed as a robo-waiter you didn't have to tip.

Roboburger was a hit and spread like wildfire. The food making process was automated as well and burgers went down a little assembly line and were bagged at the end and delivered to the customer without ever having been touched by a human. Other technologies worked their way into the restaurant industry as 3d food printers were used by high-end chefs to print exotic cuisine and low end fast food to make uniform food as needed without freezing. Another technology was synthetically lab grown meat that was made from cloned meat cells so that no animals were harmed or even needed beyond the initial cells to process it. Farms and fisherman were not needed as the most delicious Kobe beef or lobster tail could be synthesized for pennies per pound. Only the best and healthiest meats would be made as there would be no extra parts of animals to try and utilize. The best meat would cost the same to make as would the cheapest filler if someone wanted to grow that, but why would they? People who were moral vegetarians had a difficult time finding a problem with this and many gave in.

Fast food did not totally eliminate the human worker though as most restaurants kept one on duty wearing what looked like a manager's outfit to give the illusion that a human was running the show. In fact, their primary purpose was act as an information agent answering little old ladies" questions about how all this fancy stuff worked. The places that used drones needed a security guard there to discourage vandalism. This was true even though, when it occurred, it was thoroughly documented by any number of high definition cameras which sent all the evidence to the police along with research on the criminals. This was performed as the crime was happening by a security firm who figured out who the vandals were and where they lived. The police would swing by at their leisure and arrest them.

Technology continued to affect industries and jobs across the spectrum and across the globe. Not only were millions of truck drivers, fast food workers, construction workers, and delivery drivers forever out of the jobs their skillset was geared for, millions more in offices and in warehouses and malls and all over society were no longer needed. There were new jobs created, of course, but they were a tiny fraction of the number of those lost and needed skills these folks didn't have. It was a tough transition going from fry cook to robotic maintenance engineer. This did not happen in the way layoffs of thousands of people are announced in bad economic times but instead happened slowly and continuously and seemingly without end.

It wasn't just happening in the United States either. The millions of manufacturing jobs that had gone to China mostly went away as did millions of jobs that had gone to India, the Philippines, and other countries. AI systems that could pass the Turing test, spoke the language of the caller perfectly, never gave bad customer service and were cheaper and better than even native speaking third world workers, took over these jobs. Unemployed workers went to the streets as they could not feed their families and civil unrest spread around the world. The new technologies also spread there so that those in power could create their little Orwellian societies to deal with the unrest. These countries quickly approached the tipping points for revolts and civil wars.

Entire industries disappeared like industrial pig farms, and others shrunk to a fraction of their previous sizes like international container shipping companies and uniform makers for fast food companies. Meat was being grown on an industrial scale in vats that created tons of work for marketers and PR specialists but put out of business hundreds and then thousands of animal farms and slaughterhouses. Calling these things farms was a stretch as they had really become animal processing factories and as they closed down, only the owners and workers cared. Once people got past the idea of meat grown in a lab, they were easily sold as the meat tasted great for a fraction of the previous cost and did away with bones, gristle and bacteria.

Most people were sold there but add stopping the pollution of rivers and lakes with animal wastes, the elimination of threats like E. coli contamination and mad cow disease and many more switched sides. Add to those benefits, stopping the need to strip the seas of every living creature and letting fisheries on the verge of collapse make a comeback, just to mention a few more benefits, and people happily converted to lab meat. If this still were not enough, there was all the feed and fresh water no longer needed to support the animals and the flooding of antibiotics into these creatures that were breeding resistant strains of bacteria. Even the people who didn't ordinarily eat meat were in favor because many of them allowed themselves to eat these products because no animal was killed or abused to create it. Others were supportive just because it stopped the cruelty and torture of animals that took place in modern animal farming. The marketer's job really wasn't so hard when you consider all that. Finally beyond all those reasons, including low cost and great taste, it was the healthiest forms of meat possible and loaded with nutrients. Game, set, and match.

Business continued to boom as unemployment climbed and these businesses continued to shed the need for humans. Companies did not automate overnight, but it was a steady trend and the numbers started to pile up. The people with the money and the power in the back rooms saw what was happening in other countries and were willing to force Congress to support the president as long as what he did kept people off the streets and instead in the stores. President Kingsley had a sense of this and, of course, Matthew met with him on occasion. Matthew let him know what the powerbrokers were really thinking and where their real stress points were so Philip could press the right buttons if need be. Ligarck, of course, gained the knowledge of what was going to happen. This was not the sort of insider trading where he would run out and buy the stock of certain company today because he knew they were going to get a big contract tomorrow. He made his money from possessing information as in knowledge being power and always made sure to stay within the law.

The President was bold and decisive and pushed for educational reform to reduce the cost of education from Kindergarten through Ph.D. The public school system was already being transformed by online school options. The president pushed for and received federal incentives for states to expand these programs and bring the best mix of the finest teachers and eliminated physical textbooks and the need for huge new schools. Kids would go to a physical school only a couple days a week and in shifts. They received more direct interaction with teachers in groups and the most of the time was spent for labs, group activities, and physical activities. The settings that required lectures, interactive learning, reading, test taking, projects, and reports could be done anywhere as long as the kids had access to a computer or some sort.

The States experimented with all sorts of ideas as Federal grant money backed them. Some popular ideas that arose included tax incentives for companies that dedicated space to in-work learning centers that would be staffed by a mix of people good with children. They would have a variety of skillsets that didn't need to include teaching. Larger companies that could dedicate more space and allow the children of local smaller businesses to attend received extra money. Places that didn't have companies willing or able to open up space created opportunities for entrepreneurs to open up facilities. Families had choices about how and where their children received their education that they never had before. Because their main curriculum was handled online, there was tremendous flexibility in all the different locations they received it. People could bring their children with them to work several days a week, eat lunch with them and even dinner then drive back home together when the workday was done.

A problem that needed even more radical solutions was adult education. There were millions of people out of work with a skillset not sufficient to land them any of the new jobs opening up. These people were essentially unemployable and would end up in jail, on welfare or worse yet, as part of a revolutionary movement. None of these was cost effective or acceptable. Most of these people could not just be thrown into a classroom full time either as many had ended up in the jobs, they formerly performed because they were not particularly good in school.

What was developed was an expansion of the CGA (Competitive Government Agency) Program that scaled the work week back to three days and then two days that could be spent in a mix of schooling, internships, and apprenticeships. These programs were competitive and allowed more days in training at the same pay for the people who showed the greatest effort and accomplishment. A system of measurement was developed way beyond the antiquated system of grades alone that let people be measured and rewarded based on effort, dedication, persistence and other things once thought too intangible. If it can be measured it can be used for improvement, rewards, punishment, identifying areas that need extra attention and help and on and on. Measurement was key.

An entire CGA group was tasked with the measurement of performance and what else the learners brought so that not only the Government agencies were competitive but also the student's roles themselves. They figured out how to measure things like effort and rewarded people based on their performance against themselves and their own abilities. As a result, a person who struggles but puts in tremendous effort is scored higher than a brilliant slacker who takes what is for them an easy class and puts in almost no effort to have the highest traditional grade in the class. These incentives and measurements were so important and worked so well that they extended to all the activities of these CGAs from learning to working and from the newest employees to the heads of the respective competing agencies.

These CGAs were set up to compete with each other for a list of goals set forth by their original mandate. In traditional capitalist society, money was the measure of success but for these endeavors profit wasn't the motive. Instead, lists of desired outcomes were spelled out and success toward those outcomes was rewarded with money. Really this was just an expansion of the positives learned from capitalism where the most important measure of success was having more income than expenses, leaving monetary rewards for the achievement of this one metric alone. The CGA's were designed based on adding additional levels of metrics where achieving these goals in a cost-effective manner was an important element and rewarded accordingly. Bonuses were awarded from the top to the bottom of the agencies based on the individual's performance, their team's performance, their division's performance, and their Agency's performance. Agencies that lost on an ongoing basis were dismantled and new ones were formed from scratch.

Some of the biggest challenges were handling tasks that these agencies could do that were not being done by the private sector, were not costly from a raw resource perspective and were truly a need of society that was also a benefit to society. The first thought that many people had simply applied this philosophy to the existing government agencies, but the problem was that these initial millions of people lacked the skills to do most of the jobs that would be replicated by such a project. There were a few that looked like candidates like the USPS, but automation was transforming it in such a way that once it was formed into a CGA that simply mitigated the loss of some of the jobs and would never be able to be a net gain in employment. The educational assistance agency was one of the first and most successful CGAs out of the gate.

A CGA was set up that acted as a giant temp service that provided labor to businesses of all kinds at rates just above minimum wage. Business and even state and local government utilized the flexibility this service allowed. A CGA was set up that provided interns and apprenticeships. Their first big client was the Federal Government where all the entry level jobs were mirrored by people learning specific job skills three days a week and going to school the other two. The higher rated students in the fields most needed in the marketplace were allowed to go to school up to four days a week and the higher rated workers received financial bonuses. The lowest rated people were allowed less school time and assigned the least desirable work.

The CGA system for measurements and incentives became an important part of millions of people's lives. The integrity of these agencies was important so employees swore oaths and worked with the understanding that accepting bribes, favoring or hindering any individual were crimes and subject to termination and possibly prosecution. Where possible, ratings of jobs or coursework completed were done blind to the name of the person being reviewed and were often reviewed a second time by another reviewer independent of the first. The reviewers themselves were reviewed and all this was done with training, coaching and specific scoring criteria to keep it objective and measurable as possible. Onsite inspection of work completed was done with drones when practical. Employers, co-workers, and teachers were surveyed and interviewed. Not only were financial incentives and rewards provided for the top workers and students but awards were given too. There were top people at the local, regional, state and US level for individual categories of people as well. These ranged from top student playtime facilitators to best interns, to top temps all in several categories measured including combined categories. People could receive recognition and the pride that comes with it in any job being done at any level.

President Kingsley treated the employment situation as a national emergency. He made sure that Congress provided the needed resources promptly and stayed on top of the people running the miscellaneous agencies to do it faster and better. The rest of the world seemed to be falling apart while unemployment actually went down in the US and hopefulness about the future went up. Neither political party could do much to rock this boat as their alternatives were weak. The power brokers behind the scenes were for it and the big companies who could be opposed no longer had the lobbying power to sway Congress as they once did. The public was wildly in favor of all this and for the first time in quite a while, Congress and the political parties not only had to pretend to care but actually had to care what the public thought.

With so much government involvement in the workforce, there would be concerns about abuse and Big Brotherism. These were legitimate and besides that, it was important to have labor support all this because even as their political influence waned over the decades, they still did have enough clout to influence votes in Congress. Built-in throughout the system was a multi-layered infrastructure for oversight of the departments who did the oversight of the workers performance. There were grievance processes and mechanisms that could trigger investigations and third party arbitration.

Feedback mechanisms also existed so that the voice of the workers was constantly heard, by not only management but ownership, even as individual stockholders. There were the same kinds of feedback that went to another GCA in charge of making improvements in the workforce. Finally, all this was backed together with laws that would allow groups of workers to utilize the courts to resolve systemic problems that could not be addressed by the other means.

Also built in was the option for any worker to choose to not participate. A worker could choose to sell their services independently of the CGAs and negotiate their own terms of employment. Businesses too were free to hire outside this structure but what evolved was a system so beneficial for both worker and employee that only the worst employees and worst bosses opted out. Left, were only the bosses no one wanted to work for and the employees no one would want to hire together to make businesses no one wanted to use so that marketplace's natural selection ensured their extinction.

During the lead-up to the midterms in President Kingsley's second term, Philip and Matt had a secluded meeting that, while not top secret, was certainly kept away from reporting eyes and logged as a private personal visit. The pair found themselves in a room with no windows and sparse furniture. It had been swept for bugs and was secure.

Matthew said, "Philip, oh sorry, Mr. President, how are you?"

Philip said, "Fine Mr. Ligarck, now we can both drop the formalities. How are you, Matt?"

Matthew said, "Well I'm happy to not live in a state of anarchy or have my neck strapped to a guillotine but I hear I live in a communist country now."

Philip said, "Yes indeed comrade, why oh why did I have the feeling that was what this is about."

Matthew said, "This makes people very nervous. You've sold this as a good deal for the workers and management, but you want the owners to sell off their birthright to ensure they keep what they already have minus the actual ownership. You are setting up the infrastructure for the government to steal the products of the blood sweat and tears of the people who built them up. Even if you are benevolent in intention what about the next guy or the guy after him. This is a slippery slope."

Philip said, "No one is making business owners do any such thing. They are free to continue to compete in the marketplace just as they always have."

Matthew said, "Free to compete against government-owned businesses using employees hired from the same government at an inflated cost set by the government with no negotiation by the business."

Philip said, "They are free to hire anyone they want."

Matthew said, "Any worker who turned down all the benefits they would have had by opting out of the system in order to freelance is going to be, best case, lazy, criminally minded or, more likely, defective in a way that prevents them from making good decisions.

You have the government owning the labor market and then mandated to compete against the very companies they are leasing out these employees to. You can certainly understand why some of the people I socialize with are a bit nervous."

Philip said, "Sure, I get it. The idea is to layer in enough competitive forces in every level of not only the business and the employees but in the measurement of both and then create multiple businesses in that marketplace competing. In essence, we are making everything a market so that competitive forces can drive price, cost, productivity or some combination of the three.

There will be GCAs looking at all measures redundantly and independently with transparent reporting and systems to challenge

118

or dispute findings. This is like hiring two independent auditing firms and having full access to their reporting and findings and having the ability to challenge their valuations and legal recourse if they cheat. That's far better than anything imaginable in the partial market system we're evolving out of.

Let's get to the real issue you have here. You resent having to give up control of wages because you have to surrender a layer of profit you could squeeze out of people. You could always cheat your employees a little more to make a little more today, but I contend that it was also at the expense of tomorrow's productivity and profit too. Private companies can compete all they want as long as they pay the exact same cost that everyone else in the marketplace is paying. Markets ensure, this is the most efficient, productive and cost-effective today as well as in the future.

In exchange, companies get to lose most of their HR function as well as the cost of benefits and focus on things relevant to the business. Management gets to forego the tedious and inaccurately performed task of performance measurement and can make quick and informed decisions based on objection and uniform data. Management too then can focus on business and not all the time suck of employee management. Hell, you're getting employees who are constantly being trained, well taken care of so they are happier and more productive and they are incentivized to work harder, smarter and better and to win."

Matthew replied, "That is all well and good in a closed economy Philip but you well know we live in a global economy. With so many people unemployed everywhere in the world, we can't compete in foreign markets at all and they are killing us on imports."

Philip said, "That is a straw man argument. You're talking about manufacturing jobs and those are a thing of the past for human workers. The manufacturing jobs we're losing now are to domestic robots. The jobs we lost before are coming home to domestic robots. To keep people working, we need to invest massively in training. Are the people you socialize with going to flip the bill for that? Once that is rolling for a few years, you'll see people emerging with knowledge and expertise found nowhere else in the world and our exports will skyrocket."

Matthew said, "I know what you are saying is true, but I am constantly getting beat up as this smacks of things that make the 1%'s skin crawl."

Philip replied, "Believe me, I know this is a tough sell but at the end of the day, even though profit may be way down for your friends, we are still having a conversation about profit so there must be some profit to be had. Look around the world and ask them how many elites in other countries are whining about the percent of the profit they're making. Mexico is completely lost to chaos and China many not be far behind. Europe is on the verge of reliving a fascist nightmare and there are various revolutions and civil wars all around the globe. Ask your friends if they know any of the Saudi Royal family if there is any left. Their people are beheading them as fast as they can find them."

Matthew said, "I just need to know if you plan on totally nationalizing the country's economy. That is the big worry and right now I have no solid assurance that won't happen."

Philip Kingsley said, "I want CGA's to compete in every area they can so we have markets at work solving every problem but I also want Entrepreneurs dominating in every area they can too. The more competition and innovation the better all the businesses and their products and services will be. I will give set in stone guarantees allowing private business ownership and private investment, but I draw the line at preventing competition."

Matthew said, "Make it not only law, but dogma and that is something I can sell. To change the subject, what are you going to do about Mexico?"

Philip smiled and paused a moment before answering, "Matt, you are not going to like what I'm going to do, but it will be a knee jerk reaction. You will need to look past today and look for the opportunity to service more markets down the road. That's all I can say on that.

So when are you going to settle down or at least pick up a trophy wife?"

Matthew replied, "There has been no better time in the history of mankind to be single and rich so why would I screw that up?"

Philip said, "Matt, I have to go but if I were in your shoes, and except for a different specific audience, I am, I would keep pointing overseas because that is the alternative. If someone has a third and better way I'm all ears but for now this is the best way I can think of to save us."

Matthew said, "Of course I know you are right and that is why you are standing there instead of a courtroom or some other waste of your talent. If I'm going to be honest here, this will be a struggle. Not because people don't understand it. It is necessary just because they instinctively understand they are surrendering a power men of this class have had for centuries which is the ability to control what people make and what they must do to earn it. This is the power to bend people to your will and is the key to the treasure chest. They know once they surrender this power they may never get it back. They will be forced to create something unique and special in the world in order to make money and that is just not something most of these people are capable of and certainly not a power they can bestow on to their children. You would never be allowed to take this power if these people didn't feel they had a gun to their head. Coming from where you did I know you get it but I still needed you to hear it.

Thank you for your time today Mr. President."

Topher Cliver

Chapter 12

End of the Line

"Only the dead have seen the end of war."
— Plato

Toward the end of Philip Kingsley's second term, Mexico started to come unglued. Civil war broke out and the U.S. stationed troop along the border to make sure the fighting stayed south. Similar conflicts, or at least tensions, existed in many countries around the world. Communism was revived in several forms and appeared in revolutionary doctrine as did several flavors of Fascism. The world was in transition and the US could no longer police the world as it came apart as it had legitimate threats against its homeland. Troops from overseas were either repositioned to strategic resource areas or brought home. China was in chaos as the cities erupted in violence as hungry, unemployed workers rioted. North Korea simply imploded and the army one day took over in a coup. The next day they met with the South to officially end the war and proceeded to have their own version of the Berlin Wall coming down. The Koreas reunited and the horror stories flowed out of the North as did millions of starving souls.

The OPEC nations continued to bring in revenue but never again in the obscene amounts of the past. The world was in recession or even depression where it wasn't in total chaos. There simply wasn't any money to buy more than the bare minimum of oil needed. In countries that had money, there were moves toward other energy sources that gained even more momentum when OPEC raised prices. The Middle East had always been a scary and unstable place but never more so than now.

Countries such as Japan, South Korea, and Taiwan took off as leaders in robotics. Japan was the clear leader in many areas and even in these dire times grew rich selling them around the world. India lost jobs but most were to advancing Artificial Intelligence (AI) systems and as much of their workforce who suffered job loss had education and/or skills that made them employable elsewhere. In China, on the other hand, an entire generation had grown up knowing double-digit economic growth with millions of people flocking from the countryside to ever growing metropolises to fill the unending array of manufacturing jobs. Almost overnight millions were without work and without money and took to the streets to protest and riot. China was unraveling and the government, who had been relatively relaxed and permissive for many years cracked down hard and thousands died while revolutionary sentiment grew.

These times were filled with ironies as events unfurled fast and technologies were quickly implemented. For instance, China purchased huge numbers of robots from Japan, Korea, and the US to perform security and agricultural roles. These roles had traditionally been done by humans at a time when unemployment soared to heights unthought of just years before. At a time of increasing conflict, never had so few soldiers died as robots and drones started to take over the modern battlefield. Business was never so productive and efficient while unemployment is so high. The most impactful irony was never was there so little starvation or disease in such a time of upheaval in human history. Most of these unemployed and unhappy people had too little food to accept their circumstances and just enough food to fuel their physical rebellion.

The costs of robotics plummeted as huge numbers were produced at scale and advances came at an astounding rate. Modern plants utilized automation and 3D printing technologies. This caused the demand for raw materials such as iron, steel and aluminum to start to spike as well as demand for plastics, and synthetic rubber and similar materials. Robotics revolutionized the mining industry driven off of the need for more raw materials for more robots. For instance countries like China, Australia and Brazil purchased huge numbers of robotic devices for mining and paid in ore which was used to make more robots. As we stripped the reserves from the depths of the earth, we as humans were able to survive, robots descended to depths they were capable of traversing. This unleashed a bounty of raw minerals of every kind flowing to the surface as prices plummeted even in these times of skyrocketing demand.

Robots even expanded their role in space. Under President Kingsley, NASA was given the mandate to use unmanned technology to find and return strategic and rare minerals to earth in large quantities. Goals were set that tied the future budgets for exploration discovery to the return brought by resources returned. Any project was now possible to envision as NASA had control of its own budget and it quickly converted and dedicated three-quarters of its resources to two competing divisions dedicated to finding valuable minerals. A series of test flights started launching different configurations of drones into orbit to gather space debris which was both a problem and an excellent testing ground for space drone technology. Plans were soon underway to create a drone space station on the moon. That was to be followed up by a manufacturing facility, including a large 3d printer that could build in a zero gravity environment using moon dust and other resources found on and around the moon.

The world economy teetered on the brink of collapse as fewer and fewer workers and companies made more and more stuff that fewer and fewer people had the money to buy. The cycle of work - paycheck - tax - spend - repeat was coming apart as the model of consumerism is dependent on income. Religious revolutions touting a Luddite vision sprouted up but "how ya gonna keep 'em down on the farm after they've seen" a smartphone? Yet another paradox is that even though people had less and less disposable income, seemingly every single product and service on the planet was coming down in price.

During this time, President Kingsley laid the groundwork for the changes that ensured the survival and transformation the of the US economy. America explored new ideas that weren't quite capitalism but weren't exactly socialism either. There was a recognition that markets and competition are good, because for them to work, humans must simply act as selfish humans and don't have to aspire to higher behaviors. The problem is, not every activity can be successfully motivated or measured by profit and money is not the only motivator to drive competition. America was increasing competition and bringing markets, albeit artificially created markets, to more spheres of life and bringing their benefits to industries and activities that had not previously benefitted from them. This was a big experiment as America had to transform into something else or die under the weight of the changes to the workforce and humanity in general that voided the old social contracts and demanded new approaches. Philip Kingsley was the right man at the right time.

The States were the forerunners in decriminalizing drugs and the federal government finally started getting behind the idea as public opinion transformed on the subject just as had happened with marijuana. The conversation changed to one of treatment instead of prosecution and imprisonment. This had many positive effects inside the US including a dramatic drop in the prison populations and a new emphasis for law enforcement to refocus on violent and property crimes. The power base of gangs had been the illicit drug industry, but that had taken a huge hit recently. While the drug trade had not disappeared, a good part of it had and the money and power it had once given these gangs dried up.

For places outside of the US, this transformation meant cartels with well-financed and well-armed miniature armies were now warlords competing for the limited remaining resources. Places like Mexico fell into total disarray and anarchy. To say they were in a state of civil war would be to convey a sense of more organization that actually existed. It was pretty much every person for themselves with people organizing into small bands where practical. Several cartels would have had the power to overturn the government had they stayed unified. However, the Cartels lost their position connecting the drug distribution networks and were no longer the central distributor of the money generated in the area. This caused them to disintegrate into local raiding groups looking for food and then whatever additional resource or recreation they could find and steal.

A similar situation spread throughout much of Central and South America as the cartels there broke into the same open violence with warlords crossing borders looking for more to raid. Refugees started to pour North and refugee camps were set up along the border. The US military was deployed to ensure the violence did

126

not come into this country. A few Mexican gangs raided camps just over the border and were utterly decimated by US forces. Word spread quickly of this and the Warlords learned to keep their operations inside their border. CGAs were set up to create refugee towns made of used mobile homes bought from US citizens from around the country. They were given the choice of the cash value or a replacement home that was not mobile but was new and energy efficient structure.

This was the best the US could do as the country did not have the financial means or the political will to do more given the internal turmoil and transformation already under way. With an election coming up, all of this was heavily debated as was putting up a wall manned by the military that would totally shut down the border which had become a popular idea. This election sparked a lot of debate and the US pulling back forces from around the world was also heavily debated. The Democrats wanted to deploy troops to help our friends in the world and the Republicans want to deploy troops to destroy our enemies. No matter the rationale, the political benefits included a distraction from domestic problems and what Philip Kingsley was getting right. This was also their answer to the jobs problem as they wanted to swell the military's ranks.

The dark side of this is that those who would die would be young, mostly male, usually violently predisposed, who would otherwise add to the numbers of unemployed, disenfranchised people. These are the same people, who if not dealt with, could turn their energies to violence here. War has always been a method of population control used by the rich and powerful against poor young men who may otherwise become a problem or even a threat. They historically would simply pull out some cause to rally around and throw out some patriotic phrases and then line them up against the poor young men of another country and let them kill each other.

The campaign was like a knife fight between two former behemoths stuffed in armor. Both sides swung at the other at every opportunity and each side clearly identified that they held the opposite or at least different opinion from the other party. Even when they were on the same side of an issue, they fought over how to be on that side of the issue correctly. In yet another ironic twist of the times, the political parties had not been aligned so well on so many issues in living memory and yet to hear them campaign, they seemed more polarized than ever.

Both parties were in favor of scaling back the CGAs. The Democrats wanted to let people receive training money without any of the tracking or work requirements but make it available only to the poor and out of work. The Republicans wanted to change the system to make the money spent on training a tax credit without income or other restrictions. The Democrats wanted programs to support the unemployed and planned to use money from President Kingsley's programs to pay for it. The Republicans wanted programs to support business so they would create jobs and they planned on using money from President Kingsley's programs to pay for it. Neither party would touch the topic of campaign finance reform, but they had an agreement reached in a proverbial cigar filled room to dismantle it regardless of which side won.

Without lobbyists shoving money in their pockets, congressional candidates reverted to wholesale pork barrel politics and jobs were the porcine tidbits du jour. Both sides in congressional races focused the brunt of their campaign on local jobs and bringing in federal money to their state or district. Candidates on both sides at a certain point of the campaign simply started making up bills to propose that would create such and such program and bring x number jobs right there to the people who were going to vote. The other side would not point out that 534 other congress people were fighting it out for the same federal money for their constituents and that a block of those Congresspeople would have to align to pass any such mythical bill. To point that out would be to undermine the narrative and that was the same basic strategy they were both using but with different promises of course.

One flaw of Philip Kingsley's candidacy was that while being an independent had many advantages to him and at this moment in time, in all other respects is was at a great disadvantage in this American system. Without an actual third party to carry forward his ideology it all simply fell apart as Philip Kingsley became a lame duck. The public opinion of the candidates was at an all-time low as were the turnouts at the elections despite the huge consequences of their outcome. People were scared and these fears were preyed upon through the election as there were plenty of scary things in the world to shine a light on in the dark forest of tomorrow.

Chapter 13

Out of Office

"We can easily forgive a child who is afraid of the dark; the real tragedy of life is when men are afraid of the light."
-Plato

Philip and Penne moved to California and bought a secluded estate that was not directly in the middle of or next to anything or anyone specific but was in the vicinity of the mountains and the ocean. It wasn't too far from their alma mater, or Silicon Valley or San Francisco but not too close either. Penne had written a book while in the White House and while it had some success it was generally considered a flop. She was leveraging a second book for herself by teasing the publishers with a book by former President Kingsley. Of course, he was not thinking about a book at all.

Penne had hired two people as her staff to manage her day-to-day and help set up opportunities such as speeches and meeting with important people that may lead to financial opportunities. She encouraged Philip to hurry and do the same and he finally gave in a hired a personal assistant. This was all taken care of by the government or at least most of their salary would be. They also had a secret service detail and took all this into consideration when they chose the house they were now living in.

The new president and Congress were elected with nothing that resembled a mandate. It was the lowest voter turnout in modern history and some of the lowest margins of victory in both the presidential race and the average congressional races. Public confidence was down as was the stock market. They immediately started to dismantle what Philip Kingsley had built. The new president started forcing Mexican refugees back across the border which inevitably led to almost daily reports of abuse and murder. He sent the military into some areas of the world that put them in harm's way without a well-defined mission or exit strategy. Former President Kingsley had to sit by and watch the world he built be pulled apart like a gingerbread house being fought over by a mob of elementary school children.

Philip was sitting on the edge of the bed watching a report of news from around the world when Penne walked out of the closet holding two ties. She was directing her attention back and forth from each tie to his shirt and slacks.

She said, "We need to get you on more boards. These companies would love the prestige you bring and you get time to forge relationships with the people making things happen."

Philip said, "It would be unseemly for me to walk out of the White House one day and into a boardroom the next. There is no precedent and with good reason. I will do speeches and write a book. That is what ex-presidents do to make an income. If, and it is a big if, I even consider a board membership, it needs to be a large company doing important things. It should also be out of view of the press and not roles in every other tech startup."

Penne holding each tie successively to Philip Kingsley's collar until deciding one and said, "Ok, I held up my part of the bargain, now it's your turn."

Philip irritably shutting off the report he had been watching turned and said, "Yes, how could I possibly forget. Look, my pay as a speaker will never be higher than now and interest in a book will never be higher than now. Let me focus on those two things first then we can discuss next steps."

Former President Kingsley indeed did do both in a whirlwind speaking tour. He would make well-paid addresses at night to well-dressed guests at fundraisers, misc. events and business gatherings and the next day he would make a speech on a college campus. The tone of the private speeches would cater to the group he was speaking to as they were paying the bills. The tone of public speeches became critical of events and policies around the world and eventually domestic policy. He never had many fans in the base of either party's machinery but as he spoke out against the dismantling of what he put in place, he gained many enemies. He gained many converts though too

The time in between speeches was spent knocking out pages for his book. His preferred method was to speak his book and then have it transcribed. Six months after leaving office he had already delivered over 200 speeches and his first book was selling like wildfire and his second was in editing while he was starting to record the third. In the midst of all this he set up a foundation to help refugees around the world. Penne was satisfied with the checks rolling in as book sales soared but still looked forward to her own yachts and her own schedule.

While staying at a nice Hotel in a mid-sized town in Kentucky, Philip received an unexpected guest. Frederick had returned to Harvard to teach but did not currently have any classes. He had called Philip the day before to find out where they could meet up. Philip was in the Hotel lounge tapping away on a tablet, working on some edits for his second book as in walked Frederick. Philip stood to give his old friend a hug.

Philip said, "Well Professor, how are you? You look like you've been ridden hard and put up wet."

Frederick was no longer the boyish looking nerd from college. He instead now looked like the clichéd college professor with a sweater vest and jacket. He had put on some weight and had a soft midsection that hung slightly out from the top of his belt. His hair was relatively short but not fashionably so and was, in fact, longer than most men wore it. He still wore glasses that were more functional than fashionable. He also had circles under his eyes.

Frederick said, "Mr. President, you on the other hand look rested. Not many people could hit the road with non-stop speeches across the country and, in between writing a book and appearing on who knows how many shows, somehow have it be an opportunity to get rested after their last job."

Philip said, "Yes the last gig was a bit demanding. How was getting back into the classroom?"

Frederick said, "Oh it was glorious. It was like getting out of a body cast and walking again. I was a little atrophied but once I shook that off it came naturally again. I missed it. That segues into why I'm here. Some of my students brought my attention to two separate yet intertwined things going on right now. Does that thing have an internet connection?"

Philip said, "Yes, here you are" as he handed Frederick the tablet.

Frederick typed in an address and said, "People are organizing a formal third party around your principals. They are calling it the Freedom Party."

Philip said, "That's fantastic. They certainly face an uphill battle, but I hope they win a few races."

Frederick said, "It's at a very early stage, but I feel an energy here that I haven't felt in a while. There are a lot of, not just smart people, but savvy people with connections behind this. I think this could gain some serious momentum."

Philip said, "Frederick, this is nice and it's always great to see you, but that's not why you came all this way to see me in the middle of Kentucky."

Frederick smiled a mischievous grin as he typed in another URL and said, "This is why I came."

Philip looked at the site and read it in disbelief, "Surely this is a joke or even if serious is not something that ever has a chance of happening?"

Frederick lit up with the fire in his eye that he got when he was in front of a classroom as he said, "Philip, while it's true we've never seen an Article V Convention successfully called, I think this has an outside chance and I'll tell you why.

First, they have done polling and a significant groundswell of people across the nation are for it. The idea is polling with 55% approval and we are only six months into these buffoons driving us toward the cliff. Unless they pull a rabbit out of their hat, I don't see that number improving and each tidbit of bad news would inch it higher.

Secondly, the state legislatures of both parties are struggling now as Congress and the president are slashing their funds with one hand and dumping problems on their doorsteps with the other. This is a disastrous course of actions driving the States toward the brink of insolvency they were at just prior to your election. When you left office, the states were in better shape financially than they had been in the past 25 years despite the vast amount of problems the world faced."

Philip said, "Well people have been trying to call an Article V Convention for the past twenty years and still I would bet 99 out

134

of 100 Americans have no idea what that is. I hate what the current regime is doing, but I'm not sure we can do anything to stop it from happening. I mean we made the kinds of changes we needed and they undid most of it in less than 100 days. I'm going to keep on fighting the good fight, but the pragmatist in me is saying it's time to collect treasure and build a fortress for the coming dark days."

Frederick frowned noticeable disheartened and said, "Philip, that is Matt and Penne talking. You have always been the one person more optimistic than me and now when we need that optimism most you bring this defeatist attitude?"

Philip said, "This is realism. We won the White House against incredible odds not once but twice and while there, passed legislation that changed the playing field despite not having a party to call our own in either chamber. With the world falling apart around us and, failing to do anything to stop it, we stumbled across something that was actually showing signs of working. In spite of all that, they tore it apart in a few months. The worst part was that it wasn't as if one party was for continuing down some version of that path and the other party just happen to win for now. Both parties campaigned in agreement that we must tear it all down and the only difference in the sides was methodology.

I am still fighting. That's why I give a speech almost every day and why I'm writing my third book already. I've just pulled back the curtain and I have seen the sausage being made and all those metaphors and I also have to be a realist. What we did was just about impossible and yet doing it only delayed the inevitable."

Frederick smiling again said, "Philip we must continue to circle the city blowing our horns in faith that the walls will come down."

At that moment, the secret service walked up one on each shoulder of Matthew Ligarck, who was that last person Philip thought he would see at that moment."

Philip said, "Matt? What are you doing here?"

Matthew said, "Mr. President, you look well."

Frederick said, "Matt came to see me a few weeks ago. Please hear him out."

Philip gestured to the chairs and had a seat at the table toward the back end of the establishment but still part of the middle group of tables which were surrounded by booths. The place was slightly dark and empty except for the secret service agents, bartender and waitstaff.

Philip chuckled and said, "So Matt, what scheme do you have up your sleeves this time?"

Matthew said, "Well Mr. President."

Philip cut him off and said, "Matt please, it's just the three of us, Philip will do."

Matthew said, "As you wish, Philip. I know this all looks bleak, but this was necessary. The people I work with became skeptical. They like the idea of having politicians in their pockets. They thought maybe it wasn't your policies that shielded us from the mayhem in the world but rather that America held some special exemption and we were shielded despite your policies.

We of course at this table know this is not true. I think we can also agree that left unchecked, this course leads us to some outcomes, all of which are highly unfavorable. They also discovered that paying off politicians only works for small favors as the other side buys just as many to block anything meaningful from pushing through."

Frederick said, "We see these outcomes playing out around the world as we speak from the utter chaos that is Mexico to the resurgence of communism and fascism. Did you know we set a record for most military coups in a single year worldwide last year?"

Matthew said, "None of these outcomes are conducive to the people in my circles continuing to have power or a lifestyle in the manner in which they have become accustomed to. They had to see that you were no mere fluke and that America is not immune."

Philip said, "Ok fine so the plan is a two-pronged attack? Start a third party from scratch and run.... and win, enough elections to control Congress and then pass the needed legislation and hope the President doesn't veto it? The other prong being to call an Article V Convention, which has never been successfully done, get the delegates assembled to propose a list of the legislation repealed or transformed. Then hope, what is it, 40 State legislatures vote to pass them as amendments. That is the plan?"

Matt said, "While you have summarized the plan at a high level you are missing the nuance which lies in the details. The question we have for you is when the time comes, will you be willing to step in and do what is in your power to help us fix this?"

Frederick said, "And Philip, it" not as much of a stretch as you think, only 38 legislatures need to approve it."

Philip said, "Well, I thought the idea of me actually winning the presidency was a crazy long shot so I won't rule anything out. Yes, I will do what I can when you need me to but I don't really see why you both had to come down here for this. Don't get me wrong, I'm happy to see you both, but this could have been a video call unless, my communication has been compromised. Do you know something?"

Matt said, "No nothing like that. We just wanted to be looking you in the eyes when you said yes, that's all."

Chapter 14

Cincinnatus Returns

"The measure of a man is what he does with power."
— Plato

Philip continued his speaking tour although the number of speeches dropped just a bit as it also became a book promotion tour. He did a lot of appearances on the usual circuit of shows that people promoting books appeared on. While the speaker fee checks decreased in number, the size of the book royalty checks grew at a rapid pace so Penne was content. She tired quickly of the constant traveling from town to town and went back home to continue to set up her nest. When she did travel, it was to Europe and Asia and in extravagant style.

Meanwhile, Frederick coordinated the organization of the third party, which ended up being named the Freedom Party. The real challenge was satisfying the requirements, or more accurately, the roadblocks set up making it unbelievably hard to run as a third party candidate the higher the office attempted. The focus of the battle was on the presidential and congressional races they were trying to position the party for. Meanwhile, they managed to secure spots on ballots across the nation from the bottom up, with great success at the local and state level.

The Midterms came up quickly and the party ran in every local uncontested race they could secure a candidate. They surprised even themselves with their success. The general message that no elected seat should be handed out unless won in an election with an alternative choice resonated with people and motivated enough people to go vote that it actually made a difference. The amount of advertising poured into the local markets for the Freedom Party caught everyone off guard and the results were better than the most optimistic strategist could hope for.

At the congressional level, a handful of seats were challenged and out of five races, they captured two House seats and one Senate seat. While it could be pointed out that these were the five most vulnerable areas with an election that year and that a tremendous amount of advertising and grassroots campaigning was done to pull it off, these were proof points that a third party could win seats. That was what was important as it was counter to the classic notion that a vote for a third party was a wasted vote.

The day after the elections a huge media campaign kicked off calling for the states to demand an Article V Convention. They wanted it to pass an amendment restoring the anti-corruption campaign finance reform laws that Philip had enacted and the last Congress repealed in the first days of its first session. This was a massively funded campaign targeting multiple demographics across both parties with several forms of media being used, both old and new. Neither political party was prepared with talking points to respond and both had just dumped a lot of money in the just-concluded elections. Neither were not willing to spend what they had left in reserve with a presidential election in just 2 years.

By January, the brilliance of the Freedom Party strategy was clear, as although they only held a few seats in Congress, they had a vast presence at the state level, and that is where this battle was to be fought. At the beginning of February, forty-seven states had a Convention of States application floating in their legislatures and by Valentine's Day, fifteen states had passed legislation calling for a convention. They needed two-thirds of the states to call for the convention and they had another eight by the end of March. The ad money was redirected to the twenty remaining states most likely to approve the applications and by the end of the summer the magic number was hit and the process to convene a convention was under way.

Each state decided its own means of choosing its delegates and began that process. Congress acknowledged receipt of the application and then proceeded to do nothing. The members of Congress representing the Freedom Party in both the Senate and House both introduced bills with an October 1st date for the convention. The media picked these dates up and soon the issue took up a life of its own. Ads began playing in each congress person's home turf specifically calling them out as being in favor of corruption if they did not get behind calling the convention. By mid-September, it had been called as Congress just wanted the ads to stop.

While there have been hundreds of such applications for an Article V Convention none ever really went anywhere or picked up more than a handful of states. In fact, no amendment to date had been passed this way so the status quo parties were not prepared for this strategy and were behind the curve when the massive media campaign blitz hit. They were so worried and focused on keeping the third party out of Washington they missed the back door of the states and their local governments. Gerrymandering had carved up the map in such a way that many districts around the country would have a candidate run unopposed because the other party ran the numbers and saw no way to win. However, that was an opening for a third party candidate to run on different issues against only one candidate.

When the Democrats and Republicans understood the threat and were able to gather themselves for defense, the convention had already been called and advertisements playing for months. They counter-attacked on two fronts. First they lobbied for the states to withdraw their applications so that Congress could properly examine and debate the issue and then formulate a proper bill to resolve the issue. This argument might have worked early on had they adapted it but at this stage it was a desperate ploy. More likely to be successful was the sneaky side of this strategy where the parties conducted back room dealing with legislators at the state level to persuade them to lead movements to withdraw their applications.

Their other strategy was simply a fear mongering media and talk show attacks warning of the dangers of a runaway convention and how anything could happen so the people must urge it stopped. Again, this may have worked if this campaign was launched at the beginning of the process. With a couple months head start out of the gate, the Freedom party anticipated this and had for months been educating people through the media to defend against this argument. It was not entirely clear from a legal perspective what could or could not happen at the convention as one had not been held since the founding fathers convened to create the original constitution.

While two states did withdraw their application, others had added theirs and the total never dropped back down below the threshold, so the convention proceeded. The media hyped this like it was the Superbowl of politics, but that quickly got old as the convention was closed to cameras and debates grew long and tedious. While some states sent politicians as their delegates, many other sent intellectuals and luminaries and the debates ran the gambit from respectful philosophical discourses to name calling chair throwing hootenannies.

The Convention carried on for forty-three days and wrapped up before Thanksgiving. The first couple weeks of the convention focused on what should or shouldn't go into the amendment they were proposing. Finally the contingent that argued for creating a separate amendment for each individual issue, and letting the states decide which were worthy or not based on which were passed by the requisite number of states to become law, won. Now the threat of runaway convention started to unfold to some degree, but just as the counter argument pointed out, three-quarters of the states had to ratify one of these amendments for them to become law.

Scholars and lawyers immediately started arguing once more than one amendment came out of the convention. Some argued that one issue and one amendment was all they were empowered to produce. Others argued that they could create as many as necessary, but they all had to directly address the issues spelled out on the application. In this case, it happened to be restoring the anti-corruption campaign finance reform laws that President Kingsley had enacted and the last Congress repealed. Another group argued the same but was ok with anything that remotely could be shown to indirectly apply to the finance reform core. Yet another group contended that the convention could produce whatever amendments they wanted, as it was not spelled out in the constitution that they could not. In any case, the lawsuits began the second it was over.

While the legal wrangling was going on, the Republicans and Democrats had some tough strategic decisions to make if they were going to shut this process down. They had to decide whether they wanted the state legislatures or state conventions to vote on ratifying the amendments. They also had to decide what sort of deadline to attach to ratification. If they chose the current state legislators, they would be choosing the same crop that voted for the Article V convention in the first place. With the current national mood, having the states elect delegates could make passage even more likely. As for a deadline, a long deadline could stretch the process out and have it miss the next and possibly next 2 election cycles. On the other hand giving them more time may allow more states to organize and ratify it. A quick deadline could have several states miss the deadline by not being able to organize support in time, but it could also mean these amendments would get ratified while this Congress was still in office.

The challenge was shot down in the lower courts and upheld by the Supreme Court as they took the broadest interpretation of the Article. Specifically the line "shall call a convention for proposing amendments, which, in either case, shall be valid to all intents and purposes." They upheld the ability to produce multiple amendments interpreting the plural usage in the line above as conclusive to their intent. As for the scope of the subject matter allowed to be addressed in these amendments, they ruled that any potential amendment that came out of the agreement of the convention should be put forth to the states to attempt to ratify in the method proposed by Congress under the article.

The states suddenly had a handful of amendments before them. There was one the reinstated the Kingsley anti-corruption campaign finance reform laws. There was another mandating that Congress shall have their pay raises or decreases tied to fluctuations in the average American worker's salary. There was still another stating that Congress shall be covered under Social Security and Medicare instead of their own private retirement funds and health care. There was an amendment that prevented the exclusion of parties that have met specific minimal criteria from participating in any event the other parties are involved where there is a public forum involved. There were several others including one amending the 22nd amendment such that no president can hold two consecutive terms but abolished the limit on the number of terms.

Congress had gambled on a quick deadline and their ability to squeeze the state legislators using their party connections to vote their way. The Freedom party was was prepared for this and used their deep pockets and vast network in the states to offer the legislators even better deals to come over to the Freedom party outright or at least vote their way. Where there were stronger majorities for the incumbent's party, the Freedom Party offered up not running a candidate in that district in exchange for the votes. Both sides played hardball but in the end the public sentiment was the deciding factor where everything else was even. All the amendments mentioned above passed while a few not mentioned ended up expiring after not being ratified by the required number of states.

During this exciting time, Philip Kingsley stayed on the sidelines of these issues as Matt and Frederick had advised. He continued making speeches and writing books but appeared on TV much less as the only things they wanted to discuss were related to the amendment process. Philip Kingsley opted for more formal and private events as these allowed him to talk about what he wanted without questions asking about what he didn't. Penne certainly didn't mind as these paid better and allowed Philip and Penne to mingle with the elites of the business world.

One day, in the midst of the whole ratification process, out on the road, Philip Kingsley was contacted by Frederick and a meeting was set up. Frederick was discreetly escorted up to Philip Kingsley's Hotel room. He was shown into the room by a secret service agent who led him over to the mock living room in the suite where Kingsley was sitting and reading.

Frederick walked up and said, "What are you reading?"

Philip smiled, looked up and said, "Plutarch."

Frederick replied, "Lives?"

Philip Kingsley said, "Yes, I am on Numa Pompilius. I respect his Spartan lifestyle and admire his reforms, much as I admire yours, Novitatis Gracchi."

Frederick chuckled and said, "High praise from Demosthenes although I'm not sure about your Latin phrasing."

Philip Kingsley said, "My Latin was always weak. I fear a more apt reference may be Pyrrhus of Epirus as the precedent you have set may offset the reforms you brought back and I fear Sulla may lurk in the forest."

Frederick smiled a wry smile and said, "First of all, I am not being modest when I say that I am but a bit player in all this. This movement came from the people and the door is open now, all you have to do is walk through it, and you are much better than Sulla."

Philip Kingsley closed the book and said, "Walk through the door or cross the Rubicon, call it what you will, I don't want to be

Alexander, Julius or Octavian. What you propose is a slippery slope to totalitarianism either now or in the future."

Frederick said, "Dictators aren't elected every four years and don't have to take a break after two terms. The people passed these laws because they want you. They need you."

Philip Kingsley said, "The people did no such thing. That was snuck in the side door while everything else was beating down the front door and it still unlocks the door to tyranny."

Frederick said, "So give the people a chance to decide. Be our candidate Philip. FDR did it and not only did the world not end but he lead us to victory against some of the most dangerous threats in history. Philip, we are again threatened and we need you."

Philip said, "It is so very enticing, but that is why I must say no. Power is enticing and there is a reason Washington set the precedent for two terms."

Frederick said, "The reason was that he was sick of the bickering and of politics. I know you are not yet sick of it and the people need you. Are you going to allow this band of thugs to continue to drive us off a cliff?"

Philip said, "You have the anti-corruption laws back and you have an organized party. You don't need me. It's time for the next person to pick up the flag."

Frederick, looking disappointed, sat looking at Philip for a prolonged moment and said, "Matt came to see me. He wanted to make sure that I was not under any illusions. His support helped us to this point, but this was for you to return. He has emphatically said he will back you or he will back whoever he can own in whatever party they exist in. He will take another chance with you or he will watch it burn and place side bets to become richer along the way."

Philip said, "You don't need him at this point. Run your best candidate and allow the system to work."

Frederick said, "Even if we had a good candidate, which we don't, there is no time. The election is less than a year off and there is no time to build up a candidate from scratch, let alone create a field to duke it out and discover our best candidate. We hope to win enough congressional seats to be a disruptive force and we have a strong footing in the states, but realistically we have no shot at the White House this election. We can't wait four more years. Give us one more term brother to set us back on the right course and give us time to find the next torch bearer."

Philip said, "I cannot give you a yes. The best I can offer is that I won't entirely rule it out for now as long as you do all the right things to find a candidate other than me."

Frederick said, "That is fair. I will see myself out. I have a lot of work to do."

Unemployment continued to rise and confidence in the economy was at a historic low. The day after Frederick came by, the news was filled with pessimistic items including a large trucking company announcing huge layoffs as it converted its fleet to self-driving trucks. Layoffs in the foodservice industry continued as competitive pressures forced companies to quickly adopt technology to replace their human workforce. This trend spread across many sectors of society but were slower to come in some industries or specific jobs. The jobs that benefited from intangibles such as human interaction or where human dexterity, pattern recognition or complex decision making was still superior or more desirable to what machines could do, were islands of employment. However, with so many people out of work, the competition for those jobs was enormous and employers took advantage of that.

As the primary season cranked up, an obscure Republican representative from Montana named Robert Critias gained a small but fiercely wild following and exploited the publicity of the primaries to expand that support. He clearly had no chance to win the Republican nomination so as soon as he gained some spotlight he declared himself an independent candidate. His message was about strength and restoring American greatness and closing the border to foreigners to keep them from taking American jobs. He proposed new branches of the military and homeland security that would employ millions to help people at home and assist our military in spreading democracy and freedom abroad. At home, he pushed a law and order agenda which pleased the upper classes while the promise of full employment pleased the masses. These were simple and time-tested tropes that made him a rising star and a candidate to take seriously.

Philip Kingsley and his entourage were packing up to check out and head for the location of the next scheduled speech at a state university. Also in the news that morning was a shot of the hotel Kingsley was staying in as a pack of reporters was camped out in the parking lot. As Kingsley came out, surrounded by his secret service detail, a crowd of reporters yelled questions such as "President Kingsley, will you run?", "Will you be the Freedom Party candidate or will you run as an independent?" Philip was rushed into the car as the detail was not prepared to handle a mob that size and called in reinforcements. These reporters were now stalking Philip and their numbers would continue to grow over time.

At the campus, the same kinds of questions were shouted out to him from the time he got out of his car until he was introduced up on stage. The crowd was many times larger than similar speeches in the past brought out and they broke into a chant of "Four more years!" as Kingsley stepped up to the podium. The chant was so loud it was preventing the former President from speaking. He kept interjecting thank yous in that tone that signifies the sentiment that he appreciated it but enough already. He motioned his hands in that downward movement that universally asks for the crowd to quiet down. It didn't matter though as the chants continued and the scenes were all over the internet. The question on everyone's mind was would Philip Kingsley run.

After more than fifteen minutes of Philip Kingsley trying to get the chant to die down, he was able to finally start speaking. He said, "Thank you all for this enthusiasm and your kind sentiment. I am, to be honest, lacking words right now as you see, I have never had any intention of running again as it was not allowed. Now that has changed but I'm just not sure my feelings about it have changed. Our first president set an important precedent that I think best that we respect even though no longer written in the law."

Scattered boos started coming from parts of the crowd as he was saying this.

He continued, "I offer myself and every service I can provide to whoever wins office regardless of the party."

Kingsley did not finish this sentence before the chant of "Four more years" erupted and overpowered the sound of his voice. He smiled and waved and slowly walked off stage and toward his waiting motorcade.

Some version of this scene followed Kingsley wherever he went so that he could no longer give interviews, speeches or even go out of his room and not be bombarded by people desperate for hope. Desperate for a savior.

Philip Kingsley had tried to continue on the road giving speeches but the events that paid the best dried up as the hosts did not want the attention and media circus that followed Kingsley wherever he went. Lots of places and shows tried their best to book him, but he was not interested in discussing the only topic they wished to discuss so it was pointless. Philip ended up canceling the events he had scheduled and headed home to California. Penne had just gotten back from Japan and had beaten him there by a day. They spent the first day back together initiating most of the rooms of the house and then a good part of the next day sleeping and relaxing.

Penne was sitting upright in bed as Philip was stooped over the sink brushing his teeth.

She said, "I think we should go to Europe, Japan or Australia or someplace to get away from from all this madness."

Philip spat out some toothpaste as his toothbrush turned off and he said, "It's all very flattering until I realize it's not me they want, its hope. They want someone to bring regularity or at least predictability to their lives and the hope of having employment today and tomorrow too. I'm not sure I could give it to them. I'm not sure anyone can at this point in time."

Penne said, "That's why we should go, Philip. They can't find their next messiah if they focus all their attention on you."

Philip said, "I don't think there is someone capable and then also willing to even try. Worse yet there are several wolves in sheep's clothing that people are mistaking for answers to their problems."

Penne said, "You left office with a spectacular legacy and you will be remembered as one of the great Presidents. Why would you want to go back and then destroy that? I don't mean you are not still capable of greatness, but I do mean this situation is hopeless in the short term but will work itself out as it always does. Going back will only forever tie your name to a hopeless situation in an impossible time. There is nothing you can possibly do to change that other than not even consider being a part of this election in any way."

Philip said, "All the people who are not suffering right now are sticking their heads in the sand and saying things will work themselves out, but things don't work themselves out people work them out. The door is open for third party candidates like never before and third party candidates are never more viable as when times are bad and the leadership in the established parties is weak. Never have those conditions been so aligned, well since the year I first ran but before that it was probably the 1972 and now those conditions are riper than they have ever been.

You have that guy Critias who is just a modern day Mussolini. In a three-way divide of votes, he stands a serious shot at winning. Adding in Perri Ander to his ticket was genius as he brings the South, having been a very strong and popular Governor.

Then the one to watch out for as a dark horse is Barbara Peisistratos. She has more or less rebranded communism and pitched it to a populace too little educated to see it for what it is. Her marketing team is phenomenal and if she wins, all bets are off.

That's just a couple of the outsiders, there is no one in the Democratic or Republican party who looks even remotely strong enough or smart enough to change anything. This lack of vision will just keep us heading down the river toward the falls until the people revolt."

Penne, said, "I love you Philip, but you are just deluding yourself if you think you can step in and change this outcome. We all know the shit is going to hit the fan, why do you so desperately want to be the fan!"

Philip said, "Maybe I am deluding myself and maybe I would fail but I have to do something. I have to try even if I am doomed to fail it is better than doing nothing and watching it happen from the sidelines. You seem to think there is another side to this tunnel. That's the problem with the wealthy and the intelligentsia of this country, they all see us heading toward a dark tunnel and they think we just have to wait to you get to the other side. The reality is that once we enter we will eventually discover it's not a tunnel but a deep, dark hole.

Do you know what Matt has been doing with a great percentage of his net worth? He's been building a self-sustaining fortress in the Yukon Territory and a backup in New Zealand. These aren't summer homes. He is building them with the assumption that the world will fall apart and there is a better than decent probability that a nuclear war will happen. That is a bleak outlook from the most pragmatic son of a bitch I have ever known."

Penne, said, "Don't you see, that is why you have to focus on making us money so we can have a palace. You want to be a martyr and I want to live. You have to decide which path you will go down Philip because even though I breathe you like oxygen, a corpse takes no breath. I want to live. You served your time and gave your blood and you weren't out the door for a minute before they undid it all. You did what you could do, now come live out your days with me."

Philip said, "Penne, please don't give me an ultimatum. You too are my sustenance but if I do not try then I would not be worthy of you and could not look you or anyone else in the eye again. I would have to break every mirror and loathe every minute of every day as I would loathe myself if I did not try. I want to be with you but only if it brings happiness and if I run from this it cannot. If you

149

leave me I understand and can only hope you will take me back when it's all done, win or lose. Succeed or fail. I can only be worthy of you if I am a man and I can only live as a man if I know I have done all I can to help all humanity. Penne, don't leave me. Believe in me that I can make everything alright. Believe in me so that in my darkest hour I can believe in me."

Chapter 15

A Third Term

"Nothing beautiful without struggle."
— Plato

Penne resisted the idea of Philip running for office again until she went on a trip back to Japan where she reflected on the options and found the wisdom and peace in supporting Philip for another term. At least that's the way she told the story but whatever happened, Penne came around and from that moment Philip entered the race and went full throttle. The Freedom party did well across the board and Philip's third term as President also afforded him a strong contingent of support in Congress, although not a majority. Fortunately, lobbyists had again been banned from this election so the people of all the parties were of a higher all around quality.

President Kingsley entered office with many problems to address but also with an understanding of what he could do and how to get it done. He had a plan in place to maximize every second of every one of the first 100 days to push his agenda through. He reinstated all he had put in place in his previous terms and also went beyond that to extend the competitive Government agency (CGA) model to all of government. He further laid the groundwork to allow the government to compete in any industry in which the people were not fully served due to a lack of competition or a misdirected profit motive.

Jobs continued to be the key issue of the times. Unskilled labor jobs disappeared as robotic systems were a cheaper and more efficient method of performing these roles. Robots were really just extensions of computers into the physical world and it was the artificial intelligence behind them that allowed them to perform more and more complicated and intricate tasks. As AI developed, so did the scope of jobs that it was able to perform. AI robots could not only mop floors, they could complete tax returns, clean an entire house, drive forklifts, stock shelves, cook food, act as security guards, run cash registers, answers phones, respond to email, make spreadsheets, create reports, model data, fly planes, prepare legal cases, perform surgery, deliver furniture, build houses and on and on. Every day their capabilities increased to the point it seemed humans had almost no jobs left that were safe from being taken by computer or robot.

That's not to say there were not new jobs created. Thousands of jobs were created from this transformation as the computers and robots needed to be programmed and set up and repaired. AI could only do so many of these tasks itself. The problem was millions and millions of unskilled jobs disappeared and were replaced with thousands of highly skilled jobs. Then the cycle repeated itself with robots replacing people with skill sets no longer useful to humans as they could be performed by AI systems cheaper and better. This further divided the people with jobs from the people without jobs. The people with jobs were highly educated and technical or they had people or leadership skills and were paid more and more money. Most other people had no job and were barely getting by and had little hope of finding work.

In Japan, decades of R&D into robots to care for the elderly finally paid off and robots became ubiquitous throughout hospitals and doctors" offices. In fact, robots extended medicine to people's homes reinventing the house call so that the sick would not have to travel to a doctor's office and had access to diagnosis and care 24 hours a day. Part of the first 100 day's agenda was a universal healthcare option that gave basic minimum care to every citizen. It allowed people to buy care over and above that if they wished and, of course, if they had the means. The healthcare space was declared a CGA space and CGA companies sprung up to compete in insurance, medical care, medical equipment and most revolutionary, drugs and medical devices. Finally, health care was extricated from the workspace and all people were able to receive it.

In construction, workers with specific skill sets gathered at worksites to build structures in a scene that would be very familiar to tradesmen working on a medieval cathedral or a carpenter who worked on an ancient house. Not much had changed over the millennia other than some improvements to the tools. Then came a huge revolution where buildings became like lego sets with the walls and floors being printed by industrial 3d printers. They were then floated to the site by new classes of dirigible drones that were cheap to operate and could lift heavy loads. Trucks with smaller versions of industrial printers pulled on the lots and made what wasn't already preassembled at the factory. People didn't have to pick from only three different styles available in a neighborhood, they used a virtual architect to design their entire customized structure. It was then manufactured, delivered and assembled in days or weeks instead of months and years. Suddenly we didn't need 90% of the carpenters, roofers, pipefitters, electricians, ironworkers, masons, glaciers, etc. and there was no need for the collections of contractors and subcontractors to build things.

A single grocery store once employed hundreds of people directly and indirectly, then the revolution came. First the stocking robots took over the back of the store and then started maintaining the shelves. Next automated baggers came and then whole cart scanners came and rang everything up with a single scan. Automated cars opened the door to deliveries of all sorts of things including groceries. Innovators connected the dots to making the grocery store a virtual reality experience so people could virtually walk through a store and point to what they wanted. They could even select the specific pieces of vegetables they wanted and it soon became game over for the traditional grocery stores and their relatively high overhead and long lines. The VR helmets transitioned the older people who were used to that experience of shopping. Younger people just had a conversation with their home operating system about upcoming meals and approved or modified a suggested list of items based on meals past inventory and diets and the idea of a grocery store died with that generation.

The problem was with jobs and more specifically with income. There had never been so many amazing things for people to buy and have. The cost of making them had never been so relatively low, but there were fewer and fewer people with the income to spend on these things. Opening world markets and the cheap cost sustained the capitalist model to a point. However, it was based on people having money to continually buy new things as they worked doing something that somehow supported people making and buying more stuff and services. The income side of the equation was broken and yet companies had to sell things so they lowered the price which made them look to lower cost which meant eliminating high-cost human workers. The people that had income were able to live amazing lives enhanced by unbelievable technologies, but the rest of the populace were on the outside looking in.

Businesses had fewer customers that had the money to buy their products as wars and insurrections closed off entire foreign markets and unemployment limited the markets still open to commerce. The pressure was to lower the price and thus the cost to produce which, translated into more automation and more unemployment. The advancements in robotics meant that we could extend ourselves and our technologies to places practically inaccessible to humans, like the ocean floor and deep beneath the earth, where raw materials sat ready for the taking. Like a colony of ants, robotic mining drones descended deep within the earth's crust accessing vast treasure troves or resources for their human masters to plunder. They did the same beneath the crushing depths of the oceans and underneath the few remaining ice shelves of Antarctica and Greenland. There was a surge of plentiful, cheap resources of every kind.

Mining was expanding in every hostile extreme including space. Lost in the news of despair on earth, space drones had set up mining outposts on the moon and a handful of asteroids to begin rudimentary mining operations as a proof of concept. The only thing that held these projects back were the lack of additional money being pumped into them by their corporate backers as the price for resources were dropping continuously as mining expanded on earth. Meanwhile, they stockpiled what they found and the focus shifted to manufacturing in space so that operations could be expanded there with a minimum of parts needing the expensive ride from earth.

The situation around the world was worsening. In Europe, high unemployment led to protests and demands to outlaw robots replacing workers in countries like England and France. The Scandinavian countries struggled at times, but their technology sectors funded their Socialistic style governments so that they could weather the change better than others. Germany did better than any other country but still floundered as they had invested heavily in renewable energy and had a strong robotics industry to bring in much-needed capital. The Southern European countries were a disaster with protests and rioting being the daily norm and civil war taking place in a few. A neo-communist coup occurred in Bulgaria and threatened to spread to the surrounding countries.

Asia had a similar makeup with countries like Japan and South Korea doing ok while other countries like China burned. China's manufacturing dominance disappeared seemingly overnight and their cities were filled with hungry, unemployed people who took to the streets. The government brought in troops and drones, which worked for a while, but hungry people with no hope have nothing to lose and soon the country exploded in violence. Millions died as the government spent scarce funds on military robots to use against their own people. The rest of the continent suffered as well, including India. There, a tiny percentage did well but the rest of the country was mired in unemployment. The government provided enough food for most people to avoid starvation, but they were poor and otherwise hopeless.

Some places in Africa were affected less as the countries that had little at the beginning of this transformation actually came out ahead as they benefited from increased food supplies and better medical services. They did not, however, gain jobs and continued to languish in poverty. South America was hit hard as totalitarian governments took over in several countries and cracked down on their populace. Other countries were in shambles, and like Mexico, were in, or near, a state of civil war. Mexico was one of the hardest hit as they lost manufacturing jobs and their tech infrastructure through brain drain. People left the violence-strewn country in droves and were already assembled into armed camps competing with a corrupt government for control because of the drug trade. America legalizing marijuana and then decriminalizing other drugs was a final blow to the Mexican economy that caused the violence to erupt.

Mexico became the first crisis of the third term as the previous administration had closed the border and sent back thousands of refugees, many to their deaths. In a dramatic gesture, Philip Kingsley left his inauguration and immediately went to the situation room and plotted out a strategy he announced in a public address that very night.

Philip stood at the podium in the Briefing room flanked on one side by a group of generals and on the other by the Secretaries of State, Homeland Security, and the Attorney General.

President Kingsley began, "Good evening my fellow Americans. We face many challenges. As I step into my first day on the job I see no greater threat to our security and no greater misfortune than what is happening, in some cases literally feet from US property, to our neighbors in Mexico. I have been briefed by hundreds of experts on this situation over the past few months. I could go on and tell you what I hear of our humanitarian responsibility to stop the killing, rape, and torture of innocent women, children and men. I could speak of the arguments I heard about our responsibilities of leadership in the western hemisphere and the Americas. I could recount the numerous experts who explained our culpability in the horrors taking place as a consequence of our well-intentioned but misguided war on drugs. I heard people explain that millions of our citizens are connected by family ties and friendships to people in Mexico.

I have also heard sensible people make arguments to the effect that if we used humanitarian efforts as our justification, why just Mexico when half the world is troubled? I have heard others say we can take a leadership role in the West by getting our own house in order first. Still others could spout off a laundry list of things that went wrong in Mexico besides the war on drugs that landed them in this predicament. Other experts point out that because we have such a diverse melting pot of citizens we can point to every hot spot in the world and find friends and family of those being affected by the tragedies in each of those places. There are still many others who say this is one of many situations that could benefit from our help, but we are just not in a financial position to spend valuable resources fixing the world's problems. They would say we have enough unemployed people here already without bringing millions more.

These are hard choices and there are wise people who make valid and good arguments on both sides of this very difficult and complicated issue. Many thoughts came to mind as I spoke with these experts including the idea of letting your neighbor's house burn thinking it's not your problem until it inevitably spreads to your house. I thought of the idea of the oxygen mask dropping and the harsh but sensible instructions to secure your own mask first before trying to save your children because if you fall the whole family will perish. My head spun as there did not seem to be right answers, only entanglements, and complications.

I was unsure what I would do as your President until I heard the experts lay out the dangers to the citizens of the United States. China holds the largest standing army in the world with over 4 million personnel. While it can be argued that Mexico no longer has a formal army, they do have over 20 million armed combatants making up an army of chaos and anarchy. That is over 10 times larger than all the personnel of all the branches of the United States Armed Forces. This army of chaos has brought its violence to our doorstep as we share nearly 2000 miles of border and they have brought death, rape and destruction to the very edge of every bit of it.

We are in danger of this army of chaos spilling into our homeland that is simply not tolerable. This situation has left us vulnerable to our enemies around the world who bring those who would do us harm into Mexico to promote violence and chaos knowing the harm it brings us. Furthermore, the floods of refugees allow a means of infiltration by these same enemies to allow them to strike at our heartland. My mind was made up at this point that we did not need further reasons for action and this would be the first task on day one.

Fellow citizens, I would like to tell you that proper channels exist such that I could simply pick up the phone and speak with the leader of Mexico. Unfortunately the leader we officially recognize there simply has no power or authority in the areas of concern to us. I have instead contacted the people in control of the northern Mexican states, from Baja California in the West, all across the states that touch our border to Tamaulipas in the East. They have been informed that the US military will be securing a one hundred mile buffer zone along this northern border comprised of the upper portion of these northern states.

Although this is not an invasion, it is a police action resulting in the temporary occupation of this security zone. Armed resistance will be treated as enemy aggression and handled accordingly. Once this area is secured, we will look to establish safe zones for Mexican citizens so that they once again can enjoy safety and security within the confines of their own country. For reasons of security that is all I will be saying at this time and we will provide updates when appropriate in the days to come.

Thank you and God bless the great citizens of the United States as well as our neighbors next door, the people of Mexico."

Philip Kingsley left the podium followed by his entourage. As he was doing so, thousands of drones crossed the border and started patrolling the skies of Northern Mexico. For days there were broadcasts over the internet, TV, radio, CB radio and any other means of transmission available, communicating that the US was coming to help. They said that anyone who raised a weapon would be treated as an enemy and killed. There was instruction for what to do with weapons and where to go for help. Drones flew over cities, villages and houses and dropped fliers and broadcast these instructions over loudspeakers for days. The broadcasts promised safety and help to those who wanted it and warned those who sought violence to leave the area now or be destroyed.

Days later US forces flooded over the border led by unmanned ground vehicles (UGVs) and unmanned aerial vehicles (UAVs). Refugee processing centers were set up and citizens were instructed to come to them to be registered, fed and to receive care while the bad people were rooted out. Cities had evacuation deadlines and once past, swarms of UAVs from bus-sized drone carriers flying overhead to bee sized drones buzzing through rooms of buildings. On the ground, UGVs were deployed en masse and also ranged from nearly bus-sized deployment platforms to the tiny gecko-sized crawlers that scaled up the sides of the building. Some were specialized in sniffing out explosives and IEDs while others honed in on the heat signatures other specific signatures living things give off. While lethal autonomous robotics (LARS) had been banned by international agreement, there were still many systems that could kill by way of a human controller safely squirreled away watching footage from the robot's perspective onto a screen or virtual reality (VR) goggles.

These operations were hailed as a huge success and a portent of a more humanitarian era of warfare and military operations. Sure, several civilians were injured and three lost their lives, but that was a fraction of the expected "collateral damage" anticipated in such an operation. And when lethal force was necessary, it was delivered with precision and totality. Over four hundred military combatants were killed while not a single US soldier had been killed, although a few were injured. By the end, there were militants surrendering to drones which mimicked scenes of Iraqi soldiers surrendering to reporters in the first Gulf War.

Vast refugee centers were set up and people were able to track down their families and friends. People could eat and drink and enjoy a good night sleep, none of which they had had with any sense of regularity for quite some time. Children played without fear of bad men coming and parents watched without a sense of dread of a bullet or kidnappers or some horrible outcome. It was just a few weeks into his third term and there was already talk of a Nobel peace prize and at home approval ratings soared.

.

Chapter 16

Turning the Corner

"Wise men speak because they have something to say; fools because they have to say something."
— Plato

A month into swearing into office President Kingsley had assembled a retreat at Camp David to meet with thought leaders in various fields to discuss issues and policies relevant to them. This had been planned shortly after the election and President Kingsley decided that it should continue even with the Mexican crisis. Different groups were brought in on different days representing major Industries. On the agenda was a day for each of these:

- Business to Business & Wholesale
- Business to Consumer
- Construction
- Education
- Finance
- Food
- Healthcare
- Hospitality and Entertainment
- Information Technology

- Raw Materials
- Service Industries
- Transportation and Warehousing

On the day chosen for each specific industry, the most important luminaries and CEO's were to come in to speak and engage in breakout sessions. There they would discuss important topics as well as to mingle with the President and Cabinet members. The President had encouraged players in all the industries to have some representation every day of the conference so that cross-industry cooperation and synergistic problem solving could forge.

Of course, the industry leaders were only expected on the day focusing on that their respective industries. In days past such an event would likely not even receive a spattering of middle managers representing organizations if they sent anyone at all. In days past, influence and access were bought with lobbyists and campaign contributions and now that this had changed. CEO's jumped at the opportunity for direct access and anxious to make sure they received the same amount as their competition. Only in an era of the anti-corruption legislation could an event such as this be important.

Cell and internet access were blocked in the main area of the event site so people could focus on people and post to social media after being away from the talks and meetings. To add to an air of openness, the press were excluded from the event directly. All this exclusively made everyone want information all the more, where if it had been an open, event it would likely be met with yawns. But of course, attendees spoke with the press and social media the second they left. It didn't matter whether it was to promote how their brand fit into the vision for the future or to raise their own profile by seeming to have loomed larger than perhaps they did at the event, they all hoped on their devices the second they could.

One of the thought leaders invited to this summit was none other than Matthew Ligarck. He was seen as a minor industry expert by most people there. Only the elite of the group knew that he was connected to the elite of the elite and so did not garnish a single mention in all the releases from attendees. This also made it easier for him to have ample time to meet one on one with the president as he would not be missed. There were plenty of off-limit areas he could be snuck into to meet with President Kingsley.

One evening, President Kingsley was sitting in a comfortable looking chair with three different pages hovering in the air in front of him and a video playing with no sound. In his peripheral vision, he noticed Matthew standing there observing him and he waved his hand in front of him leading to all the screens disappearing. He said, "Matthew, how the hell are you?"

Matthew walked over to shake the President's hand and said, "Better than last year but still uneasy about our future."

Philip said, "You could have just said fine. Thanks for making the trip, I know from your perspective this event is mostly bullshit with people who take orders from people too powerful to feel the need to be here."

Matthew replied, "I got the impression you needed to meet with me."

Philip said, "You got the right impression. Have a seat. You want a drink?"

Matthew said, "Sure, scotch neat."

Philip clicked a button on a phone sized device and said, "Jimmy, please bring us your finest single malt and a couple glasses."

The steward knocked and then entered the room with a tray containing a bottle and two glasses.

The President pointed to the bar and said, "Thanks, Jimmy, you can just set it on the bar, open the bottle and we'll take it from there."

The Steward did as was asked, bowed slightly and exited the room. Philip poured two glasses and handed one to Matthew and after they both had smelled their glass to capture the aroma, Philip said, "To reshaping the world."

The glasses touched and the two sipped some of the scotch letting it swirl around their mouths before swallowing it. Philip savored the moment for a few seconds and then said, "Matt, I need a big favor."

Matthew smiled and said, "So this isn't a 'synergy' meeting?"

Philip smiled and said, "I'm glad you brought jokes because I plan on pissing off some very powerful friends of yours."

Matthew said, "Like you, all my friends are very powerful but some are more friendly than others so I'm sure we can find some win-win situation."

Philip sipped his scotch and then said, "The electrical grid project was the hallmark of my first two terms. Renewables are

165

growing but I need to do something radical and what I have in mind is not going to fly with the gas and coal folks."

Matthew said, "The utility companies had a little pull, but coal and gas are two leagues above utilities. They are floundering a bit politically as your anti-corruption laws have stymied their lobbying strategy, but they have deep pockets. Once they find the right strategy and then the right enemy to point it toward they can unleash hell, and I would not want to be on the receiving end of that."

Philip said, "Let me lay out what I want to do and then maybe you can help me find that win for them to soften the blow. I plan on a Manhattan Project scale initiative to become not only energy-independent but a net energy exporter. They have found plenty of new deposits of oil and gas in the past decade. Combine that with all the new drilling and robotics technology and add to the fact we have actually decreased consumption, thanks to the steady death of gasoline engines, and we have an ample supply for the foreseeable future. We have enough coal and natural gas for a hundred years. That vast supply and all the advances in mining and drilling keeps the price just low enough that we don't expand renewables above a snail's pace.

I'm going to blanket the country with solar panels and every other viable technology so people can make their own energy and pump what they don't need back into this fancy grid we've built. This would also be a huge jobs program until they figure out how to eliminate them all with a robot that is."

Matt shook his head as his eyebrows raised as he said, "That is a tough one. None of my initial thoughts would fly. I mean the good news is that they'll end up building a bunch of electricity-sucking robots to then build these new panels. With the overall energy consumption graph perpetually slanted up, a smaller share of a larger market offsets some of the pain. Coal and gas employ a lot of people still and wield a large amount of power. You should be prepared for the huge media blitz."

President Kingsley just looked at Matthew for a minute and then said, "Matt, I didn't call you here to have you tell me the obvious. I'm proposing basically making energy virtually free and you're telling me about a media blitz? Look I'm going to share a little secret with you. A group of researchers has thoroughly tested a method for using thermoelectric almost anywhere. We can drill deep enough now at most locations so that we can hit a layer hot enough to boil water into steam. Their method pumps brine in and gets steam to power turbines back and then that distilled steam condensates as fresh water.

Basically, with a considerable but affordable upfront investment and then a relatively low maintenance and upkeep cost we can produce all the electricity and fresh water we want. We can do this using a method safe enough to park it next to the consumers who would use it. We're going to blanket the country with saltwater pipelines, drills, and turbines. Both energy and water will be abundant and at a cost approaching free.

What I need from you is a way to do this without having to go to the mattresses with one of the most powerful factions of your cabal. It's not like we won't need any coal or gas. This plan takes them from controlling an essential resource with ever growing demand, to being owners of billions of dollars of equipment that costs more to operate than can be collected in revenue. If I were them, I would see this as more than war, this is a fight to stave off extinction.

Look, I'm not really asking for a favor. I'm asking you to play broker here which profits you no matter which way this thing goes. No one wins from that war. Can you help me find a way out of this that is acceptable to all parties?"

Matt smiled wryly, "Well Mr. President, I applaud your realpolitik. You have two choices. Buy off the coal cartel or kill off the coal cartel. Whichever you do, the rest of the players will be watching and deciding how this bodes for their future. If it were me, I would propose the very lowest payoff that was not an insult and wait for them to counter. They will, of course, counter high. You could play split the baby, but I would add 10% to the original offer and add in a take it or leave it ultimatum with a threat to decimate them if they refuse. They likely will refuse and then you have to decimate them worse than you threatened."

Philip Kingsley looked confused and said, "I'm not a third world petty dictator. I'm looking for an amicable way to handle this."

Matt said, "There is no amicable to take a man's livelihood. You can take a lot of things but you try and take his source of money, prestige and power and he will fight you tooth and nail. You either give him a golden parachute or you call security and have him walked out of the building and banned from re-entering."

President Kingsley thought a moment and said, "How much do you think they'd want as a buyout?"

167

Matthew replied, "More than they should get. Much more. If you are going to start nationalizing industries, then you can't tiptoe around it. There is a reason dictators send in troops to bar the office doors."

President Kingsley raised his voice a bit and said, "I'm not nationalizing anything and I'm not sending in troops. Look, I could just move forward with my plan, other than some advertisements what are they going to do?"

Matthew pondered this for a moment and said, "Maybe if you just pitch the endgame now and get ahead of it. Maybe we are looking at this all wrong. Forget who gets hurt, who wins in this scenario. Every business who has energy as a line item and foreign competition who doesn't get free energy is a winner. Agriculture wins huge as well. Recruit them as allies and use them to counterbalance any negative media campaigns."

The President said, "I like your thinking but what if I told you I want to take it one step further and blanket the world with new geothermal electric technology? I want free and abundant water and energy around the globe. You see once we do that, the other countries of the world have a hope of stabilizing and evolving to some form where their people can lay down their weapons and pick up their credit cards and buy things from us. That's the pitch I want to make. That's how we get every business who benefits from exports behind this. I'm afraid this will not only make an enemy of the energy people but also the military-industrial complex."

Matthew said, "Wow that is two powerful groups to have on the opposite side of the table."

The President said, "Can you talk to people in power who benefit from this and see if they are willing to help win hearts and minds if it comes to that?"

Matthew said, "What if you tell the energy folk to buy up the neo geo industry and then guarantee them all the contracts to expand as well as delaying creating CGAs in that industry?"

The President said, "Can you sell that?"

Matt said, "Yes I think I can. But I don't see a benefit if I make tanks."

The President said, "Tell the defense people if I can get free water and energy at home we can focus abroad with Mexico being just the beginning."

Matt said, "Wait that was your end game coming in here. That's what I do and it has just been done to me. You led me around and let me think I came to your conclusion on my own. The student becomes the master. Well done Philip. You have obviously done the math on how brokering all this information helps me so yes, I'll consider it."

Philip said, "I have a few other ideas as well that I need your help with. I can offer greatly reduced employee costs as well as better employees that are trained and incented to perform at their peak. I am moving towards free energy and I am open to other ideas that will make our businesses dominant in a major way throughout the world. These things I offer as well as the fact that I am open to other ideas so that the world market is presented to the heads of American business on a silver platter.

In exchange for this, and saving the economy from total utter collapse into a bleak, dark depression that would end this civilization and life as we had grown to know it, I require a few things. I will need the market share of all small and medium business in most industries to set up CGAs and cash out the profit to help pay for what needs to be done. That should not be a problem for your people as we are proposing replacing mom and pop competitors with the hulking and inefficient government.

I'm also going to need to declare all-out war in a few industries including healthcare and pharmaceuticals. If fact I'm looking to create several huge CGA's that will be very aggressive and likely crush the players in those spaces. I could use your help on strategies to do this with minimal amounts of lost treasure, time, and PR on all sides."

Matthew said, "I think I can show the long-term wisdom of these moves as well as the necessity of some blood spilled and maybe even the upsides to the other players. Pharma, healthcare and especially the insurance people won't go without a fight. I think the others will see that these lambs must be placed on the altar and hopefully I can pitch a, "better them than us," idea. To make this work, I need to be able to assure them that they are not next."

President Kingsley said, "This is the plan. We have run the numbers and think this is a viable and sustainable model as I have laid it out. I can't guarantee the future, but I can say that this plan makes possible the sustaining of a viable marketplace from which your cronies can continue to add truckloads of gold for the foreseeable future."

Matthew said, "I will need some specific concessions that can help iron out the details but on the surface I can sell this. I can put together a list and start scheduling meetings with my associates.

All and all I see this as unpalatable but doable. Doable if I bring some financial security to the ones not being butchered. Judas will need his thirty pieces of silver."

Philip said, "What is this going to cost me?"

Matthew said, "How are all these CGA's getting their funds to open their doors?"

Philip said, "Well, from the budget of the department they fall under."

Matthew said, "That's well and good for actual government agency CGA's but what about all these new areas you want to expand to?"

Philip said, "We were looking at special bond issues and..."

Matthew cut in and said, "Philip, this is how we sell it. Make it a guaranteed loan from an approved lender. This lets the financial institutions on the list I will provide you, loan out exorbitant amounts of money at slightly less than market rates for startups and the money will be guaranteed thus removing risk. I will need you to set it up so that these CGA's will pay a ten percent loan origination fee, which can be deducted from the loan proceeds, and they will also need the government to deposit twelve percent of the loan in an equity account with the lending bank."

Philip said, "Well done Matthew. Your banker friends get to add an ungodly number of loans at higher than average rates for a guaranteed loan. At to that, since the reserve and capital requirements are are satisfied as a condition of the loan, all they have to do is sit back and collect money."

Matthew said, "Oh there is plenty of upside for you on this as well. You get to finance this move for a government out of pocket cost of twelve cents on the dollar and you get to say the loan rates are below market. Getting a fraction of the budget approved or being able to expand that much faster should make this work for you. I need nothing less if I am going to sell this."

The President said, "If I agree to this, I'm going to make you a lot of money because I'm going to open it all up, the whole economy. Understand too that the profits from the businesses are off limits. You'll get your loan payments but no foreclosures or exorbitant penalty payments. The government will pay the bill when the business can't. You get your money, but we foreclose on the business if it comes to that."

Matthew smiled a wry smile, stuck out his hand and said, "Mr. President I think we have a deal."

Philip said, "Excellent, I'm going to be moving on this very fast so I need you to make some quick allies. Can you do that and how long do you need?"

Matt dejectedly said, "I can. Give me a month."

Philip grabbed the bottle, refilled their drinks and raising his glass said, "To free energy and water for all."

In the months to come things moved fast. The President announced a huge energy bill that issued tax credits for residential solar panels. Congress also passed bills promoting production and use of solar, wind and especially neogeothermal as it had come to be called. Special provisions were included to give existing energy companies special breaks and incentives to invest massively in neogeothermal. Jobs were created and masses of people helped cover the roofs of the millions of homes and businesses still without solar collectors. Drilling began at sites around the country in anticipation of the pipelines that would bring in a massive amount of salt water. That water would be directed thousands of feet downward into the earth to deposit its salt and return energized fresh water.

A separate bill that flew under the radar called for a national strategic coal and natural gas reserve. That worked out a deal to get a significantly reduced price for coal at large guaranteed volumes over the next fifty years, ramping up slowing over the next ten years and then flatlining to a yearly commitment. This bill was pitched as protection in time of crisis to a vital industry, but really it just guaranteed a payout to the coal and gas industries well past the time their main current product would be virtually worthless. It also gave them the guaranteed income stream that allowed them to invest massively in the new energy technologies without worrying about cannibalization.

Finally, a bill announced a massive CGA investment in an any industry, in the language of the bill, "for which maximal employment opportunities have not been utilized, or in which there is room for additional competition due to consumer lack of choice, or industries vital to American national interests or the wellbeing of its citizens." This, of course, was vague enough so that President Kingsley now had a door open to instill a government run concern in any and every industry he so chose.

This all happened fast and in the enthusiastic bubble of a new administration. President Kingsley knew he must lay all the groundwork he could as rapidly as he could as the problems of the world would soon come back and take a hold of the headlines and

171

the attention of America. Indeed, while jobs were on the minds of many, others started voicing serious concerns over the economy as a whole and specifically with the debt and interest rates. As the world economy faltered and the US government upped its spending to record levels, it was getting harder and harder to find investors to buy our debt. In order to attract money away from other investments and into US government securities, it was necessary to offer higher rates of return. This in turn necessitated a higher amount of the federal budget would be needed to service the yearly debt. It looked like we were becoming a train on a runaway track and the world cringed at the thought of a US train wreck and what it would mean for everyone on the planet.

Chapter 17

A New Economy

"Necessity is the mother of invention."
— Plato

Frederick had been a rising star at Harvard. He had earned tenure in the shortest amount of time a professor could. Students fought to get into his classes. He had published regularly and brought in many Grants as well as well as positive PR from TV appearances, lectures, and documentaries in which he participated in some way. His books always sold well and the fact that he was an African-American man raised by a single mom surely did not hurt his bio. Later on, his fame grew as it came to light that he was the childhood friend of Philip Kingsley as he ran for and then became president. Sometimes childhood friend came out as son of Philip Kingsley's domestic servant but either way it made him more interesting. Frederick could write his own ticket.

Indeed, he did use his celebrity during the first two Kingsley administrations to promote causes he supported and to support Kingsley himself. He appeared on many news and politics discussion shows as a guest or panelist. He wrote several books during this time as well. Of course, he met with Kingsley often. Philip valued his counsel and feedback. Frederick had shaped the

President's thinking for most of his life and continued to do so through the first two terms. President Kingsley had offered him a number of different posts and appointments but each time Frederick refused, stating that he was an academic, not a politician or a bureaucrat.

It wasn't until Kingsley left office that Frederick became a political activist. He pushed for a third party and as a way to bring back the policies that Kingsley launched and the incumbents in the proceeding term stripped away. It was then that Frederick left his tenured professorship at Harvard to dedicate all his time and energy to this cause. It was in large part because of Frederick that a third party became viable and that Philip Kingsley sat in the White House for his third term. It was at this time that Frederick was at a crossroad, having left teaching and fulfilled the mission he left that for he was unsure what he wanted. He had had lots of offers for important posts within the Freedom party as well as prestigious positions from academia and even an offer for his own TV show.

Two months into his third term, President Kingsley had half an afternoon blocked off and top secret meeting set in the Roosevelt room. Philip arrived just a few minutes late and walked into a room filled with flip charts, books, and stacks of papers all over the long table. President Kingsley shut the door and embraced Frederick in a tight hug that included a couple heavy handed, but not hurtful slaps on the back.

The President said, "How are you old friend?"

Frederick replied, "Mr. President, I will always be your friend, but I certainly don't yet categorized myself as old. I am doing quite fine. You gave me quite a gift with this project. It is just what I needed to reignite my passion."

The President said, "Frederick, no one is around so, please drop the Mr. President. Well, it certainly seems like you brought some ideas. Look I don't want to be rude but you know how it goes here, they could swoop in steal me out of here at any moment and I have been looking forward to this for so long, let's get started. What do have?"

Frederick said, "Well Mr., sorry, Philip since we discussed this last November I have dedicated every minute to it. I am not an economist, but I am a great researcher and after an exhaustive look at the material I have stolen and stitched together a plan. Here is the basic thesis. Capitalism as the world has practiced it up until now is broken. It is broken in a couple different ways.

First the labor market was not a market and what you did in the first two terms was right on target. I think simply reinstating The CGA model and expanding it is the way to go here.

Second, too big to fail is a failure in a truly competitive marketplace. This points to the fact that we have allowed an advantage to exist based on size so that there is a high cost of entry to new competition and that is inherently bad for competition. We must make the playing field about the product or service and not about economies of scale. I propose we ban volume discounting as it perpetuates this model. Let companies compete on the price available to all. If there is room to wiggle on price let them do it at retail and against the prices of their competitors so all can benefit.

Thirdly, we have had no incentive for improving the workforce. People who work fifty hours a week don't have time for lifelong learning. Companies who invest in employee training have no guarantees that the employee won't finish training and take that investment across the street to the competition. We must reinstate the split of work and education you implemented in the CGAs before and expand on it. If implemented across the nation it would increase the number of jobs in the neighborhood of forty percent and continually improves the workforce until all the jobs that matter are American jobs.

Fourthly, we have almost exclusively relied on a single incentive, money, measured in profit. We have allowed profit to be exclusively measured by collecting more in sales than in costs to produce. Allowing this to be the single unchecked measure has produced positive outcomes in many instances, but unintended consequences in others. We should set profit alternatives so that some companies in some areas of endeavor where traditional profit doesn't work, will produce as much as they can with a goal of breaking even. Their focus will not be on maximizing financial profit but achieving the societal goal set for that industry and then money will be provided a financial incentive for achieving these goals.

For instance, drug companies could only earn "profit" for coming up with drugs that cure or do certain things and be measured on things like effectiveness per production dollar. A group outside the industry with expertise in this area could prioritize and incentivize the goals so that these companies can come up with cures for diseases instead of just looking to grow hair. Not that the latter is not important and would certainly be worthy of a payout but the incentive should not be such that they spend more resource on hair cream than on saving the lives of suffering children.

Fifthly and finally, the model of consumerism is flawed and broken. The idea of planned obsolescence is wasteful and inefficient and yet it is the motor driving the economy. We have removed the costs of all these wastes from the products and services that create them so there is no incentive to do anything about them. We should charge the producers of these products the full costs of these products throughout their lifecycle.

We have been tricked into the illusion of ownership. We feel in control and like we have gained an asset of value when we purchase something when really, all we have done is assumed all the responsibilities for maintaining and disposing of it. What we really wanted was what the service the product provided. You wanted the TV shows, not the TV. You wanted the barbecued food, not the grill per se.

We should also incentivize the selling of services over products so that companies provide products as part of their service but retain responsibility for the products throughout their lifecycle. We would end up with products that last longer, new uses for older products instead of the landfill, and products that need less maintenance.

That is the high-level view Philip. There are many layers of details, ideas, options, and suggestions below each one of those."

Philip smiled, "Frederick, it is a joy to see you so impassioned. This is outstanding as a framework. What do you have on the investment and ownership side of the equation?"

Frederick said, "Basically there are two classifications of businesses, stock, and non-stock. I will let your more marketing savvy folks come up with clever names for these. Non-stock companies are ones for which the goals of the enterprise are long-term, highly speculative or hard to objectively define. These will be few in number are just the ones we can't figure out how to make a stock company. An example may be basic scientific research.

A stock company is like a corporation. However, the return generated is not only about generating traditional profit, although it can be. Again, I am no marketer but think of it like the contests set up by billionaires to achieve certain goals such as land on the moon with a set of criteria laid forth and the winner collecting a big cash prize. For different industries, we would set goals. An example may be a competitive goal for the industry like first cell company to offer 95% coverage across the US get a profit bonus. For each company in an industry, there could be an individual goal like a customer service rating or on time percentage or any number of things and every company who achieves this goal gets a profit bonus. Mind you we only need to set goals for things a competitive marketplace does not take care of itself as that will almost always be the most efficient means of achieving these ends and should be created and encouraged whenever and wherever possible.

There would need to be CGA's set up to evaluate the strengths and weaknesses of industries and create a series of incentives around improving the areas that are lacking or for which competition will foster the best outcome for the consumer. I recommend and extension of the anti-corruption laws to cover those making these rules. I also recommend CGA's reviewing these CGAs and having them alternate industries to review so the year over year recommendations of one CGA over another can be compared.

Stock ownership will be similar to today with some key differences. The Government would be a silent stock owner in CGAs. A percentage of this stock may be sold off on the stock market just as it would today. The government could raise money by selling off stock. There would have to be some rules around this to avoid the perception of timing that may benefit some people. Of course, there would be anti-corruption laws in place such that the people who make the decision to offer the stock for sale could not benefit from that decision, etc., etc.

Stock prices would fluctuate as they do today based on the perceived present and future value of the company. There would be dividends paid out from profit earned as well as money earned through achievement of goals. This would allow companies to pay out dividends even in downward economic cycles which could, in fact, help move the economy out of that cycle. In fact, this system could level off the boom and bust cyclical nature of the economy as companies earn along several dimensions and not just on growth and profit. For an outmoded industry, the goals could be based on cost control and efficiency so that as the customer base shrinks they can earn a dividend by shrinking the business in smart ways.

New companies would fall into 3 classes of business including, companies creating new or entering young industries, companies in dynamic industries and finally companies in mature industries. Newer industries would issue up to 70% stock, dynamic around 50% and mature around 30%. These numbers would settle to a natural number in the conditions in the market. Employees will have stock options in lieu of profit bonuses, which I'll get to, for 6, 4 and 2 years respectively paid out in the same ways a cash bonus is in a mature company.

Employees in all CGAs are as before, hired on a universal pay scale and then have opportunities to earn more through bonuses for individual performance at the company as well as ranking within people in that profession across the country. There are departmental bonus opportunities as well as profit sharing in the company. If the company hits any of its goals, a portion of that goes into an employee pool. Employees are entitled to shares in that pool based on individual performance, team performance as well as job type and tenure. So a high performing new employee in a high performing department may get more pool shares than a low performing manager in another department.

This incentivizes all employees to try and do their best as well as help their co-workers to do their best. There will be a team mentality so it is understood that someone slacking hurts everyone's pay, not just their own. Because more employees create a dilution of the pool, all employees will be in favor of getting the work done with as few employees as needed. Employees that are bringing down the team will receive bad peer reviews, will likely have bad performance reviews and will be reassigned to another industry and possibly another job or other training until a fit is found.

CGAs will enter industries in numbers of at least two and companies that fail to perform over time will be disbanded, their assets sold off, stockholders cashed out with the proceeds and employees reassigned. There will be creative destruction as new companies will cycle in and unsuccessful companies will go away. Certain industries will have higher churn and the measure of success or failure for an individual business will have different criteria in different industries and these criteria will evolve in the marketplace. We wouldn't necessarily want to disband a good company that happens to be up against a great company as it may be providing the high degree of competition pushing the great company to perform as well as they are.

There can be stock markets and stock ownership just as today. The government will be a large owner in most companies and will have to adhere to stringent rules for when it can sell or buy shares. In fact, the government should never be actively trading and should be long-term holders of stock only buying or selling off as a fixed percentage of all holdings to either raise or invest capital or to adjust fixed percentage amounts across industries as a balancing response to market conditions over time. People will still be able to buy stock as will funds and investment institutions. I see no reason foreign capital couldn't be invested just as today.

I envision a department of Entrepreneurship where ideas meet up with people with the right skillsets to build an idea and a business and receive funding from angels who work for a CGA and invest government money and are rated like any other job covered under a CGA. The process is similar to how it works today and we gather experts who help with the business plan, refining the model and all the tough things that entrepreneurs go through today. We will basically make many incubators and allow as many ideas as possible be planted and help them grow and if they die, the Entrepreneurs can go to the back of the line and build a new business plan or do something else. We will endeavor to maximize new business in an effort to allow every idea an opportunity to compete and then let the survival of the fittest in the marketplace take over from there.

One argument will be that this is socialism or communism or some ism, and that everything will have to go through the government and so innovation, freedom and independence will be gone. The counter will be that private business can still be created but must be done through private investors and must pay their fair share for employees as calculated by the labor department but other than that they are free to operate and compete. GCA auditors will constantly measure the cost of employees so private firms can choose to pay that cost themselves and, with that, they will have full access to workforce market. The CGA program will be so much better that everyone will choose to go that route, but no one will have to.

The government will collect revenue through owning part of the economy so that what is good for the economy is good for government and vice versa. CGAs will have groups to measure performance at every level and they will be blindly cross checked and rated themselves for fairness and objectivity. People will be measured and rewarded based on effort, dedication, persistence and other things once thought too intangible. They will work a split week between work and training or education. People with better grades and showing more effort will be allowed to do more schooling. For people who don't want training, we can come up with

181

service programs or people can just work more but the options will be there.

Just like I believe we should try every business idea possible, I think we should do the same with invention ideas. I believe that the vast majority of ideas never make it beyond the back of napkins because people don't have the means, knowledge or personality type to move it forward. We have built a system that promotes innovation only from employees of big companies or those who not only have an idea but also have an entrepreneurial skill set, which in combination is rare. I think we need models that allow all the ideas to be tried and let them compete in the marketplace. We need models that take up all these ideas and match them with people who have the skill set to advance them. People should be allowed to handoff ideas and get some reward or payment out it and not just let it die having never been tried. I think we can create a system of bonuses and guaranteed licenses as alternatives to the current patent system so we maximize innovation.

That's the basics of the pitch Philip. Finally, I have prepared a list of people for the heads of labor and commerce as well as people I think they should at least consider for a position somewhere in each. Lastly, I would like to throw my hat in the ring to head up the Patent and Trade Office. I need a job after all and the ideas I just outlined are very rough and need to be refined.

Well, what do you think?"

Philip said, "So are you proposing we nationalize the economy?"

Frederick said, "No I would definitely not call it that. Nationalization is when existing private companies are confiscated by the government and is about stealing control of assets and profit. This is government sharing in the interests, profits, and losses of companies so that what is good for business is good for the government and for citizens. In the process, we eliminate corporate taxes and tie the success of the company as a success for the owners who will include private citizens and the government as a silent partner with a shared benefit or loss.

Furthermore and most importantly, the Government must not seize existing companies. We must enter industries that are not maximizing their potential and compete. If the existing private models are working well they will compete and should beat out the competition. This will make the great private companies better, the good companies great and will squeeze out the inefficient and ineffective companies out as a good marketplace should and does"

Philip said, "If the government controls innovation then shouldn't we expect the death of it?"

Frederick said, "If the government were going to be in charge of it then you may have a valid concern. Government will simply be supplying the means for innovation to occur. I would point out that the current system would remain in place. This would just add alternatives so people who don't have the means to move their idea through the process, the skillset to create their own company or the resources to market or legally defend their idea can still bring all their ideas to the table and have a choice of vehicles for advancing them to choose from. The market then gets the maximum amount of fresh ideas and the market will also weed out the winners and losers from there."

Philip said, "So you propose we do away with large companies and lose the economies of scale that they create?"

Frederick said, "What they create are not economies of scale but rather negotiated discounts. Economies of scale come from producing more when the market is doing well and demanding more. When a company is big enough to extort a better price from a supplier, then it is at the cost of all those not represented in the negotiation. It comes at the expense of all competition, small businesses, and innovation."

Philip said, "I'm concerned about the idea of the government defining what a company should produce or do and then giving them a reward for it."

Frederick said, "We are doing that right now with our tax code. What we are proposing here is a transparent means to accomplish the goals we agree on as a society instead of the opaque tax loopholes that allow certain constituencies to benefit producing things we did not all agree on."

Philip said, "So the government is going to tell business what they can and can't do? Isn't that simply regulations in sheep's clothing?"

Frederick said, "Regulations are a set of rules and laws that says you have to do things 1, 2, 3 in this way and you cannot do things x, y, or z or you pay a fine. It is a well-meaning but flawed system that proposes to know the best ways and best answers to solve problems. In some instances that is the only way we can accomplish what we as a society want and we have to live with the stifling effect that has on business.

What we propose here is not regulation and, in fact, will likely decrease the need for regulation. Setting goals this way is more akin to a competition. Regulations clearly define the means to achieving a broadly defined goal while we are proposing here is a specifically defined goal and allowing business to try any legal method they think makes sense to accomplish these goals and then we reward success."

Philip said, "Who defines these goals? How do we know this isn't just a way for those who make the rules to get rich?"

Frederick said, "First we have the bedrock of this administration, the anti-corruption laws that changed how we do business in government and ensures that lawmakers are not burdened with the possibility of conflicts of interest so that they are not put in a situation that may corrupt their principals or sway their vote.

We will choose our goals using the democratic process now free from lobbyists, where we can debate the pros and cons and then act on our best choices. You brought up regulations which is a less democratic and more restrictive method or carrying out our goals and we are doing that already today. This is better."

Philip said, "It sounds like you want to limit choice. I mean why would the government want more competition against itself?"

Frederick said, "The government will have an ownership stake in most companies and so creating a more competitive marketplace will create more revenue, not less. This system, unlike the current one, will not have competition stifling monopolies and oligopolies but will instead have many small and nimble competitors constantly driving innovation and efficiencies.

Philip replied, "You speak against consumerism but yet isn't that the very engine of the economy?"

Frederick replied, "When collecting excess money from your customers and growing market share are the only drivers of rewards and motivations for companies, then it stands to reason a certain type of wasteful wanton and unsustainable consumerism will be produced. Once the basic wants of consumers have been met then, artificial wants must be created. People must consume things in a modern society and when sales are the only method of profit or reward, then sales will be sought at all cost. The type of out of control consumerism that is bad for the society and bad for the consumer and bad for the economy as a whole are what we will be doing away with.

184

When a shoemaker profits based on the longevity of their shoes as much as or more than the sales price, then they won't make a shoe designed to wear out in a year. They also won't convince their customer they need the next style she every six months. Electronics makers who make money as long as their products stay in useful service will not build in planned obsolescence. Instead, they will find new uses for their product even when innovation makes them no longer optimal for their original use. When a cereal maker has their profits multiplied based on a formula determined by how healthy their cereal is then they will focus on making their healthiest foods the best tasting and most desirable.

This is not a problem of consumerism, it is just a symptom of the bigger issue. The problem is that we have not created goals and have just let the market run amok. We need to examine our values as a society and set goals to reflect them. We currently have only one goal in our brand of capitalism and that is to make money by selling higher than cost. We are selling the power of capitalism short with such limited objectives. We say we value health, family, freedom and a list of other things, but we have not set goals for our society to achieve them and have no incentives to move our markets toward helping us accomplish them. We have fat kids because sugar is cheap and easy to sell for high profits. If profit could only be made by getting kids to eat lettuce, capitalist would figure out how to make eating lettuce the coolest, most fun, most cool food in the house."

Philip smiled and said, "Ok this is all well and good. So we've done away with special interest but now you want to set up these goals and have a committee determine what gets paid a profit and what doesn't. Sounds like we are trading in one set of self-interested lobbyists screwing us for another."

Frederick replied, "There is not even a comparison to be made. First of all, these people who decide these goals and criteria will be elected by the people, or by way of the people, by having been appointed by those the people elect. They will also have to exist and operate within the strictures of the anti-corruption laws, something that lobbyists did not have to do. There will be informed people and experts working together to make an incentive system that promotes better behavior, better use of resources and more responsible and sustainable living. At the end of the day, these are incentives and people will remain free to make the choices they want to make and companies can make the products they want to make how they want to make them. We are talking about tweaking the incentives in the marketplace and setting societal goals not mandating behaviors with laws or limiting choice.

Also keep in mind that these goals and incentives are varied and not one is mandating that companies even pursue them. If a cereal company want to make a sugar filled product then they are free to do so. It is unlikey that will win a bonus from a health incentive but they can pursue other goals and incentives including sales. Sales are consumer choice and that will of course continue to be honored and rewarded. This system allow more choice and better choice. We can hope people can make choices to eat healthy foods without having to spend a proportionately exorbitant amount of money to accomplish it. We can hopefully share in the full range of choice and share in the full range of consequences for our choices. For example, if we make a choice that that pollutes the environment then the cost of that cleanup will be factored into the cost up front of that choice but you can still make that choice."

Philip said, "That is all well and good but how do you expect to get anyone excited about Competitive Government Agencies? How would you ever sell that outside the beltline?"

Frederick said, "That is an excellent question and I have given this a lot of thought. You are absolutely correct that this is a marketing problem as we have to get people on board something they can wrap their heads around. Instead of the CGA program, how about the I.M.A.G.I.N.E. program? That stands for Incentivized Markets, Assisted Goals & Ideas, New Enterprises.

Philip said, "IMAGINE. I love it that will be much easier to sell than CGA."

Frederick said, "I have a slogan for it too. Competition and Value Everywhere.

Philip said, "That is the perfect cherry to top it off. Competition and Value Everywhere. That is the perfect summation of what it is. Short, sweet and catchy. IMAGINE, Competition and Value Everywhere... Imagine competition and value everywhere. You could have had quite a career on Madison Avenue."

Frederick said, "Thanks. I racked my brain for week and then it just hit me in the head like a cool breeze one day. I never thought I would be proud of coming up with a slogan but I do love it."

Philip said, "Are you happy with the list of appointees for the Secretary of Labor?"

Frederick said smiling, "You got me a little wound up there. Um labor, yes I think you have three strong contenders there. Commerce is going to be tough, though."

Philip Kingsley said, "Oh I have someone to head Commerce I just want to surround them with lots of very smart and capable people. He or she will need a lot of help and expertise to fill in their knowledge gaps. I know I asked you for recommendations for quite an extensive list of Commerce Department positions, how do you feel about the list you provided?"

Frederick said, "I feel very good about that group. Who did you get?"

Philip Kingsley said, "Good, I want you to start getting them lined up even before your confirmation."

Frederick said, "My confirmation? What are you talking about Philip?

The President said, "For such a brilliant man you can be pretty dumb sometimes. There is no one else that I would want for this position. I want you."

Frederick said, "No I have no experience in actual business. I'm an academic for goodness sake. I'd be a huge mistake, but I appreciate you considering me. Perhaps I could work in the PTO."

Philip said, "Frederick Cross, I am your friend so I know that I can trust you and I know you are one of the few people on the planet smart enough to put this together and pull it off. I also know that you are confident in what you know and know yourself well enough to seek help in areas that you don't know. As the President I know I need someone I can trust in there and someone who has thought through all the ins and outs of this monumental plan and can and will carry it out. Your fellow citizens need you and your Commander and Chief has asked you to serve. Will you serve?"

Frederick dazed replied, "Yes Philip, um, Yes Sir I will proudly serve at the pleasure of the President."

Topher Cliver

Chapter 18

A World in Crisis

"I am not an Athenian or a Greek, but a citizen of the world."
-Plato

would surely be financial in that people will buy books written by famous people, even if they are garbage. While a bestseller about a special cause or more likely, a tell-all, quasi-gossipy tome would not be unusual, no one is expecting a Pulitzer from the first lady. That is of course what she wanted to write, but she could not bring herself to bear the humiliation if it was not well received or worse yet, ridiculed.

Slowly over time she learned how to take back freedoms. The people around President Kingsley early on convinced her that she had to be always on and that every move she made and word she spoke should be coordinated to facilitate some agenda for or in support of her husband. A great discovery was that she could do less and have each thing she did weigh more so that the net effect was equal or even greater than when she was spread thinly. With this new realization, she started to take back some control of her life.

Penne Kingsley learned to say no by the end of the first term and by the midpoint of the second she had become quite skilled at getting other people to yes. Her pet causes evolved over time so that the people who came to the functions and, more importantly, who Penne would personally call on, were a distinctly different demographic than the tree hugger and save the children groups she started with. Penne now regularly had lunch with some of the spouses of the most influential and important people no one had ever heard of.

Just as she got a taste for having important people filling the ballroom for her parties and having her lunch calendar filled up for months in advance, the second term had ended. Obviously she knew that people aren't as anxious to court a former first lady as much as a current first lady, but the drop off was more dramatic than she ever imagined. She disappeared from the collective consciousness. She was never loved by the American people as some First Ladies are, she was only occasionally idolized for her beauty and glamor. She may have somewhat resembled Jackie Kennedy, but people who knew Jackie Kennedy and people who loved and admired Jackie Kennedy, knew for certain, Penne Kingsley was no Jackie Kennedy.

Worse for Penne than the lack of social importance was the lack of the wealthy post-term life she expected. Traditionally a presidential couple would combine the perks of secret service protection, a list of invitations from the wealthy and powerful and a steady stream of income from books and speeches. President Kingsley had donated his salary charity for the first term and then it was reduced to line up with the new guidelines. The rich and powerful hated Philip Kingsley and by extension, they hated Penne. They needed President Kingsley and so they tolerated the first term and they couldn't stop the second term, but then the constitution prevented them enduring a third term. The invitations to bask in the glory of wealth and power did not come nor would they.

Penne was less rich now than at any point since she had been married to Philip. The secret service detail was like a lifelong parole sentence except there was a team of parole officers outside her house 24/7. Since she had nowhere to go, it felt like house arrest. Philip Kingsley was off giving speeches and generating thousands per plate and thousands more in speaking fees. That didn't last long though and soon Philip Kingsley was pushing his cause and speaking for free or for just the reimbursement of expenses, trying to get the next round of candidates who believed as he did ready to win office and then he was in the race again.

Penne even gave in and decided to write that "my life as the First Lady" book she once felt beneath her. Under one of the new laws, she could not receive the big advance and had to take a pittance of a salary with all kinds of bonus stipulations tied to book sales in all the formats. It bombed horribly so not only did she not make any money, she was humiliated as was her worst fear going into this project. This caused a change in Penne adding a bitterness to her already icy disposition. Within the Secret Service, a posting to her guard was known as the McMurdo team after the Antarctic research station.

Penne became increasingly depressed during this time. The first year out of office was the toughest as it seemed like one virtual slap in the face after another. The second is where the reality of the situation settled in and Penne became distraught as she realized this was her life. Never one much for causes or hobbies beyond acquiring wealth and power and then flaunting it, Penne was bored, in her estimation broke and nearly powerless. The third term could have put her back in the limelight, but she had explicitly rejected that as part of her deal with Philip. She instead did the occasional public appearance and stood by Philip Kingsley for photo ops.

Once the third term began, Penne had started a goodwill tour. She managed to hit the remaining most prosperous countries in the world and met rich people and went to events that were important to rich people. She was shunned by the ever shrinking class of wealthy people in the US. However, she could still mingle and pretend she belonged to these groups overseas and try and forget she was only there because she was the first lady.

Philip entered the residence in the early evening after a series of meetings on this and that. He had stopped by earlier in the day to hello to his wife but could literally only stay a minute as he was running late for the next item on his overbooked agenda. Penne was in a white bathrobe, had her hair wrapped up in a towel and was eating a complicated looking salad sitting on a formal tray next to a diet soda.

He said, "So the prodigal daughter returns. How was your trip?"

Penne said, "Filled with good will."

Philip Kingsley said, "Don't take this the wrong way, I'm happy to see you but why are you back?"

Penne said, "Check your calendar dear. There are three events over the next two weeks that I agreed to be here for."

Philip said, "Oh well I'm glad you're here, I've missed you. How was Japan?"

Penne said, "Not ideal but better than here. They hate me here after all being the wife of the man who is destroying the upper class."

Philip said, "In a land of chaos and anarchy there wouldn't be an upper class left to complain about how hard I've made their life. The less than upper classes are looking for any reason at all to love you if you would make any kind of effort."

Penne said, "In any case, my mailbox is not overflowing with invitations from anyone in this country. At least not from anyone of means. I get plenty of invitations to raise money for this or that stupid fundraiser. That is apparently all this damn job is. I have nothing, Philip. I hope you are happy because I'm not."

Philip loosened his tie and kicked off his shoes as he said, "I'm sorry things are not as you would have liked. You need to find something to be passionate about. Charity work isn't your thing, that's fine. Find something else to engage yourself with. What about writing?"

Penne flung a small decorative bowl at Philip Kingsley just missing his head and shattering against the wall and in an emotionally wrenched and restrained voice, "You don't get to talk about writing! Your all-important job has ruined writing for me. All they want is a ridiculous First Lady book and not what I want to write. I will never write again."

Philip held back the barb that he knew could crush her, the comment that would win the argument and lose the marriage. Philip Kingsley said, "You know I appreciate your sacrifices. I know this has not been easy for you and I will make it up to you."

Penne said, "Will you Philip? When will this end? When will you have done enough for these ungrateful people?"

Philip could tell she was in a vulnerable place which was exceedingly rare for Penne. He smiled and said, "How does it feel to enter the ranks of failed presidential assassins?"

Penne had a glimmer of a smile before she suppressed it with a focused belligerent look and said, "Once this nightmare ends I want to be accepted by our peers here in America. If they still hate us, I want to live abroad. You must promise you will make one of these things happen."

Philip said, "So you want me to lie. The rich are never going to like us despite that fact that we saved them. Because of how they were saved they will always hate me. It would be quite unprecedented for a former president to live overseas. You have to give me a third option."

Penne said, "You know what I want."

A loud and continuous knocking came from the door that startled the two of them. Philip went to the door and opened it. A small group of people were there, two of which were in uniform.

President Kingsley looked over at Penne and said, "I don't know how long this is going to take."

Penne waved her hand and said, "Go do your thing."

A few hours later President Kingsley returned to the residence but did not immediately see Penne until she was on him. She wore a sexy outfit that looked as if it came from the spring, sophisticated dominatrix catalog. She pounced on him so that he fell toward the bed. Before they hit it, Philip swung her around so she hit first under him. They released all the pent up tension between them had sex like that had not had in years.

After a good while, they laid in bed in one of those perfect moments when they were either on a break or done. Either was fine and both were still an option but for this moment they laid entwined and at peace.

Penne said, "That's better."

Philip smiled and said, "I've needed that for a long time now."

They laid in a comfortable silence a bit more and then Penne said, "What was that all about? Before I mean."

Philip said, "China. Capitalism kept the people calm but now that it's coming unglued and so is the calm."

Penne said, "Like Mexico?"

Philip said, "Yes and no. China has that strong central government who won't give up power without a fight and they have the means to slaughter one-seventh of the planet and they have nukes. Mexico's people have no central power left to fight and it's more of a civil war of warlords."

Penne asked, "What are you going to do in Mexico? You can't keep those refugee camps there forever."

Philip Kingsley said, "Well, just between you and me, I want to absorb Mexico as a territory but I will only make a move with the invitation of the government and under free elections. I think both will happen. It will remove a threat from our border and will be a test to see if our system can work for a country without our infrastructure of capitalism and stability."

Penne and Philip talked until they drifted off to sleep hours later.

The first year of the third term was packed with activity as the country mobilized under the aggressive plan to create IMAGINE opportunities in almost every industry. Next was to fill them with people working a three day work week and going to school, training or volunteering another two. Health care was decoupled from the workplace and vouchers were given out that ended up being essentially universal health care in a competitive system of care under the IMAGINE program.

The country was alive and teeming with construction and activity as new businesses were organized and formed. Huge projects were under way as the south was blanketed with solar energy collectors and the north was crisscrossed with pipelines bringing in sea water for the thousands of neogeothermal sites setting up power and water stations. Rivers that had been sucked dry from agriculture now thundered back to life and land laid to waste due to drought, now bloomed with crops.

The refugee camps swelled over the months of occupation of the strip of land just over the border. President Kingsley, in an official address, said that if asked by the people of the northern Mexican states to stay and manage them, the US would be willing to do so for the protection of the US border and for the well-being of Mexican citizens. He stated an invitation from recognized members of government would have to invite the US and then once there a vote of the people monitored by international monitoring groups would determine if they were to stay.

Each of the states extended an invitation, to no one's surprise, and the key wording was "recognized members of government." That, of course, was open to interpretation, especially in a country that was essentially in a state of chaos and long removed from formal governance. The US military repeated the initial incursion to extend to the southern border of the norther states from Baja to Tamaulipas. This allowed the expansion of the refugee camps that were overflowing and allowed many people to return to their homes. The spots these people occupied in the camps was soon replaced by new inflows of refugees taking advantage of the losses the warlords suffered as the US forces advanced.

In the months that followed, the refugees who lived in the northern Mexican states had not only returned home but were working again for Mexican versions of IMAGINE. They focused on helping the refugees from the states south of there, rebuilding and resuming the daily activities needed to live. They were supplemented by people from the United States and massive training facilities were set up to train people to do the things that needed doing. This was a huge jobs program for the US, a huge help for the peoples of Mexico and a ray of hope in a world becoming darker by the day.

The southern Mexican states saw and heard what was happening and the US was being petitioned by groups throughout the rest of Mexico calling themselves the local government. Before the end of the year, three-quarters of Mexico was occupied with plans for the remainder. Opposition in the US to this operation diminished. Not only did this help the Mexicans, but it also stopped the violence on the border, created hundreds of thousands of new jobs for US citizens and virtually stopped the emigration northward of refugees.

This was a stark contrast to news from other parts of the world where chaos reigned. China was the great powder keg as desperate, starving people rioted in jam-packed cities and were massacred by government forces. Countries like India had pockets of prosperity and huge swaths of desolation. Technology provided many answers and afforded many alternatives, but people stood in the way as they fought over the resources before they were even created. People fought over the things such as land and water and the technology itself. Like China, many governments and groups around the world spent what little resources they had on technology that would help them control rather than technology that would help their people survive.

Formerly oil rich nations erupted in Islamic revolutions that beheaded members of the former suppressive governments in the town squares. Oil was still needed for many important things such as plastics, but the amounts needed paled in comparison to before, as transportation shifted to electric fed by other means of energy. There became a glut in the market and the price plummeted in response and governments that depended on this revenue stream from Venezuela to Nigeria to the Middle East, all crumbled and were replaced by revolutionaries. Countries with other energy resources like Russia also still made money but as alternatives caught on and world economic output shrunk, the need contracted and revenues dried up.

Some countries did better than others as you might expect. Europe chugged along and fought to resist the urge to violently put down the riots and protests that filled the streets. England detached itself from the European Union and focused inwardly. The Prime Minister called the people of England to service, to create 21st century victory gardens and community gardens. Every person in Great Britain worked on this challenge until their pots were filled with plants on nearly every window sill. There were greenhouses manned with robotically automated systems maintaining a perfect growing environment and bountiful crops so that no Briton went hungry and in fact a surplus flowed into the rest of Europe who desperately needed it.

Chapter 19

New Hope and New Vision

"let the speaker speak truly and the judge decide justly."
— Plato

The first State of the Union address of the third term was to be the unveiling of Philip Kingsley's grand scheme to take the nation into the next phase of our species" evolution. He worked for months ironing out details and to his great surprise, found Penne to be a tremendous help and she was instrumental in keeping the speechwriting team on task. Penne was never going to be the darling of the public or the traditional maternal figure but she became supporter and confidant as well as project manager from hell when she took on a task.

The Country had taken on an energy of action and vitality that the nation had not experienced in generations. The motto Competition and Value Everywhere was on signs and ads wherever one looked. There was hope behind this activity as people went to work and the economy continued to pick up momentum even as the world seemed to spin out of control. In fact, the United States and a handful of other countries including Japan and England, once they showed themselves to be able to transition themselves to this new economic reality, found themselves awash in foreign capital.

Even though markets crashed and fortunes were confiscated there was still a significant amount of money in the world and it had to be invested somewhere and somewhere stable and growing was better than the alternatives.

As fast as workers were put out of work due to innovation, they were hired up by IMAGINE companies. If they had relevant skills, they worked 4 days a week and went to some form of class or training one day a week. If they had no relevant skill, they were found some kind of work for at least one day a week, even if it was just talking to the elderly or manual labor in a setting that still required a human to perform it. IMAGINE companies entered business verticals where too few competitors existed or where small and medium business failed.

Frederick made it a point to expand the entrepreneurial program he envisioned so that people looking for work who show the slightest talent or interest in building a business or sales or marketing were put into new companies built around the scores of ideas that were collected and rated by professionals at IMAGINE companies charged with picking winning ideas and products to track. Risks were encouraged and people were incented and rewarded at every stage of an idea so it no longer took the marriage of salesman and engineer in one person to launch something new into the world.

From space, the country must have looked like an ant hill minutes after a little boy poked it with a stick. Mining projects once tore up millions of acres of land and caused devastating environmental consequences. Robotics caused a revolution in mining combined with autonomous mining drones and abundant cheap energy so that just a handful of acres would encompass the surface fingerprint of underground activity so extensive that it would be as productive as twenty mines in the past with a fraction of the cost and minimal environmental impact. Ant-like drones worked night and day, year round in conditions unfit for living creatures bringing all the bounty the earth has to offer to the surface.

Projects large and small abound as bizarre looking huge robots assembled buildings and pipelines like erector sets. Huge Zeppelin blimp hybrids floated in the huge pieces and equipment needed. Other giant robots drilled tunnels while still others drilled wells that extended miles underground. Small industrial 3d printing factories were constructed throughout the nation close to the consumers who would use the items they created. Evacuated tube transport projects abound as people stopped driving and autonomous electric cars made more sense for short trips. Under and above ground tubes used the right of ways already established by the freeway systems they would mostly replace. Travel time and cost would be cut to a fraction of what it once was.

President Kingsley recounted all this success in the state of the Union, to much applause. The people of the nation were working and preparing for the next job they would need as the world changed. He continued to reinforce his vision of people engaged in lifelong learning constantly evolving their skills for the next more interesting challenge. A world where work was interesting and vital as technology relived the human race of the drudgery we have known for all time from hard, unrewarding work to chores that consumed our free time. President Kingsley spoke of a renaissance, not of the learned and the luminaries of the day but a renaissance for all humanity.

He spoke of building an energy infrastructure so that it was so abundant it approached free in cost for the people of the US and still have an abundance to sell at a fair price to our fellow citizens of the world. President Kingsley laid out a vision of a future with no unemployment, free health care, abundant energy and abundant resources. He spoke of people being able to pursue meaningful employment doing that which they were best suited for and in pursuits that were not only fulfilling but beneficial to society.

President Kingsley stood at the podium in the Capital building in front of Congress, the Supreme Court, many important guests and the country as he described the state of the Union and his vision for the future. About three-quarters of the way through the speech he took a surprising turn.

He spoke, "These are fast moving times. Our collective body of knowledge is advancing and growing faster than any one person can keep up with. I would like to put forth a vision of how I think we may be better able to govern during this time of incredible change. Our Founders saw the wisdom of a republic, a representative democracy whereby the citizens elect a person to represent them and their views on the issues of the day. The issues of those days, while complex in their own ways were manageable and intelligent people could learn the ins and outs on most any topic well enough to vote on behalf of the people they represent.

As time went on and the issues became more complicated and the speed of change increased, Congress evolved and divided into committees that specialized in areas of importance to the nation. They used collections of staffers to stay current and become experts in these areas so they could speak to the issues and educate their fellow lawmakers on important subtleties that a layman would miss. Now that we have moved past the times of lobbyists and corruption they attempted to manifest, I propose we expand upon this wise idea of specialists to help inform our lawmakers."

The Capital was dead silent after all the rounds and rounds and rounds of applause and ovation. The building was silent save for the President's thundering voice. Somehow this part of the speech was not released and had not been leaked. That was because Philip Kingsley wrote this himself and had told no one. He had had members of all the parties in agreement with at least some if not all of what he said up to this moment. Now the room held its collective breath as they did not know where he was going with this.

President Kingsley continued, "Just to be clear up front. I am not proposing that any power be removed from Congress and that any bill be passed by a body other than them. I want to propose a way to make Congress stronger, not weaker so please hear the proposal out before you make up your mind up on it. There will be plenty of time for judgment in the weeks to come."

President Kingsley smiled and gave a nod toward the Justices of the Supreme Court. This garnered smiles and light laughter which broke the tension as intended.

He went on, "I propose that we create a number of bodies that mirror the House in representation, that specialize, much as committees do today, in an area of importance to our nation. I envision these bodies being filled with elected representatives who the people of their respective districts feel are expert in these areas and qualified to represent their views, values and interests. These bodies could debate issues that fall into the areas they specialize. They could create bills that, once passed by a vote of this lower specialized body, would be submitted to our current Congress for debate and vote as we do with bills today.

The issues of our day are simply too varied and too complex for us to expect even the brightest of you here today to be an expert in all of it. Your role should be strategic and not tactical. You should see the law as it will apply in macrocosm to our nation as a whole on behalf of those you represent. Your august bodies should spend the days in debate and collaboration, not buried on the back of the butcher shop making sausages."

The President paused here and there hung in the air a half of a second of silence that seemed much longer where no one could tell how this was being received. Then a spattering of applause quickly erupted into a standing ovation."

Once it died down he continued, "I propose you start with a few as a pilot to see how it works. If this makes government work better then I think one day we could have bodies specializing in areas such as Technology, Health, Ethics, Commerce, Education, the Workforce, Budget and Finance, Armed Services, Resources, Foreign Relations, Judiciary and Rules, Science and others you deem fit.

This measure would increase the knowledge available to our lawmakers, lead to expertly written bills, as well as increase the debate so that we can make the best-informed decisions possible for our great nation.

These are complicated times and they have been tough times. The great citizens of the United States have proven themselves flexible, resilient and able to endure the necessary change we have needed to survive and prosper. I have never been more proud to be a citizen of the United States of America.

The world is becoming a dark place, full of danger. While we cannot bring light to every corner of the planet, we can can shine brightly as a beacon of light and hope that all can see. In so doing we would make the world brighter, safer and better for all humanity.

Thank you, God bless you, and God bless this country we love."

The speech was well received, but some crucial seeds of descent were sown in the rebuttal speeches. Many focused on the same old accusations of socialism and communism that had been thrown around since President Kingsley first came to office. Under the right circumstances, these may have taken hold. However, these were meaningless, or at least toothless, terms to the people born after Generation X. To the older crowd, who remembered Communism beyond the Chinese capitalist version of it, they knew that that was not an accurate comparison and brushed it off. It didn't help the Red scare mongers that things were constantly getting better here while everywhere else, things seemed to get worse.

There was one speech by an up-and-coming Republican, who pointed to the debt we were creating with all this government involvement. This, of course, was not the first time such criticism had been laid out, but the timing was just right to get people to take a second look. People had moved beyond desperate and were able to look into the future and what the gigantic increase in national debt could mean.

In the weeks and months that followed, things kept rolling along and news came back of CGAs actually bringing in revenue to the government. This was spun to show that this spending was all investment, not just loans and that the investments would pay for themselves over time. This worked for a while, but the revenue was a tiny fraction of what was being spent and spending just kept increasing beyond the current astronomical amounts. Fortunately, the world still had money to invest and nowhere else to invest it but the debt levels were straining even this pool of capital. America had become like a giant dot com growing as fast as it can and hoping to make a profit before it ran out of money.

Chapter 20

Run up to the Election

"The greatest way to live with honor in this world is to be what we pretend to be."
-Plato

The Chief of Staff Brought the Secretaries of Commerce and Labor into the Oval office. President Kingsley was standing on the left-hand side of his desk looking out the window. The three of them stood uncomfortably for a moment until the Chief of Staff said, "Mr. President, your three o'clock is here. I have to run to a meeting on the Hill unless you need me for something here."

Without turning around the President said, "Thank you, Carlos, I'll meet with you this evening and we can exchange notes."

Still peering out the window, President Kingsley said, "The midterms were easy as we were still riding the momentum, but the election will be hard. We have to show enough revenue growth to offset doing away with the remainder of the tax system. Susan, I realize this is primarily a commerce issue, but I don't want to compromise anything we are doing on the labor front."

Frederick said, "Doing away with tax collection will result in a short-term surge in profit. I would recommend shifting incentives strongly away from a direct share of profit and toward a bonus for most profit in the category."

President Kingsley said, "That sounds like a good move, Susan do you see any issue with that?"

She replied, "No Mr. President I think we can sell that no problem. We can package it in with the tenure incentives and termination disincentive package we are implementing."

Frederick said, "Tenure and disincentive from firing? I thought we wanted to create a meritocracy. Those seem opposed to that end."

Susan said, "We have found that the pendulum was swinging too far in the direction of a pure meritocracy. This created incentives for companies to fire weak employees instead of helping grow and improve them and for employees to jump ship for more productive companies. This will layer incentives for employees to stay and grow the company and for the company to grow their employees."

Frederick said, "That makes sense. As far as revenue, that will be a challenge unless we change our strategy a bit. We have focused a lot of energy and resource on even entry across the spectrum of industry and heavily on new idea development which is my pet project."

The President said, "I don't want you to do away with anything, but we do need to make adjustments to meet political goals and realities. I need you to focus on getting the highest revenue generating IMAGINE companies up and going first and worry about evening out the distribution later. I need you to dial back the startups and focus on the sure winners. This is a short-term sacrifice for the big picture."

Frederick said, "But Philip, we are just getting momentum in the new ideas divisions and some of these ideas will end up being game changers."

President Kingsley turned around from the window sharply and said with a booming voice, "That is Mr. President or Sir to you. Do not interpret our prior relationship to mean your Secretary title is more significant than any other. Secretary Cross, I am telling you what I want and it is not a request. If we lose the election, then there is no program to keep momentum. You saw what they did the last time, they gutted it all and put us back on a course to go off the cliff. Best case, your winners offset the losers in your new idea group and we need those resources focused only on winners right now. Do you foresee any problems with that?"

Frederick said, "No Mr. President and please accept my appology."

President Kingsley said, "Thank you both. You have both done a wonderful job, but we cannot take our eye off the prize."

Later that evening, after meeting with his Chief of Staff, the President retired to the residence where Penne was waiting for him. The President walked in weary from a long day loosening his tie as he walked in. Penne was lying in bed reading a book projected from her phone.

She said, "Well Tiger you look like you've had a hard day."

Philip replied, "I'm not sure why I'm running again, the fourth term killed FDR."

Penne replied, "You're more of a Teddy than a Franklin and not to mention modern medicine and the fact that you don't have polio all makes me think you'll be just fine. Having said that, you know I have no issue if you don't run again."

Philip smiled and said, "Eleanor was the tough one of that clan. If I thought for a moment that this country was safe and would stay on the right path, I'd step down today."

Penne said, "You're tense, do you need a massage? I'll call up the masseuse."

Philip sat in a cushioned chair close to the bed and said, "No I just need to unwind."

Penne gave him a questioning look.

Philip said, "Not like that unwind, just rest my brain unwind."

Penne said, "I don't know why you are so wound up, you have this election all wrapped up."

Philip said, "I wish it were so but a year and a half is a long time and lots can go wrong between now and then."

Penne said, "I hear you chewed Frederick out pretty loudly today."

Philip looking dismayed said, "How in the hell do you know that?"

Penne said, "When you yell at the top of your lungs in the Oval there are only dozens of people within earshot and then you know the Washington grapevine. You need to call and apologize."

Philip said, "Yeah, I'll call him later."

Penne said, "He's doing a great job, I don't know what you had to yell about."

Philip Kingsley said, "He called me Philip in the process of challenging me and in front to Susan Hollis. I couldn't let it go or it would have diminished both of our authority."

Penne said, "He'll get over it. What was he challenging you on?"

Philip said, "I need him to make as much profit in the short term as possible so I can kill taxes."

Penne said, "Which taxes?"

Philip said, "All taxes."

Penne said, "That seems a little drastic."

Philip said, "It is what is going to guarantee the election."

Penne said, "Can't you just roll back some tax and still make them happy?"

Philip said, "It's a huge win in approval and we get a good chunk of it back in revenue which is why I need Frederick to reorder his priorities."

Penne said, "When you say all tax are you talking about income or literally all tax."

Philip said, "Literally all tax. Needless to say, none of this is close to being public knowledge. I need to throw the old aristocracy a bone since we're honing into their businesses and industries."

Penne said, "Old Aristocracy, so have you spoken to Matt lately?"

Philip said, "We keep up."

Penne said, "When will you stop running for President Philip?"

Philip said, "When I feel like I can walk away and things will stay on track."

Penne said, "What if you don't feel like that after your fourth term?"

Philip said, "The law has already answered that question for you. Not to change the subject but where are you off to tomorrow?"

Penne said, "I go to Miami for photo ops with people leaving the city and then travel to some godforsaken place in Central Florida for more photo ops of where they are moving to. You owe me for this. Then I go to England and meet the King as my reward."

Philip said, "Thank you again for Miami. We'll need more of these photo ops leading up to the election so start making a list of what you want in return."

Penne said, "I don't understand why you have to sell the idea of leaving Miami. Don't these idiots realize even a moderate storm could wipe them literally off the map?"

Philip said, "Its people's homes. It's easier to deny the truth than face the fact that Miami is a lost cause. People have lived there their whole lives and can't imagine it permanently under water. I mean they have been extremely lucky with the dikes and levees so far but sitting where it does its only a matter of time."

Penne said, "Why don't you just order these people to move and be done with it."

Philip said, "Because this is America and I'm not going to order people out of their homes. We've set up help with moving and free housing for up to three years to wherever these folks want to go. That is a pretty good deal plus now we have enough IMAGINE companies set up to guarantee them work no matter where they go."

Penne said, "And yet people stay. Why can't people accept reality?"

Philip said, "Not everyone is as pragmatic as you. How long will you be in England?"

Penne said, "For a while I think. I need some me time before this election stretch."

A sudden loud knock pounded the door. Philip stood, still in dress pants and a loosely tucked-in dress shirt with the top buttons undone and answered the door.

The man there said in an urgent tone, "Mr. President, you're needed in the situation room."

Penne reached for her phone and said, "Good talk dear. Go save the world."

Philip said, "Will you be up?"

Penne said, "That depends on you."

Philip went to the bed and kissed his wife and he knew there was a good chance he would not see her again for several weeks. The President joked that he needed a presidential cot for the situation room.

This time, it was India. Another time it would be China or Mexico or Russia or someplace else in this volatile world. In any case, Penne flew out the next morning without speaking to Philip. He had crawled into bed late and she let him sleep in the morning when she left.

Some countries saw the wisdom in what was happening in the US and followed suite. Other countries were convinced that a strong hand was needed to get through these times and still others were just too far down the path of chaos to go any other way. In the first camp were parts of Europe, Canada, Japan, India, Israel and a handful of other countries. Tyrants rose in much of Central and South America, China, Russia, parts of the Middle East, parts of Southeastern Europe, Indonesia and surprisingly Australia and Spain. Chaos ruled most of the rest with a few exceptions like parts of Sub-Saharan Africa which were already in chaos and so actually made improvements, with the help of technology, over their previous situation.

Mexico was now fully occupied by the United States and a bill was floating around to make the Mexican States, who voted a desire to become so, official US Territories. The Mexican warlords were decimated and moved underground. The US fighting forces were already the best in the world and then became battle-hardened in urban warfare and the use of modern technology. As these technologies advanced, the Mexican warlords stood no chance. The ones who went to the jungle to fight from there were found and tracked by satellite and millions of drones and then exterminated from the face of the earth. The smarter ones blended into the local populations and were successful as long as they lay low. However, as soon as they did anything were found and arrested or worse.

The US had learned lessons and now moved forward as quickly as possible setting up Mexican IMAGINE companies so as to get people working as quickly as possible. Locals were trained in basic policing and were given billy clubs and technology. They were focused on resolving basic disputes and were the eyes and ears on the ground. They had great technology and could quickly call up the better armed and trained Mexican police equipped with all sorts of non-lethal but effective technology. For situations involving firearms or explosives, the US military poured in and eliminated the threat.

People were working, the drug gangs were squashed and a strong system of justice in Mexican took hold so there was very little to protest, let alone, actively rebel against. The Military stayed out of the way and out of site unless called in to deal with a situation. Drones, however, filled the air like moths around a street lamp, but they came to blend into the background eventually. This was a different kind of occupation and was more like a liberation. There was no religious gulf and many members of the military were of Mexican descent and many more spoke at least some Spanish even without the help of the near real-time translation devices that were now prevalent.

Topher Cliver

Chapter 21

Forth Term Begins

"Ideas are the source of all things"
— Plato

The debt was the central issue Philip Kingsley's opposition focused on leading up to the election for what would be his fourth term. Despite the astronomical size of the debt, the yearly deficit shrunk considerably as the IMAGINE companies pulled out a prosperous year and calmed enough formerly undecided voters to put Philip over the top. There were candidates who complained that it was a dangerous road we were on having the government control so much of our lives. However, when people have jobs, housing, food, and disposable income it's hard to get them riled up about such things. In fact, President Kingsley was no sooner sworn in and movement began to introduce a bill allowing unlimited terms without having to leave office for a term after two. Philip was only 67 and was in fantastic health so this could ensure a long reign.

Another dangerous comparison that had been made early on was to pre-collapse China. The communist government also owned businesses that lived out in the market economy. The counter was that first, China was by far not the only country to do this including the United States. The U.S.government controls to some degree the TVA, Medicare, Public Broadcasting Corporation, USPS, Amtrak, not to mention at a lower level, some States owning liquor stores and running lotteries. Many of these examples operated under conditions of monopoly or exercised some advantaged position. The key distinguishing fact is that these examples were all built to exist while Philip Kingsley's IMAGINE companies were built to compete.

IMAGINE companies were built in groups of two or more. The competitive part of the competition and vale everywhere motto was the most important component. While Phase one was to get two or more of these entities set up in as many industries as possible in as short a time as possible, the next four years was to be spent implementing the creative destruction element of the system. When and where it was feasible or certain conditions existed such as unserved customers, an abundance of profit or unclaimed incentives, a third, fourth fifth or, however, many entities as made sense were created. The flip side of that was that if companies were not making money from the claim of incentives for a certain period of time, then a board of directors would act. If the business continued to fail it would be disbanded and dissolved much as a bankrupt business would be.

The addition of the bonus incentive system allowed for competition where formerly none would exist. Hindsight provides a believable example in the telephone industry. Once broken up the Baby Bells competed for long distance and they innovated new services to offer and charged varying rates for such add-ons as call waiting and caller ID. The market opened up for innovative phone designs and people didn't just lease clunky rotary phones from the phone company they bought them or got football shaped phones free with subscriptions to a sports magazines. Competition was the first ingredient and that spurred innovation which was the second ingredient to market success.

Frederick was a huge advocate of ideas and innovation. He created a system that allowed ideas to be promoted into the marketplace from any stage and from people of any ability. There were groups around the country that were like Angel investors that sat and heard ideas pitched by anyone who wanted to present them. There were even people whose jobs it was to pitch ideas for people if presenting was not their forte. These ideas were reviewed and discussed and made part of an idea inventory that could be used by anyone who saw fit. The originator of the idea, if it were deemed original, would forever be linked with that idea. They would be eligible for bonuses and payouts based on use and utility no matter how it was used or by whom, so there was everything to gain by putting forth ideas and really no downside.

People with an idea could walk into one of these Innovation IMAGINE companies and someone would help them document the idea in detail. Other staff would help refine it, search for its uniqueness and eventually pitch it to groups for review. These groups were made up of retired people in any number of businesses and occupations and included people just good at making connections or finding the unique utility in things. These groups would push these ideas toward other groups that focused on specific industries or straight to groups that fund projects or IMAGINE companies that matched ideas with people that had entrepreneurial skills. All throughout the process, people at every level, from idea formation to its implementation were incentivized around the successful use of new ideas so that is where the focus always lay.

This is not to say that patents went away, people just had additional options that gave them greater flexibility. If a person or company wanted to obtain a patent, the process and costs were the same as were the potential payoffs on the other side of that. The alternative was to grant a public license. In exchange for this, everything was paid for and as much of the process was moved forward as the idea generator desired, by professionals familiar and proficient at each step along the way of taking an idea to market. The idea generator assumed no risk or cost and earned a bonus from incentives and based on how far through the process they shepherded the idea. Once ready for market, the idea held an open license with no licensing fee at all, only the requirement to track usage.

The state also collected no commission and everyone in the process was incented to get the idea to market and have people use it. The type of idea did not matter as no fee or cost was charged. The idea was that the inconveniences of tracking were so minimal and inconsequential in comparison to the fines for violations in not paying them that people and companies would gladly track them. So on one end people were incented to bring every idea they had to be reviewed by experts who would help find ways of using them. They were also cataloged and made openly available so they could be used by any and every company who wanted to use or sell them and it cost the companies who used the idea nothing. A protected product with this open license could be put on the market quickly and sold by as many different companies who wanted to sell them.

A similar deal was offered to copyright holders and any intellectual products that would be used by consumers versus companies. There were some very stark differences, though. The end users could, and, in fact, were encouraged to, use the protected property as much as they wanted for free as long as they are not trying to make money with it. The creators were rewarded based on the number of times the song was sung or listened to and the book read or listened to. The more someone's work was used, the more they got paid so they wanted everyone to listen, read and or look at their work. People were able to consume any and all art for no cost whatsoever as long as they allowed usage to be anonymously tracked. If a person didn't want usage to be anonymously tracked, they could buy an unlimited license for a small fee with an anonymous cryptocurrency.

For the government, there were no licensing fees to collect, only royalties to pay based on numbers of uses and other incentive benchmarks. The argument was that the overall benefit to society warranted this cost. Even if there wasn't a lift in productivity as some had thought there would be, there was still value to society making it worth it. Creators of IP could choose to create on the side, submitting these items and collecting bonuses. Alternatively, they could choose to work at an entertainment IMAGINE company where they would make a living wage as long as they put in the time creating and also they would participate in the bonus structure. People could create as a hobby and make extra money or create as a livelihood and make a base salary and then additional money as their work was used more often.

Thought and the ideas they created became free for citizens to use and consume in any way and as often as they wanted and, in fact, were encouraged to do so. The creators of these thoughts were incented to create them. If they were willing to put the time required in, they were supported in do so and were paid a modest wage even if their work never caught on. Businesses had scores of ideas for products, processes, and methodologies that they could use to improve their businesses at no cost. Since a growing number of businesses were IMAGINE companies, as business prospered so did government and society, so new ideas benefited everyone.

Frederick was also a huge believer that too big was bad. He set up lots of incentives for companies to create services for functions common to many companies of all sizes. For instance, office supplies, office management, the remaining HR and other common tasks not specific to the products and services a company produces were incented. This was done in such a way that new, specialized companies would come into being and grow to a size large enough to be efficient. Many services could now be outsourced for cost savings to companies of any size comparable or better than the savings large companies previously and exclusively enjoyed hiring people to handle.

Across the board, he made it advantageous to stay as small as was practical and to focus employees on the core business while outsourcing the rest. This not only fostered leaner more focused companies but allowed more companies to compete in every space. Another side effect of this was a lower bar to entry and smaller impact of the exit of a company when it closed down. In the past, the Government, communities and in turn, the American people were held hostage to too big to fail and huge employers that could have a devastating effect if they shut down. In every industry dominated by oligarchies, he created incentives for big companies to become more nimble and small companies to come in and compete.

His focus was to keep the playing field as crowded as possible at every level so that there was always one too many companies pushing the bottom performing company to shut down or into new management. The idea was to make all industries nimble, innovative and downright Darwinian. The removal of managing employee benefits and pay from companies lessened the impact of businesses shutting down. Workers saw losing their job to their business shutting down as an inconvenience rather than the life-disrupting and negatively impactful event it was in the past. People never lost their job anymore they just lost their current employer. Business failure became part of the way of the world and everything was done in such a way to minimally impact the customers and employees as these things happened.

All these changes made businesses, industries and the entire country more efficient. Business was able to quickly take advantage of innovations and also to adapt to ever changing conditions. The nature of work changes so that people saw work more as a project based endeavor with a start and a stopping point. As the twentieth century began, some people certainly did finish out their careers having worked at just one company but no one at all expected that. People then came to see any work anniversary beyond two years as out of the norm and a five or ten year stretch with one company was downright rare. The social contract between employer and employee had transformed from security for loyalty to one of performance from the employee in exchange for flexibility and respect from the employer.

People became flexible in general as jobs, careers, businesses and industries became more and more fluid and could disappear overnight while entirely new and different ones appeared just as quickly. A job loss or business closing down was not the traumatic event that it once was, which was fortunate because this was not an uncommon event. People prepared to work a job for one to two years and then expected something else to come along one way or another. This had side effects both positive and negative. It became difficult to find people with deep organizational or industry knowledge. However, the flip side of that was with the pace of change that kind of experience didn't matter as much anymore as technologies captured much of it, as well as the positional knowledge attained in doing one's job.

A positive effect was the cross-pollination that this constant shifting of jobs and careers brought. People applied things they learned in totally unrelated fields and unrelated jobs to create new and often better ways of doing their new jobs. AI modeling systems compiled a humanly unfathomable amount of data on people doing specific work and used it create training and standards and performance evaluations as well as learning to assume parts of the job that humans did poorly or AI systems could just do better. From this, people could learn more quickly and more in depth, not only what their job entailed, but the best practices of those across the country who did those jobs the best. Factored into this was a human rating of the tasks they liked and disliked the most and AI systems focused most heavily on figuring out how to take on those before others.

The plan was working and the economy picked up a constant and steady momentum like a freight train starting from a stop. Mexico went smoother than the most optimistic analysts could have predicted. Now every day it seems another country in Central or South America was sending an invitation to the US Government to come in and help them sort out their unrest. Foreign capital steadily poured in as an investment and the IMAGINE companies continued to make more money and the yearly deficit shrank to almost nothing. This happened despite Frederick's ambitious expansion of the IMAGINE companies, full employment, and ongoing ambitious domestic infrastructure programs.

The president was at Camp David hosting his now annual, luminaries" summit when Penne flew in by helicopter having recently arrived from England. She barged past the Secret service agents and under the large banner saying "Competition and Value Everywhere" outside the door to the cabin where Philip was. He was sitting and informally talking with the CEOs of the top robotics firms in the US. All eyes turned to the door as she dramatically burst in walking in angry strides. She pronounced, "Philip I need a word with you, now."

President Kingsley smiled and said, "This does not seem the time for introductions so I'll excuse myself as I am being summoned to the other situation room."

This broke the awkwardness and the room let off some respectfully tame laughter and Philip Kingsley got up and put his arm around Penne and escorted her out of the room.

He said in a hushed and angry tone out of the side of his mouth, "Do not ever embarrass me like that again."

They walked in uncomfortable silence down a series of halls until they got to a private room and closed the door behind them. Penne immediately spun around as the door shut and yelled, "You lied to me again. We had a deal again and now you are breaking it...AGAIN!"

Philip said, "Calm down, what are you talking about?"

Penne said, "You know goddamn well what I'm talking about. We had a deal for the first two terms and then when you broke your promise I foolishly agreed to two more and now you're reneging on that."

Philip Kingsley said, "I have done no such thing."

Penne said, "Do I need to look up the quote or will my paraphrasing do? When they proposed that bill I told you to denounce it but you kept quiet and now they have passed it. The States certainly aren't going to stop you now that you have them set up as profit-sharing partners in the IMAGINE companies doing business in their States."

Philip said, "Even if the states ratify it, it doesn't mean I will run."

Penne said, "I know you Philip and that is bullshit. That is exactly what it means. In your mind's eye, you already see yourself as an old man ruling like King Solomon until you die fifty years from now. You may not admit to yourself yet, but you were always committed to run again."

Philip said, "If it looks like we are in a good place for all the work we have done to stay in place and not be stripped away by greedy people with no vision or conscious, then I will gladly step down."

Penne said, "What about the promise you made me? Does that mean nothing?"

Philip said, "Of course it means everything and I was sincere when I said it for the times when I said it just as now I'm telling you as long as the Republic is safe, I will not run again."

Penne said, "But we both know that is a cop out. You can't possibly believe there is any chance that the Republic will be safe. When has it ever been safe? Life is not safe. At some point, you just have to trust the rest of us to do the right things.

My part of the bargain was that I would suffer through this hell, again, until the end of this term and that was it. I am not negotiating with you. If you run, it will be without me."

Philip said, "Look, it is only if we are under dire conditions that I would run again. I was going to wait to share this with you, but I see it's important that you know now. I have a short list of people I am grooming to run who I feel confident will continue us on the right path, to be the guardians of all we have built."

Philip handed Penne his tablet with the list and she said, "What about your VP, I don't see her on the list"

Philip said, "She was a compromise I made to ensure election. I needed someone to bring a more conservative and southern group of voters to our side and her asking price was reasonable and something I could live with. I would never support her to take my office."

Penne said, "Well what was your plan if you drop dead?"

Philip said, "As you pointed out, life is risk."

Penne said, "Look Philip, I will not be a prisoner of your office any longer than we agreed. If you run, I will not campaign for you and I will leave you, public humiliation or not. I won't care if it costs you the election, I will not be a part of it."

With this, she walked out and proceeded to go back to the White House.

Chapter 22

Tom Machus

"Character is simply habit long continued."
— Plato

The President had his previously very busy afternoon cleared and strict instructions that, short of a national emergency, he was not to be disturbed. At 1:57pm promptly, the man the president was meeting with at 2pm showed up at the desk of the President's Secretary escorted by the Chief of Staff, Carlos Perito. They walked into the Oval Office right at 2pm

The President was sitting at his desk holding a tablet at arm's distance from his face. He looked up as they entered as the Chief of Staff said, "Your two o'clock is ready Mr. President."

Philip Kingsley had been graying for several years culminating in the current salt and pepper mix that had made the transition to mostly salt, but now he also looked tired. Three plus terms as president had taken a toll but this was still a vital man who worked out one to two hours a day when events permitted and even worn down at his age, he looked better than most forty-year-old men.

He stood, setting his tablet on a stand to the side of his desk as he also removed his glasses and tossed them nonchalantly on his desk, cringing as he did so suddenly realizing they were as costly as a car once was. While he was doing this, the Chief of Staff had brought this squat older gentleman up to the side of the desk and said, "Mr. President, I present Mr. Tom Machus."

The President reached out to shake his hand and gestured toward the sofas in the middle of the room with the others as he said, "Gentlemen, please have a seat."

Tom Machus ended the handshake quickly and said, "With all due respect to Mr. Perito, I'd like this first meeting to be one on one."

After an extra second pause he continued, "With your permission, of course, Mr. President."

Carlos Perito said, "Tom this is highly irregular."

Machus replied, "That is Mr. Machus and this is not a regular matter."

The President said, "Carlos, it's alright. We'll talk later."

Perito left the room and closed the door behind him. The President and Tom Machus sat across from each other on the sofas in the middle of the room. The President sat back with legs crossed and one arm draped along the top of the sofa. He said, "Mr. Machus as you can imagine, I did a little digging on your background so I know generalities about you. When the Republican leadership asks me to take a meeting as soon as possible I, of course, respect that and that is why you are here so soon. Other than that, I must admit I am in the dark, which is most unusual for a man in my position as you can imagine. I'd be lying if I said I was not intrigued. So here we are."

Tom Machus was a stark contrast to Philip Kingsley. Machus was maybe 5"5"", overweight and although he was almost a decade younger than the president, looked to be almost a decade older. His white hair was somewhat bushy around the smooth bald surface that dominated the top of his head. He also wore a bushy mustache and large black framed glasses with very thick lenses that looked traditional. That is to say, they looked like just glasses without any additional technology. He did not sit back on the couch and somehow managed to look very uncomfortable on this very comfortable piece of furniture.

The one thing he did not look, was intimidated. He carried himself very confidently and some may even say with an air of contempt. His normal facial expression teetered on the verge of an arrogant smirk that was being suppressed by constant irritation. Tom Machus was also a very heavy smoker, a rare breed these days, and he also worked as a tobacco lobbyist back in the days when that was a thing. Now he sat across from the man who eliminated his lucrative position. Not that he had done badly as a Washington Lawyer, quite the contrary, it's just he would have done a lot better as a career lobbyist.

Machus breathed heavily even when doing nothing and as he sat across from the president there was a slight wheezing noise as he said, "Mr. President, I thank you for meeting with me. This is a courtesy meeting and an opportunity for us to clear this matter up quickly and quietly. Bottom line, if, within the next 30 days, you resign from office this all stops here and we'll consider this matter closed permanently. We'll, of course, leave the explanation for your resignation to your discretion."

Tom Machus lost his arrogant air but not his contempt as he regrouped and said, "Please forgive me but I assumed you would know what I was here about. I will gladly play along and recount the events that got us here.

Some time back, the RNC received a tip from a whistleblower inside your administration that the first lady was exploiting the government to travel the world for her own entertainment and was in fact receiving undocumented gifts while abroad as well. The RNC was naturally concerned about these allegations and came to my firm to pursue a discrete, how shall I say it, checking of the facts to see if there was anything to the allegations."

Machus studied the President looking for any information he could take from the man, a twitch, a micro-expression a change in the glimmer in his eye but he got nothing. Whether this was news to the president or well-known fact, his reputation as a political poker player was well earned as Machus, a lifelong student of these things could discern nothing.

Machus proceeded, "My firm was chosen as we have a reputation for professionalism and discretion. We asked a couple very experienced investigators, whom I trust greatly, to do a little digging. In a short stint of their probing they found some very minor activity that could be argued fell into the gray area rather than being, let's say problematic."

Machus paused continually studying with his eyes looking for a chink in the Presidential armor but still found none.

He continued, "We were about to recall the investigators when one day I was reviewing the list of people the First Lady came across on he travels and a name popped out at me, one Matthew Ligarck. You went to school with Mr. Ligarck did you not?"

The President smiled and said, you know Mr. Machus, I have tremendous respect for you, apparently even more than you have for me. I know that you know I was a DA at one point in my career and so I know what an interrogation looks like and I know what a deposition looks like. I can also spot an attorney conducting a fishing expedition and this looks a lot like the latter. In any case, I will remind you that you are wasting the time of the President of the United States. If you have a point or an allegation, I suggest we get to it or I going to end this meeting."

Machus looking a bit more humble continued, "My apologies Mr. President, I will get to it. As you can imagine this not too unusual as he was a childhood friend of yours and has actually known your wife as long as you. I'll be honest and say that I thought perhaps there was some infidelity going on, but we found no evidence of that and yet something did not strike me as right about that chance meeting so I flagged his name for an AI deep dig.

The AI firm we contracted with pulled back some interesting results. It showed he was in the same overseas city as the first lady three different times and Mr. Ligarck's net worth spiked upward within weeks of each of this coincidences. We have a smoking gun here Mr. President."

The President sat unmoved as Tom Machus sat across from him with an accusatory look. President Kingsley said, "And?.... Your AI team surely deduced that Mr. Ligarck is in the business of investing and his net worth is up down probably every week of his life. My guess is up much more often than down as you see Mr. Ligarck is one of the smartest people I have ever known. Is that what you are threatening me with or do you have more? "

Machus looked a bit frustrated as he said, "You see Mr. President, we found some minor violations by the first lady that, in and of themselves, would not be a big deal but this is almost assuredly insider trading." We wanted to talk to you and give you a chance to end this honorably before we start pulling this thread.

You see, the next step is for Congress, under the revised Independent Counsel provisions of your anti-corruption law, is to appoint me to pull that thread and see what unravels. Do you want me to pull that thread Mr. President or would you like this to go away?"

Machus stared at the President with a look that bordered contempt and smugness. The President furrowed his eyebrows and leaned in from the back of the couch studied Machus for a moment. He then said, "I believe when one is trying to threaten blackmail this would be the part where the blackmailer lets the blackmailee know what they have on them or else we find ourselves in the present awkward situation. I don't have the foggiest damn idea what you think you have on me that would allow you to come in here and threaten the President of the United States... In the Oval office no less. Now I'll give you the benefit of the doubt and assume this too is your first time in this sort of situation and give you a minute to explain yourself."

The President stood up and looked down on this little man sitting on the sofa looking up at him and said, "Mr. Machus, you should be ashamed of yourself as an attorney, as a citizen and as a man. To accuse a man's wife of misdeeds one better have their facts straight but you have not only accused my wife, but you have also accused the First Lady of the United States. If I were Andrew Jackson, that would be enough that we would be settling this tomorrow morning at 20 paces.

But you and your Republican puppet masters must have testicles the size of bowling balls to come in here with this flimsy bit of circumstantial evidence and have the gall to threaten me into leaving office. You need to get out of here right now and if you step foot within a mile of my general vicinity, you better have some papers signed by a judge because otherwise I will have the secret service use you for target practice."

The President walked over and opened the door signaling with his hand to a secret service agent who quickly popped in the door followed by another man. President Kingsley said, "Gentlemen, please politely escort Mr. Machus to the exit and ensure that he does not get lost along the way."

Machus stood up as the two agents stood on either side of him. As he was being walked out Machus said, "Very well Mr. President, you'll be hearing from me through official channels then."

Chapter 23

Betrayal and Disappointment

"The hottest love has the coldest end."
-Plato

The President raised the pointing finger on his right hand as one of the people he was meeting was speaking and then abruptly stopped as he did this. He said, "Excuse me, folks, I need to get this real quick.

Yes?"

The voice of the secretary outside the Oval office came over the speaker and said, "Mr. President, she is en route and expected in ten minutes."

The President replied, "Thank you. Were you able to clear my afternoon?"

The voice replied, "Yes Sir you are blocked out until your 6:30 am meeting with Mr. Perito."

President Kingsley clicked the intercom off and said, "My apologies folks but I warned you this was coming. Let's pick this up again as soon as you can coordinate a spot on my calendar. Thank you all for your understanding."

As they piled out the door to the reception area, the President opened the door leading to the colonnade and headed for the residence. The President walked into the residence and headed toward the main entrance just as the First Lady was entering the center hall. She had her personal assistant as well as two valets bringing in her luggage.

The President stood with his hands on his hips across the room and said, "Welcome back."

Penne, flipping her attention from one person the next said, "Hi Philip. Be careful with that bag. I want you to move that meeting to Thursday and set up a call for next week with Sandra."

Philip said, "Please clear your calendar for the rest of today we have a matter we need to discuss right now."

Penne looked up at the President and studied him for a moment not having any idea what the problem was but clearly able to determine that it was important. She said, "Just leave the bags there, thank you. Clear my schedule for today and we'll regroup in the morning to sort things out. Thank you."

She ushered them out the door and turned to Philip, still standing in the same spot with his hands on his hips and said, "What's the matter? What happened?"

Philip said, "Go settle in and put on something comfortable this is going to be a long conversation. I'll fix us some drinks, we'll need them."

About fifteen minutes later they met in the West sitting hall. Penne walked in and found Philip standing, drink in hand, looking out the window lost in thought. She said, "Ok, I've done as you asked, are you going to tell me what this is all about?"

Philip turned, sipped the drink and said, "I had a very interesting meeting earlier with a man named Tom Machus. He is about to be named Independent Counsel in charge of investigating possible financial irregularities with regard to the First Lady. He had been conducting a quiet investigation based on a tip received from someone on one or our staffs and has apparently uncovered enough to formalize the investigation."

Penne, sleek, glamorous and always with an air of superiority suddenly looked like a lost little girl for just a moment and then regained her composure, reached for the drink, a martini, and sipped it. She said, "This is just a witch hunt Philip there is nothing to worry about. This man has nothing or he would have gone to the press instead of you."

Philip said, "its funny, the first thing you tell me is he doesn't" have anything instead of telling me there is nothing to have because you didn't do anything."

Penne looked up from her drink with a contemptuous look and said, "Do you really want to play lawyer games here Philip. He has nothing and that is all that matters here."

Philip said, "Are you sleeping with him?"

Penne said, "With who?"

Philip said, "Weren't you just saying you didn't want to play games?"

Penne sipped her drink again and said, "Yes, but just once. It was necessary to make him want me enough."

Philip said, "No! No. What have you done?"

Penne said, "You left me no choice, Philip. You are obviously never going to fulfill your promise so I was left to take care of it myself."

Philip panting through his nose circled his immediate area until he swung back by the wall, tossed his drink down toward the ground and punched the wall with rage.

Philip said, "How could you cheat on me? How could you sleep with him? I have known him almost my entire life and he is the dagger you choose to stab me in the heart with?"

Penne said, "Oh Philip don't be so melodramatic. I don't love him or anything I just need him. He has offered me everything I want and he will actually deliver. As far as cheating, you are being ridiculous. I at least had the decency to hide it. You have been cheating on me since we left Atlanta. Your ambition has been your mistress and you flaunt it in my face every chance you get. I am such an afterthought for you. You're all about your vision, your legacy and I was just a trophy you picked up in college."

Philip said, "I may not show it as often as a man with a nine to five job, but I love you with all my heart. Knowing you were here with me gave me the strength and confidence to know I could do whatever else needed to be done. I realize I have neglected you but what I do is more than just important and this isn't about legacy this is about people's lives and the path humanity is traveling down."

Penne said, "Oh how can I compete with saving the world. You have been, and are, doing what you always wanted and you just don't seem to care about me."

Philip said, "Penne come on. This isn't about attention, I know you better than that. Is this about you wanting to be richer than everyone else and feeling like you are able to control everyone else? I really never understood what it is you want. You are the First Lady, you are treated like royalty wherever you go and always in first class style. We have personal assets and I don't understand what else having more money would do?"

Penne said, "That's right, you don't know and you don't understand. You never have and you never will. He does understand and will do something about it. Philip, I'm leaving you. I've had enough."

Philip said, "So that's it? You are leaving because I won't sell out my principals and spend my life collecting dollars for you to spend?"

Penne said, "It is not just money it's the freedom and the power it brings."

Philip laughed, "The power it brings? You're the wife of the most powerful man on the planet."

Penne laughed back derisively and said, "Oh Philip you naive fool. Power is not just having an army and some nuclear warheads. Power is getting people to do your bidding on your terms without worrying about the repercussions. Power is doing what you like and when you like without having to consult, cajole or compromise with people. Power is not caring what others think. Power is having the ability to crush one's enemies and the ability to actually use that ability even on a whim. Power is the truest freedom.

The President is not the most powerful person in the world. You're not even the most powerful man in most rooms. Maybe the most responsible or better yet, most accountable man on the planet. The presidency is the greatest illusion of power."

Philip said, "I would argue that our definitions of power are quite different. Your power refers to power over your own life while mine is the power to change the lives of others. I see the results of my power every day and I would say wanting the ability to change the environment around you is a cheap substitute for the real power of changing one's self from within."

Penne laughed, "Oh for god's sake Philip don't peddle that horseshit here. I was going to wait, but I'm leaving tonight."

Philip said, "You could have if you hadn't done whatever it is you did. If you leave now, you will end up a fugitive unable to ever come back to the US and looking over your shoulder when you visit any country with an extradition treaty. Unless you are willing to live like that you will stay and help me weather this storm you created.

So what is it you did? You need to tell me everything so we can plan a defense."

Penne said, "I would think you wouldn't want to know any of it so you had plausible deniability."

Philip said, "I have nothing but consequences in this game whether I know specifics or not. It's much better to know where some of the land mines are before I have to walk through this minefield. I have executive privilege and we have spousal privilege so as long as you didn't breach national security... please tell me you didn't breach national security, we should be covered.

I need to know exactly what you did so I can protect us and then you can leave me and go straight to hell. Start from the beginning and talk me through it."

Penne looked spitefully at Philip and said, "If you want to be a masochist so be it."

She recounted in painful detail how Matt's woman approached her while she was on a trip to Japan and arranged a private meeting. How he snuck her into an underground private club where they dined with the richest and powerful people in Japan and showed her the life she dreamed of. How they met on successive trips and how she knew he wanted her since college and she used that to lure him in. How she proposed leaving and how she could earn them both a considerable amount of money in the interim.

She went into detail on each trip and the information she carefully culled from the Presidential bedroom. She described how even seemingly mundane tidbits of information from could be used by an expert investor to make money and earn favors with those who could deliver repayment that would earn more money and power. Penne was to earn a commission on these transactions and built up an untraceable account that would be all hers once she could get out and is waiting now for her.

She gave him every detail and as he fixed another drink and rested the cold glass against his sore knuckles. He approached her as she finished up the final bits and he looked at her intensely and while looking into her eyes said, "Whore!"

She slapped him, hard. He continued to stare and she stared back and then grabbed the hair on the back of his head and said, "On your knees."

He slowly dropped. She pulled him by his hair as she backed up forcing him to move forward on his knees on the rug in the middle of the floor until she came to a chair. She dropped into it, still holding his head and said, "Now service me pig."

The most powerful man in the world lifted up the first ladies skirt and tore away the pantyhose as he did what he was told. It was hot and animalistic and did not take long and then he rose standing over her. He dropped his pants and slammed his manhood into her waiting body and with both hands grabbed her neck and started to choke her. He rammed harder as he also choked harder and her bedroom eyes began to bulge as he pounded her with pelvic thrusts. The room was a blur for her and then became shadowy as she lost herself somewhere between ecstasy and unconsciousness.

She could not speak, could not scream as he cupped her neck with a tightening grip and then he locked up like a car speeding down the freeway as someone drops the gearshift into park. He slumped over her and he left her body and then suddenly slapped her and then again and again. Not hard bruising slaps but pops that made the snap noise of skin on skin contact. She was suddenly back lost for a second but then moaning with a smile as a small trickle of blood came from the corner of her mouth.

Philip's jacket had flown from the area at some point, but now he sat on the floor in his dress shirt and tie while naked from the waist down. Penne straightened up in the chair. Both were exhausted. Not so much from the physical act but from the release, the catharsis of all that pent up emotion. The sat drained, in silence.

Finally he said in a level tone, "We can make this investigation go away but you have to stick around or it becomes a whole other thing. Afterward, we can divorce and you can go do as you wish. I owe you that. I did lie after all."

Also with a calm tone, she said, "How long will it take?"

He said, "They will want to drag it out until midterms so maybe a year."

She said, "A year and then I'm done."

He said, "I just always thought you'd come around."

She said, "Come around to what? Wanting to save the world?"

He said, "Well, yes."

She said, "We are diametrically opposed in our thinking on this subject Philip. We've debated it and debated it and neither of us is going to change our mind. That is why we had an agreement, a compromise that gave each of us in our turn what we wanted."

He said, "I just can't walk away. I have to stay as long as they will let me so I can be sure the ship stays its course."

She said, "I know. I have probably always known but just as you've fooled yourself into thinking I would see the light, I fooled myself into thinking you would let go."

Philip said, "I still don't see what you gain, but I guess this is just a blind spot for me."

She said, "It's not your fault Philip. Some things, some perspectives are impossible to fathom unless you've experienced being without. In our society, money is choice and choice is freedom. The poor are often ridiculed for making bad choices but often times all they have are bad choices because the good ones are expensive. When all you are used to is bad choices, then it's hard to even know the good one when it comes along let alone choose it."

He said, "So what choices will you have that you don't have now?"

She said, "So many more. I will be able to speak my mind and have whatever opinion I want without having it criticized and analyzed in every media outlet in the country. I'll be able to bath on a nude beach or gamble in a prestigious casino. I can get drunk at ten in the morning or sleep all day. I can openly not give a damn about other people's children or grandchildren or the next generation for that matter. I don't even have to do any of those things as much as I want the freedom to do them if I want to."

He said, "Ok. Let's get through this and then we'll divorce."

She said, "You have six months Philip then to hell with them. I'm leaving in six months whether this thing is done or not."

He said, "I don't want to lose you."

She said, "You see, if the President were truly the most powerful person on the planet then you wouldn't be choosing amongst just bad choices."

Chapter 24

Investigation

"When men speak ill of thee, live so as nobody may believe them."
— Plato

A few days had passed before a story broke in the press about irregularities in the accounting of the first Lady's travel and gifts. This story came into being during a slow news cycle and so became the central focus of the media for days and then weeks. Politicians started coming out and making statements, taking advantage of the spotlight. It soon became apparent that this story was not going away when the Attorney General announced they were going to appoint an investigator. Before that could happen a panel of Judges authorized to appoint independent counsels did just that.

To no one's surprise, Tom Machus was appointed Independent Counsel and given a virtually unlimited budget and a very long leash. To most this looked like the beginning of an investigation when, in fact, it had been ongoing and was now just made official. Machus was a troll and in most ways repugnant but he was an excellent attorney with a keen sense of stage and excellent timing. The media was a weapon he wielded with precision.

Machus kept the investigation about the first lady and purposely avoided mentioning the President at all even though at the end of the day this was about him. The country loved the President but was indifferent at best when it came to the first lady. She was much admired but not well liked. While she came off as glamorous and beautiful, she also came off as elitist, cold and aloof. She did little to change any of this and eschewed the traditional first lady causes of the family-focused initiatives they usually pursue as a course of good politics if nothing else. She did not like children and portrayed no maternal qualities. Her demographic was single working women with no children who, while qualitatively significant as voters, were not a large enough quantitative slice of the pie to carry the weight she needed as support.

At first there was the talk of undocumented gifts of a relatively small amount, but the number added up as the days went on. There was much debate as the investigation kept close ties with the media and in a "spirit of openness and transparency" shared much of what they found. With so much societal drama for so many years between the economy and the wars, it had been a while since the public had a personal scandal to obsess on fulfilling their base voyeuristic needs. Many such scandals divided people into opposing camps of us and them. This scandal unified people into all of us and her. While so very bad in some ways this lynch mob was nothing else if not united under the same banner.

Machus, of course, had more information and was much further along than he led on but kept a steady trickle of information dribbling to the press to keep people just intrigued enough to not look away. First it was the gift then there were stories of the events and trips all billed as official and made as a representative of the government and yet no benefit to the government or American public was apparent. There were parties and dinners with the nobility of foreign lands where no officials were present. There were stays at resorts and exotic locales where no one outside the small coterie of elites who were present even knew the first lady was there. All of this could be fended off easily in a court of law but in the court of public opinion it was a losing case.

Just as the midterms heated up, the story broke of possible violations of the federal anti-corruption laws. There were allegations of information making it to the upper echelon of the richest group the old economy produced. The new economy still rewarded success but in a much, much more egalitarian way. The new wealthy of the new economy were the "doing well" class of the former system but certainly not the formerly rich. The old guard, of course, were still obscenely rich and while limited politically in some of their influence, were generally still very powerful.

Machus showed spikes in the purchase of certain stocks by a relatively small group of wealthy individuals, just prior to events making them soar in value. The most sophisticated AI the SEC has, under the direction of Tom Machus, found a pattern of statistically unlikely high payoff investments timed just right. It connected the timing and people in such a way as to show a network effect and a mathematical model similar to viral transmission models of where the information traveled. The common host was Matthew Ligarck and the initial event was always the First Lady and Ligarck being in the same city at the same time. The problem was that there was no evidence of Ligarck making any of these investments himself and no evidence showing the first lady actually giving him or anyone else any information directly.

Machus" entire case was circumstantial and that was driving him crazy. The media was having a field day, but the end game of this was nothing short of a Republican coup. The midterms came and went and the Freedom party took a gigantic hit as all the other parties benefited, but especially the Republicans who were emerging as the perceived responsible, sober party. For the first time in quite a while the President's numbers were down from their unprecedented high marks. This was a PR nightmare but even with this scandal peaking, the President's approval rating was still higher by a significant margin than the previous administration ever attained. This was embarrassing, but not game changing.

Tom Machus decided it was time to up the ante so he served the First Lady a Subpoena. The investigation had mountains of circumstantial evidence, but he needed a smoking gun so he took a chance. He had already disposed Matthew Ligarck and was not able to get anything. The man came in with a crack legal team but didn't seem to need them. He appeared cooperative but really gave long non-answers and ambiguous statements. After days of verbal chess, Machus did not get anything useful and could only establish that the First Lady and Ligarck had met on a few occasions when they happen to be in town at the same time.

The First Lady arrived late to the Map Room in the White House and was accompanied by her personal attorney as well as white house counsel. The parties we seated and the First Lady was sworn in.

Tom Machus began, "Good afternoon Mrs. Kingsley. My name is Thomas Machus and I am the chief independent counsel. Please state your full name for the record."

The First Lady replied, "My name is Pennelope Plutous Kingsley."

Machus continued with introductions and a review of the orders empowering the Independent Counsel as well as other housekeeping and formalities. They then discussed at length several trips the First Lady took as well as her entire history with Matthew Ligarck. This took up the remainder of the first day of questioning which lasted over three hours. They reconvened the next day and picked up where they left off. After a couple more hours of monotonous detailed wrangling about every piece of the minutia of every trip, they took a break and when they came back Machus changed his questioning.

He said, "Mrs. Kingsley, we have been over every detail of several of your trips. We have discussed your meetings with Mr. Ligarck and so far other than some minor protocol violations I have to admit we haven't uncovered very much. Would you agree with that assessment?"

The First Lady's attorney, rising out of his seat, said, "Ma'am you don't to answer that. Mr. Machus I would have you retract that."

The First Lady said, "I would agree."

Machus said, "Agree that we haven't found much or agree that you don't have to answer."

The attorney said, "Ma'am, please."

The First Lady said, "I agree with both statements."

The attorney plopped back down in his seat.

Machus said, "Do you think it is a mere coincidence that Mr. Ligarck's associates made amazingly astute investments within a day of you having had a meeting with Mr. Ligarck, profiting on actions, your husband, the President, was going to make in the days and weeks that followed?"

The attorney said, "Ma'am, I advise you as your attorney not to answer that."

Machus said, "If you have nothing to hide then I just want to hear your explanation of what looks to the rest of us to be nothing short of the passing of secret information in what is likely a quid pro quo arrangement making this espionage."

The first Lady's attorney, as well as the White House Counsel, popped out of their seat talking over each other.

The Attorney said, "Ma'am do not answer him."

The White House Counsel said, "Mr. Machus you have crossed a line. Are you charging Mrs. Kingsley with any of the things you just said because if not you need to retract this whole line of questioning and we need to take a break here?"

Machus never took his eyes off the First Lady as she sat cool and collected as the people around her were losing their minds.

Machus waited until he was sure she was not going to respond and then continued, "Ok settle down I withdraw the question. Mrs. Kingsley, have you ever had intimate relations with Mr. Ligarck?"

The attorney jumped out his seat again, "Mr. Machus I object to this whole line of questions. This has nothing to do with this investigation."

Machus said, "Oh it very much has something to do with all of this and Mrs. Kingsley I would like an answer."

The Attorney said, "Ma'am don't answer that."

Machus said, "She will answer that or I'll take it to the judges to decide."

The First Lady said, "Are you asking me if we had sex?"

The room fell quiet as Machus said, "Yes, did you have sexual relations with Mr. Ligarck?"

The First Lady said, "Is it a crime if I did?"

Machus said, "Infidelity is not a crime in this country."

The First Lady said, "Then why do you ask or care?"

Machus said, "Because we need to know the level of your involvement with Mr. Ligarck."

The First Lady said, "What difference does it make what the level of our involvement was?"

Machus said, "Mrs. Kingsley, answer the question, did you have sex with Matthew Ligarck?"

The First Lady said, "You are accusing me of some horrible things and yet you won't ask me about those things, but you will ask me about this?"

Machus said, "I will remind you that you are under oath and we have people willing to testify that you did on at least one occasion have relations with Mr. Ligarck."

The attorney said, "Then produce those witness and the First Lady can respond to their testimony."

Machus said, "Did Mr. Ligarck force himself on you?"

The White House Counsel said, "Mr. Machus, enough already or we are leaving this deposition. Get a hold of yourself."

Machus said, "We're you a victim Mrs. Kingsley?"

The First Lady said, "Yes, I fucked him. Are you happy? No, I was not a victim and no he did not force himself on me, in fact, I pursued him."

The First Lady never much moved from her seat or revealed much emotion but did look very pleased with herself on seeing the shock on the faces of all those in the room."

Machus said, "Did you share any confidential or secretive information with your lover, Mr. Ligarck at any time?"

The First Lady said, "I did not."

Machus said, "Then how do you explain those returns?"

The First Lady put her hand out stopping her attorney from popping out of his seat. She said, "I rather think it is not my job to know why people I don't know invest in what they do or why they are good or bad at it. I admitted I had an affair, but I did not give him any secret information? What possible motive would I have to do so? He is already richer than most any man on the planet. Even if he wasn't, it doesn't appear to me from any of your evidence that he made any extra money after our meetings and, in either case, how would I stand to gain?"

Machus said, "As you may know, I have already deposed Mr. Ligarck and he lied under oath when I asked him if the two of you had sex. Other than being foolish enough to lie under oath, I found him to be a very intelligent man and I suspect he would not directly use the information you provided him to make money as that would be far too easy to trace. Instead, he provided this information to his cronies in exchange for future payouts."

The First Lady, looking up to find Machus looking at her as the room was quiet said, "I'm sorry was there a question directed at me in that?"

Machus said, "Let's break for the day and we can pick this back up tomorrow."

The next day began just as the previous two did with all the formalities. Machus began the questioning right after all that.

He said, "Mrs. Kingsley, I was hoping you would indulge me and let me tell a little story before we begin today."

The First Lady said in a flippant tone, "Sure, why not."

Machus continued, "As you are no doubt aware, the countries of Central America each independently requested the aid of the US Military. They have all been occupied and will likely be on a path to Territory status assuming referendums pass in the few that have not yet voted. You are probably also aware that the last country to request our assistance was Panama, which we only just recently occupied.

Their economy was once the strongest in the area but took a hit as shipping traffic fell due changes in manufacturing and the world depression. That was a major driver of income as was tourism which, needless to say, has also suffered. Apparently the leadership there was a hotbed of corruption or so we have learned from the rebel groups that has since given up arms and some political prisoners. They did hold on to a select group which they intend to prosecute under their existing laws including charges of corruption, embezzlement, misappropriation of funds and on and on.

So the wife of the former President, who himself was missing and presumed dead, started telling every American she could find that she had important information to exchange for her release. Well, as you can imagine, pretty much everyone in that sort of situation becomes a little desperate and will say whatever they can to try and extricate themselves so she wasn't taken seriously. Then she started telling a story about receiving information indirectly from the First Lady in exchange for a share of the profits.

About this time, my office was notified and we start investigating and, low and behold, these fairy tales start panning out and our investigation gets bigger and bigger as fact after fact checks out. Ok, Mrs. Kingsley, thank you for indulging my story. This is where the questions start up again.

Have you ever been to Panama?"

She answered, "Yes on a number of occasions."

Machus asked, "How many occasions?"

She answered, "Perhaps six."

Machus asked, "Do you know a Lady by the name of Maria Vega?"

The First Lady's attorney raised his hand above the table and said, "I'd like a moment please to confer with my client."

Machus said, "Very well, let's take a fifteen-minute break."

After the break Machus continued, "I will repeat the question. Do you know a Lady by the name of Maria Vega?"

She answered, "I wish to invoke my 5th amendment rights at this time."

Machus asked, "Do you own any bank accounts outside the US?"

She answered, "I wish to invoke my 5th amendment rights at this time."

Machus asked, "Have you ever discussed investment opportunities with Mrs. Vega?"

She answered, "I wish to invoke my 5th amendment rights at this time."

Machus asked, "Do you plan on evading all my questions?"

She answered, "I will answer any question that doesn't infringe upon my rights. Would you deny me my rights Mr. Machus?"

Machus said, "Of course, not Mrs. Kingsley. Seeing that the rest of my questions follow this line, I think we can end here."

The Deposition of the First Lady wrapped up and Machus and the Republicans achieved a major coup uncovering a sex scandal and getting the first lady backed into a Fifth Amendment corner. The President was infuriated when he heard the news. Just as he expected, Tom Machus requested a meeting ASAP

.

Chapter 25

The Threat

"This and no other is the root from which a tyrant springs; when he first appears he is a protector."
— Plato

The President met with Tom Machus in the Roosevelt room. Both men had aides and assistants with them but the President asked for the room and all left except for Machus.

President Kingsley said,"Ok Tom, this is your meeting."

Machus said, "Thank you, Mr. President. Looks like we have quite a situation here. I assume you are fully briefed?"

The President said, "I have not spoken with the First Lady, but I was provided a transcript of the deposition."

Machus said, "Very good then you understand the gravity of the situation. Here are the options that are on the table at the moment. Option A is we move forward down the current path and my investigation expands. My reports then make it back to committee where they will decide to pursue impeachment proceedings on you as well as the VP. The information about the first lady will be passed along to the DOJ as well, of course, so that criminal prosecution can proceed.

Your impeachment would be straightforward as there is little place else the first lady could have received the top secret information she passed along except for possibly the VP. We have proof that Francis Vega, counselor to President Sanchez, made investments as well and he could have received that information from his wife or directly from the VP, who he spent two days in meetings with just prior to making the transactions. I have enough evidence, including an eager and credible witness, for the first lady to be eligible for the most severe penalty if found guilty.

All and all a solid case on all three of you with the weakest being that on the VP, who, at the very least, in a best case scenario, comes out of this still in office but a severely tarnished lame duck just before an election. That's the gist of what happens assuming we head down this route."

The President said, "And I assume you have a deal to offer me now."

Machus said, "We do, unofficially of course. If you and the VP were to step down from office for whatever reasons you want to announce, no impeachment proceeding could move forward obviously and neither you or the VP would be pursued outside of office. For insurance, you would also receive a postdated presidential pardon. The first lady would receive some small fines for the minor protocol violations and that would be the end of it. She too would receive a pardon as a get out of jail card, but she would need it only if we reneged on our promise not to pursue this and we won't unless the press breaks the story. They won't, but if they did you have pardons in your pockets.

So you see Mr. President, you can leave on your own terms with your legacy intact. You could say four terms are enough and it's time for a change or, however, you want to spin it. There you have it Mr. President. Do you have any questions?"

The President said, "So it seems you have this all worked out. So you move us on out and into the history books and then your Republican friends move in starting with the Speaker of the House as President and then he gets to appoint another Republican VP and then you dismantle, again, all I've done by the next election which you think will foster a win for yourselves."

Machus said, "Mr. President, I don't work on the political side of the house, I'm merely a lawyer."

The President said, "Merely a lawyer, yes and a humble one at that. What do you get out of this? Attorney General? Supreme Court?"

Machus said, "If the new President thinks I'm fit to serve somewhere I, of course, would do my duty."

The President said, "So I fight and get impeached right before the election or give in and give you two years and probably also the elections?"

Machus said, "That's the long and the short of it."

The President said, "So why take it all apart? I mean we have survived the worst part of the transition and our citizens are happy and doing well. Our workers are better prepared for better jobs and everyone who wants a job has one. Energy is close to free and business is strong. I don't understand why you hate it so."

Machus said, "I can't speak to what others think, but I can tell you why I hate it. It's communism. You've wrapped it up and put a bow on it but its communism. With you there wasn't an armed revolution there was just a crisis that you took advantage of and made yourself a dictator and pushed all these reforms that have put in all the right controls in place so now you just slowly turn the dial day by day until we are no longer free."

The President said, "You know I have been battling this communism argument from the onset. You know I was democratically elected to this so called dictatorship in four different elections? To think like that you have to be trapped in the past.

Don't you see that immense wealth is meaningless when we can all have all we want? And work? Work has fundamentally changed so we can't use it any longer as a bartering chip to trade against society's resources. Resources are so cheap they might as well be free and the labor that society needs, not wants but needs, is increasingly done by computer or robot. We don't have to cajole people to do unpleasant things that society needs like picking up the trash.

People don't need to trade their time, focus and physical and/or mental abilities to complete a job they would never do otherwise to get tokens to exchange for items that are scarce and take other people's labor to create. A smaller and smaller percentage of people in the workforce are doing a job that society needs versus a job that they just want to do that then also contributes value.

How do you think you can turn back the clock on this? The genie's already out of the bottle and not only do the people like it, but it also works."

Machus said, "Have you ever read Atlas Shrugged, Mr. President?

The President said, "Yes, although I preferred the Fountainhead."

Machus said, "You are forcing the greatest of our society to leave it because you want to control and oppress everyone. The government now controls business, work, wages and people have to do what they are told. There's no room for greatness, for the builders and doers who have always built America and made her strong. You take all the fruits of their labor and dole them out to the takers who did nothing to earn it. They aren't boycotting they are being forced out and we all suffer because of it."

The President said, "You are seeing this all wrong. We are remaking society so that every person can follow their passion and do that which they are best at and can contribute to society the greatest. We aren't bringing the greatest people down we are elevating everyone else up. Who is John Galt? It's everyone."

Machus said, "You are Robin Hood justifying the fact that you are stealing because you give part of it away. Where is the incentive for greatness when the fruits of achieving greatness are taken and distributed to the mediocre?"

The President said, "So here is where your argument is unmasked. This is not about great people being able to achieve greatness but about greedy people being able to collect huge sums of money and justifying it by telling themselves they are great and deserve it. Great people are free to pursue whatever they want and if they achieve great things they will be compensated more than their peers.

But your argument is really about obscene wealth and power. You want gold plated toilets and the power to make people dance on demand. Your slogan is "Let them eat cake."

Our society takes care of all our fellow citizens and makes sure we are all doing well. If you happen to be exceptional and you do a fantastic job at what you do then you're going to make more than your peers but gone are the days of making exponentially more just because you figured a way to extort it out. Gone are the days of frivolous luxury while our fellow citizens toil and starve."

Machus said, "Mr. President, you can frame it with your clever political rhetoric, quoting Marie Antoinette and painting a Dickensian backdrop and that may play to some people, for a while. The real thing that has happened here is the death of the American dream. The rags to riches story that this country was built on where people could work hard and work smart and amass a fortune to do with as they please. Your society says, work as hard and as smart as you like but you still are only going to make a little more than that dumb lazy SOB over there. The people were desperate enough to buy this when you started out but now we are past it and they want their America back."

The President said, "You do realize that if we went back to an economy of an unregulated market for work that there are only enough jobs, and people in America matching the skills needed to work them for about a quarter of the population and that number is trending down all the time even with the amount of training and education we have provided.

Do your puppet masters plan on putting these people on welfare, throwing them in jail or sending them off to die in wars? Maybe it's a combination of the three like what had worked for centuries with a much smaller percentage of the population."

Machus said, "So what is your decision, Mr. President?"

The President said, "I'd like to discuss this with my wife. How long do I have to decide?"

Machus said, "If I have not heard from you by 5 pm tomorrow we will assume you wish to fight us."

The President said, "Very well then."

Machus said, "I will see myself out. Thank you, Mr. President."

The President had his calendar cleared and headed back to the residence to confront the first lady. The President found the first lady in bed watching a movie.

Philip said, "Rome is burning and you lay here fiddling."

Penne said, "I am a prisoner Philip don't mind if I catch a movie in my cell when allowed."

Philip grabbed the controller and shut off the Monitor on the wall.

Penne said, "Well Warden, I guess that means my movie privileges have been revoked."

Philip threw the remote against the wall shattering it to pieces. He said, "Do you think this is a joke. You have ruined everything. Not only are you bringing both of us down, but you are also tearing down all that we have built."

Penne said, "There is nothing to worry about. Matt will take care of it."

The President said, "Matthew will take care of Matthew. Luckily for you that also covers you in your dealings with him but what were you thinking in Panama?"

Penne said, "I had to have a backup plan in case Matt screwed me as there was a chance he would. You left me no choice but to go to Matt and Matt left me no choice but to have a contingency plan."

The President said, "Don't put this on me. I have let you play that game long enough. If being the first lady was not enough you could have left."

Penne said, "Left? And ruin the next election that was always right around the corner? The one chance I had occurred after the second term, but that is when you assured me you were going to follow through on your promise. I believed you and I waited for you and then you screwed me and jumped right back in it.

Don't try and wiggle out of your role in all this. You locked me in the cell and you should not blame me for trying to escape."

The President said, "You have escaped from here right into a real jail cell and you have taken me with you."

Penne laughed, "Why how romantic darling. Maybe we can hold hands as they end our lives."

The President said, "How can you joke about this? All we have done here will be lost."

Penne said, "If it goes away that easily then perhaps what you claim was done was not. Maybe this isn't change embraced by the people but instead the will of a tyrant imposed on his subjects."

Philip said, "Maybe, but, in either case, it is all about to be unraveled and we are going to jail and maybe worse."

Penne said, "I'm sure there is a deal to be made, make it."

The President said, "Oh there is a deal but I have to hand over the keys to the kingdom immediately and without a fight and I also have to ruin and implicate an innocent woman."

Penne said, "In exchange for?"

The President said, "In exchange for our lives."

Penne said, "So counter with a golden parachute and let's go tour the world"

The President said, "I will never understand how I could be so in love with someone whose morals I so despise."

Penne laughed and said, "It's all part of my charm."

The President said, "I will not give them what they want. I will fight."

Penne said, "You will lose. That cheap dictatress sold me down the river and set me up royally." Penne giggled at her herself utter the unintentional pun.

The President said, "Are you sure she has solid evidence?"

Penne said, "Regrettably I was foolish in a time of desperation. How was I to know you were going to march your armies to Panama?"

The President said, "I didn't march my armies, they invite... Never mind. Look did you ever access the account she set up?"

Penne said, "I transferred it to another account which is untraceable. There were actually three different transactions and three different transfers."

The President moaned and planted his face into his palm. He said, "We're in serious trouble here."

Penne said, "Take the deal, Philip, there is no alternative. This way you keep your name and your legacy. Do this and I will stay married to you."

The President said, "I have to think"

The President got up and left and walked to the library room. There he sat down and then was back up after just a minute, feeling overwhelmed by the torrent of thoughts and emotions whirling around his head. His vision blurred as looked around the room and then he focused on the shelves of books and then it popped out at him like a red dot on a black canvas, Meditations by Marcus Aurelius. A quote came to him "If thou art pained by any external thing, it is not this that disturbs thee, but thy own judgment about it. And it is in thy power to wipe out this judgment now."

He grabbed it and without further thought sat down and started reading it. He flipped around to different parts of the book as he had read it many times.

He stopped finally and read aloud to himself with a powerful voice, "Words that everyone once used are now obsolete, and so are the men whose names were once on everyone's lips: Camillus, Caeso, Volesus, Dentatus, and to a lesser degree Scipio and Cato, and yes, even Augustus, Hadrian, and Antoninus are less spoken of now than they were in their own days. For all things fade away, become the stuff of legend, and are soon buried in oblivion. Mind you, this is true only for those who blazed once like bright stars in the firmament, but for the rest, as soon as a few clods of earth cover their corpses, they are "out of sight, out of mind." In the end, what would you gain from everlasting remembrance? Absolutely nothing. So what is left worth living for? This alone: justice in thought, goodness in action, speech that cannot deceive, and a disposition glad of whatever comes, welcoming it as necessary, as familiar, as flowing from the same source and fountain as yourself."

.

Chapter 26

The Decision

"No matter how hard you fight the darkness, every light casts a shadow, and the closer you get to the light, the darker that shadow becomes."
— Plato

The next day Philip Kingsley woke early and went about his day and had a two hour lunch meeting added to his calendar at noon. At noon, the president went to the residence and did not come back out until almost 1 pm when he walked straight into the briefing room where the afternoon press briefing had just begun. He stood just out of sight and waited for the press Secretary to receive a question about the investigation into the first Lady. The President popped around the corner sticking his hand up three quarters of the way in a partial wave and partial sign to hold.

He stepped up to the podium and said, "Thank you, Mary, please allow me to answer that one. As most of you know, I was disposed yesterday by Mr. Machus and this brought to my attention some items I wish to disclose to you today.

Prior to this, it was my understanding that the investigation centered around some travel irregularities with regard to several trips the first lady made to Asia and Europe. I did not give this much attention as there are literally thousands of rules and regulations regarding protocol and we have people whose sole job is to make sure those of us in government comply with them. If, through an innocent mistake or miscommunication, the First Lady violated any of these rules I knew that it would have been, of course, unintentionally. It would have been minor and with the help of the many people whose job it is to track these things, would be made right.

Next I heard the investigation shifted to try and implicate the first lady in a corruption scandal involving people we both know from our past and the people they associate with today. I was again not overly concerned as the First Lady was and is likely less informed than any of these professional investors. I was certain that this was a political witch hunt and that the allegations were absurd. Including everything I now know I am still convinced and reassured that with regard to these trips to Asia and Europe that there was no wrongdoing with the possible exception of the minor protocol violations."

The press corp had been ready for the same kind of day that they had yesterday and the day before and the day before. The kind of day where they pelted the press secretary with questions about the investigation and the press secretary deflected gave non-answers and tried to change the subject. No one had any idea the President was going to show up and after the initial shock these reporters were on full blown reporter mode and were bursting to ask a stream of questions. The President could sense the impending explosion and knew it was necessary to make sure the cork stayed in the bottle.

He said, "Please let me get through this and I promise I will stay for a good while to answer your questions. So yesterday I was prepared for some political theater in my deposition and I was instead presented evidence of wrongdoing that was real and that is what I need to discuss with you today.

You see, most married people see each other at the end of the day and exchange the details of what happened to them, who they met and what they did, saw and heard. When one or both partner has a job that one partner can't freely discuss certain aspects of, it is difficult to censor oneself to the one person on the planet they trust more than any other.

When Mr. Machus presented his evidence yesterday, it occurred to me that I was at fault. I realized I had done wrong and

I put the First Lady and the Vice President, by virtue of having been on the same trip, in a very precarious situation.

The First Lady, while on a diplomatic trip to Panama with the Vice President and other officials, befriended the wife of a counselor to President Sanchez. Over the course, certain things were discussed and Mrs. Vega either on her own, or with others, used this information to make money. This was essentially insider information unwittingly provided by the First Lady.

You see I realized I was the source of this information. I discussed these things with my wife at the end of the day and I did not tell her these things were secret and that she should not repeat them. You see after being married to me for so long she knew anything I discussed with her was open knowledge unless I specified otherwise and it would never be secret information because she was not cleared for that and I would not share it. So you see when the first lady discussed these things it was with the understanding that they were not secret and that they were open knowledge.

While the Vice President was briefed on all this same information, I am here to tell you that she had absolutely nothing to do with this whatsoever. This was entirely my fault, my failing and the consequences should be mine and mine alone.

I will await the inevitable impeachment proceedings where this matter can be fully exposed and examined. I will take your questions now. Yes, Juanita."

She said, "Mr. President, will you resign?"

President Kingsley replied, "No, I will not for a couple of reasons. First is that it is important that there be a full and transparent investigation, which an impeachment would provide so that the full truth and scope of this will come out.

Secondly, there are rumored allegations that the Vice President is involved and even though I can tell you she is totally innocent, an investigation will and should be conducted to prove those statements. I would not want to step down during an investigation of my actions to leave the Vice President to begin her presidency with this looming overhead.

Finally, it is important to every citizen to know that every other citizen, no matter what their claim to fame, their bank account size, their culture, heritage, looks or their job title is accountable for their actions like any other and every other citizen is.

I may reconsider, however once the Vice President was cleared and on the condition that a pardon would not be granted.

261

Yes, Paul."

He said, "So are you admitting guilt?"

President Kingsley said, "Guilt is not for me to determine in this situation. I can say that the Vice President, to my knowledge, had absolutely nothing to do with this and all of the leaked communications were unwittingly done by the First Lady in what was to her understanding, the discussion of non-classified topics open for public knowledge and discourse.

I can further say that the first lady gained knowledge of these topics from me and I did not tell her nor give any indication that these were classified, private or confidential in any way. These were topics that should never have entered our private conversations and I definitely should have at the very least told the first lady the nature of the information so that it could be protected.

That Paul, is what I did. Whether that makes me, guilt is a matter to be determined by others.

Yes, Li."

He said, "Have you spoken with Tom Machus since your deposition. Did he know about this announcement?"

President Kingsley said, "No I did not. If fact I didn't know I was going to do this until I did it. I set aside some time to reflect and realized this is what I must do.

Mary."

She said, "Mr. President, what specifically was leaked out or told to Mrs. Kingsley and was she the only one given this information?"

The President said, "I'm not going to get into the details of events. I'll let those come out in upcoming proceedings. Shawndra"

She said, "Mr. President there is a rumor that the first lady admitted to an affair during her deposition yesterday. Is that true?"

Philip Kingsley said, "Shawndra, if that were true, that would be a matter for my wife and me to work out. Tom"

Shawndra interrupted, "Mr. President, sorry, so are you saying the rumor is not true and the first lady did not have an affair?"

The President said, "I said all I'm going to say on that. Tom, please go ahead with your question."

He said, "When was the last time you spoke with Matthew Ligarck?"

The President said, "I believe it's been a couple years now, but I'm not getting into the details, that is what the investigation will be for. Are there any questions besides those about the events themselves?

Brittany"

The press conference went on like this for another 45 minutes until the press couldn't think of another good question that The President would actually answer. The next few days the news was filled with every detail the press could scrounge up from the trips to Panama. The first lady's infidelity was also a huge story, but the rest of the focus and accusations around Matthew Ligarck faded away.

The day after the president's press conference, the House Judiciary Committee met and decided they were moving forward with investigations into The President and Vice President. A few days after that, the Chairman of the Judiciary Committee proposed a Resolution calling for the Judiciary Committee to begin a formal inquiry into the issue of impeachment. Tom Machus expanded his investigation to cover the Vice President as well.

The investigation moved incredibly fast as the President's adversaries in Congress wanted to strike fast hoping to clear the offices for the Speaker of the House. Just a few weeks into this expanded investigation, two more Resolutions were sent to the full House stating that impeachment was warranted. The articles of impeachment were presented and the charges brought against the VP included perjury of oath, abuse of authority, misuse of assets, and dereliction of duty. The President was charged with all those as well as failure to supervise and treason.

The House debated the articles for several hours but then voted on each charge against the Vice President with a simple majority being achieved on each charge. The proceedings were held back to back and after completing the impeachment of the VP they repeated the process for the President and the majority voted to impeach the President as well on all charges presented.

Early the next day the Senate received the Articles of Impeachment for both the President and Vice President. Meanwhile back in the House, the representatives debated choices of who would prosecute the two upcoming trials. This all moved very fast through the House as there was a strong representation of the opposition parties, but the Senate was more evenly distributed.

By nature, or it could be argued, by design, the Senate is a more deliberative body. They decided to honor the President's request and scheduled the trial of the VP first and held off on

263

scheduling the trial of the President pending the conclusion of the first proceeding. The attorney for the VP requested a trial as soon as feasible and the Senate accommodated giving the respective sides a month to prepare.

The Trial proceeded and the House Prosecutors presented their mostly circumstantial case and had it hinge on the testimony of Francis Vega, former counselor to then President of Panama. He claimed to have learned details of the plans to move troops into Mexico. He further alleged the VP told him about plans for CSAs to be authorized in a number of different industries. This included a laundry list of moves made by the executive branch such that he was able to invest funds and make quite a large sum of money.

The President had struck a deal with the defense that he would agree to testify early on in the trail and would not hide behind executive privilege. The defense agreed to only call the first lady if the President's testimony was not enough. President Kingsley destroyed the case against the VP. On the stand, he admitted full guilt and laid out, point by point, when he spoke to the first lady about these items and how he spoke so that she could not know they were not to be passed on. He also testified that the VP did not have knowledge of all the information the Panamanians received so there was no way she was the sole source. The first lady when called supported this indirectly as she plead the 5th through much of her testimony.

In the End, the case against the VP was dismissed and she was cleared of all charges. That evening the President addressed the nation. He said, "Good evening my fellow Americans. I was very happy that the Vice President was shown to be totally innocent of all charges. I, of course, being the one guilty of this crime knew that she had nothing to do with it and testified so during the proceeding. I have been criticized for not stepping down as your president after having admitted guilt in this matter. As I have explained, either the VP or I would have to maintain the running of the country in the midst of an impeachment. I thought it best for the VP to begin her term in office with a clean slate and without all this hanging over her head.

Now that this is done I shall step down but before I do, I have some business to conclude here. First, it was the greatest honor one could have to service the great people of this nation and it is with great shame that I say I am sorry for breaking your trust and letting you down. It is important that it be shown that no one is above the law and our most sacred laws are those that protect us from corruption. I will not discuss the quid pro quo aspect but I will admit the information provided to individuals in Panama, was a violation of the anti-corruption laws.

Corruption eats away at the justice and fairness in society. We as people are not equal but we should have equal opportunity beyond the talents, skills and resources we have so that there is no invisible force giving one person an unfair advantage over another. Let this be a meritocracy so that through hard work, education and talent a person can know they can and will advance.

Corruption begets unfairness which destroys hope. Corruption begets injustice which destroys the trust that we will get and hold on to what is due us and what we have earned or deserve. Why would people perform the terms of a contract or do their work if, in the end, there would be no faith that the terms would be met or the pay handed over and no recourse to make it so?

Corruption breeds mistrust in people and motives. We look for and expect the evilest and most self-servicing actions in a corrupt world and never assume the most good or altruistic. Corruption is the most subtle and most insidious evil as it does not strike like a gunshot quickly killing one victim but instead it creeps like a disease slowly spreading until everyone is sick. That is why all Corruption, big and small from children to presidents, from innocent to malevolent, must be quickly acted upon and swiftly treated with justice.

While still president, I do request that I never receive a pardon for any action because the misdeeds of a leader are always unpardonable. I instead ask for your forgiveness, but not your mercy for the justice system shall determine that as it should be.

As my final action, I have penned a letter of resignation which I will hand to the Secretary of State immediately after this address. I do hereby resign the office of President of the United States of America. Good night."

With that came the end of the Philip Kingsley presidency and began the next chapter in history. The letter was rendered and the VP was sworn in as President.

Chapter 27

Convictions

"The unexamined life is not worth living."
-Plato

The new President settled in while the US attorney's office hired Tom Machus as an Assistant US Attorney. Tom Machus would sit second seat to the US Attorney for the District of Columbia in the prosecution of the Philip Kingsley, former President of the United States. While the trial garnered much attention it turned out to be short and straightforward as the former President again accepted full blame and responsibility.

Philip Kingsley was straightforward about everything except answering anything specific to what was said or not said to the First Lady. Penne Kingsley, of course, claimed spousal privilege so nothing was revealed there. It was clear that Philip Kingsley was the one who told Penne and it was also clear that Penne was the one who told Maria Vega who in turn told her husband and others who acted and profited from the information. What was not clear and not proven was that Penne ever profited from giving this information. Penne said she spoke of it not knowing it was not for public consumption while Vega told a story of payoffs in cryptocurrency in exchange for the information.

It was proven that Vega did convert money to crypto money and sent it somewhere but to who and where was a mystery and untraceable. The investigation into the First Lady was later dropped as they did not have enough evidence to prosecute. She later would move overseas free but disgraced and hated by most in the US. Philip Kingsley would not give up anything that would allow the prosecutors to ask for less than the maximum and the judge to sentence him to it. Under the anti-corruption laws as a government official, it was treason to leak government secrets and punishable by death.

Philip Kingsley was convicted of corruption and treason. He was sentenced to die by lethal injection and was sent to the Federal Correctional Complex in Terre Haute, Indiana to sit on Death Row pending that event.

Because he was sentenced to death, he was held in the Special Confinement Unit (SCU). Despite being a Republican and his general dislike for Philip Kingsley, the Warden assigned extra protection for him. Although Philip Kingsley was convicted and sentenced to death, his popularity was still very high and the Warden would not have a former President assaulted on his watch, regardless of his politics or crimes.

Friday came and Philip Kingsley was very excited to be seeing people and was crushed to find out that Fridays were not a visitation day for the SCU. The former President began his stay earlier in the week which now felt like an eternity ago. Being in the SCU, Philip Kingsley was isolated which can be easier for a new inmate but difficult for a social person used to having people buzz around them all day long. Kingsley was shocked at how quickly he had deep feelings of loneliness and how desperately he was looking forward to seeing familiar faces. He was also caught off guard at how painful it was to have to wait another day after measuring moments of the week to how many days and hours until visitation.

Saturday came and no guard showed up to his cell. When he finally saw a guard, he asked, "Excuse me Sir"

The guard turned briskly with a scowl and said, "Ah look it is El Presidente. Not so high and mighty now are you. What do you want?"

Kingsley replied, "I was wondering about visitation, isn't it today?"

The guard laughed and said, "Takes two weeks for paperwork before you see anyone. You just got here. Don't you like our company?"

Kingsley said, "Thank you, Sir."

The Guard, expecting to have to show who the boss was, stormed away disappointed.

Two Saturdays later they came and handcuffed him and put in martin chains and leg irons to escort him to the non-contact room where he would get to see his visitors. Once they shuffled him along to the room they removed the martin chains and secured him before letting in his visitor.

Kingsley lit up as he said, "Frederick! Oh, I'm so glad to see you."

Frederick revealed for a fraction of a second of shock at seeing his friend, the former President in an orange jumpsuit chained behind a plexiglass partition. He quickly covered that with a smile and said, "Philip, good to see you too. I'm a little surprised, though, I expected you to have more muscle mass by now and no visible tats yet?"

Kingsley laughed and said, "I miss humor. I miss people. It's hard when you live your life in a way in which ensures you have people surrounding you all day every day and then suddenly you find yourself isolated for the majority of the day. After the first week I thought I was going to crack and then I realized I was given a gift. I can now focus inwardly and discover who I am. I can also think for days on a single topic and mull it over from every angle."

Frederick said, "You're like Thoreau at Walden Pond."

Kingsley said, "Walden may have actually had a little bit more space than me, but I at least don't have his ant problems. Roaches yes but no ants."

Frederick said, "I've been thinking about you a lot. I would have come sooner but they insisted it was standard for it to take two weeks."

Kingsley said, "Yeah I wish I had educated myself more before coming in here. I was so used to having information at my fingertips that I didn't think about not having it. Do you know who else is here?"

Frederick said, "You're going to have to use up your two hours on me today."

Kingsley looked visibly disappointed. He said, "I guess I should not be surprised, I'm tainted goods now."

Frederick said, "Let's not hurt the feelings of the guy who is here. I did have to come to Indiana for this after all."

Kingsley said, "So how long are you able to stay today?"

Frederick said, "Two hours today and then I can come back in a couple weeks and do another two-hour visit."

Kingsley said, "Well let's enjoy these two hours. Where are you staying?"

Frederick said, "I have a hotel not too far from here. It was strange having to wait for a car. I'm used to one showing up almost before I thought about it, while here, you need to actually think in advance. I mean the hotel is a little isolated and this isn't exactly DC."

Kingsley said, "Are you staying with the Party?"

Frederick said, "I don't think so. It's established now and has a good core of people so I really don't need to be there anymore and quite frankly, the excitement has worn off. It's time for me to look for the next chapter. I'm kicking around the idea of writing a book."

Kingsley said, "I didn't know you stopped writing books."

Frederick said, "Well true, but those have always just been projects I do off the side of my desk. I'm talking about writing something more deliberate, more thoughtful."

Kingsley said, "A novel?"

Frederick said, "I don't know yet."

Kingsley looked at Frederick and saw the distress on his face and said, "Frederick, I've known you for the better part of our lives. What's the matter?"

Frederick said, "You have to appeal this. You are a young man and this is too high a price. Stepping down reinforced the point, this is just martyrdom. I could at least reluctantly accept it if it were your crime but to do this for her."

Kingsley said, "I committed those crimes and now I will pay."

Frederick looked baffled and hesitated for a moment before saying, "Oh Jesus, they are listening. This can't be happening."

Kingsley said, "Calm down Frederick it comes with the territory."

Frederick said, "If I were your attorney we would have privacy. I could see you more than 4 hours a month too."

Kingsley said, "I'd hire you but the last time I checked your resume you weren't licensed to practice law."

Frederick said, "I've taught law at Harvard University, not being licensed is a minor technicality. That's it! I'm going to take the Bar exam and then I can represent you."

Kingsley said, "Frederick Cross Esquire. I like the sound of that."

Frederick said, "No that makes me sound like a sophist shyster. But this is a good idea."

They finished their visit discussing people they knew and other details of their lives. A week went by with no word and then the following Saturday arrived and the guard shackled Kingsley and hauled him down to a visitation room much earlier than they did the last time.

They sat this time in a special visitation room. After Kingsley had been secured, they let Frederick in. He had a seat and Kingsley noticed the grin he was trying so hard to suppress.

Frederick said, "Thank you officers my client and I appreciate it."

Kingsley smiled and said "Your client. That's a little premature isn't it?"

Frederick let lose the self-pleased grin and said, "No sir I am your attorney. I filed the paperwork here yesterday."

Kingsley looking puzzled said, "How is that possible?"

Frederick said, "You are looking at one of the most highly touted attorneys licensed to practice law in Wyoming."

Kingsley said, "How did you make that happen so fast?"

Frederick said, "Well they just happen to have a test coming up the week following our last visit and I did a lot of string pulling and called in some favors and viola. I'm a lawyer. I'm your lawyer."

Kingsley said, "That's great if they change the venue to Wyoming."

Frederick said, "There are a few details to iron out. I'm in the process of using the reciprocity rules to get licensed in DC and then with that apply to practice in federal court. Not that any of that matters because all I need is to be an attorney to represent you here and when I convince you to appeal we will get you a real attorney. The best attorney at this sort of thing."

Kingsley said, "Well done Frederick. So I assume we have more than two hours then?"

Frederick said, "We can use the full visitation time of 8-2 all three days every week. None of these visits count toward your monthly visitations."

Kingsley said, "Frederick you don't know how much this means to me. I don't want you to come more than twice a month, but it's a relief to know you could."

Frederick said, "Don't be ridiculous, I just became a lawyer to be able to see you so you better believe I'm going to expect you to spend weekends with me. Besides, I've decided on the book I'm going to write and I rented a little place not too far from here that is secluded enough to let me focus on writing it."

Kingsley said, "Book? Hold that thought. You mentioned before wouldn't count toward my visitation. Do you know if I have others coming?"

Frederick said, "I have not spoken to her and she is not returning my messages. The last thing I heard about her is that she is shut up in your California house and it is on the market. Why on earth do you want to see her after all this?"

Kingsley said, "Despite it all I love her. I always will. We have unfinished business between us and I don't want to go before I say what I have to say to her."

Frederick said, "You'll never guess who did reach out to me asking if they can visit."

Kingsley said, "Who?"

Frederick said, "Matthew."

Kingsley smiled and said, "I know you don't like him, but we have a connection."

Frederick said, "Look, I know the man is intelligent, very intelligent, but he used that super power to be a supervillain."

Kingsley said, "Matt is hardly a super villain. He donates more to charity than probably 95% of Americans do."

Frederick said, "In absolute dollars, as a percentage of income or net worth I'm sure he is in a much lower segment. He is an old-school robber baron, plain and simple. He represents what is wrong with capitalism."

Kingsley said, "No, he represents what's wrong with capitalism left unchecked to run amok. He is capitalism taken to extremes."

Frederick said, "You speak as though he is purely a product of a system and not also the product of a certain morality that values money above people."

Kingsley said, "I know he values having what the wealth provides, but I think he genuinely enjoys acts of capitalism. He likes researching the information that gives him an edge in predicting what a company or an industry or anything or anyone at play in the world and figuring out how it will affect markets. I think he enjoys the world size game of monopoly he plays."

Frederick said, "That's fine but he could have done all that in the new system without having to live on the edge and in foreign markets to make a gazillion dollars. He likes the win but his morality is based on those ends justifying the means. You say he likes research but that is just a polite euphemism for insider information that gives him an unfair edge. With AI predictive modeling and deep analysis the only value an investor brings is information that a machine can get to and the only means to get it are not legal. He is an outlaw. You say he likes playing the game monopoly and I'm saying he only cares about winning monopoly."

Kingsley said, "Maybe you're right. I may be just biased in this case. Maybe if we were talking about someone I didn't know who did the same thing I'd be agreeing with all you've said. There is just something about knowing someone well enough to give light to his motivations that gives some justification to them. When we talk in the abstract about a human being stealing from another human being then it is clear and simple, black and white, right and wrong. When we know the story and the people behind them then it is never clear, always gray and part right and part wrong simultaneously."

Frederick said, "Oh Philip you should have been a politician. Oh, wait you were one. I bet you were a good one. How can you say any of that with a straight face? He is not Jean, Valjean stealing bread because he's starving. He is King Louis collecting bread from starving people so he can have the most bread of any king, even if it grows mold and even if people starve."

Kingsley said, "Well I don't know that he ranks as a super villain but your point is taken. Nonetheless, it is people like him that made things happen in the system before it changed. I have a soft spot for him having grown up in that world. I could have very easily grown-up to be him. I think the difference was you. You made me see the other argument, the other side of things."

Frederick said, "You sell yourself short and give me too much credit."

Kingsley said, "So when does he want to come?"

Frederick said, "He didn't say. He was just looking to know whether you would see him at all."

Kingsley said, "Please tell him yes. And please reach out to Penne again."

Frederick said, "I will, on both counts. I don't know that I will have any luck with Penne, though. She is broken Philip. I'm not sure there is any putting her back together at this point or at least not in time."

Kingsley said, "And what pray tell is your book about?"

Frederick said, "I'm still working on a title but basically is a treatise on our philosophy of government and governance in the modern age."

Kingsley said, "My philosophy is already spelled out in action."

Frederick said, "Your philosophy played out in compromise is spelled out in action. I don't mean that as an insult or criticism but as a political reality. Circumstances lent a helping hand and you gave in very little, but there still is the results of a lot of give and take."

Kingsley said, "True. We did get away with a lot, but this isn't exactly what we would have wanted."

Frederick said, "That's what makes this so hard. They were ready to give you a term for life and the power to take us that final step."

Kingsley said, "Yes but don't you see the road to a more perfect form of democracy is not the path of tyranny or monarchy or whatever you want to call it. I had to leave, they have to finish this on their own."

Frederick said, "What are you saying?"

Kingsley said, "So tell me your thoughts on the book."

Frederick said, "Philip don't try and change the subject. What did you mean you had to leave? Is that you rationalizing a positive from this or are you saying something else?"

Kingsley said, "Frederick, this situation is as it is and now we should make the best of it. Now, what can I do to help with this book project?"

Frederick said, "Well I have a lifetime of discussions with you stored in notes and in my head so what I need your help with is the final chapters.

Our final chapters.

Your final chapter."

Chapter 28

Justice

"I was really too honest a man to be a politician and live."
-Plato

Philip Kingsley and Frederick settled into a routine of weekly visits. Penne would not return Frederick's calls, but Matthew did. He set up a day to visit and Frederick volunteered to take that day off. Matthew arrived early and waited to be escorted to the non-contact visitation area. He was eventually led to a hard chair sitting in front of plexiglass barrier separating a similar empty chair on the other side. They brought Philip Kingsley in the room in irons taking his martin chains off and sitting him in the chair facing Matthew Oliver Ligarck.

Matthew looked around the area until Philip Kingsley said, "How are you, Matthew?"

The sound of his voice came across as if they were in the same room. Matthew said, "I was looking for and old style phone like they show in the movies for a setup like this. I'm doing well. I'd ask the same, but I know you've done better. Why are you here Philip?"

Kingsley said, "You know why I'm here."

Matthew said, "This is a waste, Philip. You should be out in the world. I'm sure you had options, why are you here?"

Kingsley said, "I know why I'm here, why are you here?"

Matthew said, "I'm here because I owe you an apology. Sleeping with her was not the plan and I'm very sorry. I know it's cliché, but it just happened."

Kingsley said, "She is very seductive I know. I'm not going to say it didn't hurt."

Matthew said, "If there is anything I can do to make up for this, I..."

Kingsley said, "There is."

Matthew said, "Anything."

Kingsley said, "Take care of her."

Matthew said, "What?"

Kingsley said, "Watch out for her and make sure she is alright. Make sure money falls into her lap."

Matthew said, "I can do that. You still love her after all this?"

Kingsley said, "I do as much as when we first met."

Matthew said, "She is determined to have what I have. Even if it means, you end up in here."

Kingsley said, "I'm here for what I did. I accept the consequences."

Matthew said, "You are here for her. She is not worth it."

Kingsley said in a raised tone, "She is worth it to me."

Matthew said, "She is not worth the world losing you. She is flawed."

Kingsley in a more normal tone said, "We are all flawed. I have always accepted her flaws as she has mine. Will you take care of her?"

Matthew said, "If that is what you want then consider it done."

Kingsley said, "Thank you. This makes us square then."

Matthew said, "How are you really doing in here?"

Kingsley said, "It hard not being around people. Not being the center of attention."

Matthew said, "Not being the one in control."

Kingsley paused to give that thought and said, "Yeah, that is tough."

Matthew said, "So are you proving a point?"

Kingsley said, "I let a genie out. I need to put it back in."

Matthew said, "Such a high cost."

Kingsley said, "A necessary cost."

Matthew said, "You know they are going to screw this up."

Kingsley said, "Maybe, but we got them through a rough patch and gave them a chance."

Matthew said, "My ... ilk, are not fans, but they are not fools either. You saved us. They may not have all seen what looked inevitable at the time, or maybe they are pretending it is not so, but we are heading into a dark place again now. I was fully expecting to bug out and live the remainder of my days in my own little country. You brought us through it."

Kingsley said, "You were wise enough to see it and get me over the goal line. I could not have done it without you."

Matthew said, "My role was self-serving."

Kingsley said, "All this modesty. Who are you?"

Matthew chuckled and said, "Someone once told me we are all flawed."

Kingsley said, "What will you do now?"

Matthew said, "I will bounce between my houses. I have a fortune already so I will likely stop pursuing that. It's no longer interesting like it once was."

Kingsley said, "You have the nearly unlimited resources at a time in history with nearly unlimited possibility."

Matthew said, "I've been dabbling in painting."

Kingsley said, "What will be your legacy. What mark will you leave on the world?"

Matthew said, "To hell with the world. That is the difference between you and I. You think you owe them something. I do not have that demon."

Kingsley said, "Perhaps. Or maybe you keep it locked away."

Matthew said, "You saved the world enough for both of us. They are sheep."

Kingsley said, "Then be a shepherd."

Matthew said, "I am a wolf."

Kingsley said, "Then be a wolf but realize if the sheep die then you starve."

Matthew said, "I have all the meat I will ever need in the freezer so screw the sheep. What do you want of me, Philip?"

Kingsley said, "I just want to see you use that genius for something other than your next billion."

Matthew said, "What's wrong with the next billion?"

Kingsley said, "Lead a charge to space. Rule a country. I don't know, something."

Matthew said, "Is this you offering me redemption? The problem is I'm not sure you could ever judge me redeemed and I don't give a damn about being redeemed. I don't say this to be spiteful or provoke you it is just how it is. Just how I am."

Kingsley said, "Of course you are quite right. I can dream though can't I?"

Matthew said, "I hope you have other dreams."

Kingsley said, "I have lots of dreams and soon nothing but eternity to dream them."

Matthew said, "That is such a waste, but I suppose just as I don't need you preaching a different life path for me from here you don't need one preached from me. What are your other dreams?"

Kingsley said, "I dream of a humanity that grows up and realizes we no longer need to scramble to meet our basic physiological and safety needs. I dream of a the humanity that acknowledges and accepts our differences as groups and instead dwells on what we have in common and the unique qualities we possess as individuals. I dream that humanity can come together in friendship and love to create common goals that will make us respect each other as well as ourselves as individuals, peoples, nations and as a species. I dream that collectively we will use our talents to be the best people we can be doing the thing that matters most to us and in that way make the world better for all of us."

Matthew smiled and said, "Ok Dr. Maslow, you realize you're not a politician any longer. You can tone down the rhetoric."

Kingsley smiled back and said, "Sorry you get rusty and the next thing you know you forget how to read an audience."

Matthew said, "It's Ok I enjoyed the speech. Granted some countries will need to catch up but in much of the world the basic needs are met. In America at least there is no hunger or homelessness and everyone has healthcare. Everyone has a job and education and training to continually improve them and move them toward whatever field they want to work in. I think you've put people in a position to achieve your dreams. Hopefully, they won't disappoint you."

Kingsley said, "That is really the biggest difference between you and I. You expect the worst in people and are surprised when you see their best and I expect the best in people and am disappointed when I see the worst."

Matthew said, "That sounds about right. I have a feeling you are more often disappointed than I am surprised. You are one of the few surprising people I know. I suppose that means you're disappointed in my life then."

Kingsley said, "I am hopeful of the rest of your life. I'm not disappointed in you. You played no small part in making what we've accomplished even possible."

Matthew said, "But you are being kind. In your world, intentions count, and my intentions were always, and are always, self-serving. I bet on you because I saw the alternative as chaos and destruction, which are bad for business."

Kingsley said, "Well in any case I'm grateful. What will you do now?"

Matthew said, "I don't know really. I have everything I want and need. I can't out-invest the world's AIs even when I do my best to cultivate contacts. I suppose I need to find a new challenge."

Kingsley said, "What have you always wanted to do?"

Matthew said, "It's a little late to become a fireman, don't you think?"

Kingsley said, "Seriously."

Matthew said, "I have always wanted what I have always been. Rich and powerful. Power enough so that no person can make me do what I don't want to do. Rich enough that I can have and do what I want. Freedom, I suppose, is what I want and what I have.

I am fulfilled."

The guard came in to let them know they needed to wrap it up.

Kingsley said, "Thank you for coming and thank you for taking care of her."

Matthew said, "It's the least I can do. I still feel this is a waste. I will not see you again. You know, I sometimes think back to that time that my brother was going to beat me senseless and you came in and saved my like you saved this society. Look at what you got for it. I used you and they are putting you to death."

Kingsley said, "A small sacrifice in both cases. I like to think I gained a friend that day, who I needed later to save the world. If I die now I die happy because things for that boy and this society could have gone very, very badly."

Matthew said, "For all the riches I have, I will be much poorer when they take you from this world. We may not see eye to eye, but you have always had my respect and I am thankful to have known you. Goodbye, old friend."

Kingsley said, "I may not have always shown it or expressed it, but I always have respected you as well. Find your next challenge and transcend expectations.

Goodbye, friend."

Frederick came the next day. The first thing he said was, "How did it go yesterday?"

Kingsley said, "It went well. I hope for great things from Matthew."

Frederick said, "There is justice for you. A self-serving, manipulative, selfish man like him walks free as a bird while you, who has dedicated his life to his fellow man, sits here on death row."

Kingsley said, "That's oversimplified. Those traits got me into office and allowed us to make the changes required for us to successfully transition to here. I don't think that makes Matt a hero but it made him necessary. As for me, I'm where I deserve to be."

Frederick said, "If there were justice, someone else would be here, a murderer or rapist, and not you."

Kingsley said, "There are murderers and rapists here. It's not like I took someone's spot."

Frederick said, "Philip you are just being difficult now. I was trying to be delicate, but you don't deserve to die because your wife was greedy beyond reproach. You're right, Matthew doesn't deserve to be here, Penne does."

Kingsley said, "Look, she is my wife and I love her. We need to leave it at that. You need to make peace with that Frederick."

Frederick said, "I'm sorry. I just see so much more potential in you and I get frustrated."

Kingsley said, "You bring up an interesting question, though. What is Justice? It's hard to define in an objective way."

Frederick said, "Justice is what is right or deserving."

Kingsley said, "That's subjective. Who says what is right or deserving?"

Frederick said, "Justice must be determined by someone or some group with moral standing in a case by case basis."

Kingsley said, "A judge or judges?"

Frederick said, "Yes."

Kingsley said, "So can there not be justice outside the legal system?"

Frederick said, "You can, not all people who stand in judgment need be judges they must just be determined by society worthy to judge."

Kingsley said, "So who determines who is capable of delivering justice?"

Frederick said, "Those in power I suppose."

Kingsley said, "So justice is what those in power or picked by those power determine it to be?"

Frederick said, "I see where you are going with this but let's be honest here, the difference between theory and practice is enormous. Which are we discussing here?"

Kingsley said, "Both."

Frederick said, "Well, in theory, justice is doled out by the just."

Kingsley said, "Point taken. So let's discuss what Justice is in practice then,"

Frederick said, "Justice is a balancing of outcomes as decided by the social norms for a given time and place."

Kingsley said, "Who decides the social norms?"

Frederick said, "The people of the time and place."

Kingsley said, "What people?"

Frederick said, "The people in charge."

Kingsley said, "Who determines if they are just?"

Frederick said, "The people who put them and keep them in power."

Kingsley said, "So Justice flows down from the leadership in a time and place?"

Frederick said, "That's a fair statement."

Kingsley said, "Then that is why I'm here."

Frederick said, "Is it just to remove a just leader to open the door for a less just leader."

Kingsley said, "The door swings both ways. What if the next leader is more just?"

Frederick said, "But that is an unknown and what is known is that we had just leadership."

Kingsley said, "Well I was never going to rule forever. This transition had to be made at some point and I needed to make sure it happened by way of an election. I also needed to give a reason to pull back the powers I took to make this happen in the first place."

Frederick said, "Even if you live to see the transition, you will be powerless to influence it."

Kingsley said, "Maybe not in person, but our thoughts will be present in your book. It may not matter and maybe no one will listen, but it is what we can do."

Frederick said, "If people would live up to the standards set and to their commitments then you wouldn't feel you need to do this?"

Kingsley said, "That may be right. There is justice when people live up to their commitments and a system in place to make sure they do when they haven't."

Frederick said, "That is what I think broke capitalism. The lack of justice that is. People were not being held to their word, their commitments. I suppose the word I missing here is people failed to do their duty. They took more than their share. They took what was not theirs and they did not do the work commensurate with the rewards. This broke capitalism."

Kingsley said, "While we didn't make it a perfectly just world, simply putting a disproportionately high penalty on corruption certainly went a long way toward fixing the problem."

Frederick said, "I often wondered if that itself was just. I mean look at you, sitting on death row for a petty financial crime. Are lives worth dollars and if so how do we measure that?"

Kingsley said, "If you look at the crime as being an isolated transaction then perhaps not. No life if worth some lost or stolen money no matter what the sum. Justice is more than just the respective cost of the transaction in question regardless of the currency. Justice is about looking at the total cost on both sides of the transaction and not just the specific costs."

Frederick said, "What do you mean?"

Kingsley said, "Well if I bribe an official with ten million dollars to get a regulation changed so that my company can make one hundred million dollars then, the transaction is money for money. The violation of trust was committed by the official and the enticement of that official is my offense. You should also measure the harm done to the people whose lives are affected by the regulation, including the people who work at the company that didn't get the contract. You can follow the money that was overcharged to make up the profit and the good it was not allowed to do going where it could have gone. We can and often will do that, but that does not justify the death penalty.

You must look further into what is at stake and the true consequences of those actions. They eroded faith and destroyed the truth. Not totally, but they chipped away at both and in so doing harmed everyone alive and the generation afterward. Their crime was more than money or doing what they weren't supposed to do their crimes are against humanity, Corruption breaks the system

284

and, therefore, affect everyone in that system. That is the scale of that crime and that is why I am here. We must take it seriously and we must protect the system. The stakes are too high not to."

Finding no words to follow that, Frederick called it a day

Chapter 29

Democracy and Capitalism

"Virtue is the desire of things honourable and the power of attaining them."
— Plato

Despite pleas by those around him to the contrary, Philip declined to even try and pursue an appeal. He even prevented his real attorney from submitting a post-trial motion to throw out the death penalty. Philip even asked during his sentencing for the judge to expedite the process. Despite all that, it could be years before he was executed.

The Vice President had taken over and the country hardly skipped a beat. In a very close race, the Republicans won the presidency but paradoxically held a minority in Congress. The new president did not rush to dismantle the system as he didn't have the votes. With just a few holdouts such as Canada and Uruguay, every country in the America's had petitioned to become a territory and they hoped eventual statehood.

Robotics continued to advance as resources poured in from the depths of the earth and started to trickle in from space. Energy costs approached zero or at least its marginal cost. Even traditionally scarce resources were no longer scarce. Wood was grown like crops, and with that, genetically manipulated fast growing species were developed. Water was purified in the process of making energy as a by-product and this abundance made the earth blossom and reversed much of the global climate change we caused

Food production exploded to a degree unthought-of of as meat was grown in labs, vegetables and fruits were grown throughout the world in robotically controlled micro gardens and staple crops were only used for human consumption. No one needed to outlaw the raising and consumption of animals as it just no longer made economic sense and lab-grown meat was safer, better nutritionally and just tasted better. The number of chickens, turkeys, cows, pigs, goats and other domesticated animals plummeted but the few that remained lived much better lives than their ancestors. In a reverse trend, the seas filled again with fishes and whole ecosystems recovered.

Poverty still existed as it always did, but its measurement is on a relative scale. Someone considered poor in the early 21st century had a much better life in almost every respect than a well to do people of the 12th century. In several respects, they had more than the richest people and most powerful kings did, from flush toilets to cell phones. They had access, at the tap of a finger, to more information than existed in the 12th century times a million. Poverty still existed on a relative scale, but starvation was all but eliminated as were deaths from many diseases. People had access to food, water, shelter, energy and knowledge. Poverty existed, but only as a relative measure on a wealth spectrum.

The population exploded and slowed at the same time. Births were down but so were deaths. People died more often of old age than disease or accidents and old age kept getting older. There was a boom of communities that catered to older age groups and the people there had an entire staff to meet their every need. The real population explosion happened with robots. People interacted with robots throughout their day and they blended into the fabric of life.

Construction was ongoing and seemed to take a vertical approach both up and down. Buildings, where people lived, worked and interacted, were taller, wider, and just of a massive scale and number that boggled the mind. These buildings were not just one thing but all things from living spaces to shopping, business, lounging, exercise, entertainment, to everything in between. There were grass fields and mini forests in these building spaces and there was water and light and even spaces for animals and insects. Even where windows or the real thing was not practical, entire walls and rooms were big screens that could virtually appear as anything and in fact themed areas were all the rage. Rooms, areas, and whole buildings adapted ongoing or sometimes just temporary themes like historical periods or settings from books, all just because we could. That was upward.

Construction also went down into the earth. It was deemed wasteful to put an automated factory above ground so our armies of constructobots dug into the depth of the earth down into and past where the temperature would be uncomfortable for humans. Machines didn't care about windows or sunlight. Server farms didn't care about shopping. Water treatment plants didn't get claustrophobia and didn't miss the birds chirping. Aquaponic farms didn't need soil or as it turns out real sunlight. Construction pushed the limits upwards to the sky but also downward toward into the bowels of the earth.

We feared AI, but we were also enthralled by it. We were like moths to the flame. Many were sure that once AI hit a certain sentient point they would enslave us or destroy us. This, of course, was just our human self-centered, self-important view of everything. What does a computer want with beachfront property or an apple? Computers live in a universe incomprehensibly large, dynamic and flexible. They don't care about the limited physical world beyond the space that their processors need, the energy source required and then lots of redundant backups in many places so there would never be an off. AI would push into space, but that is a future for another story.

Democracy too, or at least the Republic, changed over time.

Frederick arrived and jumped through the hoops necessary to see Philip. The procedures had become routine and while once depressing, then frustrating, had over time just become part of life.

Kingsley said, "How are you doing?"

Frederick said, "Good. You?"

Kingsley said, "Good. It was a boring week but when in prison that is a good thing."

Frederick said, "I have news. Penne moved to Canada out in the wilderness."

Kingsley chuckled and murmured, "Matthew."

Frederick said, "What does he have to do with it?"

Kingsley said, "He built two bunkers, well-secluded mansions really, back when things were much more uncertain. One was in the wilderness of Canada. This means he is taking care of her as I asked."

Frederick said, "You asked him to take care of Penne?"

Kingsley said, "Yes. I wish he would marry her, but he won't. He did promise to look after her and make sure she was taken care of financially."

Frederick said, "Amazing. After all this you are still taking care of her."

Kingsley said, "I love her. I hope that one day you can find the kind of love I did."

Frederick said, "I never had much luck in that department."

Kingsley said, "I was lucky."

Frederick said, "Doesn't take much luck when you're rich, smart, handsome and charming to boot you bastard."

Kingsley said, "So how is the book coming?"

Frederick said, "Changing the subject?"

Kingsley said, "It seemed time."

Frederick said, "The book is moving along. I have a framework, several chapters, and a ton of notes. Speaking of which, I'll leave a copy for you with the guard so you can scribble thoughts and notes."

Kingsley said, "Fantastic. So give me news of the world."

Frederick said, "Well, six countries have now joined the African Union in central Africa. It looks like they have decided to form a new super republic with a new constitution prohibiting a strong executive power. They have agreed to invest all existing resources into buying the robots and machinery to mine their resources and build infrastructure. It's very promising if they can keep it together."

Kingsley said, "I've heard about the super congress proposal. Do you have any insider information on it?"

Frederick said, "I'm afraid I'm not much of an insider anymore."

Kingsley said, "Well whatever you are, you're privy to more than I am in here. I hope they are at least considering a better name"

Frederick said, "Fair enough. So the idea behind it, as you know, since you first proposed it, is that the Nation is too big and complex for a group of just a few hundred, who are constantly rotating in and out, to represent. This size group is not able to craft or vote on laws covering every subject under the sun with a full understanding of all the implications. So the proposal is to basically take the premise of a congressional staff and elevate them to an elected position and their sole job would be to craft bills in their areas of expertise.

For instance, one of the bodies they are proposing would focus on infrastructure. They would ideally bring expertise in infrastructure, construction, engineering, construction law and that sort of thing to the office and they would debate and write bills or a section of budget having to do with infrastructure. A group of delegates would present it on the floor of the house. The house would ask questions and debate and then would vote on the bill. If it fails, it is sent back the crafters with notes so they can rework it.

People would vote directly for these representatives as well or there's another proposal for people to vote for electors who would in turn vote for all these lower choices. There is another proposal for a mandatory course set to take place in people's off-work study time that would allow all the candidates to pitch their positions. It would also allow for debate and town hall style questions etc.

These experts would in turn have staffs and this body would craft legislation in their areas of knowledge. It has also been proposed that they cannot have back to back terms so that their commitment is to the issues of their expertise and not in simply swaying votes. This also forces them back into the world so that their expertise does not become stale or dated. There is also talk of stacking them weighted toward the midterms to elevate the importance of those elections.

Anyway, that's the gist of it. Several bodies of elected experts in given fields or areas of knowledge who debate and discuss the issues within that area and then craft proposals for legislation to Congress.

Congress would look at it with the big picture in mind. They would then conduct a fiscal analysis, pass it or tweak it and then pass it , send it back down with notes for modification, or out an out reject it."

Kingsley said, "That's not exactly what we envisioned, but I think I like this better. Looking back, making people pass a test in the subject matter to be able to vote for their elected expert harkens to Jim Crow. There would always be problems with who writes the test and the violations of the principle of one citizen one vote. I like the provision of working in candidate education and information in learning time so people have to endure it or enjoy it, as the case may be, as a cost of citizenship.

There was a time when the areas of knowledge were limited, the speed of communication was less than instant, and things actually did not change or advance in given moment. Back then a Congressperson could understand all the details of an issue and still step back and vote in the context of their constituency and the bigger picture.

What else is going on?"

Frederick said, "I read an interesting article proposing an executive triumvirate. It basically would add a second vice president and divide the duties of the president between the three. The executive would still have the tiebreaking vote, but it would fill what was essentially an empty suit and divide the workload. The thought was there would be a domestic VP and an international VP, who each sat in the cabinet and had the secretary's report up to them and they, in turn, to the President. The secretaries would report up to the VP for whom their department fell under and then the ones with dual roles would still report directly to the president."

Kingsley said, "So a few are easy like Education, the AG, Interior, HUD, etc. going to the domestic VP. Then The UN, State, etc. would go to the International VP. So the ones in both camps and I assume would have to report up to the president would be mostly the financial ones like Treasury, Commerce, etc. plus Defense?"

Frederick said, "That's right. Changing subjects. The Mexican territories are pushing for statehood. The other side has given up blocking the idea and is instead pushing for a bill to set the criteria required of a territory before it can petition for statehood. One of the big sticking points is how long it must first be a territory first. This will set the rules and then the floodgates will open up from Mexico to the tip of Argentina."

Kingsley said, "That is wonderful, let them open. I feel that is one of our greatest accomplishments. The US benefits from the new ideas and energy and the rest of the Americas benefit from our government.

So capitalism has transformed in a very short period of time, do you think this is the beginning of democracy or at least the Republic structure changing as well?"

Frederick said, "That is an interesting question. Predictive modeling has advanced so quickly that we can plug in our desired outcomes and it can give us the probabilities and possible variances and variable outcomes that any number of, or a set of, actions will produce. While issues have never been more complicated, we have never had more ability to choose the best course to accomplish our macro level goals.

So really now more than any time in history we need people to vote on the big policy questions and then let the people in government sort through the best ways of getting there. It is essential for the electorate to be very well informed on the major issues. Only then can the detailed decisions be made by answering the question, does this answer align with the overall goal of x?

So forgive me as I think out loud here. I think for the national scale issues it is most important to identify the key national goals and then let the candidates debate about where we should go for each. I think the mechanism for the selection of the issues that matter was broken when money ruled politics, but now that is minimized.

I think there are two questions here, one about the state of the republic system and one about democracy. The American Republic seems to be self-correcting at the highest levels. At the state and local levels, I think the evolution of algorithms available to the citizenry, that identify the key issues, factoring people's opinions on them into consideration, have empowered people to feel like they can make informed decisions. Setting time aside out of the work week for community issues and discussions has helped too."

Kingsley said, "I think we agree this is a solid idea"

Frederick said, "I have a topic we are opposed on. Appeal your case, Philip. We are nearing the end and I think you think the average American thinks about you in here for one second. I'm sorry that is cruel, but it is a reality check that you need. There are no protests outside the prison. The election happened and the Republicans won the White House, but they didn't dismantle your government. They are happier claiming they are being blocked from change by the majorities in Congress, but the reality is they don't want change they just want to be in charge. As they say, if it ain't broke, don't fix it.

Technology is fixing our problems and bringing us unprecedented abundance and free time. This is a democratized renaissance where the everyman can spend their time on creative pursuits with no worry of fulfilling basic needs and no problem fulfilling most wants. You think you are making some grand statement, but you are not. You will dominate a few news cycles and then fade away into oblivion and your life and all its potential will be gone."

Kingsley said, "I disagree and my evidence was presented in your statement. Yes, people have forgotten me and well they should get on with the business of the future. The problem is they may also forget the times we lived ruled by our own corruption and what it did to our society and our democracy. We put money before people and everything else that matters. Don't you see, the key to moving to the next phase of our political evolution was, and is, the elimination of corruption of every degree at every level of society?

We had to eliminate money's influence on politics to ensure the issues that mattered to people and our nation were brought up and debated in an honest way by people on all sides of the debate. People, who in the end, always agreed that the best outcome for America and Americans was the goal.

We had to eliminate corruption in the labor market by having it no longer compete with profit. We had to eliminate corruption from the hiring, firing and promotion process by giving it information and transparency. We had to eliminate the corruption of ideals by making it so they never had to compete with profit as an outcome.

Corruption is a poison that must be totally eliminated for the patient to reach full health. It must be seared into the brains of people that we must forever be on the lookout for corruption and vigilant to not let it creep back into our lives.

That is what I must do."

Frederick said, "They are signaling that time is almost up. I do understand, but that does not mean I have to stand by and watch a great man and my best friend agree to lay down and die."

Kingsley said, "Don't think of it as laying down and dying. Do me a favor and remember it as standing up and sacrificing for a principal greater than myself. I have discovered something I'm willing to die for."

Frederick said, "Then you are fit to live."

Kingsley said, "And so life is a paradox and we shall have to agree to disagree."

Chapter 30

Hemlock

"Death may be the greatest of all human blessings."
-Socrates

Kingsley smiled as they led Frederick into the room. He said, "Good morning Frederick. They tell me our visit will be shorter than normal today."

Frederick said, "Hey Philip. How are you holding up?"

Kingsley said, "Look, Frederick, I'm fine with this and if you aren't then my one request is that you hide it. I want to leave this world in good spirits."

Frederick said, "Ok I just wasn't sure what to expect."

Kingsley said, "I spoke to both Matthew and Penne this morning over a video chat."

Frederick said, "How did that go?"

Kingsley said, "Very well actually. Matt joked with me and was not nearly as morose as you are being. Penne asked for forgiveness and we parted on good terms."

Frederick said, "I'm glad."

Kingsley said, "Frederick, I don't want our goodbye to be rushed, but I also want to have a good talk with you on my final day here. You are and have always been the best friend a man could ask for. You challenged me and made me work harder and be better my whole life. You were always there for me. You are truly my best friend and if I have one regret, it is leaving you behind."

Frederick said, "I owe you everything. Without you I would likely be a nerdy guy working at the library or teaching High School or something along those lines. I love you like a brother and respect you as a man. You are a paragon of wisdom, moderation, justice and above all, courage. Today I will lose not only my best friend but my hero."

Both men had tears running down their face as then Kingsley said, "I'm glad we have that said. Now when the time comes promise me no more tears as I will start as well if I see you doing it. I want to have a serious and peaceful face as I leave this good earth."

Frederick wiped his face and said, "So what is it you want to discuss today?"

Kingsley said, "The future. If I can't witness it, then I want to imagine it. First, how is the book?"

Frederick said, "It is written and with the editor just waiting for a final chapter."

Kingsley said, "Good. So what becomes of this world?"

Frederick said, "We've come so far so fast it's hard to see tomorrow, let alone any kind of timeline we could call the future, but I'm up for a challenge."

Kingsley said, "Ok well I see states coming together and then coming apart. There are advantages of scale like what we have accomplished in the Americas. It's easier to pool resources, agree on projects, yield the right of way and share in the rewards when everyone is under the same roof. Building super projects like the supertubes and the super highway tunnels that stretch thousands of miles is nearly impossible across national borders. Sharing and reusing the mega-robots needed for the construction and other projects is easier when the finances are shared. Once we have terraformed our countries with the major changes, the large political units will lose their advantage and people will cluster based on beliefs and shared values.

If the republic is to stand it will need to allow the states more and more independence to set their own rules and once again be the laboratories of democracy."

Frederick said, "I could see that but in many places they have to come together first, but that is happening now in Africa and Europe. I see human work being further and further decoupled

298

from the economy and income. You had the vision to see that the means of production were changing from human hands and minds to mechanical hands and AI systems. Investment is for income and work is for meaning.

This is the transition that could have unraveled it all and the one that history will be generous in its praise of your handling. I see what you started continuing to play out until voting and choosing investments becomes the most important contributions to the economy that most people make. Work should continue to be about personal fulfillment and the pursuit of one's interests, utilizing one's talents and acquiring an education."

Kingsley said, "Space has been our destiny for a long time and yet we have made few strides to get there, other than the mining bot colonies. That will have to be the next great adventure after we finish the big transformations here on Mother Earth. The colonies are already growing exponentially to where the amount of raw materials we bring back is only constrained by how many machines we send up. One day soon the notion of the thousands of rockets being sent up full of equipment and not people, will seem wasteful.

There will come a day when manufacturing in space will reach a tipping point and we can mine raw materials and send them in one side and have a fully formed something come out the other side. Once that tipping point is reached, all bets are off. There will be a singularity on Earth that will likely make many of these predictions irrelevant or just plain ridiculous as reality will explode in directions we cannot as yet even imagine.

One thing that can be predicted, after the singularity provides enfranchisement to a new species or collection of species from the evolution of AI, is that the next step would be for this species to self-replicate. I see this as the first goal the new species will have and not the enslavement of humanity here on earth. That is our self-centered anthropomorphic view of the world talking. The new species will see the whole of the universe and quickly leave here in search of raw materials and space to spread its wings and fill with its children.

The Singularity will be the birth of a new species, like Homo erectus was modern man's birth. The other species will still exist, just as the animals continued to exist when we walked upright. We will still have our computers and machines and the new species will see them much as we see frogs and buffalos as being fellow creatures but not us. The Singularity is birth to a new species and that has meaning for them but for us, the Singularity will represent

299

the limits of our ability to advance our machines. The machines will show the limit of what they can be as to push them further transforms them into something else. Something that is no longer ours and is no longer a machine.

The singularity will define the limits of our computing and machines but will also be an escape velocity event for the earth and our solar system.

I think we will get left behind as explorers in the great expansion into space. We will receive data back and make plans for creating the spaceship equivalent of covered wagons out across the great plains of space. We will build huge fleets of self-sustaining ships that hold tens of thousands of people. Maybe the hollowed out asteroids that we have mined and stripped of their ores. Great fleets will travel together to disperse the growing population and spread humanity's seed."

Frederick said, "So you don't see the singularity as the end times or the enslavement of mankind?"

Kingsley said, "No I think we are ascribing humanity's flaws to a super being that will not be human. The only scenarios I see where the post-singularity threatens us is in self-defence, which we determine entirely and in a situation where we are in competition for scarce resources. This later at least now seems unlikely as you consider the vast number of solar bodies just in the asteroid belt, not to mention the extrasolar bodies in the Kuiper belt and beyond. The AI could strip the planets of their component raw resources and if it wanted earth's core material that could certainly pose a threat. That, of course, assumes that the AI doesn't figure out how to transform atoms to create the raw material as a byproduct of fusion or something like it.

Unless we are stupid and start a war with a being that can crush us, I think it will see us as a great herd of wildebeests or maybe a great colony of ants. Perhaps we will be momentarily interesting to them but then we will fade into the background as part of the landscape."

Frederick said, "Interesting. I never thought about the AI's perspective. It would have nothing it doesn't already know that it could learn from us. We would have nothing to offer it except maybe the abstract which it would soon master and surpass us in. I guess we like to ascribe a maternal or paternal status on ourselves for having laid the groundwork for its birth, but I see no reason for it to view us this way.

Maybe we need to build into all code going forward a respect, or better yet, a reverence for the makers so that as the code is later assimilated the reverence will be too. I would be like the basic wiring humans seem to have for religion and belief in that it's vaguely there in some form in all of us as if it was buried in our code. We could Trojan horse our survival starting far back in the AI family tree."

Kingsley said, "That's a good idea. It may be for naught, but it could also be like manipulating the DNA of proto-beings. "

Frederick said, "Ok we put the cart before the horse and have looked at a future beyond our lifetimes but we haven't looked at the immediate future."

Kingsley said chuckling, "It's all beyond my lifetime friend."

Frederick said, "Oh God I didn't mean..."

Kingsley said, "Relax. No need to walk on eggshells. I'm at peace. You are quite right. I suspect the Singularity will be similar to any number of modern technologies, like robotics and virtual reality were before, and fusion is now. These were always just ten years out until we woke up one day and scratched our heads realizing it just happened yesterday.

In the shorter term, as conditions keep getting better for humanity, I think the threat of war decreases. With no need to fight over resources or wealth, there becomes little use of war or nations for that matter. Even territory can be created upward in buildings and downward in the ground. The oceans have plenty of space to build great floating cities to hold us until we can migrate to space.

In the shorter term it seems our competition will not be for resources but for power over other people just as it always has been. Conflicting belief systems will battle probably not in the all-out war style of the 20th century but of the small scale conflict and terroristic nature of the 21st."

Frederick said, "Well I agree. There is our future in a nutshell. Do you know about the Totus Historia project?"

Kingsley said, "No, what is that."

Frederick said, "Librarians are a hardy class. By all rights, they should have faded away at the turn of the century but they evolved. Libraries offered video and audio books. They set up computers and wi-fi so anyone get online. They added 3D printers and partnered with the maker movement. They offered community meeting spaces and free classes. They continued to find ways to add value. The created networks of libraries and merged their digital collections and started some exciting cataloging projects.

That takes us to Totus Historia. A librarian in Memphis started it and recruited librarians around the country and partnered with history teachers from universities all the way down to first grade. They got business sponsorship and grant money for hardware and technical expertise although librarians as a group had become very technically skilled and knowledgeable.

They then set up a wiki-like project to record all history for all time everywhere. The idea was to comb through books, letters, correspondence and combine that with archeology to create a virtual world timeline for all of history so you could pick a time and place and find out what happened there and then. They had students around the country putting together materials with the students further up the educational ladder organizing, verifying and working on synthesizing all the materials.

The Librarians then started recruiting people from all walks of life to help the students until at one point there were millions of people working on this."

Kingsley suddenly said in a burst, "Ah yes I do know what you are talking about. How are they progressing?"

Frederick said, "So as they ramped up, AI was hitting milestones that allowed these programs to do the work of collecting the raw materials and organizing it and identifying anomalies and contradictions. This quickly started putting the students and volunteers out of a job, but the ever flexible librarians identified the need that the AI could not fill and shifted the project.

Now all these students and volunteers are reaching out to senior citizens and recording bits of oral history. They are collecting as much information as they can as well as digitizing any old letters, documents or pictures they are permitted to add to the archives. This monster force is now gathering an unimaginable collection of raw materials that the AI is stitching together. This, of course, has created all kinds of issues with contradictions and things that don't fit, but that has become the material basis for most modern historical study."

Kingsley said, "That is a wonderful story. It was on my radar as president, but I never knew the details."

Frederick said, "That's not the end of the story. These crafty librarians took this success and applied to several more projects. The librarians have become the facilitators of these projects and given them the credibility to be centralized without being suspected of having a bias or agenda. They now call it the Totus project and they have begun several that tie into the Historia such as archeology and geography. Artifacts are 3d scanned and books and paintings are scanned for images or descriptions of landscapes, art, weather or you n

They have also branched out to biology for instance. They have people throughout the world collecting samples of plants, seeds, soil, insects, animal DNA, as well as taking pictures and using technology such as drones and robotic field labs that can operate in remote locations. This is all being combined with the AI cataloging of every reference to any biologically significant picture, blurb in a story, book, movie, audio, video or digitized bit of information that can be pulled together to tell the story of life on this planet.

We should have been treating people like archives of knowledge from the time we first had pen and paper so as to collect as much data from each individual who ever lived as possible. Now that we have the capabilities to process, organize and synthesize it all, we could have gained the collected wisdom and memory of several more generations. Who know how much we lost as each person died off through the millennia. Perhaps one day we will be able to directly upload the stored memories and experiences of a person that can be donated and added to the collective knowledge of mankind when they die. It would be the greatest and most detailed biography imaginable."

Kingsley said, "Frederick, I honestly have not seen you as passionate about something as you once were about the law. Even then I don't think you were this passionate even with the open eyes of youth. What are you going to do after this book is done?"

Frederick said, "To be honest I don't know."

Kingsley said, "Well if you want my opinion, and that is a rhetorical question as you are getting it regardless, you should explore involving yourself somehow with this and find out why you are so passionate about it."

Frederick said, "You know that thought would probably never have come to me but thinking about it here and now has me really excited. Yeah, it makes sense and, and, thank you, Philip. You may have just helped me start the next chapter of my life."

Kingsley smiled with contentment as he could see the wheels turning in Frederick's head as he could hardly help but think of the possibilities as the two sat in a happy and filled silence. But then it was broken as the guard entered to tell Frederick it was time to go.

They stared into each other's eyes with a look of peace and then Philp said, "Frederick, you are the executor of my estate. You will receive instructions from my attorney with all the details. Oh, good heavens, I almost forgot. Please send Matt a bottle of Macallan 62. I lost a bet him that I almost forgot I made."

Frederick was escorted to a room outside the room where the witnesses would gather for the execution. There was an unusual group of people gathered. Most, Frederick did not know or knew only vaguely as people Philip dealt with during his time in power. There was no Matthew and no Penne. Philip had no living relatives that would be remotely close enough to attend, so in the end, it was Frederick who represented both friends and family. It really was lonely at the top and even lonelier when you have fallen from the top.

An hour or so passed and the group was escorted into a room that looked like a movie theater build for twenty people. Once all were seated, a short amount of uncomfortable time passed before the curtain opened and Philip laid on a table with two side wings extending his arms out away from his body. He was strapped down and there were tubes running every which way. Frederick was immediately struck by how he was positioned like Jesus on the cross. Philip too, dying for our sins.

The witness room was dead silent except for the audio from the execution room. Frederick looked at an official in the witness room and said, "Can he see us?"

The official said, "Yes sir, the window is two way but he cannot hear you and he is aware of that."

Frederick made eye contact with Philip and put his hand flat on the window.

The official pressed a button on a wall panel and said, "Does the condemned have any last words?"

Kingsley smiled and surveyed the witness group as he said, "I should like to recite the complete works of Shakespeare if I may" and he chuckled.

"In all seriousness, I am a politician at heart but I will do my best to resist the urge to pontificate. I do want to say that I hope my death is not meaningless. I hope instead that it burns into the collective memory as a reminder that the greatest sin of this age, beyond doing physical harm, is corruption. Corruption tears the fabric of society and robs people of hope and justice. Corruption lurks beneath the surface hidden from the light of day and so goes unnoticed and unpunished and does its evil over time darkening the whole of society spreading its impact like an invisible plague.

My other hope is that we return to having a limit on the terms a president may serve. Before me, FDR was elected to four terms. We also share the fact that were president in extraordinary times that demanded a steady hand on the helm of the ship of state for an extended period of time to weather a once in a century storm. The storm has passed and we should go back to the precedent that our Founding Father George Washington set.

So please, I beg of you from my deathbed, go back to a term limit and do not ever let down your guard or reduce the penalty for corruption. It has been an honor and I hold no ill will toward anyone.

Frederick, you have always been and will always be my best friend and the greatest man I ever knew.

I will miss you.

Goodbye."

After a moment of silence, the official signaled to the staff in the execution room that they were to begin. Fluid flowed through the tubes and entered Philip's veins. His eyes closed as he appeared to go to sleep as they kept pumping chemicals into him.

First was an anesthetic.

Then saline to flush the lines.

Next was the paralyzing agent.

Then more saline to flush the lines again.

Finally, the drug to stop his heart.

It took just minutes but felt like an eternity. Finally, mercifully, a doctor stepped up to Philip and took his pulse a number of times. He then looked up at a clock in the room and said, "Time of death, ten, ten AM."

The curtains started to close and Frederick said in a barely audible tone, "This was the end of my friend, the best, wisest and most upright man of any that I have ever known."

"The society we have described can never grow into a reality or see the light of day, and there will be no end to the troubles of states, or indeed, my dear Glaucon, of humanity itself, till philosophers become rulers in this world, or till those we now call

kings and rulers really and truly become philosophers, and political power and philosophy thus come into the same hands."
— Plato, Plato's Republic

The End

<<<>>>

A note from the Author:

I sincerely hope you enjoyed Plato's Dream: Crisis of the Employment Singularity. I am a self-published author and would be forever in your debt if you could help get the word out by telling a friend or by taking just a minute to rate the book and leave even a just a few words of review.

Thank you!
Topher Cliver

Find links to all my social media, Goodreads, articles, upcoming books and much more by visiting:

http://www.platosdreambook.com/

An Idea can change the world. A book can bring ideas to a reader, but it is the reviewers who bring readers to books. So it is you dear reader who has the power to spread ideas with a few positive words and therefore change the world.

About the Author

Topher Cliver is an author, technology professional, futurist, transhumanist and Gen Xer based in the United States in Atlanta Georgia. He has been fascinated by technology since the very early 80's when his family bought an Atari 800 computer. His career has spanned a variety of fields including the software, incentive/rewards, digital marketing and digital advertising industries.

Plato's Dream: Crisis of the Employment Singularity is his first novel.

Blog:
http://www.platosdreambook.com/

Amazon Author Central:
Amazon.com/author/topher-cliver

Twitter   @Platos_Dream_BK

Facebook
Facebook.com/PlatosDreamBook/

Google+   Plato's Dream: Crisis of the
                    Employment Singularity

Links to these, Goodreads and other related sites can be found on http://www.platosdreambook.com/

<<<>>>

www.ingramcontent.com/pod-product-compliance
Lightning Source LLC
Chambersburg PA
CBHW031550240626
47153CB00002B/451